Rise and Divine

LANA HARPER

BERKLEY ROMANCE
NEW YORK

BERKLEY ROMANCE
Published by Berkley
An imprint of Penguin Random House LLC
penguinrandomhouse.com

Library of Congress Cataloging-in-Publication Data

Names: Harper, Lana, author.
Title: Rise and divine / Lana Harper.
Description: First edition. | New York : Berkley Romance, 2024. |
Series: The Witches of Thistle Grove ; book 5
Identifiers: LCCN 2023059692 (print) | LCCN 2023059693 (ebook) |
ISBN 9780593637982 (trade paperback) | ISBN 9780593637999 (ebook)
Subjects: LCGFT: Witch fiction. | Lesbian fiction. |
Paranormal fiction. | Romance fiction. | Novels.
Classification: LCC PS3608.A7737 R57 2024 (print) |
LCC PS3608.A7737 (ebook) | DDC 813/.6—dc23/eng/20240109
LC record available at https://lccn.loc.gov/2023059692
LC ebook record available at https://lccn.loc.gov/2023059693

First Edition: August 2024

Printed in the United States of America
1st Printing

Book design by Alison Cnockaert

For all the friends who hold our hands
while we go through hell and back.
This side of the veil is so much brighter because of you.

Author's Note

))) ● (((

This book deals with emotionally difficult topics, including grief, parental loss, drug use, addiction, possession, passive suicidal ideation, and physical violence.

Rise and Divine

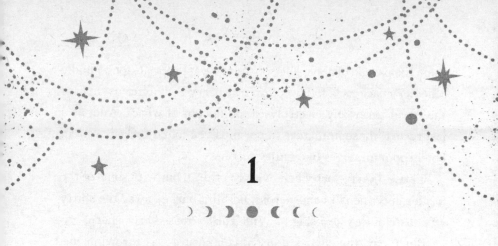

1

The Pretender

EATING DEVILS IS thirsty work.

More than the magic itself, it was that raging thirst in the aftermath that took clients by surprise. Most of those who called on me, Thistle Grove normies and witches alike, came in expecting occult accessories of a more sinister bent. Pungent curls of henbane smoke wisping from a tarnished censer, clusters of crystal shards bundled with dried herbs and feathers, arcane mutterings. (To be fair, I was more than down for the odd bit of arcane muttering when the exorcism called for it, or when an occasion demanded a sense of heightened drama. Even an outlier like me couldn't resist the Avramov family flair for the theatrical.)

It barely even fazed me now, the way their apprehension clouded over into bemusement once I unzipped my black Patagonia backpack to pull out a hefty water bottle, embellished with shrill exhortations to *HYDRATE!* in two-hour increments. Then came the parade of apple juice boxes more appropriate for a middle schooler's backpack, followed by strawberry Pedialyte, just in case the ritual threw my electrolytes too far out of whack. And, as a last resort, those miniature liquor nips you found tucked away in hotel room minibars like guilty secrets.

Those didn't exactly help with the thirst, but with some of the nastier specimens I came across, nothing burned away the shitty aftertaste quite like a slug of Wild Turkey tossed back sharp.

But today, the client's unusual composure was throwing me. When I'd arrived at the Arcane Emporium and drawn back the burgundy velvet curtain that veiled this divination enclosure, secluding it from the rest of the occult store and the series of identical nooks on either side, she'd been sitting across the table from Amrita in a posture I knew well. Head bowed, tendons standing out like steel cables in her neck, thin hands clasped on the tabletop so tightly the knuckles had paled into skeletal knobs.

Fear made flesh.

Yet the appraising glance she'd shot me when I slipped in, a keenly scrutinizing sweep of my entire person, had been shrouded by only the faintest film of uncertainty. Nothing like my normal clients.

"Hello," I said, setting my sloshing backpack down and extending my hand. I'd found that a courteously detached demeanor, the kind of brisk professionalism you'd get from a doctor, served me better than any cultivated aura of mystique when it came to setting them at ease. The worst of the haunted only wanted to feel that they were in capable hands. "Good to meet you. I'm Daria Avramov, Amrita's colleague. Dasha, if you like."

"Right," the woman said, with a crisp nod that made her glossy cap of chin-length brown hair sway, its caramel highlights glinting in the candlelight. She looked in her mid-to-late thirties, a handful of years older than me. Not my type, but a fresh-faced pretty, with the kind of dewy skin that meant either excellent genes or the budget for premium skincare and cosmetic intervention. Her handshake was cool but surprisingly firm; I was accustomed to a much clammier and more tremulous greeting experience. "The . . . the specialist. I'm Emily Duhamel, but just Emily's fine."

I withdrew my hand, considering her more closely. Anyone who required my niche services tended to show up beside themselves with terror—and unsure of whether they should be more afraid of whatever it was that plagued them or of me, yon fearsome exorcist witch. Given the breakdown of Thistle Grove's normie population, they were also often the love-and-light types who drove me especially batty. The low-effort, high-commitment kind who outsourced their chakra cleansings and flung indiscriminate amounts of money at the spiritual life coaches they invariably found through social media.

Alas, this insufferable subgroup came with the territory. Many Thistle Grove transplants were drawn here by the allure of living in a town steeped in witchy history, as if the act of paying property taxes in a place ostensibly founded by four witch families might awaken some dormant psychic talents of their own. Even the Arcane Emporium's signature herb-and-incense scent wasn't enough to mask the patchouli they seemed to emanate aspirationally rather than physically. The irony of it was, when something sly and eldritch *did* come creeping in at their open-ended invitation, it often turned out that these were definitely not the vibes they'd been looking for.

That was when they came running to Avramov diviners at the

Arcane Emporium—the only game in town that cut their teeth on shadows, specialized in dealing with manifestations from the other side of the veil.

But this woman wasn't so easily rattled. And I didn't catch so much as a whiff of figurative patchouli drifting off her, only the sweet, floral notes of some top-shelf perfume by a designer I'd never recognize, much less be able to name.

"Thank you for coming out for this, especially on a weekend," she added, with a light laugh and a semi-incredulous shake of her head, as if the absurdity of her circumstances—the fact that the "specialist" in question was an alleged witch, with the alleged power to banish whatever monster it was that lurked under her bed—hadn't escaped her. "I, uh, I'm looking forward to your expert opinion."

"Glad to hear it," I said, even more taken aback. For one of the haunted, this Emily had her shit impressively together, I decided, revising my estimate of her upward by several more notches. Despite the deceptively soft, flower-embroidered cashmere sweater over a preppy collared shirt and distressed jeans, I suspected she did something high-powered in her weekday life. The kind of demanding work that left her encased in an enamel shell that never really chipped off. "And happy to help with your problem, of course. I assume Amrita has discussed our rates with you?"

"Oh, yes." She suppressed a tiny smile, as if she found our hourly rate laughably low but didn't want to offend. I felt my first twinge of annoyance with her; whatever it was she did, not all of us were in the business of fleecing people by overcharging for essential services. "It won't be an issue."

"Perfect. In that case, let's get started. Amrita?"

I glanced over at my half sister, who, though her everyday role was store manager, was bedecked in the clichéd fortune-teller regalia we all wore for our divination shifts—plummy lipstick, a cascade of gauzy maroon shawls shot through with shining thread, elaborate earrings, stacked rings on every slim finger. With her huge, thickly kohled dark eyes and lacquered spill of black hair loose over her shoulders, Amrita looked like my polar opposite, as if the entire palette of decadent color that should've been split between us had somehow ended up hers alone. Her hair inky dark to my white-blond; skin a warm golden brown to my year-round pallor; clothes a bright riot of color to the black cowl-neck sweater, black jeans, and black knee-high suede boots that comprised my fall uniform.

Compared to her, sometimes I thought I looked like a shade myself. A living ghost.

Appropriately enough, maybe.

Unlike me, Amrita blended seamlessly into the arcane décor. Three wooden chairs sat around a small table draped with a silky altar cloth, styled after the tarot starter deck we all grew up using, the one that had been designed by Oksana Avramov two centuries ago. On the tabletop, an ornate silver platter held a gray pillar candle with a high-licking flame, anchored by a dried pool of its own wax—along with an onyx scrying plate, a bowl of black salt, and a scattering of crystals mostly for appearances' sake. A maroon damask canopy swooped over the tops of all the cubicles in the divination area, to blot out the Emporium's brighter overhead fixtures. In here there was only candlelight and the soft bluish glow of a Turkish mosaic spiral lamp tucked into one corner, its azure glass-chip globes swaying on their brass chains every time one of us shifted in our chair.

"Catch me up on the details?" I said to Amrita. She'd summoned me by text once she realized Emily had a problem more in my wheelhouse than hers, but she'd been vague on the specifics.

My sister gave a smooth nod, though I caught the flicker of concern that flitted across her delicate features, the same disquiet I often saw in the mirror. Sometimes her expressions were unsettling replicas of mine, a side effect of us both having inherited most of our father's face. "This is the tainted object," she said, sliding a velvet jewelry pouch to me across the table, touching it as gingerly as she could. "I believe it's the locus for whatever has attached itself to Emily."

"So it's definitely an entity, not a curse?" Sometimes our clients came in with heirlooms that had, either by accident or ill intent, become infused with malign spellwork that affected the wearer. The effects could appear similar to a haunting, but unpicking that kind of nasty tangle was a completely different undertaking, and not my forte.

"An infestation for sure," Amrita confirmed, with a shudder so faint that someone less familiar with my sister's poise wouldn't even have caught it. "A pestilential one, too, I'd guess."

"There's no need to put it that way," Emily cut in with a startling edge of reproach, a flash of temper flaring in her brown eyes. Under closer scrutiny, she looked worn-out beneath that tasteful makeup, the skin under her eyes the tender, predawn hue of purple that came from more than one restless night. Something was disturbing her sleep. "So crudely. Like she's *evil*. An affliction. I told you, it isn't like that. I'm not afraid of her."

She, I noted. *Her*. So Emily thought she already knew what had taken up residence inside her jewelry.

Also unusual.

My sister drew the inside of her lower lip between her teeth, clearly refraining from comment. "Then why don't you tell Dasha the story, Emily?" she suggested delicately, cocking her head. "It's better that she hear it from you, anyway. More precise."

Emily gave a clipped nod and relaxed back into her chair, appeased; as per usual, Amrita had struck the perfect note. The idea of precision obviously appealed to Emily, and I marveled again at the strangeness of it, of someone so stable and collected needing our services. Most of the people who traipsed through the Arcane Emporium were tourists chasing the giddy thrill of having their cards or palms read—though unlike your standard carnival experience, Avramov diviners never lied or sugarcoated unpalatable truths. Only a small handful of our visitors came afflicted with actual paranormal manifestations that had glommed on to them, made them desperate enough to seek the kind of help they likely didn't even *really* believe in.

And an even smaller segment had acquired the sort of malevolent hitchhiker that I specialized in.

"It was my aunt's," Emily began, untying the pouch's drawstring and fishing out a heart-shaped locket on a delicate chain, letting it pool in her palm. Candlelight caught its links with a sinuous, flickering gleam. Again, I saw Amrita stiffen with distaste, but Emily's fingers curled protectively around the locket, betraying no trace of fear or distress. She toyed with it fondly, running her fingertips over its edges as she spoke. "Passed down from my maternal grandmother, her mother before that, and so on. It's belonged to the women in my family for at least four generations."

I nodded, committing this to memory. The age of the substrate mattered when it came to infestations. Something old, infused with decades or even centuries of emotion, tended to be a more attractive and sturdier medium, a better home for malevolent entities than an item without its own patina of history.

"How did it make its way to you?"

A fine tremble of emotion rippled over her features. "My aunt passed away, a little over six months ago," she said, swallowing hard, a corner of her mouth twitching. "An aggressive cancer; we had almost no warning. Most of her estate went to debts, the rest to me and my mother. This piece in particular, she left to me."

"Your aunt didn't have any daughters of her own, I take it?"

"Not anymore." She licked her lips, tightened them against the slight quiver in her chin. "But she used to. My . . . my cousin, Scarlett. Lettie. She died when I was fifteen. We were almost the same age; my mom and Aunt Percy, they had us less than a year apart. They used to call us Irish twins. And that's what it felt like to us, too. Like we were sisters instead of cousins."

"So you were close," I prompted. The mention of a dead cousin as well as a dead aunt had piqued my interest, but I didn't want to lead her or bias myself. Still, any kind of tight entanglement with the departed was promising.

"Yes." A faint smile ghosted over her lips. "I lived with them for a while before Lettie died, for almost a whole year back when I was twelve. My father wasn't in the picture, and my mother was weathering a rough patch. She has bipolar disorder, with a panic disorder on top of that, and meds back then were even more of a guessing game. It took a while for her to reach something like an even keel. So we agreed I'd move in with Aunt Percy and Lettie, just until Mom found her footing."

"How was that? Living with them?" Emily seemed willing enough to reminisce about her cousin and aunt, but two teenagers circling each other in close quarters could create a frothy turbulence. The sort of psychic turmoil that sometimes left a contrail, a delicious impression that drew some entities like bees to nectar.

"Wonderful," she said wistfully, no bitterness whatsoever. "I'd been living with my mom in Boston before that, in one of the college student neighborhoods she could afford. It was pretty much what you'd expect. Loud, crowded, parties at all hours. But Aunt Percy, she had this gorgeous restored farmhouse in Vermont. Acres and acres of land, a few horses. So much quiet and sky, exactly what I needed at the time. And Lettie and I, we had the run of the place. I even went to school with her that year, and it was like . . . I don't know, an endless sleepover with your best friend in the world. Like I'd fallen into this cozy fairy tale."

"What happened after that?" I asked.

"My mom got better, and I went back to Boston." Emily's face darkened like a storm front. "I'd been gone for almost three years by the time Lettie died, but I visited every summer, sometimes even for holidays. It was a drunk driving accident, the kind where everyone else walked away practically without a scratch. Just awful, cosmically shitty luck."

Amrita flicked a subtle glance at me, gauging my reaction. My mother had died in a car accident, too, six years ago, though that had been a highway pileup caused by an ice slick rather than any human recklessness.

I gave Amrita a tiny, reassuring nod in response. Corkscrew twist in my stomach aside, I'd come a long way since the days when the slightest reminder of my mother's absence could send me spinning out, where nothing and no one could reach me.

"I don't think my aunt ever really recovered. If you even can, from a loss like that." She toyed with the locket again, turning it over and over between her fingers, her drawn features softening a little. "That's what's in here. A lock of Lettie's hair. I assume that's partly why Aunt Percy left it to me. She knew . . . she knew the way I loved her, too."

My interest sharpened almost tangibly, like a lens focusing. So there was an organic component involved, which could be a powerful locus for sympathetic magic.

"Then weird things began happening," I guessed. "Once the locket passed to you."

Emily nodded, a rapid bob, throat spasming as she swallowed. "It was just the odd thing here and there, at first. Lights flickering, creaking noises, thumping in the walls. The kind of stuff you can write off as faulty wiring, an old house settling, maybe mice. Or, you know. Pipes."

"Pipes," Amrita and I deadpanned in long-suffering unison. As far as explanations for the paranormal went, crappy plumbing really played an outsized part. Sometimes I wondered if we even needed the oblivion glamour that was cast over Thistle Grove to prevent its normie residents from retaining memories of magic, when eighty percent of the time you could blithely pin the blame for anything from a rogue demon to a rampaging poltergeist on "pipes."

"But then," she went on, a little smile tugging at her lips, "I started *feeling* her. Lettie."

My shoulders tightened by reflex. Now we were really getting somewhere. "How do you mean? Cold spots in certain areas of the house? A sense of presence?"

"No cold spots, nothing like that. But a presence, yes. It was only in my dreams at first. Lettie and I'd be lying together by our creek at sunset, like we used to." Her brow furrowed. "She'd be talking and talking to me, telling these long, winding stories. Holding my hand, or with her head resting on my stomach. Always touching. And I . . . I've missed her so much, for so long now. It was like really being with her again. I'd try so hard to remember what she said to me after I woke up, but I never did. I could never hold on to the words."

A chill trickled down my spine, and I could feel the prickle of the sideways glance Amrita stole at me, to confirm that I'd registered this aberration, too. Normal shades didn't behave this way, not even the punchier ones. They didn't have the bandwidth or the cohesion to affect the living like this, trespassing on their dreams.

But other things did.

"You said 'at first,'" I probed, resting my forearms on the table's edge. "What happened after that?"

"Um." She licked her lips again, strained gaze darting between the two of us. "After that . . . well, a few months ago, Lettie started getting into bed with me."

"I see." I strove to keep my tone neutral, though even as someone on first-name terms with a variety of chthonic entities, the notion of something inhuman slinking into my bed gave me an instant case of the willies. "Did you feel a dip in the mattress, something like that? Or has she made physical contact?"

"Contact." She smiled, an expression of such sheer joy and affection that it only unnerved me more. "She spoons me sometimes. Snugs her arms around my neck, all warm. Exactly the way we used to sleep, the nights I snuck into her bedroom so we could stay up and freak each other out with ghost stories."

All warm. That wasn't right at all. Shades felt like nothing to most humans, completely incorporeal—and on the rare occasion where they manifested an ectoplasmic form dense enough to emit a temperature, the living experienced it as a freezing, bone-burrowing cold. I should know. As an Avramov, ectoplasm had been my magical clay since I began casting, and decades later I still wasn't immune to its slimy, icy texture.

"And this happens every night?" I asked, my pulse kicking up.

"No, but it's gotten more frequent. And I'm not—I'm not saying I have a problem with it, per se," she added hastily, lest I get the wrong impression about nighttime snuggles with Alleged Dead Lettie. "It feels so precious to be close to her again, after all these years of missing her. Like a gift. Like she's missed me, too, so much that not even death could keep her away from me forever." She huffed out a tearful little laugh, tucked her lips behind her teeth. "You're . . . This is the first time I've even told anyone else. Believe me, I know exactly how unhinged this all must sound."

Amrita reached across the table and gave Emily's free hand a quick squeeze, her eyes warm with compassion. I noticed that Emily's cuticles were raw and inflamed, as if she had been worrying at them while avoiding the glossy coat of her polish. "Not at all," my sister assured Emily. "It's your experience, and you're doing a wonderful job describing it for us. That's what we're for—to hear stories just like this. And then help, if we can."

"That's the thing," Emily said, mouth twitching in a brief, pale smile. "I'm not completely sure I even *need* help. For the most part, I love having her there. It's just that . . . I've been waking up so tired, the mornings after she spends a night with me. And I used to run hot, but now it's like I'm freezing all the time. It's gotten bad enough that I went in for a check-up, but everything seems fine. And I—I guess what I'm asking is, would that be normal? In, in situations like this?"

That posture I'd seen when I first arrived *hadn't* been fear, I suddenly realized, but a desperate, ferocious hope. Emily didn't want to be saved, delivered from any evil—she wanted confirmation of what she hoped was the truth. That this was truly the ghost of her beloved cousin reaching out to her from beyond the veil, wanting nothing more than to cozy up against her living kin's back. That sounded sublimely fucking creepy—even to me, someone who, not that many years ago, would have given anything for the smallest sign of my mother reaching out to me from beyond that depthless dark.

But part of Emily—the part that had her gnawing at those ragged cuticles—at least suspected that something here was terribly wrong.

"And I can handle it," she continued before I could reply, gaining conviction. "The fatigue and the cold, whatever else happens. It's a ridiculously small price to pay for having gotten her back, in any form. If this is what I can have of her, then I'll take it. But . . . I want to be sure. That it's really her, and not . . . I don't know. Something else."

"It's very brave of you," I murmured, holding her eyes. "On both fronts. To be willing to make that sacrifice, *and* to be willing to know the truth. But I do have to tell you, even if it is Lettie's shade—what you might refer to as her ghost—that's attached itself to the locket, I wouldn't advise allowing her to stay with you. For one thing, it isn't really her. Shades are only shadows, echoes of unresolved emotions. Not the person you knew."

I could see from the unyielding defiance on her face that this wouldn't be a convincing line of argument; she didn't care which part of Lettie she might have gotten back. Grief could be like that, hollowing you out enough to make you starved for crumbs you could barely see, much less taste.

"More importantly," I went on, trying another tack, "the living and the dead aren't meant to mingle, to entangle so closely. Their presence wears on you. Long term, there would be both spiritual and physical consequences. Progressively more severe."

Without conscious thought, my fingers drifted up to the hollow of my neck, where the protective Avramov garnet hung on a slim silver chain. It was the gem ward we all used to keep ourselves grounded, given the way our mere existence attracted anything of an ectoplasmic bent. Because we Avramovs weren't just necromancers, or speakers to the dead—something in our blood made us into living beacons, the human equivalent of standing stone circles. A walking invitation for possessions and infestations of every stripe.

My own especially volatile nature meant I sometimes needed the garnet's anchor even more than most.

"I'll make that decision for myself," Emily said, with a stout lift to her chin. There was such a vibrant energy to her, an electric sense of leadership, loyalty, and fearlessness that burned in her like a brand. Luminous enough that even I could see it, having known her for all of fifteen minutes. I could understand why something would have wanted to feast on that vibrant part of her. Maybe even I wouldn't have minded just a little bite of all that zest. "That's why I'm here. I want to know for sure."

"Understood." I reached a hand across the table, palm up. "May I?"

Reluctantly, as if she was just a tiny bit afraid I might steal it from her, she relinquished the locket, letting the chain pool onto my palm. It was a vintage heart etched with whimsical little flowers drawn from curlicues, its edges rubbed lopsided by years of handling, the raw brass still warm from her skin. A sweet curio, with a warm, feminine energy to it. Likely just as appealing to whatever now lived in it as Emily herself was.

I closed my eyes, grasped at the locket with my mind, and tumbled headfirst into darkness.

2

The Other Side

I STAGGERED IN place, struggling to gain my bearings. The transition to the other side of the veil always felt vertiginous, a sickening lurch followed by crawling panic as my senses acclimated. Red clouds, every shade from rust to velvet cake, stuttered overhead—hovering in place, swirling like mist, flashing across the sky in fast-forward. As though time here moved not regularly, but in ragged, leaping, senseless increments. Aside from those bloody clouds, the sky was a watery smear of grayscale with no hint of color, no bright sliver of moon or sun.

Stillness reigned absolute, an absence of movement alien to someone used to a world rife with circulation, its air whipped into currents and cross breezes. Nothing stirred here, not even the profusion of pitch-black flowers that sprawled over this field—orchids, lilies, roses, and peonies, laced with strange, angular little sprays of baby's breath. Alongside them grew a riot of bulbous blooms and trumpet-shaped blossoms dangling from thick vines, unnatural specimens unlike anything I'd ever seen. All of them that same sleek and glistening black, the centers an even deeper, void-like dark. I'd knelt to touch them a few times before, rub them between my fingers; they felt chilly and brittle and somehow dusty. And they smelled like nothing, too, as though scent required hot-blooded reality to underpin it, not just a flat mimicry of life.

Spindly trees poked up in the distance, naked black skeletons hung with faceted, geometric approximations of fruit. Big and heavy as gourds, in crimsons and purples so wine-dark they were also nearly black. I'd never seen these trees change in any way, sprout buds or leaves, let their fruit drop or rot. Everything here was like that, besides the clouds. Immutable, ever abiding. The opposite of the living realm, where nothing could be counted on as a constant, not even oceans or mountains or the bedrock itself.

I looked down at my hands, like I always did to steady myself. Tracing my eyes over the familiar shape of my fingers, the road map of lines on my palms, the crosshatched texture of my skin. But even though I appeared and felt corporeal to myself, I wasn't *really* here. Only my soul and awareness passed over when I visited, the fiery, enduring core of my spirit and consciousness. The essence of who I, Dasha Avramov, truly was. Enough of me to create this lifelike avatar, to lend me shape and matter on this side.

As soon as that initial sense of terrible dislocation passed, a flood of shimmering euphoria rushed in to take its place.

In a land of death, of a vast, flat nothing, I was stunningly alive. The only truly living thing. And this awareness felt *wonderful*, like a river of warm honey crashing through my veins. An all-encompassing ecstasy that surpassed any human high I'd ever felt.

Fighting it was useless, I'd learned long ago, not that any part of me had ever truly wanted to resist. I tipped back my head and let the elation rollick through me, yielding to it until it reached a nearly unbearable crescendo, a deluge of gamey, decadent pleasure that felt too much in every respect. I'd tried to describe it to Amrita once, and the closest I'd come had been telling her to imagine the most mind-blowing orgasm of her life, crossed with a mouthful of dark chocolate and melted butter and caviar, all washed down with some bloodred wine.

And even that didn't graze the surface of how sublime it felt.

Once it waned enough to let me master myself, I opened my eyes to see the Lettie pretender watching me, head cocked.

"Hello," it said, its voice a triple-pitched harmonic warble, a malicious smile playing on its lips.

It looked convincingly like a teenage girl, the way it must have appeared in Emily's dreams. Big hazel eyes under thick, straight slashes of brows, long brown hair parted down the middle, chipmunk cheeks and a pointed little chin. I could even see some of Emily in her, the shared bone structure that in Lettie hadn't been given the time to surface. It wore low-slung jeans that sat beneath the hip bones, and a lacy cami under an unbuttoned flannel shirt with the sleeves rolled up, the fabric juddering like static with the effort of trying to be blue and green; most color didn't fare so well here. A pair of sparkly Skechers were on its feet, and rows of chunky friendship bracelets clustered around one wrist. This must have been a favorite outfit for Emily to have remembered it in such lovingly meticulous detail.

"How are you here?" As human as it looked, its eyes glittered with the shellacked gleam of a wholly alien curiosity. "You should not be."

"I was born to death, and I have an appetite for it," I told it, lifting my chin. "So I'm given leave to visit."

That was the truth, as far as any of us knew. As the only living Avramov devil eater, there hadn't been anyone to teach or guide me. My father had suspected what I'd become when I was born en caul, the slippery film of amniotic sac clinging to my face— though, given my Harlow mother, even he hadn't been sure what might happen until my magic began manifesting as Avramov. We had records of a few others like me, but I was the only one to be born in Thistle Grove. Even for a family of necromancers, witches like me were an aberration, travelers who could briefly cross the diaphanous border of the veil. Where the rest of the family took every precaution to ground themselves firmly in the mortal world, I straddled the realms, one foot on either side. As if I wasn't exactly human myself.

It made even seasoned necromantic practitioners uncomfortable. And while I normally wouldn't be so forthcoming with an entity like this, I wanted this one to consider the wisdom of being afraid of me.

"Curious," it replied instead, its overbright gaze shifting between my eyes. "I have never heard of such a thing. Are you some abomination, then? Do you mean to try to eat me?"

I tilted my head from side to side, like, *jury's still out*, though I took a lot of exception to being called an abomination by something wearing a dead girl's shade like a hide. "That would depend on what your intentions are. Toward Emily Duhamel."

"Emily." The thing all but purred her name, stretching its

syllables out like taffy, its eyes rolling back with pleasure. "Have you met my delectable Emily, my ambrosial trifle? My pretty, sticky pudding fresh from the oven?"

Fury roared up in my belly, helpfully blotting out all that distracting euphoria. "I've met her. And she isn't your *dessert*."

"Oh, *of course* she is," the thing crooned, mimicking my emphasis as it bared its teeth in a terrible imitation of a smile. "She likes me close, allows me in her bed like a favored cat. Shares her honeyed mortal heat with me, bite by little bite. And all I must do in return is present this face to her, and sweeten her dreams with stolen memories while she sleeps."

My suspicions crystallized with a hard snap. I knew exactly what this entity was—a revenant demon. They were notorious shape-shifters and siphoners, taking on the guise of some well-loved departed to ingratiate themselves with their prey, while they sucked the living's memories and life essence away exactly as it had said, bit by precious bit. It might take years for Emily to die with this thing stuck to her like a leech, maybe even decades. But she *would* die, withered and hollow eyed and long before her time. With only a scrap of soul left.

There was no way to know when it had affixed itself to the heirloom locket. But now it was using the locket as both an anchor and portal, whenever it wanted to cross the veil to feed on Emily.

"So she gets to be tricked into believing that part of her cousin is still with her, and you get to feed until you burst like a tick." I shook my head, flexing my hands into fists by my sides. "Afraid that's not going to work for me."

"Why not? It is a fair enough bargain," it said, flicking one shoulder in a repulsive shrug, like the twitching of an antenna.

"Fairer than many others I have seen struck. And if you had ever tasted her for yourself, death hungerer, I am certain you would agree."

"You will leave her alone," I ordered, swaths of ectoplasm coalescing around me like a cloud of billowing dark fog as I began drawing on my magic. Ectoplasm hung thick in the air here, ripe for the shaping, much more readily available than it was on my side. Sometimes I wondered if this entire lifeless world might be made of it. "She isn't for the likes of you."

"Or what?" it whispered mockingly, taking a slow, dragging step toward me, scuffing a sneakered toe through the black flowers. Then another step, this one at uncanny stutter speed—bringing it less than a foot away, close enough that I could make out the details of its features, down to the pollen smattering of freckles. The visual memories of Lettie it had stolen from Emily.

Over its shoulder, the outline of a towering black castle sprang up from nothing, its tapering, needle-thin spires spearing into the charcoal sky like finials. The only shape on the horizon besides the jagged mountain range looming in the far distance, like the serrated vertebrae of this world.

Besides the cloudscape, the castle was the one other mutable feature of this side. Sometimes it appeared like a mirage, other times it never showed itself. I had no idea what it was—or who it might belong to—the same way I didn't know the true nature of this place. Was it an entirely separate realm of its own, existing in parallel with ours; maybe one of the many netherworlds of Avramov mythology? Or was it what we thought of as purgatory, a way station for shades on a journey that ended in some other destination?

All I knew for sure was that along with shades, devils roamed here, too.

"Or I'll be the final death of you," I replied with measured calm, though my heart thundered furiously in my chest. The electric adrenaline of facing down a demon never really dulled, no matter how many of them you'd dispatched. Now I could feel the scorching heat coming off the thing, in rolling, infernal waves that baked my face like desert wind. It wouldn't have been this hot curled up against Lettie's back, but here it was in a more natural habitat, closer to its innate form. "For a change."

It chuckled at that, a guttural sound between a cackle and a rasp. "I think not," it replied, that grotesque smile spreading until its girlish cheeks quivered with strain. "You, who do not even know my deepest name, could never cause me harm. But such sterling human hubris does always make my day."

"I don't need your name, you devious, hungry little *shit*," I shot back through clenched teeth. "All I need—"

Without another word, it pressed a searing palm to my sternum and gave me a brisk, hard shove that sent me reeling back.

MY EYES FLEW open, and I was in my chair at the Emporium once again, a fist clutched against the burning spot on my chest where the demon had forcefully expelled me from the other side of the veil. Though my body hadn't been there, the lingering heat felt very real—as disturbing as the realization that I'd underestimated this entity's strength. Very few denizens of the other side had the firepower to dismiss me in such a casual way.

For a moment, I leaned into the sweeping sense of loss that always accompanied return, heaving ragged breaths as the despair of no longer being a bright torch of life in a dead world settled over me, like some funereal cape. Amrita reached over and gripped my wrist, giving it a grounding squeeze. She knew these first few moments back could be devastating. "You okay?" she asked, low and calm, not wanting to frighten Emily.

"Fine," I said curtly, swallowing against the chalky dryness of my mouth. "It was stronger than I expected. Made for a more abrupt departure than normal."

"So?" Emily demanded, gripping the table's lip, eagerness blazing in her eyes. "Is it her? Is it Lettie?"

"I'm sorry, it's not," I said, as softly as I could, my gut clenching in sympathy as disappointment drowned the hope in her face. "I'm afraid you've been infested with something called a revenant demon."

"Demons aren't real," she said, but gingerly, as though testing the waters of an unlikely theory. Already halfway to belief.

"Unfortunately, they're very real. And very dangerous." I gritted my teeth, infuriated once again by how easily the demon had expelled me. "And this one wasn't exactly open to civil discourse. Its kind are siphoners—they feed on the heat of your life, and the sweetness of your memories. Tell me, have you been forgetting things? Things to do with Lettie, or other pleasant aspects of your life? Memories you cherish?"

She opened her mouth, then closed it, a thoughtful, fear-tinged expression settling over her face as she tested her memory for gaps. "I would've said no, because it's nothing overt. But, yes. I was trying to remember something about an old friend the other day, a road trip I took with her our sophomore year for spring break, and it was just . . . blank. A bunch of nothing, like it had never even happened. I *know* we had a wonderful time, we always talk about it when we get together. You know, the glory days of 99 Apples and fake IDs and Forever 21 under fleece jackets. But now . . ."

"The memory's gone. And it'll only get worse," I finished for her. "It's already eaten many of your best memories of Lettie; you just haven't noticed because you have so many. But this entity . . . it wants to kill you, and slowly. It's a parasite, and it can't coexist with you in any other, less lethal way, even if it wanted to. Which it doesn't. I talked to it just now. It spoke about you like you were food."

Her face went taut with revulsion, even as confusion brewed in her eyes. "What do you mean, you *talked* to it? When? You only held my locket for a few seconds!"

"It's hard to explain. You came here for our expertise, and this is it. You'll have to take my word for it that what I'm telling you is the truth." I leveled a solemn gaze at her, because I wasn't going to do this against her will, without her active consent. If she wanted to die because an ersatz dead cousin was better than none, then that was her choice to make. "Knowing that it means you harm, will you let me exorcise it? Once it's gone, you'll be able to safely keep the locket. But the thing you've thought of as Lettie . . . it'll never be back."

She gazed at me, wavering. Part of her wanted to keep on going as she had, clinging to the beautiful illusion the beast had conjured for her. But that other part, the staunch, burning warrior who intuitively understood that something here was badly amiss, wouldn't be so easily swayed. And I knew that in situations like this, my appearance helped lay skepticism to rest. I'd always been an otherworldly kind of beautiful, with the filigree of my features and the creamy pallor of my hair and skin. The ghostly tracery of violet veins at my temples and eyelids, the silvery blue-gray of my white-lashed eyes. A pale, pale girl with shadows swimming in her irises, like black minnows in some frozen-over pond.

I personally credited Vera Farmiga for normalizing the idea that an exorcist worth their salt might look more like me than a male Catholic priest. In my case, the overall pallor gave more Victorian Consumptive Chic × *The Exorcist*, but it still seemed to do the trick.

"Okay," Emily said in a deflated whisper, dropping her gaze. "Do it. Whatever it is you do."

I released a pent-up breath, and beside me, I could hear the soft exhale of Amrita doing the same. It went against our Avramov grain to leave something baneful unexorcised; both of us would have hated watching Emily walk away with that locket curled like a sleeping snake around her neck.

With a nod, I set the locket on the table and began unloading my hydration supplies, unscrewing caps and stabbing in straws so that after the exorcism, I could suck down my liquid of choice with the least amount of fuss. Emily watched, only slightly bewildered, a wrinkle appearing between her neat brows. "You must be *very* thirsty," she said, wryly enough to make me smile despite myself.

"Not yet, but I will be soon," I said, glancing over at my sister. "Amrita, if you would?"

Amrita scooted her chair toward a corner of the enclosure, gesturing for Emily to do the same, until they both sat huddled near the mosaic lamp, a healthy distance away from me and the table. I could feel the glittering dome of the protection spell my sister cast under her breath as it settled around them, making sure the demon couldn't lash out at her and Emily once I drew it out of its cozy little lair. My sister was an expert at this kind of protective ward—part of the reason we worked together as often as we did. Someone needed to act as my foil, the shield rather than the sword.

As soon as they were safely settled, I began my work.

As far as I knew, all Avramovs could banish or exorcise both shades and demons, though with wildly varying degrees of success. But they needed spells to do it—premade magical workings gleaned from the Grimoire, the spell repository used by the four witch families of Thistle Grove. A series of words and gestures, sometimes helped along by the use of occult arcana, in formalized rituals they committed to memory.

For other kinds of spells, I also relied on words and tools crafted by others, handed down over the centuries. But to eat demons out of existence, I'd only ever needed myself.

First, I pushed my chair away and knelt on the floor; these workings were always easier when I felt connected to the earth, the loamy soil beneath the pour of the Emporium's concrete foundation. Then I cast a circle just wide enough to encompass me and the table, above which the demon would manifest—though this was just a precaution, since it would be bound to my will as soon as I summoned it. Next, I reached out to the locket with my mind, sensing the now-familiar shape lurking just beyond the veil, the way its malignant essence entangled with the locket in an ugly snarl. And I instinctively knew just where to push and press with my magic, the psychic lockpicking I needed to pry it loose.

It resisted as soon as it sensed the insistence of my call, its struggle like some ferocious thrashing, a giant squid flailing against a harpoon. But I didn't give it so much as an inch, not a moment to wriggle itself free, though I could feel the sweat springing up along my hairline at the tremendous effort I was expending, a flush traveling like brushfire down my spine.

Arm wrestling matches with chthonic creatures were not for the faint of heart.

Once I'd loosened its sucking hold enough, I shaped my will into a snare and looped it around the revenant demon's nebulous form. Then I raised my hands and made a come-hither gesture so forceful it ended with my nails digging into my palms—accompanied by a colossal wrenching of my will, the single-minded intent of dragging the demon into our plane.

Ectoplasm began roiling out of the locket in a raging river, swirling like a maelstrom over the table and emitting a furious hiss. The demon churned like poisonous smoke above a boiling cauldron, before settling into a manifested form—something be-tween a leech-like blob and an octopus, with twitching stubs of tentacles instead of full-length limbs. A hideous approximation of a face protruded from its soft underbelly; two gelatinous black eyes like clumps of roe, a circular lipless mouth lined with rows of gnashing teeth. Its slick hide glittered like black mica, as if it were studded with tiny stars.

I had to hand it to the beast—the shimmer was a nice cosmic touch. I'd definitely seen uglier.

"Cut-rate Cthulhu," I remarked, screwing up my face in mock disappointment. "Huh. You know, I would have put good money on your true form being, well . . . more *original* than this."

"Oh my god," I could hear Emily repeating in the background, in a high-pitched tone somewhere between full-fledged panic and wild laughter, though I didn't dare shift my gaze to her to check. Amrita could manage it; that was her role. "Oh my fucking god, *that's* been getting in bed with me? *That's* what I let in?"

"It's not your fault," came my sister's low reply, and though I couldn't see it, I knew this would be when she'd draw Emily against her into a side hug. "You didn't know. And you still knew enough to come to us, which is what counts."

"LET ME LOOSE, YOU INSOLENT MORTAL *BITCH*!" the revenant demon roared at me in that hellish timbre, ear skewering and bone rattling all at once. Hopefully someone on duty would have drawn an aural privacy glamour over our enclosure by now; everyone at the Emporium knew the kind of work I did and how noisy it could get. Even if not, they'd probably just blame it on sound effects bleeding through the walls from our haunted-house experience next door. "BEFORE I SUCK YOUR EYES OUT OF YOUR HEAD, AND BURST THEM BE-TWEEN MY TEETH LIKE BOILED JELLIES!"

I feigned a bored yawn, though my blood had whipped up into a screaming gale of exhilaration and terror, the taste of metal tanging in my mouth. The hotter I could stoke its fury, the more easily I could break it down. I knew that from long experience.

"Right, right, your teeth are so very sharp, et cetera," I said, stifling another yawn. "Slurp up my brains like crème brûlée, blah blah. Though I'm pretty sure I run more savory than sweet, which doesn't seem to be your thing."

"FOR YOU I WILL MAKE A JOYOUS EXCEPTION, YOU DECAYING SLU—"

"And that's enough," I cut in, splaying my hands open before clenching them back into fists. The demon's roar stopped as if it had been sheared off, severed by my will. In the sudden silence, broken only by Emily's harsh breathing and the heavy thudding of my own heart in my ears, I drew a shining thread between my intent and my devil-eating magic—the coil of raw, dark, ravenous power that curled tight at the very center of my being like something hungry and serpentine. I could feel it stirring with interest at the prospect of a treat. As if it were almost sentient, something that existed both as an integral part of and independently from me.

Then I channeled the full force of my will into dissolving the revenant demon into something it could eat.

This deconstruction demanded such single-minded strength and focus that the real world around me seemed to recede, take several steps back. Leaving me stranded in some liminal space, a tiny amphitheater that contained only this small battle, this intimate face-off between the demon and me.

It fought me hard. This was an ancient entity, likely born before the cosmos had even begun contemplating the possibility of my own existence. The souls it had fed on were legion, fattening it up and strengthening it. And as I whittled it down bit by bit, imagined its form breaking down into an inky slurry of ectoplasm, it resisted me with every iota of its own formidable will. Whatever concept of "alive" this beast possessed was just as precious to it as mine was to me. It wasn't about to go gently, not when it was used to being the one snuffing out other lives on a whim.

I could feel it battering ferociously against me, even as its form began to lose material cohesion, becoming translucent and gelatinous as it thinned down into a floating sludge.

"EAT ME, THEN!" it roared directly into my mind, no longer able to vocalize aloud. My focus wavered at the colossal drone in my brain, like a clash of cymbals shot through with a keening whine, though a glance at Emily and Amrita confirmed that only

I could hear this. "IT WILL NOT SAVE OUR MILK-SWEET EMILY IN THE END. BECAUSE *HE* IS COMING, THE ROUGH BEAST BREACHING THE HORIZON. FOR HER ABOVE ALL, AND THE REST OF YOU ALONG WITH HER!"

Who the fuck was this approaching "he"? I thought wildly, my heart bucking in my chest. And what did it want with Emily? Normally I'd have thought it was only trying to scare me; demons spewed whatever lies worked best to foment despair and fear. But there was a note of awestruck reverence to the words that felt troublingly sincere.

"And when he comes . . ." it hissed, its voice in my mind abruptly dropping to a sibilant whisper. Somehow the quieter timbre registered as infinitely more sinister, sending a chill scuttling down my spine. *"When he comes, all of you will fall to your brittle human knees and weep, a flood of salty, futile, delicious tears for him to—"*

"I said, *enough*," I repeated, in a ruthless whisper of my own, clamping back down on my focus and bringing it to bear. Even halfway unraveled, the demon was still strong, and the raging of its struggle might have blown some weaker witch's soul to smithereens.

But unlike almost anyone else, I'd been born for exactly this.

Even though my garnet burned against my throat—my talent might have been something I was born with, but that didn't mean using it was good for me—I refused to give in. Indomitable as a steamroller set to pulverize, a boulder rolling downhill.

With a final squelch, the demon melted entirely. What came next was the trickiest part. If I hesitated, left the slightest gap in my resolve, I'd give it a chance to recoalesce, gather up the free-floating fragments of its own will and manifest again. Demons were resilient like that, tenacious as cockroaches. You had to stamp them out, brutal and quick.

So as much as I hated what came next, I had to fully commit.

I let my head fall back, my jaw hinging open, and drew the demon's sludgy remnants toward me in thick gray skeins that spiraled through the air. For a moment, they hung above me like an ominous thunderhead. Then the ectoplasm began to drip into my mouth, drop by drop like a slow rain, before merging into a sluggish stream that sluiced directly down my throat. As always, I fought to swallow, to keep my mouth levered open. In its living form, the demon had been heat incarnate—but inert, ectoplasm as a substrate was a bone-chilling cold, the essence of death. And it tasted fouler than foul, like acrid venom infused with dry ice. The world's shittiest artisanal cocktail.

Whatever force had seen fit to instill me with this "gift" could've at least tweaked my palate to match, I'd thought more than once. But life wasn't that kind of fair.

And while the human part of me—most of me—loathed every moment, that dormant hunger yawned wide open like a living chasm. I drew strength from it, let it gird me, so I could do what had to be done without allowing the revulsion to overwhelm me.

As if from a distance, I could hear Emily pose some shrill question to Amrita that I couldn't catch, followed by the low murmur of my sister's reassurance that, despite all alarming evidence to the contrary, everything was actually proceeding according to plan!

Once the last of the demon had dripped into my mouth, I choked it down with a final, convulsive gulp. Then I pitched forward unsteadily, swiping the back of my hand across my mouth.

The world snapped back into place around me, a bath of warmth and candlelight and sound, an oasis of normalcy. Amrita hurried over to help me up, warm hands closing around my upper arms. The thirst was already raging inside me, a desperate need for mundane liquid, anything to counteract the deathly matter I'd just absorbed. I lunged for the apple juice first, crushing box after box, pulling so hard on each straw that the cardboard sides crumpled in on themselves. Then I chugged two-thirds of the water bottle, eyes fluttering closed at the soothing cool coursing down my ravaged throat. When Amrita held out a Wild Turkey nip, eyebrows raised, I shook my head.

"Not this time," I said hoarsely, head still swimming a little. "It tore up my throat too much. I'll take the Pedialyte, though."

With the salty sweetness of strawberry-flavored electrolytes sloshing in my belly, I finally felt steady enough to shift my attention back to Emily. She still sat hunched in the farthest corner, her face leached of color, tear tracks glistening on her cheeks. I noticed, a little giddily, that her foundation had managed to hold through what must have been a full-blown existential crisis crossed with a nervous breakdown. The hells kind of primer did rich people even *use*?

"That . . ." Her voice broke, throat working. "That was fucking horrible. Was it . . . was it as bad as it looked? For you?"

"Yes," I said simply, seeing no reason to sugarcoat it for her. "Not that it's ever enjoyable, but as they come, this infestation was pretty vile."

"Thank you," she whispered, wet, dark eyes fastened on mine. "For doing that for me. I . . . I really think maybe I'm not paying you enough."

I chuckled through the rasping pain in my throat. "Well, tips are very welcome. But it's what I do, and I'm glad to have helped."

"We do recommend you cleanse your home with purging and protective herbs, as a prophylactic measure," Amrita added. "Sometimes the negative energy of it having fed on you can linger, draw other psychic predators."

"Other psychic predators," Emily echoed with a weak burble of a laugh. "Of course. Why not."

"I'm happy to set you up with our purification bundle, if you'd like. It's the routine protocol."

She nodded, dabbing at the corners of her eyes with a knuckle. "But she . . . I won't see Lettie again?"

"The revenant demon's gone for good," Amrita said, with infinite gentleness. "So, no, you won't be exposed to any more illusions of your cousin. No more dreams or nighttime visits. None of that."

Though I'd known it was coming, it still hurt to see Emily's face contort, the renewed gush of tears. "This is so stupid," she said damply, thumping a vicious fist against her thigh. "I don't even know what I'm crying about. It wasn't ever really her, I know that now. It was that awful thing the whole time. But I'm . . . I'm just . . ."

"You're going to miss her," Amrita finished. "You were tricked into believing you'd been given something precious, and now you have to come to terms with the loss anew. Of course it's hard. *Of course* it hurts. Don't judge yourself for it too harshly. Or at all, if you can spare that much grace for yourself."

With a beckoning glance at me, she crossed the enclosure to sit next to Emily, taking her hand and folding it between both of hers. I moved next to them to kneel by Emily's other side, head bowed. Lending her my presence as she wept, bookended by the two of us, her shoulders racked with sobs. Just the way Amrita, my niece, and my stepmother had once done for me.

Because this was part of it, too. We didn't just deal with ghosts, walk dark paths that wound deep into the forest gloom.

Tending to grief, bearing witness to the ponderous weight of loss, was just as much what it meant to be an Avramov.

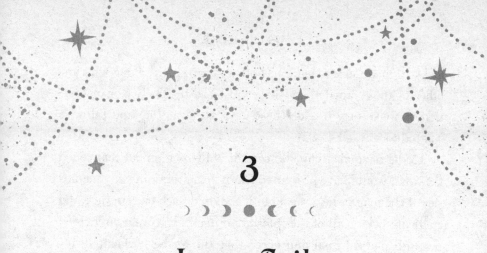

3

Lesser Evils

"HOW ARE YOU doing?" Amrita asked again as we walked through the Emporium's aisles together, the otherworldly choral music that always played in the store drifting around us like the auditory equivalent of the incense. I still felt tweaky enough that even its ethereal strains grated on me a little, but that was good.

It reminded me that I was really here, both feet solidly planted in this realm.

"Better than Emily Duhamel," I replied with a half shrug. "She was a lot tougher than most, I'll give her that. But I'd still bet she's in for a rough few weeks, coming to terms with having let a life-sucking hell squid spoon her every night."

Once she'd composed herself, we'd sent Emily home with the bundle of purification herbs and the reassurance that we would be here if she ever needed us again. Even as shaky as she'd been, she had still made sure to leave us both a generous tip, along with another of those sturdy handshakes. If I had the energy or inclination to make new friends these days, she was the kind I'd have wanted for myself.

Under normal circumstances, the oblivion glamour that veiled the town would have prevented Emily from retaining any memories of the magic she'd seen, but it couldn't reach back in time and eradicate her recall of the infestation itself. And we'd discovered through painful trial and error that the formerly haunted, infested, or possessed *needed* to remember the exorcism. Otherwise they'd never shed the subconscious memory of what they'd experienced; the physical imprint would live on in their bodies, as if stamped all the way down to the matrix of their cells. We'd only be leaving them differently traumatized, haunted by their own minds. So we'd made it one of our best practices to tweak the oblivion glamour during any banishing ritual we performed, letting our clients heal from their own psychic injuries.

This loophole technically flew in the face of the prohibition against allowing normies to witness and remember any of our magic—but the Blackmoores did the same at their Castle Camelot attraction, allowing tourists to retain the magical "special effects" they saw during their cloyingly cheesy musical performances, twisting the rules purely for their own profit. And in all the years we'd been bending the rules, making such exceptions had never come back to bite us. As best we could tell, most of our clients went about their lives keeping what they'd seen to themselves—or if they didn't, no one believed what they had to say.

Amrita looped her arm through mine, cutting me an impressively keen side-eye. "Except she isn't my sister. And she sure as the hells isn't the one who just pounded liquefied devil after getting a hit of the other side. So no more deflection. How are you *really?*"

I took a deep breath as we meandered between ornate wooden shelves, stacked with everything from hand-painted tarot decks and scrying mirrors in hammered copper frames to cut-glass chalices and ceremonial bowls. Above us, handmade besoms— witches' brooms used in rituals—hung from the exposed rafters of the high ceiling, strings of drying herbs swinging between them like rustic ornaments. The familiarity of what we all affectionately referred to as Ye Witchy Walmart, the megastore of occult arcana I'd grown up with, helped ground me with each step. But I still shook a little, a fine tremor that coursed through my limbs and left my fingers twitching.

It clearly hadn't escaped my hawkeyed sister. Not much did, alas.

"It's still fucking hard," I admitted, picking at loose threads dangling from my sweater hem. "It would almost be easier if I could, I don't know, build up some immunity. If just being there wasn't so damn potent every time. But it never fades. Every time feels exactly like the first."

"Do you need to come home with me?" Amrita asked softly, no censure in her tone. "Saanvi would love to stuff you full of whatever's for dinner tonight, I'm sure. And you know Kira can never get enough of you."

I smiled at the mention of my stepmother and niece; Amrita had been living with her mother since my sister's less-than-amicable split with Kira's father four years earlier. After my bleakest period a little over two years ago—the dark, lost days of my complete infatuation with the other side—part of my slow and scattershot recovery had included moving in with the three of them.

I'd needed that immersive contact with the living, especially my own kin, and all the full-blooded human joys that came with it. Saanvi's spectacular food and hugs, late-night wine with Amrita, Kira's rollicking toddler giggles, the warmth of her little body on my lap when I read *Grumpy Monkey* and *How to Catch a Unicorn* to her before bed. Even after I'd felt steady enough to move back out, just over a year ago, they still kept the guest room reserved for me.

Sometimes I forgot how complicated our unconventional little family must seem to anyone on the outside. But it worked for us, so well that it had gone a good way toward saving my life.

"Thank you, but I don't think so. I can't keep relying on you every time I cross," I replied, just as gently. "If I'm not going to stop sliding over altogether, I have to be able to safely withstand it on my own. You know that."

She nodded, only a little reluctantly, concern still etched into her features. Slipping through to the other side came as naturally to me as other forms of necromancy did to the rest of my family, and even at my worst, none of them had suggested that the answer lay in never crossing the veil again. As much as my visits there were a dangerous temptation, a slippery slope I needed to navigate on my own, I was an Avramov. The connection with death was in my blood, part of my father's legacy. Even if I did happen to have a much riskier case of it than most.

"Well," she said, "you know the invitation stands. In the meantime, are you feeling up to a quick meeting with Elena? I let her know you were coming in for an assist, and she wanted a final check-in with you on the Cavalcade preparations."

In my more mundane role, I was the Arcane Emporium's event planner, which meant that any special events or festivals fell under my purview. I'd always enjoyed my job, but more recently, the organizational aspect of it had become something of a lifeline. It demanded constant contact with living people and an endless array of spreadsheets—the kind of substantive and administrative juggle so firmly rooted in this world that it kept my mind from drifting toward the metaphysical.

A debrief with my boss—who also happened to be the Avramov family matriarch—was exactly what I needed to take my mind off the other side and banish the lingering unease of the demon's parting words.

"I'll be fine." I held up a hand for her. "See? Shakes already fading."

"I'll walk you. I need to check in with her myself anyway." She frowned, elegant nose wrinkling, light winking off its two dainty studs. "Something odd's been going on with the apothecary inventory. The numbers aren't squaring up at the end of the month."

"Are you thinking shoplifting?" It had been an occasional problem in the past, though rare; the few cases we had tended to be Thistle Grove teens on a dare to steal from the town's spookiest witch family. It was unusual enough that we'd never even bothered putting wards in place for it.

"Possibly? But who's got sticky fingers for henbane, wormwood, hound's-tongue, vervain, and mandrake, specifically?"

"You're right, that *is* odd." I rummaged through my mental repository of Grimoire spells that might rely on those ingredients, and came up empty with any combination that required all five. "Have you talked to Wynter about it?"

"She's the one who brought it up to me, which is frankly astonishing in itself, given her powers of observation." Amrita gave a massive roll of her kohled eyes. Sweet-tempered as my sister was, especially for one of our family, Wynter still managed to wriggle under her skin. "I know she's a superlative pusher of merch or Elena wouldn't tolerate her. But Mother and Crone, that is one aggravating bitch."

Wynter—a name I hoped to the hells and back her own mother hadn't actually saddled her with—was one of the few local normies employed by the Emporium. My personal suspicion was that she'd been hired only because she also happened to be one of our most reliable purchasers of occult paraphernalia and herbs. She was a self-styled "solitary practitioner," complete with an Etsy craft store and revoltingly devout social media following, despite the fact that she didn't belong to any of the four Thistle Grove witch families and exhibited not even the slightest inkling of real magical talent.

"Dim as a dead bulb," I agreed. "And the worst kind of wannabe. Buys one thousand percent into her own bullshit, which is either an impressive amount of delusion or total commitment to a bit. Not to mention contagious."

Amrita gave me a warning squeeze as we neared the Avramov Apothecary section of the store, where Wynter herself was delivering an ardent lecture to a customer who seemed to be hanging on her every word.

She *was* cute, I suppose, if you went all in for the CW Glam Witch™ aesthetic. Her waist-length hair and heavy bangs were dyed pitch-black, framing a pert face with a ski-slope nose, hazel eyes fringed with eyelash extensions below a pint of shimmery gray shadow, and a tragically overfilled pout glossed to a taupe gleam. Above the gauzy bodice of her gown—all her necklines were filmy and low-cut, to showcase the kind of balloon boobs that needed no scaffolding—tattoos sprawled over her neck and chest.

An intricate jewel necklace curled around her throat and across her collarbones, spiderwebs and snakes creeping up each porcelain shoulder. At least she wasn't wearing one of her witch fascinators, sheer black veil included.

It was all the kind of much that did absolutely nothing for me. But I could see why it worked for her when it came to the hordes of horny, lonely, witch-fetishizing strangers who drooled over her online.

"The thing is, like, if you're trying to restore the lost sanctity of your love," Wynter was saying, gesticulating broadly with her tiny hands, tipped with the kind of pointy nails that looked like they could spear a passing eyeball in an overzealous movement, "it's all about, does the cosmos will it so, too. But you can always grease the wheels a little. I recommend a wax-sealed jar of turmeric, dragon's blood, crushed violet petals, and moon water for this type of thing, ideally assembled during the dark of the moon. And I know this is going to be gross—that's how you know it works, right?!—but you're going to need some of your period blood and his fingernail clippings in there, too. They're the special sauce."

The poor, beleaguered woman bit her lip, looking torn. "I . . . his nail clippings? I'm really not sure how I could get those. I'd rather not, I don't know, stalk him. Or break into his *house.*"

"Hmm, yeah, sourcing that can be tricky for sure. But veering into TMI territory for a sec, is ex sex maybe an option?" Wynter's face turned conspiratorial, and she leaned across the counter, propping her dainty chin on her palm. "Because if it is, that's even better. You could always just save his—"

"Mother and Crone, I cannot with this," Amrita muttered

under her breath, hastily steering us out of hearing range before we were subjected to the rest of Wynter's advice. "Special sauce, indeed. She's gonna spiritually advise that chick right into prison."

"But she's definitely also going to drop a small fortune on those herbs, right?" I suppressed a shudder. "Before she even . . . *sources* the rest of the ingredients."

"Yup," Amrita bit off, with an exasperated pop on the *p*. "And then when this deranged love spell doesn't work, fifty bucks says she'll be right back here for more of Wynter's sage counsel and another pricey batch of herbs."

"Painful to watch, but hey. At least the cycle of absurdity helps keep our lights on."

Amrita gave a doleful nod. "Believe me, I know. Elena's going to keep her around *forever*, which means I will never not be supervising her. She has become my eternal millstone."

"She might still poison herself with one of her own concoctions," I consoled, patting her shoulder.

"Working here is her whole personality. Ten to one she'd be back for her next shift right after getting her stomach pumped. Nothing short of the end of days is likely to deliver us from her evil most banal."

I spurted a laugh, raspy against my still-sore throat. "Damn, sis, tell me how you *really* feel."

"And now I have to admit to the boss that my archnemesis was actually useful, for once." She gave a dramatic groan as we reached the door to Elena's back office. "Why me."

"Think happy thoughts," I instructed, leaning back against the wall with my arms crossed and one foot propped up as she knocked on Elena's imposing mahogany door. Our matriarch had a very Avramov thing for the more intimidating woods. "Saanvi's epic leftovers sandwiches. Kira's dramatic reads of *Dragons Love Farts.* Evrain Blackmoore busting his smarmy face open on a sidewalk and then getting terrible veneers."

"The dipshit father of my child already has veneers for a soul," Amrita muttered, leaving me chortling outside as she let herself in. "At least they would match."

While I waited for my turn with Elena, I tried to keep those same happy thoughts—warm, mortal thoughts—front and center of myself, as afterimages of the other side slid across my mind like enticing trespassers. The faceted glitter of that strange fruit that grew on the spindly trees. That sweep of shale sky billowing with streaks of crimson clouds. Those motionless flowers, black and bizarre and uncannily perfect. And me among it all, ablaze like a bonfire, burning with so much delicious life. Like a living sun rising against the cold expanse of that unending dark.

The thought whispered delicately across my mind, like a scrap of silk being drawn over stone, the way it always did. *You could go back,* that hunger inside me prompted in a tantalizing hiss. *Anytime you wanted. Right now, even, without moving an inch. And you wouldn't ever have to leave.*

It was right; the other side was never closed off to me. Even with the grounding influence of the garnet at my throat, some crucial part of me was simply unmoored, untethered, in a way that other members of my family weren't.

Some part of me naturally belonged there, more than it did here. I aligned with it magnetically, like a compass needle straining toward true north.

But I knew what this line of thinking led to, its inevitable conclusion. I knew what it had done to me when I'd given in to it; what it had done to those who cared about me the most. And so

I'd do what it took to resist, even if committing those lesser evils sometimes hurt almost as much.

FIFTEEN MINUTES LATER, I sat across from Elena Avramov's massive desk, in the beautiful yet perpetually wobbly antique Queen Anne chair that always made me feel like a penitent child. I had no proof, but I suspected its lopsidedness was the matriarch's subtle way of getting the upper hand in every conversation conducted in here before it had even begun. Not that she needed the help, being larger than life simply by existing. Her entire person, from those penetrating, feline-green eyes and cascade of fox-pelt hair, to the heavy scent of perfume and pipe tobacco that permeated the office, exuded authority. Even the formidable mahogany bookshelves rising behind her, stacked with leather-bound ledgers and carved with ivy, hellebore, and capering imps, couldn't dwarf the dark-star immensity of her presence.

"Amrita tells me you've exorcised a revenant demon for one of her clients," she said, her eyes alight with the thought of a successfully dispatched demon. "Ghastly creatures, aren't they? I could hear that one bellowing its uninspired obscenities from here before someone thought to cast a dampening glamour over the divination enclosures. You'd imagine, given the length of their existence and taste for stolen human memories, they could muster at least a touch of creativity."

"It did say something . . . odd, right before I dissolved it." I closed my eyes, quoting the demon from memory as best I could. "Does that mean anything to you?"

"'And what rough beast, its hour come round at last,'" Elena said, rolling her eyes a little. "Yeats, 'The Second Coming.' A demon cribbing from classic apocalypse poetry, how terribly cliché. I wouldn't put much stock in deathbed threats like that. Perhaps it ate a melancholic English professor somewhere down the line."

I chuckled at that, the last of my unease dissipating. "Maybe that's why it went down so harsh. Left me with a solid case of exorcist strep throat, but nothing a hot toddy or three won't fix."

"How are you feeling otherwise?" Elena asked, leaning forward in her hobnailed, crackled-leather chair, those jade eyes sharpening until I shifted in my uncomfortable seat. "I assume you traversed the veil before exorcising the wretched thing. Did you have any trouble finding your way back?"

I clenched my teeth, bristling a little at the question—even though she, of all people, had every right to ask. Both as the head of our family and the witch who'd done the lion's share of clawing me back to life when I needed it the most.

"No. I'm doing well," I said stiffly. "No . . . relapses to speak of. Time with family helps; so does work. Especially planning something as ambitious as the Cavalcade."

Elena nodded, elbows resting on her blotter, fingers steepled under her chin. "I imagine putting it together hasn't left you with much room for ruminating. And I'm glad to hear you've been prioritizing it on our behalf. I take it we're all set for launch next week?"

I nodded, giving the agenda a quick mental once-over. The Cavalcade was Thistle Grove's most elaborate festival, and like the Gauntlet of the Grove, it was one deliberately laid out in the Grimoire as opposed to being a more modern, tourist-trappy invention. It marked the September anniversary of Thistle Grove's founding, in the form of a historical re-creation of the four founders' staking out of territory in the town nearly four hundred years ago. Every twenty years, the families came together to give tourists the opportunity to retrace the founders' footsteps, and enjoy performances inspired by our different magics and set against the backdrop of the family demesnes. This was the only instance in which tourists, locals, and Thistle Grove vendors were allowed to both witness and participate in magical displays as part of the celebration—the Grimoire specifically called for this exception, even as it omitted any reason why—and it made for an outlandish spectacle that outshone almost everything else the town put on. (And even without the oblivion glamour, these days you could always pass off real magic as high-end special effects.)

The preparations involved were extensive, even for a town that ran on witch tourism year-round. Fall was the most beautiful and beguiling time in Thistle Grove, a season that felt charmed even to the magicless, not to mention a gateway to the chaos of Halloween month. Which meant that every two decades, the Cavalcade gave us a tourist boost that equaled two back-to-back Octobers.

"The planning committee's holding a closing meeting on Tuesday, but it's mostly a formality," I replied. "Everything's set for the Friday opening. We've already completed the scheduled dry runs for the Avramov spectacle, and they've all gone off without a hitch."

"Wonderful." Elena clicked the tips of her shining candy-apple nails against each other, making a pensive moue. "And everyone's behaving? No issues with the other families?"

"Well, I wouldn't say our collaboration has been an epic joy, but no, nothing worth noting. Gawain Blackmoore pitched only a manageable number of prima donna fits when it came to his 'creative vision' for our closing lakeside spectacle. I think having Big Brother Gareth at the Blackmoore helm has actually been good for him."

Elena gave a small smile, presumably enjoying a fond memory of Yule past. During the Yule celebrations, our current Victor of the Wreath, Emmeline Harlow, had summarily dethroned the former Blackmoore elder, Lyonesse, on account of some egregious misconduct and treachery. Little love had been lost between Elena and the older Blackmoore generation, and so far, Lyonesse's scion, Gareth—previously best known for being an infamous fuckboy-about-town and overall degenerate—seemed to be doing a surprisingly fair job running things at Castle Camelot and the Blackmoores' Tintagel demesne.

"And to her credit," I continued, "Genevieve Harlow is sensible enough to have kept him well in hand."

Our Harlow planning committee chairperson was so relentlessly minutiae oriented that her detailing of bullet points occasionally made me want to slide into catatonia. It was possible that the timbre of her voice managed to lull even Gawain's hyperactive nervous system into rest and digest.

"And the Thorns? I know we've had an easier time with them overall, what with Issa and Rowan's ongoing dalliance." Another inscrutable smile flickered over the elder's lips at the thought of her younger daughter's partnership with the scion of the Thorn line. What Elena actually thought of the pairing, given our complicated history with the Thorn family, was impossible to decipher, at least to someone like me. I was a relatively distant cousin to the Avramov main line, and beyond my work at the

Emporium—and Elena's involvement with my checkered necromantic past—I'd never had a close relationship with our matriarch. "But we haven't been collaborating directly with the official
Honeycake event coordinator, have we?"

I swallowed, my stomach bucking with a reflexive lurch of sadness at the mention of my Thorn counterpart. Otherwise known
as my ex-girlfriend—and quite possibly the love of my life, before
I'd fucked that up on every level humanly possible.

When it came to leaving relationships in smoldering, apoca-
lyptic ruins, no one could accuse me of any lack of natural talent.

"That's correct. Ivy Thorn's assistant, Indigo, has been working with us instead of Ivy herself, due to . . . scheduling conflicts
on Ivy's end, I believe," I added, running my tongue over my teeth.
Not a wholesale lie; Ivy Thorn's unwillingness to tolerate the
sight of my face *could* be perceived as a scheduling conflict. In a
certain light. "But it's been relatively seamless. Indigo's a consum-
mate professional, and doesn't seem to have bad blood with any of
the families."

"A gift from the Mother and Crone herself," Elena commented,
arching a feathery copper eyebrow. "Let's hope her blessing will
carry over to the ceremonies. Involving mundanes in our festivities is a tricky enough business to begin with, and the last time
around, we didn't have a storm-riddled Lady's Lake to contend
with."

I sat back in my chair, a shiver skittering down my spine. The
mountaintop lake that served as the town's overflowing font of
magic—and the sacred, underwater sanctuary of the goddess
Belisama's stone avatar—had grown increasingly tumultuous over
the past few months. Boiling storms now raged just above the lake
at least once a week, bolts of sapphire lightning forking like

serpent tongues down to the water's churning surface. The turbulent weather never seemed to extend past the Hallows Hill summit, and somehow Thistle Grove's magicless inhabitants seemed to have readily accepted "climate change" as a viable explanation.

The families were much less nonchalant about it, though as far as I knew, we were equally in the dark as to what was causing the disturbance.

"It's come up in our meetings," I told Elena. "Since the Hallows Hill ceremony is families only, we don't have to worry about normie spectator safety. And if we wind up with a stormy night, the Blackmoores seem confident they can calm the weather enough to allow for the rite." As elementalists, the Blackmoore family had the strongest aptitude for storm-wrangling atmospheric magic. "But I'll bring it up again on Tuesday just to make sure."

Elena nodded vaguely, an abstracted expression stealing over her face—as though the conversation had reminded her of some subterranean concern that she'd been grappling with before I'd even walked in. Something that was clearly on a need-to-know basis that didn't extend to the likes of me.

"Let us hope that's indeed the case," she finally said, gaze shifting back to me, something murky and unreadable still swimming in its jade depths. Unease stirred inside me like the slow shift of tectonic plates; the ominous sense that what I'd managed to glimpse of her disquiet was only the tip of a very large, very daunting iceberg. "Thank you, Daria, that will be all. And enjoy your hot toddies tonight—along with something stronger, if you're so inclined. You've earned it."

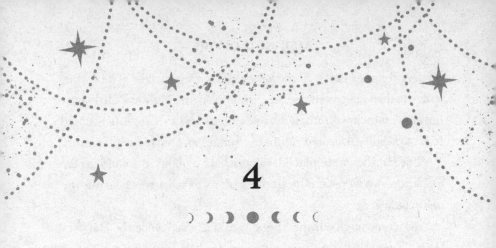

4

Seams of Liquid Gold

SHE WASN'T SUPPOSED to be there.

When I walked into the Harlow House library for the last meeting of the Cavalcade planning committee, I'd been in what passed for a good mood by my admittedly low standards. I'd had a productive morning, and the weather was Thistle Grove's early fall perfection, vibrant and flawless as a stained glass window. Brilliant slants of sunshine, fiery leaves swirling in patterns intentional as omens, a breeze tinged with woodsmoke and the faint cider tang of the Thorn apple orchards, just chill enough to pinch a gentle flush into your cheeks. The sky was pure cobalt, every passing cloud a shape inviting dreamy interpretation. A bichon's fluffy head, the silhouette of a cat with its tail swept over its arched back, a spouting whale.

I'd strolled the two miles here from my little cottage at the edge of the Witch Woods, the sun settling like a warm crown on my head, breathing in that crisp autumnal air with its incensey undertone. Thistle Grove never smelled more keenly of the lake's magic, a smoky perfume of melted beeswax, amber, and frankincense, than it did in fall. It was nearly enough to make me forget the constant undertow of yearning for the other side that rushed inside me like a dark river. Even if only for an hour or so.

Which meant I'd let my psychic armor slip, leaving me even less prepared to find Ivy at Harlow House instead of Indigo.

My gaze barely skimmed the rest of the library: cluttered bookshelves, a cushy assembly of mismatched furniture beneath the punched-tin ceiling fixture, the crackling leap of flames in the stone hearth. From its handsome but understated colonial exterior to the homey elegance of its rooms, Harlow House made much less of a fuss over itself than the other family demesnes. As usual, Gawain Blackmoore lolled in one of the overstuffed chairs, in a close-cut blazer over a T-shirt for a band I didn't recognize the name of—probably fictional, meant to signal that Gawain's taste in music was just That Impossibly Cool—golden curls swept back from his disaffected-front-man face. Under different circumstances, I'd have been annoyed by everything from the obnoxious way he sat to the hairy ankles above the turquoise Converse emblazoned with his initials, his distressed jeans hitched up too high.

But the sum total of these irritations barely registered, because all I could focus on was her.

The glorious, devastating, all-consuming shock of her unexpected presence.

Ivy sat near the fireplace, curled up on one end of a love seat, argyle-socked feet tucked under her. The firelight gleamed off the sculpted curve of her cheekbones, highlighting the lushness of glossed lips and the dense wings of her eyebrows. Its reflection flickered in her near-black eyes, played over the luster of her dark brown skin. She'd let her buzzed hair grow out a little, but it was still only a neat shadow over the elegant shape of her skull, tapering down to the swan neck I'd run my lips over so many times. The moss-green ribbed sweaterdress she wore clung to the familiar full curves of her body, its sweetheart neckline revealing the delicate struts of collarbones, skin drawn taut over them. A tiny silver snowdrop necklace glinted in the hollow of her throat.

She was so impossibly beautiful, and her liquid gaze so shuttered as it met mine, that it made me want to keel over where I stood.

The last time I'd seen her had been only a handful of weeks ago, at the Lughnasadh celebration. We hadn't spoken, but we'd been fresh off a favor I'd done for her and her best friend, Delilah Harlow. Ivy had been just a little softer toward me then, thawed enough to at least acknowledge me whenever our eyes caught over mugs of celebratory mead. Something like the memory of sparks flaring between us.

The steely person holding my gaze like a cool challenge looked nothing like someone who'd once called me "Starshine," or smiled into my face like a flower unfurling as a prelude to a kiss.

"Dasha, you finally made it!" Genevieve Harlow chirped, a tart note of reproach to her bright voice. She wasn't the type to overlook seven whole minutes of tardiness, though she was also too Midwestern to call me out on it directly. "I was just starting to worry we might have to kick things off without you."

"Never fear," I managed through a tight smile, somehow tearing my gaze away from Ivy as I turned toward the closest available armchair. Genevieve sat at the round conference room table I assumed didn't normally live in the library, a platter of gourmet pretzels and a stack of napkins and paper plates arranged in front of her. Genevieve *was* the kind of person who'd rustle up a conference room table for a planning committee meeting of four—even if she was the only one who ever sat by it—and feel obligated to provide premium snacks. "Wouldn't miss our last moments together for the world."

Gawain snorted a laugh into a fisted hand, but Genevieve beamed like a glad-handing congresswoman, smiling so hard she nearly dislodged the chunky glasses perched on her freckled nose. Unlike passive aggression, sarcasm was somehow a foreign language to her. She'd even twisted her hair into a glossy brown chignon, like this was her last chance to play the role of Madame Chairperson to the hilt.

"Same, clearly. And we're lucky Ivy managed to find the time to attend our last little recap. Though, of course, Indigo has been *so* on point with everything!"

Again the subtle sniping, this time at Ivy's expense. I caught the brief spark of irritation in Ivy's heavy-lidded eyes, the flare of her fine nostrils. Genevieve also happened to be her best friend's not-quite-estranged little sister, and I knew the fierce loyalty Ivy felt toward Delilah Harlow meant she wasn't Genevieve's biggest fan even at the best of times.

"I'm just here to make Indigo more comfortable," Ivy replied, with enviable mildness. The low, honeyed texture of her voice resonated right in my solar plexus. "An event like this is way more than she's ever had on her plate. She's been a rock star covering for me, but we both wanted to make sure she hadn't let anything slip on our end before I take over for the duration of the Cavalcade."

I caught my breath, the pit of my belly blooming with

excitement. So Ivy *would* be there for the Cavalcade itself, overseeing Thorn involvement. I knew not to read anything into it; Ivy was a paragon of responsibility, and it tracked that she'd be willing to show up when her presence really counted, even if it meant dealing with me. But at the same time, I'd get to see her every weekend, for a whole month.

Which meant opportunities.

"Right, right." Genevieve peered at the sleek laptop open in front of her. "So, why don't we run through the full sequence of events? I'll start! Every Friday, Saturday, and Sunday morning, Tomes & Omens will be the first stop of the Cavalcade, with hot chocolate and breakfast pastries from Wicked Sweet available for purchase. From eight to eleven, Delilah and Emmy Harlow will be there to greet tourist groups, provide background on Thistle Grove's founding, and hand out brochures containing the town map, the schedule of events, and affiliated vendors."

Technically, Tomes & Omens wasn't the Harlow family demesne, and an educational tourist meet and greet wasn't exactly a spectacle. But given Elias Harlow's historical role as the scribe of our Grimoire and Harlow House's relative modesty, it made more sense for the tourist procession to kick off at the family's indie/occult bookstore on Yarrow, allowing visitors to explore the other storefronts along our picturesque main street before heading to the next event.

"The Honeycake Orchards spectacle will begin promptly at two," Ivy picked up smoothly, without consulting any notes. "Plenty of time to walk over to the orchards, or take a shuttle if they prefer. Those visitors who didn't grab lunch on Yarrow can choose to eat at the Honeycake restaurant or bakery. For the spectacle, we'll be doing an avian summoning at the entrance to the hedge maze, in recognition of Alastair Thorn calling down birds as witnesses to the founding."

Ivy flicked a gaze up at the ceiling, absently brushing the pad of her thumb over the silver hoop in the center of her lower lip in the achingly familiar way she always did when consulting her memory. I'd done it myself many times, too, grazing my finger over the plush pillow of her lip to part her mouth open before I kissed her.

The hollow space below my ribs clamped down so hard that I crossed my arms low over my stomach, curled over them to curb it a little.

"A normie contemporary dance troupe will perform as well," she went on. "After that, everyone's welcome to wander the orchards before heading to The Bitters."

"Uh, the Avramov spectacle begins at five thirty. Peak dusk," I said after a beat, so thrown by Ivy's gaze shifting expectantly to me that I almost forgot I was up next. "We'll be featuring normie aerialists, against an ectoplasmic shadow play evoking Margarita Avramov's ceremonial gathering of shades. We'll also have food trucks catered by the Shamrock Cauldron and Cryptid Pizza, and cocktail trucks courtesy of Whistler's Fireside."

The cocktail trucks had been my brainchild, and fuck if I wasn't proud of it, especially since we couldn't go as hard as the other families with our "special effects" lest we trigger a mass possession event.

"Is your demesne even big enough to mount that kind of production? I mean, *cocktail trucks*, really?" Gawain said, wrinkling his patrician nose, as if the Little Lord of Castle Camelot Musical Theatre somehow had the nerve to find cocktail trucks trashy. "That takes, like, some serious real estate."

"You were there for the opening ceremony of the Gauntlet of the Grove two years ago, were you not?" I retorted, infusing my tone with as much "do you even have spatial reasoning and basic recall, you relentless box of tools" as I could without making it explicit. From the corner of my eye, I caught Ivy almost-smirking, a dimple denting her smooth cheek. My heart leapt unreasonably at this tiny evidence of harmony between us. To be fair, when it came to loathing Gawain, you could probably find common ground with any random stranger plucked off the street.

"So you might remember that we can comfortably fit all the members of the families in The Bitters' backyard," I continued. "Which means plenty of room for everyone, plus a *bevy* of cocktail trucks."

Gawain held his palms up in mock concession. "Okay, chill. I'm not *implying* any lack of foresight on your part, or whatever. I was just *making sure*, given that we're about to go live three days from now."

"Right, except the cocktail trucks have been the plan for"—I glanced down at the nonexistent watch on my wrist, cocking my head—"a month and a half? Would you say that's how long it takes the average fact to fully penetrate your consciousness?"

This time, I caught the corner of Ivy's lip twitching dangerously, before she bit down on the inside of her cheek. A swell of satisfaction surged up my throat, sweet and heady as a mouthful of mulled wine. I'd always been able to make Ivy laugh herself silly, and apparently that much hadn't been irretrievably lost, swallowed up by the yawning fault lines that had consumed everything else good between us.

Fault lines I'd carved into place, fracturing them open like the human earthquake I was at my worst.

Genevieve cleared her throat with a schoolmarm's prissy disapproval at our bickering, breaking in before Gawain could mount a retort. "The cocktail truck box is officially checked, so let's keep things moving, shall we? Gawain, the Blackmoore spectacle?"

Gawain shot me a final azure glare, then sullenly set his gaze somewhere above Genevieve's shoulder, as though this entire tiresome exercise was beneath him.

"Eight sharp, in Castle Camelot's courtyard," he recited in a grudging monotone. "And we will not be using any normie performers."

"'Using'?" Ivy echoed under her breath, her face scrunching with distaste. "Ugh."

"Instead, we'll feature an incendiary charm extravaganza, spellwork shaped to mimic fireworks and lightning," Gawain went on, demonstratively ignoring her. "In memoriam of Caelia Blackmoore's historic founding storm. We'll still be running both matinees and evening performances of *The Green Knight's Folly*, for tourists who want to spend more time at Castle Camelot over the weekend. But the evening performance will be over well before eight, so no conflicts with the spectacle."

I swallowed back the same futile complaint I'd lodged a number of times already, about the inherent unfairness of holding the elaborate Castle Camelot musicals at times that would conflict with both the Thorns' spectacle and ours, potentially drawing tourists away from us. As far as Gawain was concerned, he'd already made a massive concession by agreeing to hold only a matinee on Sunday—though I suspected that even this token gesture of goodwill came from Gareth or Nineve Blackmoore, Gawain's older sister and Gareth's advisor.

Given the Cavalcade's fluid format, it didn't matter as much as it otherwise could have, anyway. Since we'd be running the spectacles on the same schedule for all of September, tourists would be able to either enjoy the entire Cavalcade in one packed day or split the experiences up between the three weekend days, giving themselves more time to explore Thistle Grove in between. We were also offering guided tours that included all four stops, discounts, and meal vouchers, and the circulating shuttles would add an extra layer of flexibility. There'd almost certainly be more than enough tourist money to go around.

My seething at Gawain's Blackmoore selfishness was mostly a reflex at this point, but damned if I was willing to give it up.

"And finally, the closing lakeside spectacle," Genevieve said, clicking away at her laptop. "Last Saturday in September, so it doubles as a Sabbat for us. All four families will converge on Hallows Hill, and the four elders will cast a joint ceremonial spell above the lake as we've discussed, to commemorate the founding. No normies will attend the rites, obviously, so it should run like any of our more customary Wheel of the Year holidays. Any questions on that front?"

"Elena's wondering if we feel confident about safely executing the closing," I offered. "Given how temperamental Lady's Lake has been lately."

"We do," Gawain replied testily. "As I've explained before, Nina will handle any weather-related contingencies."

That made sense. For a brief time, Nina had enjoyed a particular kinship with our Lady of the Lake, who'd granted her a mysterious goddess's favor that had lent Nina's own magic an exponential boost, along with other unexpected fringe benefits. As far as I knew, Nina had willingly relinquished the favor, but her unique familiarity with Belisama likely meant that she still felt attuned to the lake's weather patterns.

"I assume you've run Nina's stewardship of the weather by Emmy Harlow?" I asked Gawain, who ceded a stiff nod. "In that case, it's good enough for us."

"Oh, thank the triple goddess," Gawain muttered. "Imagine if it *weren't.*"

For another fifteen minutes, we discussed outstanding logistics. We'd divvied up the affiliated Thistle Grove vendors, along with point-person responsibilities regarding the shuttles and tour guides.

"That should be it, then," Genevieve said with relish, closing her laptop with a triumphant click. "Well done, team! I was thinking, if you all had time, we could go for a celebratory lunch at—"

The library instantly dissolved into a chorus of demurrals and the screech of pushed-back chairs, as the rest of us flailed for any excuse to not spend any further time together. Gawain was the first to duck out, sneaking a handful of pretzels for the road without even cursory thanks to Genevieve, the cheap bastard. I scrambled up next, heart pounding as I hastily shrugged into my trench coat and slung my satchel over my shoulder, hoping to catch Ivy before she left.

Yes, she'd looked at me like a stranger . . . but she'd also smiled twice, I thought, a foolish flood of hope rampaging through me. Maybe that meant something, some internal softening if not an outright invitation. Maybe the rattling collection of sharp-edged fragments between us could still be salvaged if I found the right words this time. If I finally managed to rein in all my fear, and the worst tendencies that came with it.

I'd seen a *kintsugi* exhibit once, in Thistle Grove's tiny art museum. Maybe we could be like one of those broken vases that became art once it was pieced back together, made whole with seams of liquid gold.

But by the time I'd gathered myself to go after her, Ivy had already slipped out.

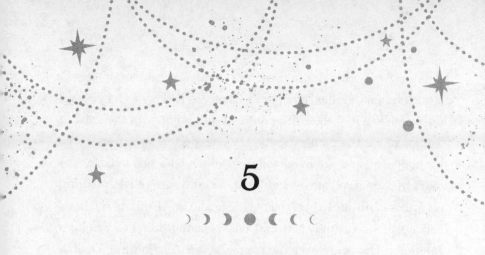

5

Something Hallowed, Something Dark

OR FRIDAY LAUNCH, the planning committee had agreed that we'd each attend all four of the events in case anything needed tweaking. I slunk into Tomes & Omens just after eight—as much as it galled me to drag myself out of bed that early—hoping to catch Ivy there. She woke at six every morning to run through her sun salutations, so I'd assumed she'd be dropping in on the earlier side to watch Emmy and Delilah Harlow regale a throng of rapt tourists with a theatrical lecture on the town's founding, and their roles as Elias Harlow's descendants.

Both of them stood resplendent in their family's dove-gray-and-white robes, their curls braided with tiny glimmering crystals, flowers, and owl feathers, Delilah's bright-eyed raven familiar perched on her shoulder. Tasseled curtains had been drawn across the storefront windows to thwart daylight, creating a suitably esoteric gloom. Candles in hurricane lanterns flickered everywhere, the warm smell of their dripping wax mingling with the must of legions of weathered books, and the unexpected sweetness of the hot chocolate and sugar-dusted pastries set on a side table for the tourists. I lingered for over an hour with no sign of Ivy, nibbling on a pistachio-cream croissant and enduring Delilah Harlow's barrage of increasingly serrated looks. Having been privy to Ivy's emotional wreckage over the course of our relationship, Delilah had long since committed to loathing me on principle.

Just as I was contemplating giving up, I caught sight of Cat Quinn, Delilah's paramour, prowling toward me through the crowded maze of bookshelves.

More than a few of the tourists turned in her wake to gape at her lithe form, the gleam of her amber skin in the candlelight, the sheaf of white-blond hair falling over one pale green eye. Where a tiny spider tattoo had once nestled next to it, there was now only a silvery patch of scar that somehow lent her face an even more intriguing flair.

The half-cat sith I'd saved from a brush with death over the summer tended to have a very pronounced effect on mortals—and witches—in her vicinity.

"Waiting for someone, are we?" she asked in her smoky voice, black-cherry lips curling, one dark eyebrow arched in question.

"I'm sure you know I am," I said shortly, trying to ignore her closeness, the dew-drenched wildflower scent that always surrounded her like some fae pheromone. Which it probably was.

"Rough," she remarked, in a genuinely sympathetic tone. "You won't catch your girl here, though. Waiting for an all clear from that one." She tipped a sultry wink at Delilah, who caught her gaze and flushed a deep crimson even against her olive coloring, faltering a little in her dramatic delivery.

"Sorry I don't come bearing better news," she said with a little shrug, turning back to me. "Still owe you one, after all. Though if I'm being honest, I'd rather not poke the bear by returning the favor anywhere near this particular sore subject. Especially given how much I'm still atoning for myself."

"I exorcised that wraith venom for Ivy, not you," I said after a moment, wondering what exactly had passed between her and Delilah. Along with the rest of the witch community, I knew the half fae came from Chicago, where she'd once lived in an enclave of creatures with what sounded like a very complicated pecking order. But the details of why she'd traded her high-octane former home for the relative sleepiness of Thistle Grove—aside from Delilah Harlow's prickly allure—weren't common knowledge. Maybe she just preferred Thistle Grove's much more temperate seasons. "So as far as I'm concerned, we're square."

"Not according to the fae code of conduct, unfortunately." A corner of her mouth twitched in a wry smile. "I might not be at the Shadow Court anymore, but some habits die hard. And one of our most important rules is to never find yourself in someone's debt. Or, if you can't avoid it, to be in it for as brief a time as possible."

I shrugged. "I'll keep that in mind." I couldn't really imagine myself needing her help, but there were worse things than a powerful half fae owing you a favor.

With a parting nod, Cat plunged back into the crowd. Fair play to Ivy and Delilah, I thought to myself as I turned to leave, but two could play that game. Ivy wouldn't miss her own family's opening spectacle just to avoid me, so at least I knew exactly when to find her at Honeycake Orchards.

As I headed toward the door, Delilah's raven familiar croaked a good-riddance caw, harsh enough to slice through the hubbub of the crowd. Suppressing the urge to flip both it and Delilah the finger on my way out—I more than deserved all that attitude—I headed over to the Shamrock Cauldron, Cryptid Pizza, and Whistler's Fireside to make sure the trucks were set for the Avramov spectacle. Once I'd ticked them off my list, I stopped by some of the other Yarrow storefronts, checking that everyone was displaying the Cavalcade signs and brochures Genevieve had designed.

I made it to the orchards twenty minutes before the Thorn spectacle was slated to begin, weighed down by way too many impulse purchases. I'd bought a set of goat milk soaps from Bespelled, which peddled hand-dipped candles, cosmetics, and tea; a framed map of Thistle Grove in a poppy neon palette from our paper goods store; and three scoops of witch-themed green-and-black gelato from Hell Frozen Over. I had an irresistible sweet tooth at the best of times—something about sugar-triggered dopamine dulled the call of the other side—but never worse than on a day when I was already afire with nerves.

When I finally homed in on Ivy, I'd worked up a sugar rush that at least tasted like courage.

She stood a few rows back from the stage erected in front of Honeycake's towering hedge maze, its flower-strewn walls a riot of unseasonable color against the brilliant blue of the sky. Her gaze slid to me before I'd even elbowed my way over to her through the crowd of tourists waiting for the spectacle to start. So she *had* been on the lookout for me, too, I thought, satisfaction spreading through me like warmed oil.

She wore a fitted and flared double-breasted peacoat, clearly vintage, the black fabric printed with cabbage roses. Silver earrings like elongated teardrops hung from her ears, and her lips were glossed a dusky violet to match some of the floral print's darker blooms. Ivy's ensembles were always like that, a seamlessly elegant blend of thrifted and modern. It made me feel drab in my simple black trench and gray infinity scarf, and also like the only thing I wanted was to pop those oversized buttons and peel the coat right off her like a rind, expose all the gorgeous softness beneath.

"Hey," she said coolly, gaze flicking down to the paper bag slung over my elbow. "What's all that?"

"Souvenirs?" I offered, feeling a flush creep into my cheeks. I blushed at the slightest provocation, like any other nearly translucent person, and I knew Ivy liked to see me color. Predictably, her eyes drifted to my cheeks, lips parting a little before she remembered herself. We stood close enough that even against the powerful perfume of sun-warmed grass and apples that wafted across the orchard, I could smell her. Shea butter and vanilla and sweet pea, even the fruity tang of the lip gloss. "I went to check in on our vendors. Possibly got a little carried away during my inspection of the goods."

"You always were the worst magpie," she said, smirking. "Zero impulse control."

In front of us, the normie dance troupe began assembling onstage, filing into graceful lines. They wore layers of gauze and feathers in mauve and dusty rose, their hair loose beneath floral wreaths. When they turned in unison to face the crowd, lifting up their arms, their dolman sleeves flared wide like wings. Behind them, the magically animated flowers twining through the maze's leaves—freesia, iris, and eglantine, alongside morning glory and pale anemone—perked up and burst into an ethereal three-part melody. A ribbon of delighted laughter wove through the crowd, underpinned by the hum of curious chatter as the more skeptical spectators among them began speculating on how this effect could possibly be achieved.

"Guilty," I admitted, my heart speeding up at the trace of fondness in Ivy's voice that she hadn't managed to conceal. "I do have a notorious weakness for color. And glitter. And sugar."

"And spice," she added, this time with an edge in her tone, dangerous as a glass shard half-buried in sand. "Can't forget that, can we? *Variety*, the spice of life."

I bit the inside of my lip, my shoulders hunching as the dart hit home, sinking right into the guiltiest, most tender part of me.

When Ivy and I had met a year ago, I'd been fresh off another in a series of relationships that I'd torpedoed into shipwrecks. Even before my near-deadly stint of obsession with the other side, I'd been shit at sustaining healthy relationships. Committing to another person made me feel trapped and panicky, a fox with its paw caught in a snare. If you loved someone completely, you could always lose them—and that kind of pain never fully waned, no matter what the platitudes would have you believe.

But after my mother died, and the dark days that came after, I'd been so much worse. Because by then, I'd discovered that there *was* an antidote, something that felt nearly as intoxicating as the other side—and luckily for me, it wasn't mundane drugs. Instead, it was the outermost edge of falling in love, its event horizon. Butterflies swarming in your stomach; the electric zing of anticipating every touch; the feral, insatiable quality of that initial lust. It drove away the temptation of encroaching darkness, forcefully infusing you with light. It was dizzying and gorgeous and all-consuming—and while it lasted, I was virtually untouchable, shielded from the dark that nipped at me like some ravenous temptation. Safely anchored to the shores of the mundane world, immune to the riptide that otherwise drew me inexorably toward the other side.

And then, inevitably, the first hot blush would fade. Those thrilling touches and tokens of affection would become familiar, commonplace—and the desire to tumble headlong into the dark would come rushing back. When that happened, I *had* to move on. I couldn't risk seeing what might happen if I stayed.

But being with Ivy had made me desperately want to try.

"It wasn't like that," I replied, low and intent. Onstage, the dancers had risen en pointe in their mauve ballet shoes, weaving around one another in hypnotic patterns. Sleeve-wings and loose hair whirling as they shifted into a formation that resembled a flock of birds aloft. "I know what it must have seemed like to you, but I swear I was trying to make things work."

Incredulity flashed over her face, followed by a wash of outrage. "You were trying to make things work?" she demanded, soft lips thinning. "Is that what you're telling yourself these days? Dasha, come the fuck on. You dumped me seven months in because I was *boring* you. Because things weren't zesty and spontaneous and wildly romantic one thousand percent of the time, or however the hell you put it. All I know is, you flat-out hated it as soon as we got anywhere near comfortable."

That last part was true, though not for the reasons she thought. Not even close. "Ivy, that's *not* what happened. I—"

She held out a hand stacked with antique rings, forestalling me. "And I *understood*, right? It hurt like a bitch, but I didn't even give you all that much shit because I got it, that maybe you weren't ready for something real. That maybe you'd never be ready because you weren't even capable, given . . . everything. Your dad, your mom, your whole terrible ordeal. Or at least the part of it you felt comfortable sharing with me, which I'm still pretty sure wasn't the full extent of it."

It hadn't been, I thought, shame welling up my throat like blood. Almost no one outside of my immediate family knew exactly what I'd been through, and telling someone like Ivy—such a naturally overflowing font of light, and a practitioner of green magic to boot—about the allure of the other side, what it had done to me, had felt so daunting as to be impossible. What she knew were only the most palatable bits. The more easily digestible, sanitized version of events I could stand to give.

And if I couldn't even bring myself to share that full truth with her, how could I have told her that once we'd settled into each other, once the passion had dampened enough to allow for true closeness and comfort, once I'd felt the happiest I'd ever been— and the most terrified? As soon as those initial sparks between us faded, I'd begun to feel the delicious drone of darkness at my periphery, the haunting siren song of the other side. If I gave in to it, I knew exactly what would happen. I'd lose myself to it again, and by abandoning my life on this side of the veil, I'd lose Ivy, too.

Hells, I would probably lose her anyway in the long run, because if I'd learned anything in the wake of both my parents' deaths, it was that nothing and no one ever stuck around for good. This world simply wasn't made that way.

So I'd run from her like I had from the others, thinking it would be better, cleaner, if I were the one to cut the tether. Easier for us both.

What I hadn't accounted for was how different Ivy was, how much more I loved her than I'd ever loved anyone before. The way

I'd open my eyes every morning feeling like I was waking into the miserable, endless nightmare of her absence, an aching pit of yearning in my stomach that wouldn't dull. That had never happened, not with anyone else. Being with her had broken down some essential ramparts inside me, defenses I hadn't even known were there. And once they were gone, I hadn't known how to build them back.

"Then you came crawling back a few weeks later," Ivy went on, lips quivering with hurt. "Groveled for all you were worth, begged me for another chance. And like the worst kind of trusting, oblivious asshole, I *gave* it to you. So let's not forget I swallowed my pride—and that shit went down bitter for me, Dash, you know it did—and I took you back. I did that for you, for us. And then what happens, huh, not two months after that?"

I gritted my teeth and looked away, knowing where this was going, the inevitable condemnation.

Just then, a gasp raced through the crowd—the clear sky above had begun darkening with birds. A slow, stately procession of them, dozens if not hundreds, falling into a precise murmuration that swirled to the rhythm of the flowers' song, subtly echoing the intricate movements of the dancers that still wheeled beneath them in their own rapturous circles.

It was a nod to Alastair Thorn, the Thorn family founder, who'd commemorated the founding of Thistle Grove by calling down birds as witnesses to the momentous event. And judging by the audience's sudden awestruck silence—most of them overcome by the visual splendor, the more dubious few likely wondering how so many birds could have been trained to fly in such complex tandem—it inspired exactly the kind of reverence that must have marked that original moment so many years ago.

Beside me, Ivy cocked her head and swept an imaginary length of hair over one shoulder, drawing my gaze back to her just as she widened her eyes in what was clearly meant to be mimicry of me.

"'Ivy, I've been thinking. What would you say about, you know, maybe, opening things up a little?'" she said, imitating my cadences, the high lilt of my voice, with searing accuracy. "'I'm not saying I want us to be poly or anything, if you don't want to try that. Obviously I wouldn't want to do *anything* you're not comfortable with. But maybe it could be . . . interesting. More long-term sustainable, if we both had a little freedom.'"

"There's nothing wrong with open relationships," I said on a harsh exhale, even though I knew full well that in this instance, that was a completely bullshit take. My cheeks were blazing now, fueled by some incandescent alchemy of regret and guilt. I hadn't said those exact words, and certainly not in that sweetly scheming way. But it had been damningly close. I truly hadn't meant to hurt her with the suggestion, though part of me must have known Ivy would never accept anything less than a fully monogamous commitment. It simply wasn't what she wanted, and if I'd been thinking more clearly, I could have predicted the pain it would cause, the way she'd immediately leap to the conclusion that our relationship wasn't enough for me.

But on my end, once the darkness resumed its inevitable incursion, the suggestion had been a desperate, terrified attempt to splice together a solution. A path that would let me love Ivy even past infatuation, while allowing me the prospect of dating more casual partners, if I ever needed them for those newness endorphins that helped keep the darkness at bay. I'd thought of it as a safety net, not something I actively wanted to pursue.

Of course, I hadn't explained my intentions to her in those

words, hadn't been anywhere near vulnerable enough with her to admit what I was trying to solve for. There'd been no way to tell her how afraid I was—of losing her, myself, this world at large—when I'd always been too ashamed to admit how bad things had been before we'd met. How close I'd come to never returning to this world, how much I'd hurt my family at every step.

By the time I understood what I'd done, the trust had broken between us. There was no way to take the words back, to make her believe that she mattered more to me than anyone else.

"Of course there's nothing wrong with it!" she tossed back. "That is *not* the point, and you know it. The point is, you were trying to have your cake and eat it, too. Because you use people, Dasha. Yes, you do, don't shake your head at me. As ridiculously sweet and fucking delightful as you can be . . ." Her eyes glittered, and she pressed her lips together hard, her chin bunching like a little girl's. "That's still what it's called when you throw people away like that. It's why you're so damn confusing. At first you're all in, so passionate and warm and sexy, an incredible partner. But then as soon as someone's not ticking off exactly the right boxes for you? Off with their head. Because *your* health, *your* sanity, *your* journey is more important."

"You're right," I forced out, licking my lips, my heart beating so hard it felt like a hummingbird lodged in my throat. This kind of confrontation was very much not my speed, but if there was ever a time to explain to Ivy how I'd actually felt, this was it. Even if it ended in an aneurysm. "It was terrible of me to suggest it in the first place. Horribly selfish, even. But I've been doing better, working on myself. I'm going back onstage with Amrita; you know I haven't wanted to do that in years. And I've been meditating, just like you taught me."

It was true. The yoga flows and breathing techniques she'd shared with me back when we were together *were* helpful, keeping me grounded in a more stable way even if I still wasn't very skilled at either. They weren't nearly as good as a love high, but they worked in a way I could control, and I'd been making a real effort to integrate them into my life.

Her face softened a touch, the raw flare of hope in those dark eyes impossibly inviting. "Every day?"

"Yeah. Every day." Emboldened, I reached for her hand, just a grazing touch. When she didn't pull back immediately, I tucked my fingers under hers, light as a shallow breath. "And I . . . Ivy, I miss you *so much*. I miss you all the fucking time. And I know asking for a third shot is way, way more than I deserve, but it was different with us. We both know it was. And I swear to you, I won't be fucking things up again."

She paused for a long moment, that lucent gaze shifting between my eyes, boring into me as if auguring for truth. Against the beautiful backdrop of wheeling birds and dancers set to the flowers' chorus, the moment seemed rendered in a palette of infinite possibility. Hope expanded inside me with such force that it almost hurt, straining against the confines of my ribs—driven through with just the faintest, sparkling seam of panic. What if she actually said yes this time? What then? Could I truly be trusted to handle her with the care she deserved, to not run away from her again when the darkness came knocking?

Then a frightened yelp from one of the spectators jolted us both.

My eyes flew skyward, where a handful of birds had drawn together into a clump that disrupted the harmony of the whole. Even worse, they were being openly aggressive, wings thrashing at one another, talons clawing. One of them a small bird of prey, tearing viciously at another's fanning tail with its beak. Their screeching was so loud it overwhelmed the flowers' song, turning it into an unnerving cacophony.

"What the fuck?" I breathed, a funnel of cold roiling in my gut, as if a chill wind had blown its way inside me. "That—that's not part of the spectacle, is it?"

"Definitely not," Ivy replied, sounding as disconcerted as I felt. Despite everything, my heart leapt when her fingers tightened around mine; she still hadn't let go of me. "We've practiced dozens of times, with Rowan and Linden communing with and directing the flock. Nothing like this ever happened during the trial runs. They never . . . *went* at each other like that. So violent, for no reason."

As I watched them battle, a familiar sensation began nudging at my ribs—the part of my magic that intuited the intrusion of the other side. The taste of iron began twanging on the back of my tongue, tiny hairs prickling on my neck. I could feel the urge to summon ectoplasm tingling in my fingers, the inbred Avramov instinct to defend, to meet dark with dark.

But a sweeping glance around me confirmed that nothing had manifested anywhere in my field of vision. No shades, no entities, nothing that snared my attention. Except those feuding birds, still so intent on drawing blood in the skies. Their frantic, flitting shadows fell over the dancers, who'd paused their own rotations and craned their necks to watch. Even the flowers had trailed off into an uncertain, stuttering echo of melody, as feathers drifted down from the battle raging overhead.

I glanced over to see Rowan Thorn, the family scion, his twin sister, Linden, and his partner, Isidora Avramov, peel off from the crowd, gathering beneath one of the fruit-heavy apple trees a dozen feet away from the stage. The grim expression on Issa's pretty, freckled face, the way her black-polished hands were spread by her sides—as if primed to summon ectoplasm at any moment, just as I was—set my gut to an even more nauseating churn.

Something was amiss here. Something malevolent that Issa felt brewing, too.

Rowan reached for Linden's hand, and they lifted their free arms to shoulder height, palms up to the sky. Their eyelids drifted closed in tandem as they began to murmur some cantrip, their faces setting in concentration. Both went so still that their only movement was the breeze-stirred sway of Rowan's locs, the fluttering tassels of Linden's tawny scarf, the synchronized movement of their lips. As far as I could tell, no one in the crowd was even looking their way, captivated by the bloodthirsty spectacle above.

Issa had gone dangerously quiet, too, her green eyes flicking intently between Rowan, Linden, and the birds, as if gauging when to intervene. Even in the starkly modern teal wrap coat she'd likely designed herself, her auburn hair woven into a playful coronet braid, she looked like a necromantic warrior queen torn from the pages of one of our Old World storybooks. An energy vortex trapped within that deceptively quirky exterior.

Issa might not have been the Avramov heir apparent like her older sister, Talia, but she was still a powerhouse unlike any our family had seen in centuries.

Our gazes snapped together, blood singing to blood as we nodded silent agreement at each other. *Ready when you are, sister.*

"Dasha?" Ivy said questingly. "You . . . you don't feel right. You're scaring me."

Before I could respond, the aggression in the skies began to wane.

In response to the green magic that Rowan and Linden were weaving with their combined will, the feuding birds drew reluctantly apart, wheeling away from the rest of the flock and off toward the horizon. The apprehension inside me abruptly deflated, too, that feeling of imminent invasion dissipating like a vanishing shade. I glanced over at Issa for confirmation, and she gave me a nod and a relieved smile, her shoulders sagging with relief.

Whatever had been edging its way over onto our plane, infecting the birds with malice, had beaten a retreat. Dispatched by Rowan and Linden's joint mastery over the flock, and likely the green magic that permeated every leaf, petal, and blade of grass in this entire orchard.

But as the spectacle resumed, the flowers taking their chorus back up and the dancers and remaining birds realigning with their delicate rhythms, the thought continued to peck at me. If something had managed to leak over into a place as inhospitable to deathly magic as the Honeycake Orchards naturally were—enough to momentarily wrest control of the birds from the Thorn scion and his twin—how powerful would that unknown something have to be?

The last time any necromantic working had happened at the orchards, it had been a curse cast by one of my family, under extenuating circumstances. But this . . . this hadn't felt like any spell I knew.

This had felt like something more, and worse.

With a shudder, I pried myself loose from the thought. "I think we're fine now," I said to Ivy, who was still peering nervously at the sky. The familiar swoops and flourishes of her profile, so delicately sketched against the dazzling blue, made my breath catch in my throat. "Must have been some kind of fluke."

"Yeah," she said reluctantly. "Must've been."

I cleared my throat, giving her hand a careful squeeze. "We still have time, before I have to head over to The Bitters," I said. "Do you . . . Maybe you'd like to get coffee or something? Talk a little more?"

She looked over at me, her eyes pensive, dark pools beneath her winging brows. And with a sinking heart, I could pinpoint the exact moment she changed her mind. As if those feuding birds had registered as a symbol of doom and ruination, a reminder of the way something beautiful could turn on you, grow savagely unpredictable. Sink its talons directly into the soft flesh of your heart.

When we'd been together, she'd been the dance and I had been those birds. Not once, but twice.

"What is it that you want from me, Dash?" she said, her face hardening like setting clay, her voice devastatingly soft. "For me to just gamble my heart on you again, hoping you've finally figured things out for yourself? Because any roll of the dice, any risk I might have to take is worth it, for the chance to be with the incomparable Starshine Avramov again?"

I swallowed hot tears, salt in my mouth. "You know that's not what I think. I'm not—between the two of us, I'm not the incomparable one. *You* are, Ivy. And you'll always be. And that's why . . . that's why I keep asking."

"Even if I said yes, what would be the point?" She snatched her hand away, cradling it against her stomach, where I knew she kept her hurt. "You'd just get tired of me, eventually. And then you'd run away, and I'd be ruined again."

"You don't know that."

"And neither do you, not really." She reached out and gently traced the outline of my face, regret and longing swimming in her beautiful eyes. "And *that's* the point. You broke my heart, Dash. Two whole times. I can't trust you, no matter how much I want to let myself be that person again. That naive, that open . . . That willing to throw caution to the winds just to have you back. Because it's my responsibility to keep that from happening again. Do you understand?"

"I do," I whispered, quashing the urge to nuzzle my cheek into her palm. I didn't deserve the comfort—just as much as she didn't deserve having to say no to me over and over, when rejecting me clearly only hurt her more. "I'm sorry I asked, I really am. And I won't . . . I promise I won't ask you again."

"Thank you," she whispered, her own eyes glossed bright with tears. "I would really appreciate that, Dasha."

6

From Shadows Hewn

THANK THE MOTHER and Crone for cocktail trucks. Best damned idea I'd ever had, and straight to fuck with all of Gawain Blackmoore's snotty commentary on the subject.

As I waded through a sea of tourists wobbly from a day of sun, food, and drink, I had to admit that my family demesne looked downright bewitching, exactly as planned. Against a dusk-dipped sky of velveteen blue and indigo, the horizon still ablaze with syrupy streaks of peach from the recent sunset, The Bitters loomed like a temple consecrated to some enticing darkness. If anything, its peeling gray façade and gothic Victorian splendor—crookedly set widow's walks, spike-tipped towers, a wolf-and-snake weathervane clinging to the steeply pitched black roof—seemed cut from the same shadowy cloth as the approaching night. A legion of candles had been lit in each of its many arched windows, all framed in a stone tracery of stylized brambles. The effect was a penumbral kind of sacred. The equal and opposite of those Thorn orchards singing their blooming songs of life.

I'd already made my official rounds, checking in with all the food trucks and ticket kiosks, skating around visitors gawping at the scattering of oversized firepits burning with multicolored flame. Avramovs in carnival masks and our traditional gray-and-mulberry robes mingled with the normie crowd, offering palm readings and mini séances in the fortune-telling tents pitched all across the yard. It had been another of my, dare I say, more brilliant ideas. On-theme entertainment for the tourists as they waited their turn for a spooky candlelight tour of the inside of the house—and, of course, the spectacle itself.

With everything running smoothly so far, I'd given myself a little leeway. Enough to sample a sriracha-honey beef kebab and even sip a spiced old-fashioned to dull the memory of those vengeful birds and Ivy's regretful eyes.

Normally I didn't drink during events I was overseeing, but tonight the darkness groped at me, its claws hooking into my frayed edges. Reminding me how sweet it would feel to slide across the veil, to sink into that delicious burn that scorched everything else away. It was always worse when I felt vulnerable, and the confrontation with Ivy had thinned my reserves of restraint. The finality of it had struck deep; the way it had felt like this time, there was truly no hope left with her.

"Almost time!" Amrita announced, appearing at my elbow in her spectacle regalia, a feathered jet-and-amethyst domino mask concealing her eyes. My sister had an uncanny sense of when my control was slipping—or else it was incidental, a side effect of the way she scrutinized me whenever we occupied the same space. "You excited to see all your hard work bear some highly dramatic fruit?"

"I am," I said, and to my surprise, I found that it was true. Alongside the churn of all that negative emotion, a banner of pride had somehow managed to unfurl without me even noticing. Our demesne had drawn a crowd that, to my practiced maximum-occupancy eye, outstripped the throng of tourists I'd seen at the Thorn spectacle, even though they had an entire orchard of attractions on offer.

I'd done that. Even with most of my days still a struggle, I'd pulled off something pretty damn memorable.

I breathed in long and slow, letting myself sink into the simple satisfaction of a job well done as I inhaled smoke and flame and nippy autumn night, the savory smell of grilled food dueling with the deeper scent of dead leaves and damp that wafted from the Witch Woods. I felt at home, I abruptly realized. Even with the other side tugging at me, I felt more like I belonged here than I had in a long time.

"Everything really is looking fantastic," I conceded further. "The food and drinks are both fire, the candlelight tours seem to be proceeding with only the expected number of jump scares, nothing overly dire is being prophesied in the tents. I'd give it a solid 8.5 so far."

"I'll bet the spectacle tips it past that half point for you." She glanced over to the stage, set a few paces in front of the wrought iron fence, where stomach-droppingly high circus silk rigs had been erected for the normie aerialists. I'd had the stage placed for maximum dramatic effect, with the depthless dark of the Witch

Woods spreading like an inky tangle behind the billows of silks. "How did the Thorn show go, anyway?"

I looked over at her, my stomach flipping a little. "You haven't heard?"

"Heard what? I came straight here from my shift at the Emporium, barely had time to change. We were fucking slammed—in the best possible way, clearly, tourist crush being an excellent problem to have. But of course Ms. Wynter chose to take the day off, get balls-deep in those Cavalcade launch *vibes*." The unabashed crassness, and the way her "vibes" somehow came across as a verbal eyeroll, yanked a giggle out of me. "So I had to pick up her slack on top of everything else. I'm sure she's roaming around here somewhere, high off her perky little ass on that skunky mugwort-and-weed vape she carries everywhere. So yeah, I've talked to no one and heard nothing. Why, what happened?"

I gave her a brief recap of the unexpected aerial combat show, along with that noxious sense of necromantic manifestation I'd felt as the birds fought each other. The visceral unease I'd seemingly shared with Issa that something wicked was cresting the horizon.

I considered telling Amrita about what had transpired between me and Ivy, but the reopened wound still felt too raw for that. And I didn't want to dwell on it, not when I was finally feeling like I might be edging a little closer to acceptance. I'd tell her eventually, because I told my sister everything that mattered. But this wasn't the night for that kind of vulnerability.

Amrita let out a low whistle. "Mother and Crone, that's fucked. And on *Thorn* grounds?"

"Exactly. Not unprecedented, given what happened two Beltanes ago. But damn close."

"It sounds like Rowan and Linden managed to get it under control without too much trouble, though," she said. "And without you and Issa having to intervene. So maybe it registered as necromancy, but was really just some . . . weird spike in the normal flow of magic?"

"Could be," I waffled, though I *knew* what I'd felt, that bubble of maleficence expanding in my chest.

"And the lake's been so strange lately," Amrita added, still trying to put me at ease. "Maybe it's causing fluctuations. Besides, we're lifting the oblivion glamour for the spectacles, which means a bunch of normies are witnessing magical displays en masse and actually retaining the memories." She flicked a robed shoulder in a shrug. "Who knows how that's affecting things."

"But do you think I should find Elena before we start, give her a heads-up?"

"You said Issa was there, right? So she'll have reported back if she thought there was anything worth flagging." She squeezed my arm, her eyes twinkling in the mask's dim holes. "Quit being such a worrywart, sister mine. This is *your* night. Your spectacle, practically."

I snorted at that. "I won't even be casting any of the shadowplay—Adriana and Morty are in charge of that entire piece of things."

"That's because you're the theatrical director, the creative mastermind. Now's your moment to rest on your laurels, revel in your masterpiece a little." She tipped her head against mine in an affectionate bonk, then gave me a tug toward one of the cocktail trucks. "Also, I've got Saanvi on Kira duty all night, and I'm planning to get very comfortably tipsy, if not early-twenties-drunk. So come grab another drink with me, and let's enjoy your show."

))) ● (((

BY THE TIME the aerialists slipped onto the stage, lithe in their sequined bodysuits, I'd had a glass of mulled wine on top of my cocktail, and such a hefty dose of Amrita's relentless optimism, that I was finding it hard to cling to any qualms.

We stood in the very front, behind the bespelled barricade that separated the audience from the stage. Although there wouldn't be any summoning, the shadowplay portion of the performance did depend on a lot of raw ectoplasm floating around to be molded; we didn't want any of its tendrils slinking over into the normie fray. The normie aerialists were all shielded against its influence, of course. Each of them had been assigned an Avramov handler, who'd be preventing any stray ectoplasm from interfering with their performance.

Below the center silk rig, Morty Gutierrez, the owner of the Shamrock Cauldron, caught my eye and winked, the silver sequins and glitter in their dramatic cat's-eye makeup glinting in the firelight. I'd spoken to them earlier today when I checked in about the food trucks, but in their performer's guise, with the liquid spill of the bloodred silks pooling behind them and the gloom of the Witch Woods hulking beyond, Morty was nearly unrecognizable. Their dark hair slicked back as if lacquered, eyes a piercing azure against that extravagant makeup. The snake-scaled bodysuit clinging to long muscles, strategic cutouts exposing obliques and shoulders that were at once cut and delicate.

As far as I knew, Morty and the prim, staid Nina Blackmoore had been happily partnered since the previous winter, but the mechanics of that match continued to elude me.

"Ugh, they're so fucking delicious, I can't even stand it,"

Amrita groused beside me, as if she'd read my mind about Morty. "What did Nina 'Boring' Blackmoore ever do to deserve all *that*? I need the details, because whatever it is, I bet I could top the—"

And then, in a spectral billow of fog just beyond the wrought iron fence, the spectacle began.

I'd hired an (extremely pricey) twelve-piece band to create a lush score for the aerialists, and at the initial burst of fog, they launched into a haunting, violin-forward melody that evoked the sensation of night falling, the last glimmers of daylight winking away. As the aerialists wound themselves in their silks, a driving percussive beat kicked up, the kind of rushing thump that felt like an external heartbeat, the sound of blood surging wildly through veins. When the performers began their routine—tangling and untangling themselves from the silks with liquid ease, tumbling like falling stars before hitching themselves into place—the entire audience settled into mesmerized silence.

As they clung to their silks with tightly fisted grips, I could see that all the performers' hands had been painted with stylized brambles that echoed The Bitters' window traceries, the same pattern repeating on their cheekbones. Besides the palette, it was the one thing I'd specifically requested from Morty when it came to costumes and makeup; I thought it would be a nice touch, paying homage to the ancient Avramov crest. Beyond that, based on their performance portfolio, I'd trusted Morty to be exactly the kind of independent creative who'd craft something this unforgettable.

Chills stippled my neck with every abrupt plunge and effortless ascent, the music skirling around them like something equally alive. I'd already seen all this happen three times in dress rehearsal, but watching it now left me no less rapt and breathless.

"Fucking perfection," Amrita whispered beside me, squeezing my arm. "Like I said. You absolutely killed it."

"You know I was just the logistics bitch," I protested, but none too insistently. Without my guidance, the spectacle wouldn't have come together this extravagantly—and I was making more of an effort these days not to sell myself short when I actually did something good. "But agreed. The whole aesthetic turned out even better than I hoped."

"Didn't I always say you should've gone into dramaturgy?"

"Just wait," I said, pride tugging at the corners of my mouth. "It gets even better."

Behind the stage, the rising fog roiled and thickened, condensing into a backdrop like a swirling canvas strung against the night. I could have used a mundane fog machine for this, but I'd wanted a more controlled effect, so I'd reluctantly hired one of Gawain's Blackmoore elementalists to conjure this malleable mist for me. Now I was glad I'd handed over the exorbitant sum—especially once Adriana Avramov, the youngest daughter of the main line, began casting her own necromantic shadows against that milky screen.

Ectoplasm was a tricky substrate, semi-sentient and averse to being manipulated into anything that didn't birth shades, demons, or something equally sinister. But where there was a ferocious will, there was a way—and the youngest Avramov was an uncanny wildling of a girl, unafraid to wrest even ectoplasm into something bizarre and beautiful. Where she stood tucked away behind the rightmost corner of the stage, I could see the intent concentration on her pale, angular face, dark hair braided tightly away from her temples, hands twitching in front of her in a cat's cradle of casting gestures. Using the ectoplasm's ferny roil like paint, she shaped a landscape of Hallows Hill, twisting and turning the image until our sight line hovered right at its summit.

A grayscale likeness of Lady's Lake, ringed by sketchy depictions of its encircling trees.

Then, above the landscape, she conjured a legion of drifting shades like some dark and gathering flock. Just the way they'd swarmed four hundred years ago, when the Dread Lady Margarita Avramov called upon them to come bear witness to the founding.

They were so lifelike, so close to what true shades looked like when they manifested—vaguely human silhouettes, with only trailing impressions of hair and limbs and roiling vortices for eyes—that I had to remind myself that these weren't the real thing. Just clever shadow puppetry that posed no danger to the mundane spectators. As Adriana brought them darting down toward the lake like a colony of bats, the music shifted into something even more ominous, an eldritch drone like a wordless Gregorian chant. The creeping thrill of it seeped through the crowd, parents clutching their children a little closer, lovers cuddling each other tight, tucking their faces into their partners' necks.

That pride bubbled up in me again, at having orchestrated this celebration of the essence of the Avramov spirit—our passionate devotion to the dark, the way the veil between worlds sheered around us naturally—with such authenticity. Because I felt it in my bones, the way my spectacle made the audience squirm with both delight and the slippery slither of fear. As if they could sense the truth that hovered behind the facsimile of our magic, how all this hinted at something very real.

Focused as I was on the ambience, I was probably the first to feel it when the energy turned, curdling like spoiled milk. My spine went rigid, insides shivering with dread. Amrita stiffened beside me, too, brow furrowing above her mask as she picked up on the shift.

Then a wall of pure, massive malevolence struck us like a sudden storm.

Every Avramov in the crowd sucked in their breath at once, the hiss of air over teeth loud enough to hear even above the orchestral score.

The normie spectators flicked curious glances at us over their shoulders, unsettled by the mass intake of breath but clearly oblivious to what had incited it. We ignored them, our eyes pinned to the canvas of fog—where the ectoplasm had begun to coalesce and somehow *multiply*, like petri dish bacteria blooming in fast-forward. Growing larger and denser until the whirling shadow mass of it hovered at least ten feet across, spinning slowly like some lightless nebula.

I flung a frantic *what the fuck?!* look at Adriana, but she was staring at the ectoplasmic mass with the same shock-tinged confusion as every other Avramov, those formerly busy little hands limp by her sides.

That malevolent taint surged again, like a red-bloom tide. Once, twice, three times, in ripples like silent sonic booms that made all the witches in the crowd stumble as one, even the non-Avramovs.

"Shit, is *this* what you meant?" Amrita demanded, poking an elbow into my side. She'd shoved her domino mask up onto her forehead, and the glossy mass of her hair bumped up behind it like a beehive. "When you said something weird happened at the orchards? Because I'd say you severely undersold the situation."

Before I could answer, I heard Ivy's familiar low register through the sudden shifting of the crowd, witches weaving through the throng to find knots of their own to huddle with. "Dasha? Dash, where *are* you?"

"Ivy!" My heart lodged in my throat with sudden terror, the knowledge that she was here, exposed to whatever evil this was. "Over here!"

Moments later, she slid into place next to me. My heartbeat slowed incrementally as soon as I knew where she was, close enough that whatever happened next, I'd be able to keep her safe. "What is this?" she murmured, eyes wide. "Is it like the birds?"

"I think so," I whispered back, licking my lips. My throat had gone the terrible sawdust dry that I usually associated with exorcism aftermath. "But this . . . whatever it is this time, I think it's much worse."

"What do we . . ."

The nebulous dark floating above us began to spin itself into shape, and whatever else she'd been about to say withered away.

Legs came first, shadowy yet well-defined. Bulky and powerful, corded with ligaments and tendons and veined bulges of muscle, ending in high-arched feet with curling, clawed toes. A tapered torso slabbed with shadow muscle emerged next, followed by a pair of equally colossal arms, shoulders broad and mighty enough that they looked like they could balance some monstrous orb of a world between them.

It was a male silhouette, I realized with dawning horror. Carving itself out of the ectoplasm as if some invisible sculptor were chiseling it out of black smoke.

Next came a bull-thick neck, topped with a shadow-hewn face all the more terrifying for its unearthly precision, beautiful and brutal features sculpted much too fine. Full lips drawn back in a vicious snarl over even black teeth and a pair of fangs, a square jaw and cheekbones as blunt and broad as steppes. Above the jutting forehead was an upswept riot of shadow curls, topped with an ectoplasmic crown of spires and spikes.

Finally, just as I thought the hammering of my heart might pulverize my ribs, a pair of tremendous wings exploded from the colossus's back—shaped like a bat's with barbed claws at the tips, but lined densely with glistening feathers of ectoplasm. They flared wide around him, flapping in languid flicks, as if he didn't even need them to keep himself aloft.

"Oh shit," Amrita whispered beside me, aghast. "Just what in the actual, utter *fuck*."

When Ivy's cold hand slipped into mine—afraid enough that she was reaching for me again—I knew we were in an entire sideways universe of trouble.

7

Out, Away, Begone!

THE SHADOW TITAN opened his eyes.

They glowed like spectral searchlights, shedding an unnatural, poisonous green light as they swept over us, narrowing
with a menace that made the pit of my stomach bottom out like a
sinkhole. *Wrong, wrong, wrong,* the petrified field mouse part of my
brain chittered at me. The part that knew full well that even I still
counted as prey to some.

Somewhere in the stupefied crowd, I heard the high, terrified
wail of a toddler who knew in their guts that this was some abject
nightmare shit, even if the adults in charge still seemed absurdly
ambivalent.

"God*damn*," a normie beside me exhaled, taking a reverent
swig of his IPA as he stared at the entity hovering above us. "That
is some fucking epic craftsmanship right there. Check out those

details. I mean, that goth angel dude's got fucking toenails, bro. And serious junk."

"Yeah, they're not holding back, are they?" the guy next to him said through a grimace, sounding both stoned and a little repulsed. "Why's he gotta be packing like that, man? There's little kids here. That's messed up."

The other guy shook his head, apparently unfazed. "Kinda reminds me of some *BioShock Infinite* shit. How'd they even pull this off? It's holographic lasers, must be. But on such a wild *scale*—"

Then the colossus tossed back its head and roared.

Somehow, we still couldn't hear it, but we sure as the hells could *feel* the staggering impact of that world-rending bellow. Such an enormous surge of power, a tremendous, silent knell of it, that it nearly brought us all to our knees, normies included. I'd never felt anything like this before—not even with the major arcana demons I'd exorcised, nor from any spell I'd seen cast at the Gauntlet of the Grove or one of our Wheel of the Year ceremonial rites.

Then the canvas of Blackmoore-conjured fog behind it began to tear itself into milky streamers, recoalescing in front of the thing like a sheer curtain rippling in a breeze. The creature—*the goth angel dude*, I thought, a wild urge to laugh building in my chest—tore into it, shredding at it viciously with his curving claws.

"He's still behind the veil," I said, realization crashing over me. Because that was what the fog was doing—clinging to the invisible veil that separated the other realm from ours, rendering it visible. I'd never seen normal fog do any such thing before, but this was an elemental conjuring by a Thistle Grove Blackmoore, infused with their will. It was possible that it had some special properties, especially given the distorting effect of whatever the hells was going on here. "Close, but not fully manifested in our realm. That's why we can't hear him. Whatever—whoever—is bringing him here hasn't pulled him all the way through."

"You can't let him through, Dasha," Ivy said in a petrified whisper. I glanced over to find her ashen and trembling, beads of sweat tracing the outline of her upper lip. "No matter what, you *cannot let him pass.*"

Amrita and I both froze, appalled at the sight and sound of her, the way she looked like someone poisoned. "Why?" I asked, gripping her shoulder with my free hand, the one not crushed by hers. "Ivy, why? Do you know what he is?"

"Death," she said simply. "Eater of light. Quencher of flame. The destroyer. The nemesis. He doesn't belong here. Dasha, make him *leave.*"

Before I could ask her how she knew any of this, the clarion of Elena Avramov's raised voice suddenly pierced the noise of the crowd. "House Avramov! *To me!*"

The command in her voice was so implacable that both Amrita and I instinctively moved to obey. But then I paused, turned back to Ivy. "Are you going to be okay here on your own?"

She gave a twitch of a nod, gnawing frantically at the inside of her lip even as she unlaced her clammy hand from mine. "I'll be fine. Now *go.* They're going to need you."

When I hesitated for another moment, she gave me a push, forceful enough that I turned and plunged into the crowd after Amrita. My sister, nurturing as she was, had also never hesitated to throw elbows or hands in her life. She sliced through the crowd for us like a scythe, carving a path to where I could see a knot of Avramovs already tying itself around Elena and the rest of the main line.

As we charged past both bewildered and openly fearful normies, I brushed by Wynter, who darted out a hand to snag my arm.

"Do you fucking see that?" she gasped at me, her face so stricken it bordered on rapture, tears pouring down her cheeks. Her eyes were glassy, likely from that mugwort-and-weed vape that annoyed Amrita so much; I thought I caught a whiff of it on her. She swayed in place, one hand curled against that over-wrought bosom, clutching a handful of pendants. "Do you *see*?"

For the first time ever, I could identify with her, even if she was likely high as shit. If ever there were a time for "oh fuck" weeping, it was now. Unfortunately, the Avramovs in this crowd didn't have that luxury.

"I do," I assured her. "And don't worry, we're going to take care of it."

"What do you mean?" Beneath the glam witch-queen makeup, her face crumpled with confusion. "But—"

I swept past her in Amrita's wake, no more time for comfort.

By the time we reached Elena, she'd already orchestrated a circle of Avramovs, with herself, Talia, Issa, Adriana, and Micah standing at its epicenter, holding hands. The Avramov main line, surrounded by the rest of the family in a circumscribed circle, one of the most powerful magical configurations.

"In here with us, Daria," she instructed, and even as I moved toward her, I quailed at the sight of her face, the dire gravity of her eyes, the depth of her pallor against the copper blaze of her hair. Even Elena Avramov, dauntless matriarch, was afraid tonight.

"We're going to need you to take point. Amrita, you'll join the outer circle."

Issa and Micah parted to make room for me, and somehow their somberness—in such stark opposition to the wild-child partiers I'd known them both to be in the past—shook me even worse than seeing our matriarch so rattled. Even when Talia had been possessed by a horde of rampaging shades several years ago during the Gauntlet of the Grove, Elena had maintained her composure, stoically led us through what had to be done to exorcise them all and save her daughter.

Which meant that whatever the threat here was, it was unfathomably worse than a mass possession of her own scion.

"Inner circle," Elena went on, her clear voice betraying none of the trepidation in her eyes. My gaze strayed over her shoulder to the stage, where the dark titan still tore at the fog-veil in front of him, fury rippling over his colossal face. The milky veil had grown more threadbare, leaving ragged patches like unraveled holes in a shawl. Whatever we were about to do, we needed to do it fast. "We're casting Alyona's Aversion. Outer circle will amplify. Daria, I assume you know the Aversion by heart?"

My insides clenched painfully tight. "Yes," I all but squeaked. "I know it."

Alyona's Aversion was the most powerful banishing spell in our arsenal, so ancient and cataclysmic that it had never been used here in the New World. Because nothing had ever warranted it, not even Talia's possession. I'd only ever learned it because the spellsmith, Alyona herself, had been one of the few other devil eaters in our line. She'd lived centuries and centuries ago, back when we laid claim to stone castles across the seas, presided over craggy mountains black with pine. Learning it felt like forging some deep connection to my own strange blood, knowing that I wasn't the only weird offshoot, some one-off Avramov varietal.

I'd never expected to actually *use* those barbed incantations in my lifetime. And the fact that it was traditionally cast to repel incursions of what translated from ancient Russian to "the Kings of the Many Hells" didn't exactly help my state of mind.

"You . . . you think that's what he is?" I asked Elena, knowing she would understand what I meant.

"That, or worse," she replied grimly, jade eyes glowing like witchlight. "But we either show him our bellies or strike as hard as we know how. Daria, you'll lead. Begin *now*."

I closed my eyes and drew my will into the finest point I could muster, sharp as a pen nib, even as my heart rioted in my chest. I couldn't remember ever having been this terrified, and yet, there it was again—that coiled hunger that curled at my very center, opening a lazy, slitted eye as it stirred in anticipation. That I'd catcn a revenant demon only a handful of days ago barely mattered to that sleepy inner beast that was never sated. Nor did it care that we were about to try to banish a *goth angel dude* that dwarfed an entire crowd.

As far as the hunger was concerned, there was always room for one more.

I launched into the first incantation, my voice wobbling like a top before it stabilized, gaining in intensity and power, feeding on the energy funneled to the inner circle by the outer. On the second incantation, the rest of the inner circle joined me, intoning the words and cementing them with will. On the third, the outer circle bolstered us, a harsh choir of voices like the opposite of angels.

I didn't know exactly what the ancient Russian words meant, but I could *feel* what the language and form of the spell were meant to convey. The intent that crashed like luminous silver waves, an ocean lit by some internal moon swimming in its depths:

> OUT, you scourge you plague you otherworldly taint
> AWAY, you beast you monster you pestilence
> BEGONE, you foulness you curse you nemesis;
> OUT by silver, out by light
> OUT by the one and endless might
> OUT OUT OUT OUT OUT OUT OUT!

As the primary caster, the full strength of the spell stampeded through me with all the force of a natural disaster. An avalanche, a mudslide, a volcanic eruption. A purging cataclysm, something so implacable it would not brook even the notion of opposition. Even if that opposition was a King of the Many Hells.

I knew then why Elena had chosen me to lead, rather than herself or Issa or even Talia, all three of them stronger Avramov witches in most ways that counted.

It was because someone else—someone who hadn't been eating devils since they were seven—might not have survived being this ruthless casting's conduit.

At the final incantation, the spell whipped out of us—or rather, out of me, its focal point. Loops of silver light like chains tore themselves free of my mouth, emerging in a seemingly endless spool of light that burned and burned, a flood of molten metal rising in my throat.

Released, the Aversion whirled itself through the air like a flung lariat, shining so blindingly bright against the night sky and the even deeper darkness of the Witch Woods that the crowd shaded their eyes. It pierced that foggy mimicry of the veil—or what was left of it, after the behemoth's savage attack—as if it wasn't even there.

Singeing right through it, scorching as it looped itself around his body.

Everywhere it touched, that dark ectoplasmic flesh began to hiss and fade, wisping into nothing. The banishment broke down the behemoth's form, boiling it into the nothing from which it had come. Casting it out and away from this realm.

This time when the colossus bellowed in rage and pain, all of us heard the rattling roar of it, all the way down to jellied marrow. Screams erupted in the crowd, a wild surge of movement as true terror finally infiltrated even the normie throng, though the danger had already passed.

But just before he vanished entirely, the creature locked eyes with me, as though he could sense that I'd been the one to channel Alyona's Aversion. As though that lariat of spellbound chains still connected me to him.

And as he huffed out, I felt that familiar tug just beneath my solar plexus.

The sharp fishhook pull that meant I was about to fall into the other side of the veil.

8

Child of Dark

I LANDED IN that field of glistening black flowers like I always did, stumbling a little as I gained my footing. Listless air pressed against my skin, rust-red clouds skittering above my head across that pewter sky. In the distance, the orchards stood skeletal as always, bearing glittering loads of bruise-dark fruit, heavy and sharp and never to ripen.

Again, I wasn't alone. But this time, it wasn't the Lettie pretender who stood across from me.

On this side of the veil, the behemoth was human-sized, scaled to me. Still tall, well over six and a half feet, enough that I had to tip my head back to meet those limelight eyes—a gentler, more jeweled green on this side than they'd appeared on the other. Those spectacular wings still flared behind him, both leathery and feathered. And he was naked, but sheathed in what appeared to me as real flesh and proper skin, still black as onyx but gleaming taut over that powerfully muscled bulk.

The real difference was that on this side, he was less sheerly terrifying and more deathly beautiful. That night-hewn face of unnatural symmetry, black curls swept back from a high forehead and shining beneath the weight of a jagged crown, spiraling horns curling away on either side of it.

I wasn't much for men in general, but on rare occasion, one of them managed to catch my eye. And this one . . . this one was the kind of ferociously gorgeous that couldn't have existed on our side. A dreadful, inhuman, magnificent wonder to behold. Brutally and perfectly made, from those clawed wings to the taloned bare feet, as if someone had carved him out of the fabric of the night.

Goth angel dude, indeed.

For a moment, we simply stared at each other with heads cocked, unwitting mirror images of each other. He hadn't pulled me here on purpose, I realized, even as my blood began to blaze with the unspeakable glory of being here while alive. My presence was probably a side effect of the spell itself, the fact that it had lived briefly in me before unleashing itself on him. That incubation, and the fact that I'd served as its conduit, had created a temporary connection between us. One strong enough to hitch me along for the ride when it banished him.

Probably it wouldn't have happened with someone else, someone less untethered than I was. But a piece of me always yearned to be here, anyway. It must have been easy to latch on to that wishful segment of my soul and tug me along.

He took one step toward me, and then when I didn't flinch away, another. I stood still, trembling like a doe, knowing full well

I couldn't outrun him here. That he was something else, something vastly different and much more than any devil I'd eaten before. And some small, treacherous part of me—the part of me reveling in the intoxication of being back here, wallowing in the luxury of being this side's living torch—didn't even *want* to run. Wanted, instead, to find out what would happen if he touched me, ran one of those claws down my pliant human cheek. Down the column of my throat and over my clavicle, where the skin was thinnest.

In two more steps he closed the distance between us, until I stared directly into those eyes, a green so cold it made me think of glacier hearts, the deepest core of some bottomless ice.

"Child of dark," he whispered, hunger and curiosity vying in his tone, his voice like satin sliding over a sheet of frigid metal. As he leaned closer, nosing my cheek and then my hair, I stood still, breathing in panting little gasps like a trapped animal. And with a judder of surprise, I realized I *understood* him, even though the language he spoke was unlike anything I'd heard before. Closer, in fact, to the shape of the words in Alyona's Aversion than any living language I knew. "You ousted me! *Me*. But why?"

"To . . . to keep them safe," I replied shakily. "Me and mine. You don't belong on the other side. You would have hurt them."

"Is that so?" Something close to amusement rippled in his tone, and goose bumps prickled along my skin. "Who are *you* to say where I belong? And how are you to know what I would have done?"

"Uh." I swallowed hard. "Context clues?"

A chuckle against my cheek like honey dripped over coals, deep and dark and stirring. "How strange you are," he remarked in that sharp-edged language, nuzzling my ear. "Shadow-full to the brim, and still you glow with life. You smell of death, and yet. And yet you also smell of *her*."

The way he said *her*—venom and longing, all entwined—shook loose a memory that should have surfaced long before now. What had that revenant demon said to me?

Because he *is coming, the rough beast breaching the horizon. For her above all, and the rest of you along with her! And when he comes, all of you will fall to your brittle human knees and weep, a flood of salty, futile, delicious tears . . .*

At the time, I'd assumed the revenant demon was talking about Emily. But what if that hadn't been it at all?

"Who?" I asked, my lips trembling. "Which her?"

"She who is the font of light," he replied, still against my ear, the ice of his breath sweeping down my entire side. "Your fallen star. What other could there ever be for me?"

Before I could reply, he slid those powerful arms around me and clasped me against the bulwark of his chest, drawing me close. His sigh of satisfaction curled like a purr inside my ear, tinged with a wisp of melancholy.

"No, you are not her," he crooned, cheek against my cheek, that despondency intensifying. "Though I do not fault you for what you could never be. But for now, you are close enough. For now, you are here. With me."

Then the glory blazed up inside me, infinite and dense and sweet, like some thick custard scorched to a perfectly crisp caramel finish. Such an ineffable euphoria that I felt like I might burst, die of all that honeyed heat and light pulsing under my skin.

With my flesh feverish against his—because he was cold as the

LANA HARPER

very void, the chill antithesis of light—I felt something beyond transcendent. Being held by him was like gulping down the quintessence of what it felt like to exist here. My eyes fluttered shut, a deep moan twisting itself from my throat. And what would happen if I turned my head, found his lips? My arms were already wound around his neck, clinging to him with all I had, though I didn't even remember returning the embrace.

What bliss would it be, to angle my head into a kiss with something like him? Wrap my legs around those strong hips and let him lift me up, until the blazing light of me swallowed such a length of living shadow?

"Ah," he murmured against me, throaty and deep, a hand sliding down to the small of my back. "Is it so, child of dark? Perhaps . . ."

The fishhook lodged beneath my ribs tugged again, sharp and insistent—yanking, this time, back toward the other side. The garnet at my throat pulsed to life, a hot, insistent throbbing against my skin.

"What?" I mumbled, still too enraptured to understand what was even happening. "Wait, no, I don't want—"

Then came another, much more fearsome pull—cast on a reel that I recognized even through my stupor as the line of Elena Avramov's formidable, unmistakable will. Dragging me away from him.

"THERE YOU ARE," Elena said, her peaked face hovering above mine as I blearily came to, my back pressed against hard ground. The night sky beyond her head swam as I struggled to focus, stars doubling on themselves like a crystalline swarm, the dissipating skeins of all that conjured fog still twisting around each other. My ears felt like they were stuffed with cotton, like they needed a sharp, elusive pop.

Relief lit in Elena's eyes as I stirred, groaning, and managed to prop myself up on one arm. "You're safe now, Daria. You're back with us. Now let's see if . . ."

The sound of her voice faded as a wave of anguish broke over me, bleak and heavy as a ton of earth dumped over my soul—the equal and opposite to that sweet, heady flame that had engulfed me on the other side. I felt like I'd been interred, buried alive. Stripped of everything hot and rich and joyful, mired once again in the sticky bog of despair that was this side of the veil.

And yet again, it was Elena who had brought me back.

A wrinkle furrowed her brow as she registered the shift in my expression, the rage that must have begun creeping into the blankness. "Daria? Are you—"

With a wordless roar, I hauled off and slapped the Avramov matriarch full across the face, hard enough that my palm stung from the impact.

"*Why?*" I shrieked at her as she reeled back, hand clapped to her cheek. Her face a picture of such absolute consternation that under different circumstances, it might have been funny to imagine how utterly unacceptable it was of me to slap not just my boss but the absurdly intimidating Avramov family head. "Why won't you ever just leave me the fuck alone? I want to go back! I want to stay! That's *all* I want, that's all I ever wanted. I just want to *stay!*"

Elena made an abortive little movement, as if to brush my hair away from my eyes, though the imprint of my palm still blazed like an angry weal over her cheek. For a moment, the sympathy on her face nearly pierced my desolation. "Daria, I can't let you do that. You know I can't."

I set my jaw and scrabbled back away from her, enraged and devastated beyond all logic, all reason. "Then why don't you fucking try to stop me!"

Closing my eyes, I reached for the other side of the veil as I'd done so many times, fumbling for the path that was normally as familiar to me as the length of my own limbs, the fleshy drumming of my heart, the patterns of my breath. But that meddling bitch was blocking me somehow; I could feel the hulking obstruction of her like a menhir looming in my path, a standing stone that would not let me pass to where I needed, craved to go. Back to the other side, to that fiery caramel flood of a feeling.

Back to him, and his dreadful and glorious embrace.

But no matter how I clawed at or grappled with her will, I couldn't get past it. She wouldn't let me through.

"Daria, stop," I heard her plead, and this time there was anguish in her voice, too, along with a thread of strain that filled me with a bitter twist of hope. Maybe I could wear her out, if I just kept battering myself against her. Maybe even she couldn't stand between me and the other side forever. "You'll hurt yourself, and I still won't let you through. Not like this. Not when you're in this state, and especially not while *he* might still be there."

I began to cry in dry, soundless sobs, my insides aching with fatigue and need. I was so spent, brittle as shale, yet somehow still overflowing with fury and want.

"Just please let me go," I begged Elena, pitching forward and burying my face in my hands, shoulders heaving. "I don't want to be here! I don't *need* to be here, don't you understand? I belong over there, like I always have. So just . . . just let me go this time."

"No," a different, determined voice said a little while later, cool fingers sliding over my hands. Gently, those fingers peeled my own away from my face, then clasped them against the softness of her chest. Through a blur of tears, I made out Ivy's luminous face in front of me. Those huge bright eyes, the way the naturally darker outline of her lips faded to a softer color toward the plush center, the glimmer of the silver hoop that sat flush against the cleft of her lower lip.

She'd taken Elena's place, kneeling so close that her knees pressed against my own. Over her shoulder, one of those multicolored bonfires still blazed, its flickering rainbow gleaming off the curve of her left cheek. Somehow it made her look like a gorgeous warrior, a slash of brilliant color painted beneath one eye.

"Ivy?" I said, perplexed, twining my fingers more tightly through hers. "Why . . ."

"Elena tapped me in," she replied. "She thought I might be better equipped to hold you down."

The idea that Elena had been forced to call in reinforcements gave me a perverse rush of triumph that I savored anyway, as the first positive emotion I'd felt since I found myself stranded back here.

"Kinda funny, right, given that Thorns don't exactly choose violence every day of their lives like you all like to do. But she's goddamn right about me tonight, Dash," Ivy continued, those soft lips setting in a very familiar expression of dogged stubbornness. "Because I am not letting you slide back over. Not after you just saved us from a doomsday angel with an overly literal understanding of 'swinging dicks.'"

I sputtered a wet laugh, shaking my head—though just the sight of her had made the darkness recede the slightest bit. "And what do you plan to do about it?"

Her eyes sparkled almost mischievously. "I was thinking some fairy-tale bullshit," she said, cocking her head. "If you're good with that?"

When I gave a wary nod, she cupped my face with a palm and leaned forward to cover my lips in a soft, sweeping kiss.

I caught my breath from the shock of it, my heart feeling like it was shuddering instead of beating in my chest. I'd been thinking—dreaming—of kissing Ivy again for months now. And this wasn't anything so cautious or hesitant as what I'd been imagining. She buried her hand in my hair, murmured, "Damn, you still taste like starshine," against my lips, and then drew me flush against her with an arm around my waist until I was halfway on her lap, one of my legs draped over her thigh. My insides clenched with an immediate flare of desire that blazed up from everywhere we touched; the silken graze of lush lips against mine, the warm press of thigh to thigh, the hand tangled in my hair and the other at my waist. The sweet, hot whisper of her breath as her mouth parted open against mine. Inhaling her perfume, that commingling of sweet pea and vanilla and shea, felt as crucial as the very act of breathing. Expanding my lungs, anchoring me in place.

She lit all the dark places, filled up the bleak yearning. Chased the desolation away like the orange sweep of a torch cleaving the night.

There must have been people in distress all around us, but I couldn't spare a single thought for them, for whatever damage control was transpiring beyond us. The crowd—maybe the entire world itself—seemed to have peeled back, withdrawn from me and

Ivy. Maybe Elena had drawn a tactful privacy glamour over us, or maybe it was simply Ivy herself, the same effect on me she'd always had, especially lightheaded and hazy as I was. When the kiss deepened, a slick, singeing rush of tongue against tongue, I sighed into her mouth, snagging her lower lip with my teeth until she rewarded me with a sharp intake of breath.

But when I leaned in for more—*more more more*—she pulled back, her eyes at once heated and deadly serious on mine.

"So? What say you, Dasha Avramov? Will you stay?"

I hesitated, still torn. Coming from her, the question seemed to double on itself like blurred vision. It didn't just mean did I want to stay here, on this side of the mortal plane—but also did I want to stay here with her or run again?

"I don't know," I finally said, the craving for the other side still throbbing inside me, though weaker now. "I do want to, Ivy. I want to be wherever you are, more than almost anything. But it's . . . fuck, how do I even explain it? It's so hard to be on this side. So empty. Over there, everything else is dead, but me? I'm so, *so* alive. It feels like nothing else."

An unexpected smile curved her lips, where I'd expected disappointment. "So what you're requesting is more life? Did I hear that right?"

"I guess that's what it is, yeah."

She leaned closer again, until our lips just barely brushed. "Lucky for you, life is kind of my specialty. So listen, and breathe with me. Beat with me. Let me show you what it can be like over here."

I closed my eyes, uncertain, but trusting her enough to at least try to follow where she led. We'd done things like this before, when she guided me through one of her longer and more demanding yoga flows (usually with a good bit of grumbled complaint from me, which always felt like it halfway defeated the spirit of the practice). As our breath mingled, our rhythms slowly syncing up, she took my hand and wrapped my fingers around her other wrist, pressing their tips to where her pulse leapt beneath warm skin. I focused on it, the rapid but steady ticking of her heart, along with the peaks and valleys of her breath matching up with mine, until it felt like we were perfectly threaded cogs in a strange and delicate two-part machine.

"That's it," she murmured, brushing a tiny kiss over my mouth, like a little zing of static electricity. "Stay with me, okay, just like that. This is the good part."

She lifted her other hand and curled it around my nape, tilting my forehead against hers. And on the next joint exhale, a wave of rich, violet-and-green Thorn magic came sluicing into me. Mellow and sweet as maple sap, a gentle elixir of well-being and renewal.

I'd felt this healing Thorn magic before; Ivy had never had any compunction about using it during sex in many delicious ways. But she'd also never let it flow as openly as this, until it coursed so indiscriminately between us that I couldn't tell which of us it even came from, as if I were a tributary to her vast river. There was such a sweetness to her magic, such grounded yet tender hope, the precious perseverance of something new and green nosing its way past cold, stiff earth, toward a still-weak sun. And she was right. This *was* life, at least the fragile, burgeoning beginnings of it. Not the overly extravagant glut of it I felt within myself on the other side, so wildly blown out of human proportion it was nearly too much to bear. This was simple, nourishing, natural. A smear of wildflower honey across a slice of freshly baked bread.

The taste of hearty home cooking with the windows flung wide open, letting in the breath of spring.

"There we go," Ivy murmured against me, the softest shade of triumph to her tone. She dug strong fingers into my nape, into the sensitive knobs of my skull where I loved to be rubbed, adding a simple but enthralling physical sensation to the mix. "There you are. And now that I've got you, time to turn it up."

I huffed a breathless laugh against her, frankly amazed that I even had it in me to laugh. "What are you talking about?"

"If you let me focus, you just might find out."

Sliding her hand free from my hair, she lifted it slowly toward the sky, palm cupped like an empty chalice.

Then flowers burst through the trampled grass all around us, like an enchanted bower transplanted from a storybook in one gorgeous swoop.

As far as I knew, no garden had ever grown on The Bitters' grounds. The pall of our necromancy seeped into the soil itself, turning it sere and unhospitable, until the only things we managed to cultivate were hardscrabble patches of grass that grew to weird and unpredictable lengths, like Baba Yaga's storied chin hairs. Yet somehow, Ivy was managing to coax night bloomers of all kinds to grow. Jasmine crawled over our legs, shedding its overpowering perfume from a profusion of tiny, tubular flowers. Heavy moonflowers twined up on their stems as if climbing an invisible ladder, until they nudged our cheeks with silver petals. Evening primrose like sprays of sunshine hovered in the night air, little yellow sparklers in the periphery of our vision. And finally, Japanese wisteria burst to life, so feathery and purple that its fronds made me think of fireworks as they grew into a net that bowed over our heads.

Living plants were usually antithetical to Avramovs—especially animated ones like these, imbued with Ivy's will into something like semi-sentience. They instinctively knew just enough to recognize the magic in my blood as something that repelled and frightened them. But connected as Ivy and I were, heart to heart and breath to breath—bound up so tightly with the threads of her green magic—tonight they seemed to accept me as part of her. Someone to bend to, to equally worship and adore.

This time, not one of them shied away from me.

As I closed my eyes to revel in the soft tickle of their leaves against my skin, the droop of heavy blossoms settling onto my head, I realized I could feel them back. I felt them the way that I imagined Ivy must always feel them, at least to some degree. The brash way their roots corkscrewed into the soil, the fizz of chlorophyll in their tiny cells like green champagne. The intricacy of their wordless, chemical language with one another.

The way they existed wasn't loud, but it was ferociously tenacious nonetheless. In its own way, so much more formidable than the death I wielded with my own hands.

"Well?" Ivy said as I opened my eyes, awash in wonder. She was smiling so wide that the dimples on either full cheek looked like crescent moons. "That enough life for you yet?"

I shrugged, as if considering. "Well, you were dead-on about the fairy-tale bullshit. Though I guess you *could* have made them sing, if you wanted to go that extra mile."

She widened her eyes at me in mock outrage. "*So* greedy!"

"I was just thinking, imagine this . . ." I swept my free hand up to encompass our vibrant cage of flowers, dazzling against the night sky. "But set to something like 'Big Energy.'"

She burst out laughing, throaty and delicious, a sound I hadn't

heard in so long it made my stomach clench with pleasurable longing. "You want me to make animated night bloomers cover Latto
for you? Are you for real right now?"

"I actually think I'm being pretty reasonable. It's not like I'm
requesting Taylor Swift over here. I mean, 'evermore' would really
hit right now, but you know. Too on the nose."

"You are out of your mind, truly." She pressed her lips together,
sobering in an instant. "Seriously, Dasha. Is this enough? Does it
feel like enough to make you want to stay?"

"Why are you even doing this for me?" I asked, finally steady
enough to fully grasp the magnitude of what was happening between us. "After everything I did, how badly I fucked up with you.
Why do you care what happens to me? Why are you going out on
such a limb?"

"I take it you wouldn't accept 'just being a good neighbor' as
an answer?"

When I raised an eyebrow, she took a shaky breath.

"I'm doing this because, as it turns out, I can't stand the
thought of this world without you and your chaos in it," she said,
her eyes welling. "Okay? And . . . well, there's more to it than that.
But I'm not talking about it with you tonight. Not until I'm sure
you're not going to poof away. So? Are you planning on poofing?"

Even without everything else she'd done for me, seeing the
ache in her eyes, that painful hope, would have been enough to
banish the last of the raw yearning still clinging to my edges.

"No imminent plans of poofing, thanks to you," I assured her,
setting my hand on her thigh. "Not tonight. Not anytime soon. I
swear."

I could see her relax, the tension leaving her body in a way that
the bower around us echoed, each petal and leaf nestling more

comfortably in place. This was why so few Thorns bonded famil-
iars, I realized. Why would you need to, when all flora bent to you
like something that mimicked the shape of your thoughts, like you
were born grafted to anything green?

"Alright, then," Ivy said, with another sunrise smile. "In that
case, buckle up. Looks like we're about hear some very zesty
covers."

9

Shoulder to Shoulder

I STILL CAN'T believe we had to glamour *everyone*," Amrita said, tucking her bare feet under her on the couch. Puffy purple moons stood out beneath her eyes, her heavy mass of hair pulled up in a precarious topknot on the verge of collapse. It was well past midnight; the day had been a very long one for both of us. "That was some shit for the history books."

I sighed deeply, taking another fortifying sip of the still-hot rooibos with a dash of brandy that Saanvi had brewed for us before she finally managed to pry a very reluctant Kira off my lap and whisk her back to bed about fifteen minutes ago. "Just imagine future Thistle Grove generations reading about this Cavalcade," I said, lifting my mug in a mock toast. "Never thought we'd actually be those people living in interesting times."

Back at The Bitters, Ivy's flowers had sung to me for hours. Long enough that by the time I'd trusted myself to be parted from her and ushered home by Amrita, the large-scale damage control had been completed. Elena had led a small circle of Avramov casters in working a modified version of the oblivion glamour that would allow all the normie attendees to remember what had transpired at the spectacle—but only up until the moment the Potential King of the Many Hells had appeared. They'd remember the food and drinks and masked fortune tellers, the candlelit tour of the inside of The Bitters if they'd taken one, and even the performance of Morty's aerial troupe. But after that, they would recall nothing except being herded out of The Bitters and shooed off toward town, where they'd head to dinner or to Castle Camelot for the Blackmoore spectacle.

Too much tinkering would have done more harm than good, so Elena apparently hadn't even tried to instill any fabricated memories. Anyone who didn't automatically assume they'd had too much to drink would simply think their attention had wandered somehow, that they'd accidentally missed the grand finale by chatting with a friend, getting lost in thought, wondering about dinner or when they could go pee.

The human brain was unparalleled at confabulation, at stitching dreams into the holes where bits of reality had gone unexpectedly missing.

At least, that was the case when it came to a single mundane, or even a small group of normies. A glamour of this scale had never been performed before, which meant that no one, not even Elena, could predict any possible repercussions or ripple effects.

"So, the show must go on?" I asked Amrita. While I'd been clinging to Ivy for dear life—or the other way around, maybe—Amrita had been part of the mega-glamour casting, and then close enough to overhear Elena conferring with the higher-ranking

Blackmoores who'd been at the spectacle. "They went ahead and held the Blackmoore spectacle at Castle Camelot, even after what happened?"

"From what I heard, yes. The Grimoire is very clear on the fact that nothing should be allowed to disrupt the flow of the Cavalcade, which always includes all four spectacles. But the Blackmoores agreed not to use magic tonight—Elena suspects that was what attracted his attention, somehow, both there and at the Thorn spectacle earlier. They went with mundane fireworks instead, mimicking what they would have done with elemental spells."

"I wonder why he wouldn't have fully manifested at the orchards?" I said, rubbing the underside of my chin. "The Thorns used a lot of their magic today."

Amrita shrugged. "No idea. Maybe Thorn magic isn't conducive to building gateways for whatever kind of thing he is? Maybe he's more potent at night? No one seemed to know anything for sure. I do know there was an emergency quorum meeting tonight after the Blackmoore spectacle, with the elders and scions. So some decision will likely already have been made about what we're doing tomorrow and Sunday. We'll probably find out first thing tomorrow."

She took a final sip of her boozy tea, stretching awkwardly over the couch arm behind her to set the empty mug on an end table before fixing her gaze on me. "At least the decision-making is above our pay grade. What I'm much more worried about is you, Dash. What *happened* to you on the other side? Because that was bad, the way you came back. Extremely fucking bad, even. Worse than it's ever been, at least since the last time Elena had to wrench you out."

"I don't understand what happened, exactly." At Amrita's half-skeptical look, I bristled, spreading my hands. "Honestly, Ree, I don't. All I can really say for sure is that he wasn't a demon, at least not like any I've banished before. He's something much bigger, much more. And I know this is going to sound fucked up, but he's also very . . . enticing, somehow. Over on the other side, he's beautiful, this highly monstrous kind of sexy. He hugged me, and then I wanted . . . Amrita, I wanted to stay over there with him. And he wanted me to stay, too."

"Well, that's horrifying." She tucked her hands into her armpits, sinking deeper into the oversized folds of her slouchy, heather-blue sweater. "Did he say why?"

"Because I smelled like her," I said vaguely, struggling to remember all the details, overwhelmed as I'd been while they were actually happening to me. "He kept calling me 'child of dark.' He thought I smelled like . . . shadows, I think, but also like light? It confused him. Because I remind him of whoever he's looking for, but I'm also definitely not her."

"Well, we do have quite the number of contenders for this monster-seeking-partner reality show," Amrita remarked dryly. "Two of our current family elders are women—and one of them also happens to be the Victor of the Wreath and the Voice of Thistle Grove."

"That's true," I murmured, mulling it over. I hadn't even considered Emmeline Harlow, but as the Voice of Thistle Grove, she was intimately connected to the living essence of Thistle Grove itself—the town having been rendered a certain kind of sentient by centuries of being bathed in the magic that spilled over it from Lady's Lake. "He did call the 'her' he's searching for 'a font of light.'

Doesn't Emmy glow blue somctimes, when she's reaching for her connection with the town?"

"She does. Then there's Nina Blackmoore, former recipient of a goddess's favor. And let's not forget the full-blown goddess avatar in our lake, if he's more into magical statues." She shuddered like a cat, a full-body tremor. "Thank Mother and Crone Elena managed to snatch you away from him. The way you were when you came back to yourself, so feral . . . I can't imagine what might have happened if you'd been exposed to him for much longer."

I hung my head, a steady drumbeat of guilt thumping through me. "I'm so sorry to have scared you like that." I groaned, burying my head in the crook of my elbow. "And everloving *fuck*, I cannot believe I hit Elena Avramov in the face. *Hnnnngh*. Think I'm fired?"

"Oh, sweetie," Amrita said, on a soft exhale of a chuckle, propping her cheek up on a fist. "Elena surely doesn't give a shit about that. She appointed you—*you*, of all people—to channel Alyona's Aversion. That shitty consequences were a possibility, especially for someone as vulnerable as you, was eminently foreseeable. I'm not saying she was wrong to do it. It was the definition of an emergency, and you were the obvious choice." She shifted around until she was sitting tightly cross-legged, closer to me, the sleeves of her oversized sweater flopping over her hands like a little girl's. "But you absolutely can't blame yourself for this like it's some personal lapse in discipline or control, not when you didn't even choose to slide over of your own accord. I will not have you treating this as a relapse, you hear me?"

"Loud and clear." I gave her a two-fingered salute. "And just this once, I will indulge this endearing delusion that you're the older sibling."

"We all know I *am* older. In spirit and temperament."

"Is that what we're calling 'dementedly bossier' these days? Because that's a lot closer to how I think of it."

"I think what you mean to say is 'intentionally nurturing.'"

We smiled at each other, both abruptly awash in a sepia-tinged bath of nostalgia for our shared childhood, as unusual yet perfect as it had been.

I was actually a little over three years older than Amrita. My parents, Lev Avramov and Jacqueline Harlow, had been partnered for four years by the time they had me, but they had never chosen to pledge the witch bond. I was not quite one when they separated, and two when my father met Saanvi—a first-generation Punjabi American who'd recently moved to Thistle Grove from Chicago to start a solo CPA practice, away from a faster-paced consulting career and the dismal aftermath of a miserable divorce. They'd fallen headlong into what had clearly been the kind of once-in-a-lifetime love that my parents had never shared. They were witch-bound within the year—which meant that beyond the empathic bond all witchbound couples enjoyed, Saanvi had also become an honorary Avramov, a witch by marriage. Amrita had arrived soon after that, and I remembered how fiercely I'd loved her from the very start. That tiny, squalling face, bunched up and furious; the way she'd melt whenever I held her, even at her most colicky. Like she recognized me from birth, knew me already.

Somehow, the fact that we had different mothers swept away most of our sibling jealousy and rivalry, drew us closer where it might have been a wedge. I may have shared my father with my new favorite little person, but my mother would always be mine, and that was its own kind of security.

In the beginning, I spent every other weekend with my father and Saanvi. But as I got older, I alternated weeks between my mother's and father's houses, conveniently only two streets away from each other, so I could walk or bike between them by myself once I was old enough. As a result of all those years spent here, the warm homeyness of this house, with its creamy yellow walls and antique furniture—picked and restored by my father and step-mother as one of their mutual hobbies—had always been as famil-iar and welcoming to me as my mother's. As an adult, I recognized that there must have been at least *some* chafing, a fissure or five tucked somewhere in there; no blended family was ever perfectly harmonious. But all three of my parents managed to shield me and Amrita from it, bubble-wrapping us away from adult discord. Enough that I had no memories tainted by acrimony, not so much as a raised voice between the three of them.

Instead, if a tight-knit bond between all five of us had been some kind of purposeful arrangement, the three of them nailed it. There had been shared parties for anything that passed for an oc-casion, birthdays and BBQs and Wheel of the Year holidays. The five of us had spent so much time together that I couldn't remem-ber a time when Saanvi hadn't felt like blood kin to me, in the same bone-deep way my parents and sister did.

"And don't act like you ever got the shorter end of any stick. You *always* had meltiest-s'more dibs when Dad took us camping up on Hallows," Amrita pointed out. "And he taught you how to tickle trout way before he did me."

I cleared my throat. "That was, um, actually a spell. You'd spurt a little ectoplasm at them to stun them into flopping over. I was just better at it because I'd started spellwork school already."

Amrita mock gasped, clapping a sweater-floppy hand to her mouth. "You nasty cheater! And all these years you let me think you just had *better hands*!"

"Who's to say it wasn't both?"

"You know what he'd have said," Amrita murmured, her face softening. "That wonderful sappy little rhyme."

"'Sisters are soldiers, comrades-in-arms,'" I recited. "'Sisters are always on the same side.'"

"'Shoulder to shoulder, steady on their feet. Sisters don't judge, or compare, or compete,'" she finished, a wistful ghost of a smile hovering over her lips.

"Kind of weird martial imagery there, now that I think about it. You'd think he'd have enrolled us in aikido or karate or something, to go with it."

Instead, we'd both participated in decidedly pacifistic, un-Avramov extracurriculars. Gymnastics, dance—contemporary for me, ballet for Amrita—singing and violin lessons, musical theater when we got older. It helped that we had similar talents, but there was a certain throughline there I'd never really considered before.

"You know, it makes me wonder," I said slowly. "Maybe he nudged us toward what one might call highly life-affirming activities because of me. Because things like dancing and singing and tumbling would ground me in my body, on this side. And doing it with you would only reinforce it."

And it had worked. I had been highly resilient, even joyful, for most of my life. Pre-orphan Dasha was spirited and energetic and luminous. Full of the trademark Avramov charm, but with a much lower helping of darkness than most of us, despite the fact that I'd been born to eat devils and traverse the veil.

Amrita gave a thoughtful nod. "It does sound like him, the way he thought things through so meticulously. Always with the pedagogic theories. And he worried about you so much, once it became clear what you could do. It wouldn't surprise me that he'd have planned for it in some elaborate way—molded your whole life into an anchor on this side of the veil."

"To be fair, you'd probably have worked out an action plan, too, if Kira had eaten her first demon at the age of seven, and without any training to boot," I said dryly. "I imagine that might've been a little unsettling for everyone."

Amrita flung an instinctively adoring glance in the direction of her daughter's bedroom. Saanvi had never reemerged to join us, probably because she'd fallen asleep in the rocking chair while singing lullabies to Kira, a not-uncommon occurrence. "You know I'd have come around. Even if she turned out to be a full-bore, creep-ass devil eater like her Auntie Dash."

I flicked her a casual finger, and she blew me a kiss in return.

"Seriously, how could I not love any magic that makes my baby who she is?" she said, face hardening. "Unlike that bigoted shithead Evrain. Sometimes I want to kill him with my bare hands for not wanting any time with her aside from the occasional random Sunday. She's clearly not the one missing out, but how can he handle not seeing his own daughter grow up? Making her think, Mother and Crone forbid, that it might somehow be her fault? She's too little to think that now. But it'll occur to her one day."

"We'll make sure it doesn't," I assured her, wondering myself how anyone could help but adore the perfect nugget that was my little niece. Kira had done so much to heal me when I needed it the most, back when I lived with them during my recovery; intuiting how much her sweetness, the wealth of loving energy in her

))) 121 (((

generous little body, acted on me as a physical balm. She was forever clambering all over me like a kitten or a puppy, scrambling onto my lap, demanding piggyback and horsey rides. There was even a stint during which she'd only accepted Auntie Dash as the provider of her bedtime routine, from her mango-scented bubble bath to the minimum of six board books deemed necessary before she'd even consider sleep.

"I really thought he would, no matter what," Amrita said, with a somberness to her tone that she usually kept locked up tight. The small hours were good for lowering defenses—or terrible, depending on where you fell when it came to vulnerability. "Just the way our father loved us. I mean, I always knew Evrain could be kind of feckless, self-centered. You know—Blackmoore-ish. But he really *did* love me. And when I got pregnant with Kira, he seemed so genuinely happy about it, too, even if it was so much sooner than we thought. I figured it would be impossible for him not to love her, no matter which way she manifested."

In Thistle Grove, inherited magic ran unpredictably down bloodlines. There were no percentages, no probabilities that anyone had been able to discern over the centuries. As the child of a Harlow and an Avramov, I'd had just as much a chance of inheriting the quieter version of Harlow magic as Avramov necromancy—just like Kira could have taken after her father and become an elementalist. The predisposition usually made itself clear no later than three or four, sometimes even earlier. Once it was set, the child officially took that bloodline's last name.

Fucking Evrain certainly hadn't let the door hit his ass on the way out, as soon as he'd absorbed the fact that his precious daughter was going to grow up an Avramov rather than a Blackmoore. I still hadn't forgiven him, and never would, for how he'd made my sister cry over the illusion of love he'd conjured for her; the way it had brushed away like sticky cobwebs as soon as something hadn't fallen in his favor. Saanvi and I had quietly discussed the possibility of sending a subtly malicious little hex his way many times—always concluding it wasn't worth the trouble it might cause for Amrita if the judiciary ever caught wind of it.

"You were young, and in love with him," I consoled my sister, reaching out to squeeze her sweatered hand. "You couldn't have known. Much as it pains me to admit, not all Blackmoores are inherently trash. Look at Nina with Morty. Hells, look at Gareth. He's been leading them on something like a semi-righteous path ever since Emmy let him have the helm."

"I know." She cleared her throat, blinked back incipient tears. "I just . . . I wish that at least Dad had gotten to meet Kira. Can you imagine how wonderful he'd have been with her?"

I could. Our father had been a rare person, in many ways. Unlike most members of the Thistle Grove witch families, he'd never held down a mundane job. Instead, he'd been one of the few modern spellsmiths we still counted among our ranks, and for his paid work, he'd been a spellcraft teacher—one of the members of the community tasked with teaching baby witches the lessons of the Grimoire, how to control their own magic, and eventually how to cast. It had been perfect for him. As raucous and larger-than-life as he'd been, huge on elaborate pranks and with a memorized encyclopedia of jokes on tap, he was also infinitely patient. Slow to anger, quick to thrill at a child's most minor magical achievement.

I'd never been able to decide whether my favorite memories with him were outdoors—him teaching us the Avramov names for the constellations when we slept outside for solstices and equinoxes—or inside with one of our favorite books. The way he nailed all the voices and never tired of rereading our dog-eared favorites.

The way he'd died had been one of those fluke tragedies you could mourn without regretting. I'd been seventeen, Amrita thirteen, when it happened. A student had cast a practice summoning that had spiraled out of control, and our father had died in the process of reversing it, and shielding the student from the necromantic blowback.

"He'd have been the best with her," I said quietly, my own eyes stinging. "So many pranks. So many Best Grandpa mugs. So many homemade Lucky Charms peanut butter cookies."

"Those were fucking disgusting," Amrita whispered, her voice cracking. "I loved them so much."

For a moment, we sat in silence broken only by the occasional sniffle, just remembering Lev Avramov. We hadn't had a night like this, of overtired reminiscing, in a while—though I couldn't count the times my sister and I had shared this couch, drinking wine and swapping confidences. But something about a goth angel dude invading the Cavalcade and stealing me away apparently had both of us wishing for our father.

"I don't know how to ask this," Amrita said, breaking the muffled silence. "But I think I should, given what happened tonight. So just, I don't know. Stop me if it's bullshit, okay?"

I nodded, a touch of apprehension flaring in my chest.

"Why do you think you didn't . . . get lost, after Dad died? So consumed with the other side, the way you did after Jacquie died? What was different about it?"

I wrapped my arms around myself, reluctant to talk about this of all things, tonight of all nights. But I could see why Amrita had asked, why it might be important for both of us to understand, especially if the encounter with the Potential King turned out not to be an isolated incident. Because she was right. I'd always dabbled with the other side of the veil, been fascinated with it and the bright feeling it gave me, ever since the first time I'd accidentally slid over as a child.

But the obsession with it—the dark days—hadn't happened until after my mother's death.

"After Dad died, things were terrible," I finally said. "I don't have to tell you that. But they were terrible for *all* of us, and Saanvi especially, because of the witch bond. It felt like grieving together, as a family. Less lonely. Remember how much time Mom and I spent here, just because it seemed the tiniest bit easier to face when we were all together?"

"Yeah," she murmured. "And then there were those few weeks, a couple months in, when Saanvi just couldn't get out of bed. And Jacquie took care of all of us."

My mother and Saanvi had always been friendly with each other, despite the unusual circumstances that had brought them together. But after my father died, they'd grown much closer, into real friends. The kind that spent time together even when Amrita and I weren't around, just for the pleasure of each other's company. In a way, they'd been almost like platonic partners, giving Amrita and me a joint well of reliable gravity to orbit like satellites.

"But when I lost her, it suddenly felt like . . . I don't know. Like being an orphan for real. Even though I knew," I hastened to add, at the aghast look on her face, "Amrita, no, of course I *knew* that I still had family. That I had you and Saanvi, who loved me so much. But Jacquie and I . . . we were so close, in a different way. Inseparable. You know how I adored her. She was so funny, so smart, so completely strong. Such a golden person. And she made me the center of her world. You remember how she barely even dated while we were growing up, not that anyone would have judged her for wanting companionship."

The ache fissured inside me like it always did when I thought about my mother, fracturing outward from the star crack embedded in my very center, no less sharp even four years after the fact. It was as though her death had been a form of grievous physical injury, an insult that my body would never fully forget. The loss of Jacqueline Harlow, from whom I'd inherited my corn silk hair, pale skin, and veiny eyelids, along with my mezzo-soprano and perfect pitch. She'd given me the shape of my mouth, and the bony, weirdly small feet for my height.

What I hadn't gotten were her gift for numbers or single-minded academic focus, specifically the fascination with infectious diseases. It might have seemed strange for a Thistle Grove witch to carry a torch for something so mundane as viruses and bacteria, but this was a Harlow witch we were talking about, not particularly magically powerful, but devoted to the pursuit of knowledge, thrilled to share all sorts of revolting germ facts with me upon request. By the time I was ten, I'd probably been more conversant in the pathogenesis of rare diseases than your average second-year medical resident.

She'd worked at a medical research lab in Carbondale, her normally easy commutes much longer in bad weather—like the blizzard we'd had the night she died, when I was twenty-seven. Almost exactly ten years after we lost my dad.

For the first two years, I'd been mired in such deep denial I'd thought something was wrong with me, that after having lost my dad I'd become pathologically incapable of grieving. That was the era of desperate, frenetic partying, relationship after doomed relationship, me cutting the moorings as soon as it felt like I might be getting in too deep with anyone. Then something tectonic shifted; some deep part of me grasped once and for all that my beloved mother was never, ever coming back. That vault had slid closed, and could not be opened again.

And then the darkness had truly come calling.

I discovered what it felt like when I lingered on the other side, spent more than the odd few minutes there. The blazing glory of it, the way it blotted out the loneliness and grief like the most perfect antidote to the endless ache of missing her every single day.

But I couldn't think about those details tonight, not when I'd just experienced the ultimate distillation of the other side. Not when the memory of *him* still fluttered like moths at the edges of my perception, a soft, brushing beckoning that threatened to raise goose bumps on my skin if I let myself think about it too long.

"I don't think I can talk about this tonight, Ree," I said, ducking my chin. "I'm sorry. It's too much. Not safe. Another time, maybe? When we're both operating on less recent trauma and more sleep?"

"Of course," she said hastily, unfolding herself from the couch and offering me her hand. "I shouldn't have . . . I'm sorry to push. Let's both try to get some rest, before we discover what kind of fresh hell we're in for tomorrow."

10

That Hot, Wrong Honey

I T WAS PAST two by the time I finally snuggled under the fluffy comforter of the "guest" room, a space that had always unofficially been mine. The acanthus-carved empire canopy bed had been bought at my request; Little Dasha had indulged in some very grand tastes. The vibrant wallpaper, an indigo, teal, and beige print of curling florals and birds stealing tiny strawberries— a family project, from back when I'd had a thing for antique Morris prints—had never come down in favor of something more neutral. Saanvi even kept the brass censer on the vintage vanity stocked with my favorite incense blend from the Emporium, a mix of vetiver, amber, and bergamot.

It all declared, just as clearly as they constantly repeated to me, that I was always welcome here.

After a long shower to wash off any lingering miasma of the

other side—along with drinking it, submersion in water helped banish unwanted necromantic energy—I'd spent a little time in the oasis of Kira's room. Cuddled next to her in the pink glow of her ladybug night-light, stroking the warm curve of her cheek and the glossy black strands that threaded over it, so like her mother's and grandmother's. I couldn't allow myself to impose on their little trio as often as I sometimes wanted to; I was an adult, and one who'd already trespassed on their life enough, even if they were family. I didn't ever want them to consider me a burden, horrified as they'd be if they knew that the thought had even crossed my mind. But sometimes I couldn't resist the draw of my little niece, the peace of her.

After I'd brushed a kiss over her golden cheek and tucked myself into the guest room bed, I'd passed out within minutes. Encounters with the other side often left me with weird lucid dreams, the dark and sludgy dregs of whatever I'd seen swirling around in my head like silt in a churned-up riverbed.

But tonight I found myself on this side of the veil, hovering between a dream and a memory.

It was the first farmer's market of the season, always held at the beginning of March on the emerald swath of Thistle Grove's commons, close enough to Hallows Hill that you could smell the incensey magic lapping down from Lady's Lake above. The year had been unusually warm even for us, the hill already aflame with the vivid purple of Scottish thistle that grew alongside the trails winding up the little mountain. That day, a cascading mist had also been coursing down Hallows Hill like a steamy waterfall, rolling across the commons and refracting sunlight into miniature rainbows.

Against the lemon-curd sunshine and pristine sky, it had felt ridiculously enchanting even for Thistle Grove.

I'd been to the last six inaugural farmer's markets as the Emporium's event coordinator, to help set up our stand. But I remembered this one like it had been etched into my memory—because it had been the first time I'd properly met Ivy Thorn.

Because nothing was ever perfect, I'd had Wynter in tow. Despite Amrita's grumbling, Wynter was undeniably one of the best salespeople at the Emporium, and we'd have been silly not to use her for something like this. She'd hung up black-and-silver bunting in artfully trailing loops and wound tiny purple fairy lights around the stand's posts before I even arrived, and we'd moved on to arranging our wares over a mulberry altar cloth that pooled to the ground like a bridal train. Bundles of premixed incense, "bespelled" hand creams, "enchanted" potions in bejeweled vials (magically inert, but safe to drink), edibles infused with herbal mixes that actually *were* psychoactive to (mostly) legal degrees, and our centerpiece—the coffin-shaped "dollhouses for ghosts" that one of the Avramov main line cousins had recently begun to craft.

They were adorably macabre, like something made for a gothic nursery. Each perfectly rendered little room a mimicry of one of The Bitters' rooms, with a bunch of teeny, white-sheeted ghost dolls you could place wherever you wanted. Not the kind of goods usually sold at a farmer's market, but a novelty that would pique interest in visiting the Emporium.

"Sorry to bug you, but I've been trying to understand this whole situation from across the way," a low, clover-honey voice said, a shadow falling over me as I fiddled with the final spread of incense. It hardly mattered anyway, since Wynter was going to rearrange it into a superior aesthetic as soon as I turned my attention elsewhere. "And failing. Would you mind just explaining these . . . mini coffins to me, please? Because the not getting it is *killing* me."

I looked up and met Ivy Thorn's doe eyes, huge and dark and beautifully lined in a way I'd never been able to master. I knew *of* Ivy, but we'd somehow never crossed paths before—a damned shame, I remembered thinking, considering the bold architecture of that striking face, that decadent mouth. I'd certainly noticed her before—and noticed the way she looked at me, as if thinking very similar thoughts.

I'd blown a sheaf of white-blond hair out of my mouth, smirking up at her. "They're artisanal coffin dollhouses for miniature ghosts, obviously. Cottagecore, but make it goth. Because, you know, Avramovs. Does that help? I'd really hate to play any part in your untimely demise, Ms. . . . ?"

"Ivy," she said, smirking back. "Thorn. Not that you don't already know my name, Daria Avramov. Just like I've heard plenty about *you*."

The way she said it made me think that she'd been privy to some less-than-complimentary details about me from any number of my exes. Or, more likely, all of them, given the way witches talked in this town. If any tea was ever left unspilled, you could bet it was by oversight.

"I prefer Dasha. And I do," I assured her, dropping a tiny wink, even more committed to winning her over. "I just thought it'd be sexier to let you tell me. And more respectful, clearly. So, what do you think, Ms. Ivy Thorn—did it work for you?"

She burst out laughing, a multilayered sound like some complicated dessert, so warm and sweet it immediately sparked heat low in my belly.

"Where the hell did you learn this flirting technique? A pervert at the mall?"

"Oof, was the wink too much? I was afraid it might be." I cocked my head, tucking my teeth into my lower lip. I could see her gaze flicker down to my mouth, before she very intentionally dragged it back up to my eyes. *Oh yeah, this is happening.* "But I remember 'finish overture with a subtle wink at the lady,' from the Victorian manual on flirting in public spaces I recently read. *The Brash and Brazen Wanton's Guide to Wooing Other Wantons*, I think was the name?"

"First of all, that wink was an entire parallel universe away from subtle." Her eyes narrowed with amusement. "It wasn't even subtle's third cousin twice removed. And I'm sensing a certain . . . implication here? Which is kind of out of pocket, if you ask me, given that 'Why did you bring tiny-ass coffins to sell at a farmer's market?' seems like a pretty innocent question. Not to mention reasonable."

"I think we both know this isn't *really* about the artisanal coffin dollhouses, Ms. Ivy Thorn. But points for effort and consistency."

Next to me, Wynter coughed demonstratively. "Hey, Dasha, not to be rude or anything, but do you think, like . . . maybe you two could converse about *Victorian porno literature* elsewhere? I'd really like to sell some shit today, and your cringe pheromone cloud is obscuring our entire deal." She waved a hand dramatically in front of her face. "I mean, you can practically *see* the fug. No one's gonna come over here while you two are doing all that."

I flung a brief glare at her, noting the delicate pendant that hung around her neck on a black chain—an amethyst obelisk with some unusual faceting—before I swallowed a retort. I wasn't technically her boss, and she also wasn't technically wrong. The stand was hers to run, anyway; I was only here for setup and initial oversight. And I *did* want to continue this conversation outside of judgmental Gen Z earshot.

"Would you like to take a turn around the commons with me, Ms. Thorn?" I said, sliding out from behind the booth and offering Ivy my arm. "We can discuss coffins further. Or wantons. Or *Victorian porno literature*. Or anything millennial dowagers like us feel moved to chat about, really. Lady's choice."

She smiled at me, long and slow, lush lips curving over bright teeth, before slipping a hand into the crook of my elbow. "A turn sounds like just the thing. Why don't you come check out the Thorn stand with me first? For some much-needed perspective on normalcy."

This was where the dream forked away from real life, or at least my memory of it.

In real life, Ivy had taken me to her family's stand and bought me a piece of strawberry-rhubarb pie, breaking down for me in hilariously pedantic detail why this was a more "normal" choice for a farmer's market than toy coffins. Then we'd wandered around the other stands, marveling over intricately braided bread, wildflower honey, herbed butter, cheese, and limoncello—all the while riffing off each other, inventing increasingly absurd practices from my fictional manual on flirting. As the hours passed, we'd segued into talking about her hobbies; she taught yoga in her free time and sang in a local choir. The fact that I'd been in semiprofessional musical productions at the Carbondale theater with Amrita had especially confounded her.

"Avramovs, singing in *musicals?*" She'd wrinkled her nose in disbelief. "And not one but two of you? This shit is not computing."

"Such shade, from a Thorn who just dropped not one but two antihistamine pills because she couldn't stop sneezing out here, in her natural habitat."

Ivy's eyes—now much less watery—widened with outrage. "Oh, is hay fever not green-magic enough for you? Did you think it maybe made us immune to pollens and grasses and—"

"Just saying." I bumped her shoulder. "Glass houses."

Then we'd moved on to family. She'd told me about an ongoing rift with her little sister, while I'd done my best not to bring up anything too alienating about myself, instead regaling her with stories about Kira's toddler exploits and some of the wilder clients I'd had at the Emporium.

It had been our first de facto date, ending in an intense make-out session in the copse of trees that shaded the north side of the commons. Both of us half-tipsy from the limoncello stand that should've really come with a high-proof warning. Ivy's back pressed against a sturdy sycamore, her mouth against mine like free-verse poetry, or maybe something too sublime for any words at all.

In real life, I'd felt the darkness lift for once, falling from my shoulders like a horsehair cape.

But in the dream, as soon as we drifted away from the stand, Ivy wheeled to face me, setting her hands on my shoulders. Flowers sprang up all around us, a riotous profusion just like the one she'd woven for me at The Bitters. Then she closed the distance between us until her lips were only a whisper away from mine.

"Promise me you're really staying with me, Dasha," she said fiercely, her face taut with trepidation. "Promise me you're not going back to *him*."

I shook my head, not understanding, even as that swirling fog around our feet began to rise, curdling like landbound clouds, billowing up around our waists. I could feel its sudden clammy chill leaching into my legs. "What do you mean? Of course I'm here with you. We're going to . . . we're going to go have strawberry pie, and then we're going to walk and talk and kiss. That's what happens today. You know that."

"I hope that's what happens." Fear and regret brimmed in her eyes. "But look, Dasha. Just *look*."

Slowly, she turned me around, until I faced the Avramov stand again—where Wynter stood still, a disconcerting smile curving her dark lips, her fingers toying with that amethyst pendant. The fog around the stand had coalesced into an inky darkness, no longer mist but a churning river of ectoplasm. And as I watched, Wynter's familiar Bratz doll features morphed into an onyx darkness, her hair shortening and curling, a spired crown and coiling horns appearing on her head. Her clothes melting away to reveal a masculine form carved from granite slabs of muscle, a pair of wings tucked behind her back, their clawed tips curving high above her head.

His head. Because it was him, the Potential King of the Many Hells, the Avramov stand having vanished entirely. Instead, the other side of the veil loomed behind him, fields of black flowers under oxidized clouds, bristling orchards heavy with unnatural fruit. The jagged outline of a castle suddenly reared up, too, against the distant mountain range that was the crooked spine of that other world.

"Child of dark," he crooned at me, lifting a clawed, beckoning hand. His nostrils flaring, as if he could smell me even in this dream. "Do not think that I have forgotten you so very soon, even if I cannot touch you from here. Do not think that you will not find yourself by my side again."

"But I don't want to," I whimpered—even though I *did* want to, had as soon as I'd seen him. My feet were already scuffing in his direction, Ivy's hands falling from my shoulders as I trudged helplessly toward him.

"Dasha, don't!" Ivy begged, grabbing for my hand, whirling me around to face her again. Behind her, the farmer's market was still as it had been that day—sunlit and mundane, as if this dreamscape were split in two, with the other side of the veil hovering at my back. And myself strung up between them, like a makeshift boundary. "You can choose to stay, I know you can. This world is for you, too. Please, Dash, stay with me."

But I could feel them already, the chill tendrils of ectoplasm winding around my ankles, enticing me toward him. And the urge building inside me to taste that hot, wrong honey that would come after the slide, that scorching blaze of life that was me alone among the dead.

"I don't know," I admitted. "Ivy, I'm sorry. But I don't know what I'm going to do."

She leaned forward and pressed her lips ferociously against mine, a palm flat against my cheek. It was so furnace hot against my skin I nearly flinched, before the heat dissipated into a mellow warmth like a spreading balm.

That didn't make sense, not even in a dream. Ivy had *never* been hotter than me.

"When the time comes, you will know," she whispered against me. I opened my eyes, my breath catching to see the new light that glowed in hers, pulsing a searing amber like the first filaments of breaking dawn. "I know, I *trust*, that you will. But before then, Dasha . . . there's more for you to do."

11

Please

I BURST AWAKE with my heart hammering, my insides still aching with the dream.

As I sat up, propping myself against the pillows with the duvet a rumpled mess around me, snippets of images floated in my head, glistening queasily like a rainbow sheen in an oil puddle. Ivy's stricken face, the curve of Wynter's coy smile before she transformed into *him*. The fact that the real-life Wynter was such an obnoxious but mostly harmless poser somehow made the sinister dream version of her even more unsettling.

I leaned back against the headboard, jaw hinging wide with a massive yawn. A thin film of sleep still clung to me; a glance at the window confirmed that it was still at least an hour before daybreak, the sky only just bruising toward morning. Which meant I'd slept maybe a handful of hours at most. But my heart wouldn't settle, my skin antsy with wakefulness. I wanted to be up and moving—weird enough by itself, for someone who normally did whatever it took to avoid being conscious before eight.

And I didn't just want to be up. I could feel myself straining toward Lady's Lake like a bloodhound on a scent, an arrow quivering on the bow. I yearned to be up on the Hallows Hill summit, in the same powerfully compelling way I usually craved the other side of the veil.

Like most Thistle Grove witches, I loved our magical lake and the ceremonies we held beside its shimmering waters. But unlike others, I'd never been particularly drawn to commune with it by myself, to find solace there. Maybe my deep connection to the other side of the veil was so demanding it left too little room to long for anything else. Or maybe my inherent Avramovness was that much stronger than my mother's Harlow blood, as sad as it made me to think that I had inherited so little of that part of her. She'd often taken me up there with her for picnics, just the two of us; I'd seen the way she responded to it. Always leaning into the sweet magic-scented breeze that drifted off the waters as it ruffled her flaxen hair, the accumulated stresses of the day melting away with every breath. She so clearly belonged up there, as naturally as the bright sprays of thistles blooming along the banks.

It had made me feel a little lonesome and somehow homesick, to know this feeling wasn't something I shared with my mother.

But after the massive toll last night had taken on my system, maybe I needed to recharge. The dream had most likely been me processing the shock of it all in my sleep—and maybe now, the balm of the lake would ease me the rest of the way back.

At any rate, I had nothing to lose by spending a quiet half hour up on Hallows Hill before the day descended on us all. Shit, maybe I'd even properly meditate, and not just half-ass it the way I usually did.

Groaning, I swung my feet to the cool parquet, goose bumps prickling up my bare arms. This was not a household of early weekend risers, especially not after such a late night. It would be hours yet until the smell of French press coffee and Saanvi's home-made biscuits permeated the house. But if I borrowed Amrita's car, I'd probably be back before anyone even noticed I was gone.

I MADE IT to the Hallows Hill parking lot, nestled two curves of the road down from the summit, just before six. No cars were al-lowed anywhere near the little forest that surrounded the lake. A brisk ten-minute walk brought me up to the lakeside, the moun-tain air bracing with crisp leaves and the beeswax-and-amber smell of the lake itself.

It wasn't storming today, the way it often had been recently. Instead, the circle of sky right above the water looked oddly pris-tine, as if a cookie cutter had been used to slice away the dense clotting of clouds that trailed off in every direction besides di-rectly overhead. And even though the horizon had already taken on a rosy predawn blush, the deep blue of the sky above was some-how still cluttered with an improbable number of stars.

I gaped up at them, at that bright and frosty throng like a bliz-zard crystallized, sparkling and clear-cut as they normally only were at night. This was unusual, even for the lake. I'd never heard of anyone going stargazing up here in the early mornings. A sliver of moon still hung among them, too, so sharply rendered I almost expected it to glint, like Ivy's lip ring catching the light. The mirror-smooth surface of the lake reflected it all, an earthbound universe in miniature, framed by the dove grays and charcoals painted by the early light. Aside from the lap of the water against the shore, there was a numinous quality to the almost perfect silence, like the hush of an empty cathedral. It was too early for birdsong, the rustle of woodland animals in the brush.

Too early for anything but me, apparently, the slow thud of my heartbeat in my ears and the sound of my own breath.

It struck me that I couldn't even remember the last time I'd been up here by myself, and that this might be a terrible shame.

You had a point, Mom, I thought, wrapping my arms around myself and snuggling deeper into my coat. As soon as I'd set foot up here, the coil in my chest had begun to unwind, replaced by that glimmering sense of existing in a moment carved out by the cosmos with exactly you in mind.

This isn't half-bad. Not even a quarter bad, in fact.

"Excuse me? Hello?"

Shock crashed over me like a bucket of ice water. Defensive whorls of ectoplasm already coalescing around my hands, I wheeled toward the voice echoing from the trees, squinting through the low light.

Because I wasn't alone. As solitary as I'd felt, someone had been huddled just beyond the tree line since I'd arrived. Watching me.

Then a petite silhouette came stumbling toward me from the ring of pines, tripping down the uneven grassy incline that led toward the lake. As soon as I focused in, I could tell it was just a girl—or a young woman, rather, wrapped in an oversized jean jacket, the sleeves rolled up to reveal a plaid flannel lining.

"Hi?" I called back, still wary, but feeling safe enough to allow the ectoplasm around my hands to dissipate. This person didn't seem like any real threat, especially given that unsteady gait. More likely, I thought, my belly tightening with concern, something bad had already happened—to her. "Do you need help?"

"I . . ." She slowed, then came to a full stop about ten feet from me, swaying a little. "Yeah. I think I do."

Then she burst into heart-wrenching sobs, the kind that rolled up from the gut, and slowly crumpled to her knees. Almost gracefully, like an autumn leaf seesawing from a tree.

I broke into a little trot toward her, that bud of concern blossoming into full-blown fear. For all my experience with haunted people, most of my more dangerous encounters were under controlled circumstances, directed by me. Whatever had happened to this woman, of the many things that *could* happen to women, I was going into it blind.

"Hey," I murmured, sinking into a clumsy squat next to her. She was still sobbing into her hands, the red-and-gold ringlets that framed her face shaking with the force of her tears. "It's okay. I mean, it's not, clearly. But I'd like to try to help if I can. I'm Dasha. Do you want to tell me your name?"

She keened into her palms, a hopeless sound I could actually feel inside me, like a knitting needle driven through my sternum.

"I can't," she said, almost furious, dropping her hands to meet my gaze. Beneath the tears and badly swollen eyes, she was lovely. Delicately pointed chin, light brown skin, and honey-hazel eyes, their corners tilted up and the lashes wet and starfish-splayed. At least ten years younger than me, maybe in her early twenties—though those tears made her look even younger, tugging pitifully at my navel in how much they reminded me of Kira crying. "I'm sorry, it's not that I don't want to. I just *can't*."

"That's okay!" I assured her hastily, as a fresh wash of frustration and anxiety flooded her face. "Are you hurt? Do you need a ride back to town? Or is there someone I can call for you?"

What was she even *doing* up here by herself, I wondered, mind racing with possibilities. She wasn't a Thistle Grove witch; members of the families all knew each other by face if not by name. And I was sure I'd never seen her before. I ran a critical eye over her, scanning for obvious injuries, but she seemed reasonably put together, if disheveled. She was wearing heavily distressed mom jeans—the kind that Ivy killed in, and which I'd never even tried to pull off—with a ribbed white top tucked in, under that oversized and flannel-lined denim jacket that looked like she might have borrowed it from someone else. Overlapping chains of necklaces with delicate little pendants hung around her neck, lacy rings on her fingers above and below the knuckle. Her short nails were a kaleidoscope of color and pattern—matte black lined with gold foil, dove gray tipped with white, mulberry with charcoal chevrons, and marbled sage and brown.

The colors of the four families, I realized—the ones we'd used in all the brochures advertising the Cavalcade. Which meant she was either a normie local, one who went all in on our witchy traditions, or a tourist who'd come to town specifically for the festivities.

But my eyes snagged on the scraps of leaf caught in her copper ringlets. Had she *slept* up here in the cold woods, or just fallen by the trees? And then, with a chill that rippled through me like an icy trickle, I saw a feathered domino mask hanging from her other wrist, its band wrapped around it like a bracelet.

Whoever she was, she'd been at the Avramov spectacle yesterday—which meant that she must have been glamoured, like everyone else who'd witnessed *him*.

She shook her head, a helpless, despondent gesture. "I don't have a phone on me, I checked already. No purse or wallet, either, and nothing in these shitty shallow pockets. Doesn't matter anyway. Even if I did, I wouldn't know how to unlock it."

"And why is that?" I asked, struggling to keep my voice calm.

"Because I don't remember," she forced out in a trembling whisper, her voice breaking on the *r*. She wrapped her hands around the nape of her neck and rocked back and forth, teeth bared. That red-and-gold hair shone like a blaze with the motion, catching the warm glint of the morning that had finally broken over us. "I don't remember *anything*. I—fuck, I don't even know my own *name*."

I rocked back on my own heels, trying to stay composed. If I was right, something like this had happened before—to Delilah Harlow, Ivy's best friend. She'd been struck by a superpowered oblivion glamour, and according to Ivy, it had taken a week to piece her mind back together. But where Delilah had spent months randomly spiraling back into oblivion, this woman seemed much more generally lucid. She clearly understood the concept of a locked phone and the fact that she was supposed to have one in the first place, along with a wallet or purse.

But then again, we'd never seen the long-term effects of such a large-scale glamouring, especially after a magical manifestation as immense as what had happened last night. Who knew what it might have done to this particular woman's brain, how it might have slotted into any existing trauma or neurological conditions? The glamour that had afflicted Delilah had been completely different, nothing to do with a glamour cast by a circle of Avramovs. It made sense that whatever was happening to her might present differently.

"Do you know where you are?" I asked carefully, feeling out how far the amnesia extended. "It's okay if you—"

"Lady's Lake, on Hallows Hill," she replied without hesitation, before her face crumpled in confusion. "Okay, the fuck? How do I know that? And why do I know *that* if I don't know my own name, or how I got up here in the first place?"

"It is curious," I agreed, giving in to my burning thighs and kneeling next to her, the wet chill of dewy grass immediately seeping through my jeans. "Can you remember anything from before you came up here? Where you might have been?"

She closed her eyes, delicate face pursing with concentration, the tip of her tongue poking out like a little girl's as she thought about it. Another wash of protectiveness flooded over me, a raw tenderness that I'd only ever felt for Kira, twinned with a powerful urge to help this woman however I could.

Because this was someone terribly lost, maybe even more lost than I'd ever been. And I knew exactly how it felt to be so unmoored.

"No," she said after a moment, brow knitting. She toyed with her ringlets, pulling them tight and letting them spring back, the tiny piercings that marched up her ear glittering under the play of light and shadow. "There's just . . . light. Like a—a very, very bright fog? Maybe a fog with giant headlights behind it? I don't know. None of that makes sense, and I know it's not right." She flinched a little, as if the memory, or lack thereof, was physically painful. "And then, after that, nothing. Big old blank. The last thing—or first, I guess?—that I remember is seeing you standing by the lake."

"Would you like to go to the hospital? Get checked out?" There was always the chance that she'd come up here late for some ambiguous party purpose and gotten a concussion, though that wasn't something I'd ever heard of happening. Hallows Hill didn't exude the kind of vibe that made thrill-seekers want to rampage around its gentle, magic-soaked woods. In the whole of the town's history, there'd never even been an accidental drowning. "I could take you, if you want. I have a car here. We could—"

"No!" she broke in, shaking her head furiously, dread flashing across her face. "I definitely, absolutely don't want that. I'm not hurt, not like that. No doctors, no hospitals, no police. *Please.*"

That plaintive *please* twisted my stomach as much as the beseeching expression on her face, the shifting murk of fear in her eyes. Whatever the subconscious reason, the idea of going to a hospital or the authorities clearly terrified her. And given the domino mask on her wrist, I was willing to bet that it hadn't been a knock to the head that had gotten her into this predicament, anyway. If this really was the side effect of a glamour gone awry, normie doctors wouldn't be able to make heads or tails of it.

"We're not going to do anything you're not comfortable with," I soothed, resting a light hand on her shoulder. She eased into my touch immediately, like a lost puppy pressing against your leg. Again, the pit of my stomach clenched with instinctive sympathy. Beneath the jacket, she radiated heat, so at least exposure wasn't on our list of worries. Which had, apparently, somehow already become *our* list. "But if it's okay with you, I do have a friend I could call. Someone with some . . . medical-adjacent expertise."

"'Medical-adjacent'?" She cocked her head. "Is this like in the movies, where you take the gunshot wound victim to the vet to keep things stealth?"

"So you remember vets? And that particular movie trope?"

She made a perplexed face, scrunching up one eye. "Apparently, yes? Don't think I could give you an example of one, though. So, is that what it is? Your friend's a vet?"

I snorted a little, thinking of the many animals that roamed Honeycake Orchards, the horses and cows and baby pigs that Ivy had grown up around. Sure, why not; she'd probably helped out with all that at some point. "Something like that. She might be able to help, with no doctors or hospitals involved. Would you be comfortable with that? It would mean coming with me."

Ivy was going to murder–death–kill me for dragging her into this, especially if it *was* the Avramov mess I increasingly suspected it to be. But technically speaking—if we completely ignored last night—she still owed me one for the time she'd called on me to exorcise Delilah's partner, Cat.

The redhead looked me full in the eye, surprisingly forthright and unflinching, those honey-hazel irises shifting between mine. As if appraising me before arriving at a decision.

"I'll come with you," she said, with a solemn nod. "And meet your vet friend. On one condition."

"Oh, we're negotiating now?" I asked, with a chuckle, genuinely amused. "I wasn't aware this was evolving into a bargain."

A smile tugged the corner of her chapped mouth. "Maybe not a condition, then. More like a wish. I'm *starving*, Dasha. Problem is, I'm kind of broke right now. So before we see your friend, do you think you could spot me for something to eat?"

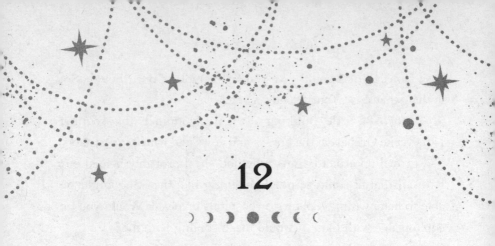

12

Starshine Moves

YOU TOLD HER I was a *vet?*" Ivy hissed at me through her teeth, eyes wide with accusation.

I shushed her frantically, throwing a harried glance over my shoulder toward the doorway leading to the tiny space that served as both my kitchen and very-mini dining room.

I'd inherited this glorified caretaker's cottage from my great-aunt, who'd passed it down to my father first. It had been an Avramov property for generations, mostly due to its off-putting proximity to the Witch Woods, and had originally been on the same parcel of land as a much larger Victorian that had eventually been sold separately. The cottage's owners tended to be Avramovs with an affinity for our haunted forest, like my great-aunt Akilina, who'd brewed concoctions from the strange, bitter flora that grew in the Witch Woods, selling them to the witch community for the psychotropic spells we cast during our Samhain celebrations and full-moon esbat circles.

My dad had held on to it after Akilina passed, not that people were lining up to live in a cottage that needed to be perpetually warded against curious shades nudging up against its windows. I'd chosen to move in when I turned eighteen, despite my mother's protests. But it turned out I actually *liked* living with its low beams and boho-rustic feel, the gloom of the Witch Woods hovering at my back. It felt a bit like an extension of the other side, a little piece that I could safely borrow and make my own.

"What was I *supposed* to tell the amnesia-stricken normie?" I hissed back. "Hmm? That you were Ivy Thorn, of the green-magic Thorns of Thistle Grove, blessed with the healing powers of root and earth? I was thinking maybe we'd keep that on the low to start."

"We do not say any such corny shit about ourselves." She tipped her head to the side, pursing her lips. "Not bad, though, to be honest. Kinda like it. Still, a *vet*. Dash, that doesn't even make sense."

"I was thinking on the fly, okay? My stranger-with-amnesia management skills are, weirdly, kind of rusty. Hence why I called you—at least you have actual experience. Next time I'll tell her you bring flowers to life and make them sing bops, if that's your preference."

Ivy thumbed her lip ring, looking pensive. "Well, at least she knows what vets are. That's something."

"That's what I thought, too. Her long-term memory doesn't seem impaired at all, at least not in that sense. She understands how the world works, what things are. Just not who she is."

"That can happen with some forms of mundane amnesia." Like most Thorns, Ivy actually *had* received fairly extensive (human) medical training as part of her magical education—standard fare for a witch as powerful on the healing scale as Ivy was. "How is she now?"

"Still eating, I think."

We glanced back toward my kitchen in unison. As promised, I'd granted the little redhead's wish and stopped by one of the few fast-food joints within town limits, loading up on a variety of breakfast sandwiches, wraps, and hash browns, in case she didn't know what she preferred. She'd tucked into it all as soon as we'd gotten here, surfacing only to inform me that "wow, your place is *colorful*," before diving back in. Ivy had arrived ten minutes ago in answer to my frantic summons, and from the faint wrapper rustling and munching sounds emanating from the kitchen, the pace hadn't slowed any in the meantime.

"A lot," I added. "Housing it, really. I don't even understand where she's putting it all, from a physics perspective. I think she might have spent the night up by the lake—maybe even been there since right after the Avramov spectacle. She seems pretty young, and probably a witch-town tourist rather than a local. Who knows how much she ate yesterday, or how much money she even brought to spend on food?"

Ivy nodded, nibbling on the inside of her lip as she thought it through. Even under the strange circumstances, my mind swam with the way her perfume had expanded to fill all the available air in the room, the way it seemed to steal directly into my lungs as if it had seeped into the oxygen particles. The memory of last night's kiss hovered over us like a (very sexy) ghost. And it didn't help that we'd spent so many nights right here, cuddled together on my teal couch among the peacock-patterned pillows and throws, snacking on pastries Ivy had nicked from the Honeycake Orchards store and watching trashy shows until we couldn't keep our hands off each other anymore.

Now, we sat a circumspect distance apart, knees not even brushing. But the memories layered over each other like onionskin, as if all of them still existed—maybe were even still happening right now—in a series of painfully close alternate realities.

Worlds in which things hadn't gone wrong between us, and the right branch had been taken. The one that kept us together.

"And you're thinking it was the Avramov glamour that did it?"

I gave a broad shrug. "It seems like the most reasonable explanation, though it doesn't tell us why she wound up wandering Lady's Lake alone at night. It's not a terribly difficult hike; we've all done it enough times, for fun and ceremonies. But still, alone, at night, disoriented . . . why would she have done that?"

"The lake does feel very inviting to some," Ivy speculated. "Maybe she's one of those normie sensitives, and in the absence of any other touchstones—if her memory loss was sudden and she had no idea what else to do, or if she was in a fugue state for a while—it might have called to her. Felt like a safe haven."

"Do you think you'll be able to feel anything when you examine her?"

"We'll see. The more receptive she is, the more I'll be able to glean. So I'll start with making her comfortable."

"Thank you," I said stiffly. "Look, I know this isn't your problem. I know you didn't have to come."

"Technically, it's not your problem, either," she pointed out. "You could've just taken her to the hospital or the police station. Someone's probably looking for her."

I flashed back to the terror on the stranger's face when I'd suggested it, the sense of primal protectiveness that still paced inside me like a caged tiger. "I couldn't, not after how she reacted to just the suggestion. Traumatizing her further doesn't seem like the way to go, and if she's that afraid of the idea? Maybe she's also afraid of whoever's looking for her, in a way that we shouldn't ignore. Obviously, I'll keep an eye out online for missing person reports, to see if we can at least find out her name. But I don't want to push her into anything she doesn't want to do."

"Still." Ivy's face softened, her eyes lustrous in the early morning sunshine that poured through the window above the couch. "It's good of you to choose to get involved."

"Thanks," I said, just as softly. For a moment, we just stared at each other, that old magnetism thrumming in the air between us like a struck chord.

Just before I gave in to the urge to reach for her hand, she cleared her throat and heaved herself up, narrowly avoiding one of the vintage Yule ornaments hanging from the rafters. The little redhead hadn't been wrong in calling my place "colorful." One entire wall was a vibrant collage of Broadway musical posters—Amrita's and my handiwork, back when I'd first moved in. I'd matched my teal couch with a plush hobnailed chair the color of raspberry jam. My cedar curio cabinet held everything from petrified snake skulls to crystals to my old dancing shoes, tattered to bits, along with about a million framed photos of my family. And the stuffed, sequined unicorn Ivy had once won for me at a Castle Camelot carnival booth.

She hadn't said anything, but I'd seen her notice it. This was probably the last place she wanted to be, given everything, but still, she'd come. For me.

"Not like we have anything better to do today, anyway," I said, trying to lighten the atmosphere.

Right after we'd arrived, I'd gotten a series of both texts and emails—missive spells might have been more appropriate, but sometimes modern technology was simply more reliable—informing me that the spectacles would continue as scheduled, only without the magical components. As the quorum's reasoning went, we knew from the Grimoire that the Cavalcade was necessary to Thistle Grove, but removing the magic might block further intrusion attempts from the entity while keeping the general vibe of the experience intact.

This was obviously only a stopgap solution, given that we had a whole month of weekend performances to go, and I suspected I'd soon be called in for a debrief on what had happened on the other side. No one had experienced the entity more intimately than I had, and the quorum would want every piece of information they could get.

But no summons had arrived for me just yet. I'd also texted Amrita to let her know I'd borrowed her car to meet Ivy for a breakfast chat about the previous night—a rendezvous with Ivy being one of the few things that could have plausibly gotten me up that early—and would be returning it a little later in the day, with plenty of time for her to drive to the Emporium before the tourist crush began. So, Ivy and I had at least some time on our hands for this mystery within a mystery.

"Alright," Ivy said briskly. "Let's do this. Let me take the lead, okay? I'll need to establish my own rapport with her."

I gestured to the kitchen with a flourish. "All yours."

As we ducked through the low doorway, the girl—it was so hard not to think of her that way, though I kept correcting myself to *woman*—looked up, chipmunk-cheeked with whatever cheesy biscuit and mystery sausage she'd been tearing into. As soon as she spotted Ivy, she swallowed the impressive mouthful with effort, then broke into the first real smile I'd seen from her. Apparently the quick and dirty calories had gone a way toward perking her up.

"Hey!" she said, with a little wave. "The vet, right? Nice to meet you. I'd offer my name but . . . well. No information available."

"I'm Ivy, and I'm not *exactly* a vet," Ivy clarified, smiling back. "More of, ah, a holistic practitioner. You know, Reiki, energy work, pressure points. Things like that?"

"Acupuncture," she said, nodding sagely. "Sure, I'm into that, I think. I know what it is, for what that's worth."

"I'm pretty well versed in first aid, too," Ivy went on. "And I've had some field training in more extensive medicine. Would it be cool if I took a little look at you? Just preliminary exam?"

The redhead wiped her mouth and hands with surprising daintiness, considering the unabashed way she'd wolfed the food, then crumpled up the napkin and nodded, patting the chair next to her. "Please. I'd love to know just what the fuck is rattling around in my head. Bring on all the holistic disciplines."

As Ivy moved to sit by her, I shifted from foot to foot. "Would you, uh, like me to leave? If you'd be more comfortable, I could—"

"No, no." She gave an adamant shake of the head, those fiery ringlets bouncing. "You didn't have to do any of this for me, I know that. But you did. You brought me into your home without knowing the first thing about me, literally. Shit, without *me* knowing anything about myself. So I'd . . . I'd like it if you stayed for this."

I nodded, a warm, unexpected rush of relief surging through

me so hard it nearly weakened my knees. Why was I feeling so attached to this unfamiliar person? To be fair, she was adorable, and shockingly upbeat for someone undergoing such a traumatic experience. But I felt almost bonded to her, as if it would hurt to relinquish the role of protector I'd taken on by finding her.

As I sat down, Ivy was instructing the redhead to shift in her chair so they could face each other. "And I'm going to touch your face now, okay?" Ivy said. "Kind of weird, I know, but it's what works best."

"That's fine," the redhead replied, instantly relaxing into Ivy's touch the same way she'd done with me up at the lake. Even her voice mellowed with pleasure at the physical contact. "It's nice. Feels warm. And really good, actually, making me a little sleepy. I'd leave a bomb Yelp review for this if you wanted, tell you what."

Ivy chuckled, her eyes sliding closed. "Just relax into it if you can, and keep your breathing nice and steady. Now, let's take a look."

For a few moments, nothing happened. They both stayed quiet, the redhead's breathing slowing to a steady lull as that sweet, mellow Thorn magic funneled through her, presumably questing into her mind as Ivy gently probed for answers. I was just beginning to relax myself when Ivy caught her breath in a sharp gasp, snatching her hands away from the woman's face and backing her chair up with a scrape. Then, she flapped both hands frantically in the air, as if she'd accidentally touched a still-hot stove burner.

"What?" I barked, a spike of fear lancing through me. The redhead flung a startled glance back at me, and I struggled to soften my tone. "Ivy, what is it?"

"Nothing," she eked out. But from the tension in her face, I could tell she was still in pain. "I'm—I'm sorry. I couldn't, ah, detect anything out of the ordinary. It just took me by surprise, is all. Usually I'm . . . a lot more intuitive than this."

For a moment, the girl appraised Ivy with watchful eyes, rightfully dubious; it seemed obvious that whatever Ivy had felt, it hadn't been a raging case of the nothings. Then she sighed, deflating.

"Well, bummer. Guess it was a long shot anyway, right? Thank you for trying. I . . ." She broke off, yawning hugely. "You know, I'm still feeling really sleepy. *So* sleepy. Dasha, I know this is a major ask, but do you think I could crash here for a while? Sleeping bag, air mattress, the floor. Whatever you've got would be great."

"Of course," I said, rattled. Ivy was still staring into space as I stood, clearly trying to gather herself. "I have a very cozy guest room, if you're into sleeping in the equivalent of a walk-in closet. There isn't even an overhead light fixture. But the sheets are clean; it's all set up. Does that sound good?"

"More like fantastic," she said through another jaw-cracking yawn, knuckling at her eyes. She stood, too, tottering a little bit, as if she were about to fall asleep on her feet. "Thank you."

As she trailed me out of the kitchen, I cast a look over my shoulder at Ivy. She mouthed, "We need to *talk*," widening her eyes emphatically at me. I nodded, trepidation whipping up inside me like a dust storm.

What the hells had she felt in the stranger's head that had shocked her that way—and even caused her pain?

"SOMEONE BUILT A wall in that chick's head."

We sat on my screened-in back porch, watching the light rain that had begun to fall. The festivities wouldn't be affected; there were so many meteorological spells in place at the family demesnes that it was a wonder the Blackmoores had time to be casting anything else. But over here, in the unprotected area near the north end of the Witch Woods, what looked like a thunderstorm was gathering, gunmetal clouds churning above us. It rarely stormed in Thistle Grove, but when it did, the fall weather brought the appropriate melodrama. The kind of lightning-struck backdrop befitting a cackling crone bent over a bubbling cauldron.

I could already smell the tang of ozone crackling in the air, along with the delicious petrichor that mingled so well with the Witch Woods' damp mulch. Every once in a while I even caught a draft of the wild garlic that grew in the woods, a pungent, nearly skunky odor that had become an acquired taste.

Before settling in out here, we'd dropped Amrita's car off at Saanvi's. But despite her earlier urgency Ivy had been uncharacteristically quiet as she drove us back, still mulling over what she'd felt.

"I'm sorry," I said now, "did you say a *wall*?"

"Yes, and not just a wall. A hot one," Ivy elaborated, making a face. "That shit felt like pressing your hands against a furnace on full blast." She winced, turning over her unmarked palms to examine them. "It's not like anything I've ever felt before, I'll tell you that much right now."

"But Avramov magic is almost always cold. I've never known a glamour to feel hot," I mused, bewildered. "Especially not an oblivion glamour. It doesn't make *sense*."

"No," Ivy agreed grimly. "That, it does not."

"And you don't think it's something mundanely medical? Some neural condition that might register that way to your, uh, magical scanner?"

"Almost definitely not. Whatever that was, according to my *magical scanner*, it wasn't mundane." She shuddered a little, curling her hands into fists. "It wasn't anything I've ever sensed before, and certainly nothing from the Grimoire. But magic for damn sure."

"Do you think you'd even know if it were an Avramov working? Some vestigial remnant of last night's glamour, maybe, like what happened to Delilah?"

"I can't be sure, obviously. But I do know Delilah's mind never felt that way, and I'd be able to tell if there were parallels. I used to spend hours with her, trying to balance her out a little. She was a whole mess, but it was nothing like that."

We heaved sighs in weary unison, then caught each other's eyes and shared a little smile. Beyond the screen, the rain had begun to fall harder, in a needling sheet that lanced sideways and made the screen tremble with each lash. We were both already wrapped in the fuzzy blankets I kept on my rocking chairs, but I felt a little chill course through me at the next damp waft of breeze that blew over my face.

"Want some mulled wine?" I asked Ivy. "It's the perfect weather for it. And are you hungry? I'm suddenly realizing that I haven't eaten all that much since yesterday afternoon. There's gotta be some leftovers, even after those intense amnesia munchies."

"I wouldn't mind a nibble of something." She stretched long arms above her head, arching her back like a cat, and I made a herculean effort not to let my eyes linger on the high, full curve of her breasts straining against her caramel-colored sweater. "And mulled wine sounds heavenly, if you wouldn't mind. It's a little early, and I'll have to sober up before I head over to the orchards for the spectacle. But yeah, the weather does call for it. And . . ."

She made a broad gesture that encompassed the boggling quality of our entire morning, pulling an expressive face.

"Exactly." I pushed up from the rocking chair, letting the throw fall back from my shoulders. "Just give me a minute. I'll pull together a little porch picnic for us."

She smiled at me, so full and sweet I felt a sharp yank at my heart, like tugging on an unraveled thread. "You always were epic at bringing the snacks."

"Next-level girl dinners—another trademark Starshine move," I said, winking at her the tiniest bit, even as my stomach tumbled into an entire series of somersaults. Maybe I was wrong, but her willingness to linger here with me, even now that our mysterious stranger was asleep, felt like a possibility. The cracking open of a door that I'd thought firmly shut. "And I'll have you know I've only upped my game since us, due to all the solo meals. So prepare to be impressed."

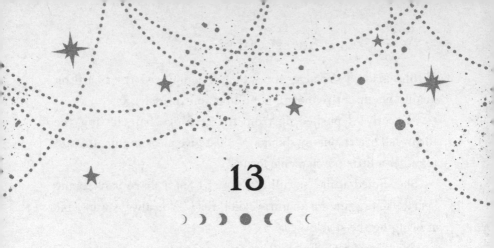

13

Mulled Wine and Confidences

THERE'D BEEN PRECIOUS little left of the fast-food breakfast
smorgasbord. But while the red wine simmered, I'd cut the
sole remaining bacon-and-egg biscuit into quarters and spooned
pine nut hummus and harissa-spiced Greek yogurt into little
bowls for us, along with cubed cheese, olives, and the seed-flour
crackers I'd started buying because Ivy liked them, and then kept
stocked because the taste reminded me of her. I topped off the im-
promptu mezze platter with some of the champagne truffles I
always kept in the pantry, for dessert emergencies.

"A little unconventional, but I'm here for it," Ivy concluded,
dipping one of the biscuit quarters into the harissa yogurt. "Mmm,
who'd have thought cheesy bacon paired so well with a yogurt dip?"

"What can I say?" I snagged a quarter for myself. "Creative
tapas are one of my love languages."

"Are they?" She gave me a little glimmer of a smile, lifting her mug of wine in a toast. "Good intel."

"Is it? Because I know I'm starting to sound like a broken record, but this is the second time you've shown up for me. And it seemed like . . ." I swallowed hard, past the dry lump in my throat. "It seemed like you were so firm yesterday at the orchards, about us being *over* over. Friendship didn't appear to be on the table, either, if that's what this is. Not that I wouldn't welcome it."

"It's not friendship," she said quietly, eyes on her plate. "Last night . . . I don't think I ever fully realized how bad it could get for you. You told me about it, but it was always the abridged version. Surface-level stuff. I didn't *really* appreciate just how awful it was, how difficult and dark it must have been, until I saw it happen. Not that it lets you off the hook for all the shit you pulled with me, but . . ." She shrugged, flicking me a little sideways look. "It does change things. I'm not sure how just yet. But it does."

"What can I do?" I asked, shifting in my chair until I was angled toward her, my heartbeat pulsing at the base of my throat. "How can I change them more?"

She rocked her chair a little, pushing off with her socked toes. "Well, like I said. You never gave me any details, except to say that after your mom died, you'd had a rough patch with controlling how much time you spent on the other side. I always felt how turbulent you were, how much pain you were still in, but I never understood it. What was it really like, when that happened? And why didn't you ever tell me more?"

I licked my lips, torn between fear of pushing her away now that we were at this tentative inflection point, and the urge to finally tell her everything. Hold none of the darkness back.

"Because I was ashamed," I said, so quiet it was nearly a

whisper. "I was addicted to that feeling, Ivy. No one ever said it out loud, but maybe we *all* should have. It might not have been in the traditional sense, but functionally, that's what it was. Still is, I guess. And I hurt people who cared about me the most. I scared them so much, so many times."

"It wasn't your fault," Ivy said, twisting sideways to throw me a fierce look. "That's not how addiction works."

"I know that. Intellectually, I get it—but I don't *feel* it. I wanted to atone for that lost time and all the worry, to be a better person for them. And I never wanted to be in that space again, which at the time meant I needed a substitute, something to take the edge off a little. And for a while, new relationships were it. The butter-flies, the sparks, that warm energy. The way you feel so buzzy and alive when things are just beginning. So I thought if I could have you to love, and the safety net of those more casual relationships, too . . . that maybe we could make it. That I wouldn't have to ever lose you." I caught the way she winced at that, and hastily added, "It was never about you not being enough, Ivy. Never. I was just so afraid that if I let go of the only antidote that's ever worked for me, I eventually wouldn't be able to resist anymore. And I couldn't do that to my family, Ivy. Or myself. Or you."

"I think I get it," she said, nodding slowly. "It . . . it really hurts to hear, I'm not going to lie. But it also helps to understand."

Tears stung in the back of my nose. "I should have explained it all to you at the time, I know that. And I'm so sorry that I didn't. That I felt like I couldn't. It was cowardly of me, and so unfair to you."

"It was," she agreed, and somehow that admission didn't even sting—because it meant I was finally doing something different. The right thing, maybe. "Do you think you could tell me more now, about how you got to that space in the first place? When spending time on the other side became so unhealthy for you."

"Ivy, I'll tell you anything you want," I said—and I meant it, with a ferocity that clawed at my chest with the pleasant pain of scratching at an itchy, healing wound. "Like I should have done to begin with. But it's ugly. It's fucking sad. Are you sure that . . . do you really want to hear it?"

"I do." She reached out in the space between us and took my hand, gave it a tight squeeze. "All of it. I can handle it, Dasha. I promise."

I blinked back tears, swallowed them down, holding off until I was sure my voice wouldn't waver.

"In the beginning, it wasn't a big deal," I started, swiping under my eyes with a thumb. "I've spent time on the other side since I was little. That much you know. But then after Mom died, it was such an easy escape. The only place I could leave the constant fucking grief behind. The way it feels on the other side, Ivy, it's . . . Mother and Crone, it's such euphoria, like your blood turning to hot honey. And it's gorgeous there, too, in this terribly bleak and deathly way. Dialed up high on the nihilism. Which, at the time, really spoke to me."

"Understandably," she said, with a small, sad curve of a smile. "Then what happened?"

"I'm not sure when I started losing control, exactly," I admitted, hanging my head, letting my pale hair curtain my face. "The hikes—that's what I called them, just to make it sound more acceptable—kept getting longer. There are these fields of black flowers there, and orchards with this weird not-fruit. And beyond them, there's this wide gray river like quicksilver that never moves. I'd sit on its bank for hours sometimes, just letting myself burn with that feeling. And it's not a Narnia situation over there, when it comes to time. I don't even know what the other side actually is—the afterlife, a parallel universe, some sideways realm?—but time *does* pass here, too, if you spend enough of it there."

"Oh," she said softly, seeing where this was going. "And then all of a sudden, you were there more than here."

"Yeah. I wasn't eating, sleeping, showering. For a while, everyone assumed it was just the grieving process. But then I started missing work, being late to family dinners at Amrita and Saanvi's, or just skipping them altogether. And at some point . . ." I drew a trembling breath, my chest aching with the memory. "I kind of decided I didn't want to come back at all. That I'd rather roam there for as long as I could, instead. I didn't get hungry or thirsty while I was over there, anyway. So why come back ever, when being here hurt so much? Couldn't see the point."

"Dasha," Ivy breathed, squeezing my hand tight. I clutched back at her just as hard, as if I'd finally caught a lifeline in a bucking ocean. "That's . . . I can't imagine."

"There was a part of me, too . . ." I closed my eyes, waiting for the intense swell of emotion rolling over me to recede a little. "I actually haven't told anyone this. But there was a part of me that kept thinking I might find my mom there. I do run into the occasional drifting shade, from time to time. So it's possible that it *is* a way station of some kind, if not a destination. I didn't . . . I didn't think it was very likely. But even just the 'maybe' felt like more hope than I would ever feel again."

"Oh, Starshine." Ivy pressed her lips together, the corners of her mouth trembling. "I'm so, so sorry."

"Thank you." I dredged up a tremulous little smile for her.

"Lucky for me, I have a bulldog of a sister and a stepmom who'd probably literally move mountains with her bare hands for me. They figured out what was going on, and one day, they came barging in here and found me in the stupor—I enter a sort of vegetative state when I slide over, and I have to will myself back. They both tried, but they couldn't budge me. So they called in reinforcements."

"Ah. Hence the Elena bitch slap. It's all falling into place."

I dragged my hand over my face, groaning. "Yes. Really a total champ at gratitude over here, someone get me my trophy. Anyway, as Avramov elder, and just an unconscionably powerful necromancer, Elena managed to hook her will into me and drag me out. Kicking and screaming, I might add. I wasn't any more gracious about it the first time around, though I managed to keep my hands to myself that time."

"Just barely, I bet," Ivy remarked wryly.

"Then she bound me with my garnet, using some ancient, really nasty bind that definitely isn't Grimoire approved. I couldn't take it off, couldn't slide across the veil. Hurt like shit if I even tried. Elena told me she wouldn't remove it until I was better, and had proven myself capable of managing my time on the other side. And if that turned out to be never, then so be it."

I closed my eyes briefly, my fingers tracing the garnet's now-cool facets, remembering that separate grief of being trapped, the agony of being unable to slide over the way I had done my whole life. The searing pain when I tested the limits again and again, and then the endless sense of longing.

I'd really become an expert at all the flavors of loss, given everything.

"So that was when you lived with Amrita and Saanvi for a

while," Ivy said, her eyes huge and bright with sympathy. "They were taking care of you."

"More than that. They were basically teaching me how to be alive again, on this side of the veil. And it worked. It was slow going, but I got better, found my footing. Not in any perfect way, clearly. What I was doing with relationships . . ." I shook my head, guilt swelling against my ribs. "You were right, about what you said at Honeycake. When it came to you and me, it might not have been exactly what you thought, but I *was* being selfish, using other people. Of course I'm not the only one who matters. Whatever my anchor's going to be, it can't be a thoughtless pheromone parade. I'm so sorry I ever even suggested it to you."

She nodded warily, pressing her lips together. "So what are you doing instead? How are you coping?"

"I'm doing whatever I can think of to ground myself. Long walks with Amrita and Kira, refocusing on work, meditating like I told you." I wrinkled my nose. "Or trying to, at least. I still kind of suck at it. And . . . okay, this is going to sound ridiculous, but the theater over in Carbondale is putting on a production of *Wicked*. Absurd, I know, but Amrita roped me into auditioning. So come October, the sisters Avramov shall be playing Elphaba and Glinda."

Ivy cackled, actually throwing her head back. "Man, what a twist. Did not see that one coming."

I smacked her shoulder, grinning. "Are you mocking my rehabilitation? Ivy Thorn of the green-magic powers of root and earth, that isn't very *nice* of you."

"I'm not, I swear I'm not. But which . . . oh my god." She wiped at her eyes, still burbling with giggles. "It's too much. Which *witch* are you gonna be?"

"Fucking Glinda," I muttered, rolling my eyes. "Perfect hair for the job. I won't even have to wear a wig; they'll just put me in curlers. Amrita's going to play Elphaba, that lucky bitch. She gets to be green and *everything.*"

"Real-life witches playing iconic fictional witches." Ivy chortled to herself, shaking her head. "The level of meta humor here is *wrecking* me."

"Yes, I can see that," I retorted, arching an eyebrow at her. "Pretty rich, for someone who once drunkenly insisted on dueting Seal, Usher, *and* Miguel with me at Whistler's karaoke night. With your sunglasses on. Inside. At night."

"Come on. That was so different." She tipped her head back against the porch chair, still giggling a little. "You have to admit, we totally killed 'Kiss from a Rose' and 'Sure Thing.' Jury remains out on 'Lemme See.'"

"None of those songs are even duets! How did we pull it off?" I chuckled at the memory, shaking my head. "As my erstwhile karaoke partner, don't think you won't be coming to take in our grand debut. I'll be expecting my backstage rose."

"I assure you, there is no way I'm missing something like this." She crossed her arms over her chest, still fighting back laughter. "Okay, I can be chill, I really can. Seriously, though—good for you, Dasha. Fucking fantastic for you, even. You're putting in so much work. I'm . . . I'm really proud of you. And I'm so glad you finally trusted me with all this. That took work, too."

"You did grow me flowers to order," I reminded her. "I think maybe that deserves some confidences. But we're always talking about me. What about you? How have things been with Juniper?"

"Ugh." She scrunched up her face, tilting her head back against the chair. "I'm gonna need a refill for that, please."

Once I was back—having briefly peeked through the cracked guest bedroom door to determine that our stranger was still dead to the world, sprawled facedown across the twin bed like she'd collapsed onto it and never budged—Ivy accepted her mug with a deep sigh.

"June and I are about the same, I guess? We just never really recovered. And it seems so nuts to me, that we can't find a way past this. But she keeps pushing me away, and we were so close before. I don't get it. Like, you're going to let one argument ruin years of all the good sister stuff?"

This conflict between them was an old one, especially by Thorn standards; empaths that they were, most issues tended to be resolved quickly, given how uncomfortable friction was for all of them. But the previous year, a few months after Ivy and I had met, Ivy's little sister Juniper had taken over for Holly Thorn as May Queen, after a rogue Avramov curse had incapacitated Holly and taken her out of the running to lead the Beltane festivities. Holly was one of Ivy's closest friends, and a second cousin to her and Juniper. Ivy had felt that under the circumstances, it sent the wrong message for Juniper to leap at the chance to replace Holly as Queen—or for any of the Thorns to take her place.

"I still think she shouldn't have done it," Ivy said. "And that's the problem—I won't back down on that. It *should* have been someone else. A Harlow, a Blackmoore, whatever. But Holly isn't just family. She's our friend, mine and June's. We should've been circling the wagons around her, not stepping into her shoes while she recovered from something that nearly stole her magic."

"I hear you," I said, taking a sip. I knew all this, but I'd been hoping both their stances had softened in the meantime. "But she felt you were picking sides, right? Choosing Holly over her?"

"Yeah. Stealing her moment, or whatever." She snorted softly into her wine. "Which, honestly, is just silly. June's so talented; she could've been Queen this year, or the next. It would've happened eventually. There's no mad rush, seeing as it's almost always one of us anyway. But to hear her tell it, I *undermined* her in front of the whole family, took our cousin's side over hers. And I can feel how resentful and hurt she still is over it."

"I'm sorry. That's rough on both of you." Amrita and I, for all our playful squabbling, had never really had a fight like that, the kind that seemed to shake the foundation between us. We were too tightly bound together, and we'd experienced too much shared loss; even during my dark days, Amrita had never been truly angry at me. Just frustrated and terrified and sad, but never blaming me, no matter how difficult I made things for her and Saanvi.

"It doesn't help that our parents are with me on this. So you can imagine how it looks to June. Like I turned everybody against her. I barely see her these days, and we used to . . ." she pressed her lips together, fixing her eyes on the ceiling to clear tears from them. "We used to be so tight. Inseparable. And losing her while Delilah was so precarious, needing me so much . . . man, it was a lot on me."

Now I was the one to reach over and lace my fingers through hers, swinging our hands together in the distance between us.

"Do you ever wonder why life must contain such a very great amount of shit?" I mused. "Angry sisters who won't be appeased, needy best friends with memories on the fritz. Dead dads, dead moms. I'd be totally cool with the balance tipping the other way, if any of the higher-ups ever asked for my two cents. Like, when's *that* satisfaction survey landing in my inbox?"

She laughed through her nose. "Maybe it's the toll for living in a magical place like this. Price of admission?"

"Yeah, a magical place that turned into a gothic horror show last night." Something occurred to me—the look on Ivy's face when he had first manifested, what she'd said to me before I'd run to join the Avramov circle. "Hey, how did you even know to call him those things? Quencher of flame, destroyer, nemesis."

She nibbled on her lip, her face clouding. Beyond us, the sheets of rain seemed to gust almost intentionally, in billows that shook even the sturdy timber of the cottage.

"Honestly, I barely remember saying all that. I could just . . . *feel* him." She shuddered, drawing the blanket closer around her shoulders. "And I know this is going to sound fucked up, but he felt kind of like *you*, Dasha. Like your family's magic, the essential opposite of mine. But worse than that, because you all aren't malevolent. At least not for the most part."

I made a little face at that, then gave a grudging nod. Some of us did tend to be a little sharper than others.

"You just *are*," she went on, "the way death is just a fact of life. But he's . . . he's hungry, and empty, and pissed. And something even worse than that, I think."

A brilliant bolt cleaved the sky, like an incandescent artery pulsing against the angry roil of clouds. A roll of thunder followed, so booming and instantaneous it sounded like the lightning might've struck only a few feet away. We both flinched, releasing matching little squeaks—then turned to each other, the startle melting into amusement.

"Should we go inside?" I asked her. "Not that it won't be as loud in there, but it might feel a little less immediate than this."

"Yeah," Ivy said, trailing her thumb along mine in a deliberate, languorous way that sent an instant spiral of heat curling in my center. Her dark eyes glowed against the rain-washed gloom of the porch, a heavy-lidded sultry look I knew well. "Hey, remember how we used to . . . nap together sometimes, during storms?"

"Oh, I do," I said, my voice emerging at least an octave lower than normal. "I remember those naps very, very vividly."

"Good. Cause it turns out, I'm kind of in the mood for one," she said, standing slowly enough to draw me up with her, close enough that the warm fan of her wine-scented breath brushed over my lips. "What about you, Dasha? Do you feel like a nap today?"

"Hells yes." I slid my palm against hers, fingers interlacing. Heat racing over my skin, chasing away even the memory of that last billow of damp breeze. "Never been readier for one in my whole fucking life."

14

That Hot, Right Honey

In MY BEDROOM, we undressed each other slowly and deliberately, though the clothes got tossed to the floor in a haphazard fashion that was very unlike Ivy. She'd somehow retained enough presence of mind to cast a one-way sound-dampening glamour on the locked door, so when we sank into my queen bed, the wood-paneled room felt like a forest haven. A private little bower in which we could hear the crashing of the storm against the windows, but no one would hear us. No matter how loud we got.

"Hey," she said, as we lay on our sides facing each other, nose to nose. Her near-black eyes glittered in the gloom, like the light from some far-flung galaxy that had managed to make its way to me against all odds.

"Hey yourself." I leaned forward for a grazing nuzzle, the plush silk of her lips barely brushing against mine. "Fuck, you smell so good."

"So do you," she whispered, running a palm over the back of my head, brushing my hair away to follow the long line of my neck, the curve of my shoulder, my arm where it lay tucked against my side. Everywhere she touched, she laced with a warm, syrupy swirl of Thorn magic. Heat rushed up to meet her touch, as though my blood wanted to surge toward and meld with those little spurts of magic.

"Unfair advantage," I murmured throatily, running my fingers down her throat before I dipped lower to cup the full swell of her breast, roll the soft weight in my hand. "Not like I can reciprocate."

She chuckled against me, leaning in to nip at my lower lip. Under all that sweetness, Ivy could be a ruthless tease, and much more dominant than you'd expect.

"You never used to mind before, Star," she said. "Still a hard no on you returning the favor, though. I don't ever want to know what ectoplasm feels like against skin."

"No problem," I assured her, rolling her nipple between my fingertips until her eyelashes fluttered, a low, breathless moan slipping past her lips. "I have other ways."

With a gentle push, I rolled her onto her back, straddling her hips in one smooth motion. Then I bent to cup her face and kiss her in slow, shallow grazes, my hair sliding down to veil us—until she reached around to give my ass the kind of firm squeeze that meant "stop screwing around."

"So it's like that," I said against her mouth, swallowing a laugh. "Such a *rush* we're in."

"You know damn well it's like that," she replied, giving me a swift, deliberate smack that stung just enough to make me catch my breath. "So kiss me like you fucking mean it, and finish what we started last night."

I didn't need to be told twice.

We'd kindled this fire the night before, but there had been a desperate edge to it then, Ivy's determination not to let me slip away from her and back to the other side. Now, this, was just her and me. Intent on each other until everything beyond us melted away—as though reality had always been merely an illusion, the two of us nestled at its core like seeds. The only real thing, embedded in the dream that was the world beyond.

I kissed her slow and deep, my thumb against her chin to keep her mouth open wide under mine, sliding my tongue against hers in long, searing sweeps. I could feel her hips writhing beneath me like waves, lifting and lowering me with their force. I ground back against her just as hard, setting a driving rhythm that was still only a promise for what was to come.

Once she was panting against me, sinking her teeth sharp into my lower lip and moaning into my mouth, I slid farther down, licking a long line down the column of her arched throat, nestling my face into the sensitive crook of her neck. I lingered there, sucking and biting at her, her hands buried in my hair.

"Fuck," she exhaled on a shuddering breath. "Fuck, I missed you so much, I missed *this* so much."

"Me, too, sweetness," I whispered back, my insides quaking with how much I meant it, how terribly I'd longed for exactly this so many nights. "You know how bad I've always wanted you. And I'm so glad you're back."

I flipped my hair over my head and let it trail across her skin, a long, silken caress that followed the line of sucking kisses I pressed into her chest and belly. I might not have had warm magic to send spiraling into her skin, but she'd always loved the caress of my hair spilling all over her. Then I propped myself up on my forearms, pressing her breasts together so I could suck both of her nipples into my mouth at once, drawing them through my teeth. Mother and Crone, Ivy had always had the most unearthly perfect pair of tits. Teardrop shaped and slung low and lush, at least three cup sizes bigger than mine.

She let out a high, helpless yelp, tipping back her head and grinding it against my pillows. "More, more," she hissed through her teeth. "Don't you stop."

Shifting to one side, I slid a palm down the softness of her belly, letting my fingers slip between her legs. She was so wet already, so slick and heated, that the demanding throb between my own thighs tightened into a hollow ache. I parted her with a finger, trailing slow, firm circles around her taut clit, then skimming lightly over it, the way I knew she liked when she was this sensitive. If I kept going, flicking my tongue against her nipples and working at her like this, she'd come for me not once but sometimes two or even three times. Just the thought of it sent a ferocious, pulsing thrum through my middle, a seismic tremor of desire.

"*Fuck*," she moaned, flinging up an arm to grab a handful of pillow. "Fuck you're so good at that, I can't . . . I . . ."

"Keep going?" I asked her, lifting my head even as my fingers kept up that circling, skimming rhythm. I'd never seen my own face when I was like this, wanting Ivy with every fiber of my being. But she'd once told me I looked like something semi-feral, a wolf or a succubus or whatever other creature might want to eat all of her at once. "I can, if you want. Whatever you want. But if you let me taste you—"

Before I could finish, she slid both hands down to grab me by the waist, gripping me hard enough to make me gasp before flipping us over, landing me effortlessly on my back. We were nearly the same height, but Ivy had always been much stronger, all that hard yoga muscle beneath voluptuous curves and satin skin.

"Oh, I'm definitely gonna let you," she said, her lips curving with wicked promise, that clover-honey voice raw with desire. She traced my profile, running her fingers from my forehead down the curve of my nose and over my lips. Letting them linger until I sucked at her fingertips. "But right now, I want it like this."

Two scoots forward brought her just above my face, soft thighs pressing tight against my cheeks. The sudden scent of her was overwhelming, perfumed skin mingling with the salty musk of her desire, so enticingly close to my mouth I could barely stand it. I slid one arm under and around her thigh, pinning her in place for when she inevitably started squirming. My other hand, I let wander down my stomach to the cleft between my own legs, fingers skimming over my own heat.

Arching my neck, I started lapping at her the way she'd always liked to start, in slow, tantalizing ice-cream licks. She tasted just like I remembered, sweetness and salt tinged with the faintest hint of bitter, like salted caramel and aniseed. Complex as wine, so intoxicating I could feel myself go dizzy at both the taste and the sound of her full-throated groans.

She bore down on me, head thrown back in abandon, grinding against my open mouth. I moved into deliberate, swirling figure eights, tracing the silken contours of her, feeling that wet heat slickening my cheeks. I moved my other hand in a slower rhythm, much slower than the frantic beating of my heart against my ribs. But I could still feel the relentless pressure building inside me, like water surging against an increasingly porous dam, trickles of pleasure already seeping in.

"Ah, damn," Ivy was moaning, rocking back and forth, clinging to my headboard with both hands. "I'm so close . . ."

I took that as my cue to latch on hard, sucking the hard nub of her into my mouth, my own fingers dipping in and out of me, speeding up to match her pace. Then I unwound my other arm from around her thigh, gently sliding a curved finger inside her, the searing heat of her clamping down around me like a fist. Ivy could be sensitive to too much penetration too soon, but when she was this close, already hovering on the precipice, sometimes that careful pressure was enough to tip her right over the edge.

"Oh, god," she groaned above me, ratcheting up into little half shrieks. "Fuck, Star, fuck, I'm going to come . . ."

I could feel the clench of those powerful muscles around my finger even as her legs trembled with the force of her climax, and I instantly couldn't rein myself in a second longer. I kept licking and stroking against the rising tide of my own pleasure, until that sweet explosion rocked me like a tiny supernova, a flush of heat surging up my belly and down my own shaking legs.

"Again," Ivy demanded breathlessly before I'd even spiraled all the way back down, hips still bucking. "Please, *again*."

With a little growl, I powered through that liquid spill of pleasure and kept at it; the same insistent sucking and pressure, fierce enough to make my jaw ache, my wrist burn. But it was worth it to feel Ivy unravel above me again and again, dragging me along with her each time. Across peaks and valleys like some ecstatic mountain range we'd never finish summitting together.

I didn't stop until Ivy pitched forward against the headboard, her entire body quivering.

"Okay," she whispered, through a low, semi-astonished chuckle I could feel vibrate against my face. "Oooh, damn, alright. I think maybe that was enough. For now."

"WHAT DO YOU think it is about storms," Ivy asked, "that always makes you so horny?" I lay flopped on my stomach with an arm flung over her, while she'd curled up on her side with her knees tucked up against me.

"Um," I said, voice muffled by the pillow. "I believe it was *you* who instigated."

"I was just catching your vibe." She trailed a warm fingertip down my spine until I arched into her touch like a cat, mock purring until she giggled. "You were wanting to jump me before we even went out on that porch, don't even lie."

"True. And I'm not sure about why storms," I said, turning my head to face her. "Maybe because they're so dramatic. Turbulent, decadent. Kind of like the way I feel on the other side, but good. Normal. Right."

"Yeah, I'll buy that," she said, nodding slowly, that limpid gaze shifting between my eyes. "You were pretty phenomenal, you know that? Blew my mind very thoroughly."

"What can I say? Maybe I learned it from *The Brash and Brazen Wanton's Guide.* Or maybe I'm in my hedonistic mind-blow era." I leaned in for a kiss, both of us heedless of the fact that I was still sticky with her, having given my face only a cursory swipe with the sheets before we both collapsed. "Which, now that I think about it, is maybe the only era I've ever been in. And likewise, damn. A bitch can *ride*."

"Come on, now. Saying it like you didn't already know what's up." A corner of her mouth quirked in that cocky grin I'd always loved so much. Ivy was normally so mellow, so dedicated to catering to other people and putting herself second, that it felt like the most delicious kind of secret to see this other side of her. "But yeah, you certainly haven't lost your touch. Or that very talented tongue."

"Keep talking like that, and we're going to have to find out if another round might actually kill us," I threatened, stroking the curve of her ass before giving it a grab-and-jiggle to make her laugh. "And my guest might start to wonder where we are. I don't know about you, but I'm going to need a very hot and soapy shower before we venture back out into the world to go oversee our respective spectacles."

"I bet she's still asleep. Something as heavy-duty as that spell-work in her mind would hit anyone like a ton of bricks. But, you're right." She sat up, began winding sheets around her. "We should probably get our shit together."

"Ivy . . ." I reached for her and gently drew her back down, trepidation scorching up my throat, burning away the playfulness. "Today. Us. What does this mean? You don't have to answer right now, if you don't want to. I just . . . I'd like to have an idea? So I know what I'm allowed to feel."

Her face softened, warming with empathy at whatever she felt emanating from me. Thorns weren't quite was attuned to others as they were to each other, but their psychic antennae were certainly sensitive enough to pick up on partners' and lovers' emotions.

If that was what we were, again.

"I'm not really sure yet, Dash," she said softly, stroking her knuckles over my cheek. "And you know what, that's okay. But for starters, I'm really glad it happened. Not just the sex, but everything else—everything you told me. And I do think it could mean something good. For both of us."

15

Matters of Life and Extremely Grisly Death

MY SUMMONS TO The Bitters arrived immediately after the Avramov spectacle—which, while featuring no invading hell kings, had been considerably less spectacular without Adriana's necromantic shadowplay.

Now, I found myself in The Bitters' imposing library, sitting across from Elena on one of the stiff pieces of baroque furniture that managed to make you feel unworthy while also looking like it had seen much better days. A mangy but still plenty menacing wolf's head with one missing eye hung above the heavy doors, mid-snarl. A variety of other taxidermied beasties, skeletons, and murky preserved specimens leered from the curio cabinets scattered among the weathered bookshelves. One wall was hung with oppressively framed portraits of previous Avramov elders, all billowing hair, jaws like blades, and icy, portentous glares. The air was so thick with swirling dust it felt almost deliberate, meant to underline the spookiness of the ambience. Even the moonlight that managed to filter through the single leaded window looked watery and weak, as if it were expending unusual effort to penetrate The Bitters' perpetual gloom.

"Thank you for coming on such short notice, Daria," Elena said, recrossing her legs. Her feet were bare, I noticed, the writhing tangle in my stomach easing just the slightest bit. Maybe this encounter wasn't going to include the reaming out I'd been expecting if she'd gone this casual. "And you're looking well today, considering your ordeal last night."

I heaved a quiet sigh. It could certainly be worse, I told myself; she could have called me up in front of the entire Thistle Grove quorum to give testimony on what had happened on the other side. But she'd chosen to keep it in the family for the time being, likely to spare me the pressure of all that scrutiny. Embarrassing as it was to be the recipient of such an uncharacteristic gentleness from her, it was also something to be grateful for, to add to the already too-long list of kindnesses for which I owed the Avramov matriarch.

The idea of that much gratitude made my skin feel itchy.

"Thank you," I said, clearing my throat, "Elena, I . . . I wanted to apologize for what happened last night. That was reprehensible behavior on my part. I shouldn't have—"

She cut me off with a brisk wave of a crimson-tipped hand. "Oh, not at all. Think nothing of it. If an apology is called for, it should be me delivering it. I don't regret having put you in such a vulnerable position—it was an unfortunate necessity. But I do regret having caused you additional pain, after everything you've been through."

I nodded unsteadily, pressing my lips together lest I do something truly unforgivable, like going dewy-eyed in front of the mordant elder. This unexpected softness nearly made me want to confide in her about my amnesiac houseguest—but as soon as the thought surfaced, that ferocious protective instinct reared up again. The unwillingness to expose her to anyone who might insist she be taken anywhere she didn't want to go. Elena's priorities were clear. When necessary, she'd use whatever tools she had at her disposal, including the human ones—and it was almost a guarantee that she'd be more ruthless than me in determining what was wrong with the stranger's memory. Especially if it did have something to do with Avramov magic.

"That's why I lifted the bind on your garnet," Elena continued. "I'd seen enough to trust you with your unique talents again." Her lips quirked. "So if I have to tolerate a slap or two for all the hard-won progress you've made, and for what you did for all of us in helping banish that . . . entity, then it's a small price to pay."

I cocked my head. "Why the pause?"

She mimicked my movement, the softest brush of mockery. "Pardon?"

"You took a beat, before you said 'entity.' As if you were going to call him something else. Were you?"

"Observant girl." She took a sip of amber liquid from her cut-glass tumbler, which made me wish someone had offered me my own stiff drink. "No less than expected, from the daughter of Jacqueline Harlow and our brilliant Lev, may he rest undisturbed in the nether realms. Yes, I *was* going to say something else, but I won't tell you what just yet. First, I'd like to hear it in your words.

What you saw on the other side when you encountered him, if any conversation passed between you. Whatever you remember will be invaluable."

Her face grew somber as she set the glass back down on her side table with a rattle of ice.

"And please, hold nothing back. What happened at our spectacle . . . I'm not exaggerating when I say that this might be the gravest moment Thistle Grove has ever witnessed. The direst threat yet to our town. Anything you know about him, we *all* need to know."

I nodded soberly, my throat tightening. "I understand. I'll do my best."

I walked her through everything as meticulously as I could, leaving no detail out. What he'd looked like on the other side of the veil, what he'd said to me, how it had felt when he touched me. The intoxicating vastness of that cold and empty power emanating from him, the way it had heightened my experience of the other side to an almost unbearably delicious degree. Her eyes narrowed in the telling, and every once in a while she'd give a tiny nod, more to herself than me, as if my account was confirming her suspicions.

"I see," she said once I'd wrapped up, my heart pounding just from reliving the memory. It scared me that I still found the idea of him so compelling, when I should have been only terrified of him. "Not, alas, what I'd been hoping to hear. Though one rarely does, in situations like this."

"Situations like what?" I asked, with rising alarm. "Elena, what is he? An elder demon? A dark angel, if that's a thing?"

"They are indeed a thing," she said, pulling a disgruntled

face—as if maybe she'd had an encounter with one herself, and it had gone annoyingly. "And one of the fallen would be far preferable to what we're dealing with here—which, I'm afraid, is a trespassing deity. Worse yet, one of the dark gods. Harbingers of death, destruction, potential apocalypse. Et cetera."

I struggled to clear my throat, which had turned to sand. A dark god, for fuck's sake. A harbinger of death, in Thistle Grove. "So which one is he?"

"I don't know yet. But I'm hoping that with your help, and Talia's, we may be able to find out."

As Elena led me to Talia's room, I was still wrestling with the notion that the doomsday angel I'd been cheek-to-cheek with had been no less than an actual fucking god.

It wasn't that the concept of deities was all that alien to me; Avramovs generally believed in the Slavic pantheon of pagan gods, and many more besides. And shit, we had a slice of a goddess encased in stone at the bottom of our lake, throwing tantrums with the weather and spilling her divine magic across the town.

But the idea that I had interacted not with a demon or a paranormal creature, but a literal *god*, in whatever passed for their flesh and blood? No wonder he'd felt like a living void, albeit a weirdly sexy one. As I understood it, deities were a constellation of energies in animate form, sentient manifestations of forces far beyond mortal grasp. Beings so many orders of magnitude higher than us that we couldn't even fathom the fullness of their reality— which was why they only appeared to us in one of their many aspects. And this one had not only barged into Thistle Grove, but also nuzzled my cheek, crushed me hard against that obscenely ripped chest, called me a child of dark. Maybe even considered kissing me.

Even for this town, it was enough to blow your mind a little.

After winding through The Bitters' meandering corridors, the dark wallpaper hung with cockeyed, mismatched mirrors that reflected flashes of shades you could only catch from the corner of your eye, Elena left me in front of Talia's open door.

"My scion will take it from here," she said, gesturing toward the doorway. "The Dread Lady doesn't appreciate a larger audience."

"The Dread Lady?" I squeaked, my voice reaching a mortifyingly high register. I normally considered myself a pretty sturdy little bastion of fortitude when it came to the supernatural, but today was really taking a turn. "Wait, are you saying Talia is going to summon *Margarita Avramov*? The centuries-dead founder of our house, herself?"

"That would be correct!" Talia broke in, having appeared to lean against the doorway with her usual insouciance, a black dolman top sliding off one sleek shoulder. "Or rather, *we* are going to summon her. I will say, our dear departed great-great-great-great-grandmama does not take kindly to being bothered these days. But needs must, right?"

"Right," I said faintly, following Talia into the bedroom with a final, desperate look flung at Elena over my shoulder. She mouthed "good luck" and turned away, headed back to her dust-choked enclave.

Inside, Talia's massive suite was a marked departure from The Bitters' shab-glam aesthetic. Her bed was roughly six times the size of mine, with a teal button-tufted headboard and a heaping of

snowy pillows and comforters, a colorful quilt draped over one corner. The gray walls were hung with celestial artwork, bespelled to
make the violet and sapphire nebulae swirl and stars revolve in
mesmerizing circles. A contemporary-looking wrought iron light
fixture like a decorative cage glowed above her bed, set on low.

"I'm assuming your room isn't part of the haunted mansion
tour," I commented wryly. "This all looks, dare I say, alarmingly
pleasant."

"I prefer my space this way," she confirmed with a blithe shrug.
"More order and color in here than our resident shades are comfortable with. Saves me from waking up to one of the more obnoxious Bitters denizens dangling above my face. Trust me, that'll
fuck your REM sleep right up."

"I'm sure." I glanced over to the wall opposite her bed, where
a huge, antique mirror hung on the wall, at clear odds with the
rest of the décor. The gold frame peaked in two delicate spires,
the rest of it an intricate profusion of leaves and lilies, between
which ornately rendered snakes and wolves stalked each other.
The glass itself was so heavily foxed it looked like silvery mist
made solid. "Is that a scrying mirror?"

"It is. Ancient Avramov heirloom, passed down from matriarch
to scion."

With a tilt of her head, she led me over to kneel in front of it.
An altar had already been set with ritual items, so that its reflection took up the bottom of the mirror—a bowl of hellebore heads,
an antique tea set, and a lush slice of what looked like Black Forest
chocolate cake, the cherries on top glistening where they nestled
between curls of chocolate shavings. Seven candles circled the arrangement, along with a scattering of crystals and semiprecious
stones.

LANA HARPER

"Are you familiar with summoning spells?" Talia asked, shifting to sit cross-legged behind the altar, me beside her.

"In the academic sense, yes. My father wouldn't have let me get away with not learning them. But I'm more on the exorcising end of things, given my skill set. And even if that weren't the case, I've never seen the point. Why summon entities that have no business being here, that you're just going to have to banish later?"

Talia chuckled at that. Her raven hair gleamed blue-black in the room's low light, so dark it seemed impossible that we might share common genetics. But then again, her eyes were magnetic, glacier pale, even more uncanny than my own softer gray.

"I should have you talk to Issa about that," she said, rolling her eyes. "When it comes to summonings, she has . . . some ongoing trouble grasping that kind of reasonable perspective."

Before I could ask her to elaborate, she conjured a flame above one of her fingers, a sharp sting of sulfur singeing the air. Once the candles were lit, she huffed the incendiary spell out and trailed her fingertips over the assortment of crystals and stones, her eyes growing distant with concentration.

"White quartz, blue lace agate, and amethyst," she murmured, for my benefit. "To enhance the summons and cast it wide across the veil. I threw in some wulfenite and red beryl this time, just to butter her up. According to the books about her, she often worked with those. Plus they're beautiful, which never hurts."

"Right." I knew this part. "And the flowers and cake are . . . also offerings?"

"You got it. The medovukha, too," she said, jerking her chin toward the tarnished silver samovar. It tracked that this spell wouldn't call for something so gentle as tea. "The tea set was hers, too. A few of the Dread Lady's favorite things."

I brightened at the idea of medovukha, a Slavic honey-based liquor a bit like mead, somewhere between wine and beer. It wasn't for everyone, but I'd always liked the delicate flavor, followed by the potently sour aftertaste. My great-aunt Akilina had distilled her own, for both fun and rituals; there was a good chance this was tapped from one of her premium casks.

"It's still pretty early," Talia remarked, nudging the bowl of hellebores closer to the plate of cake. "Usually it's best to cast this summoning just after midnight. She's not going to be happy about the deviation, but we do need her insight ASAP, and she's likely to be sour about it either way. So why wait."

I made a noncommittal sound, uneasy at the idea of conjuring up the Dread Lady's irate spirit at the wrong time, on top of everything else. But I wasn't in charge here, and I certainly wasn't about to argue with the Avramov scion when it came to a summoning.

"Any advice before we start?" I asked her. "Since I've never done this before?"

"Just relax and follow my lead," Talia said. "And, uh, try not to freak out too much once she manifests. I know she can be tough to look at, but overt displays of fear are like blood in the water for her. So just . . . do your best to keep your shit together. Cool?"

With that casually delivered warning, the chandelier's light dimmed before going out altogether, plunging the room into sudden darkness broken only by the dance of candle flames. Then Talia brought her hands up in front of her chest, positioning her fingers in the complex arrangement I recognized from Grimoire diagrams as the starting point of a spirit summoning. I stayed quiet, goose bumps stippling my spine as I watched Talia work, admiring the precise dexterity of each fluttering movement, her low incantation intoned at a register that hummed with sepulchral resonance. Though this wasn't my area, I could recognize both the innate talent and expertise this spell demanded, the total focus and amount of sheer will she was funneling into it.

Taking a pause, Talia poured us each a splash of medovukha and sliced off two bites of the cake with a fork. I took a sweet, burning sip from my teacup, then let her feed me a mouthful of cake, dense and indulgent, the cherries bursting tart against the dark chocolate and frothy whipped cream. Dread and austere though she might have been, our ancestress had clearly also had a taste for decadence. It made me feel the tiniest bit more comfortable with the idea of her.

Setting down the cup and fork, Talia resumed the chant. The crystals began to glimmer one by one, as if lit from within, the candle flames flickering as if caught in an invisible wind. I could feel the room's atmosphere yaw sharply toward the other side of the veil, that familiar, beckoning chill curling against my skin. The mirror's murky glass roiled with what looked like ropes of gray smoke, twisting and coiling into hypnotic wreaths.

Then the glass cleared, to reveal the spirit of founder Margarita Avramov, her black hair coursing around her head like a dark aurora, incandescent fury blazing over the bold, lovely lines of her face.

"Greetings, Dread Lady," Talia began, inclining her head. "I call upon y—"

The Dread Lady lunged forward like a rabid dog, snapping at the glass, revealing bright teeth with pointed canines. One palm splayed out in front of her, as if she were actually trapped within the mirror, her hand pressing flat against her side of the glass.

I jerked so hard I nearly knocked the altar over with my knee, but Talia simply waited out the rage. Her finely drawn profile shone serenely in the candlelight, while my heart tripped over itself in my chest, nails biting into my palms.

"My apologies for the intrusion," she said, once Margarita had subsided into a low, menacing grumble of a growl, her teeth still bared. The founder's eyes were mesmerizing, morphing from black to cobalt to a brilliant green, then an amber yellow I'd only ever seen in cats. Her face seemed to strobe between two states, beautiful and monstrous, flickering with black filaments that flashed across that porcelain skin like cadaverous veins before melting away. "We did not wish to disturb your repose. But we—"

Margarita threw back her head and issued an ululating banshee scream so shrill and penetrating I could actually feel it rattle my ribs like castanets. It was so hugely loud its acoustics seemed to fill and then overwhelm the entire space, bouncing off the walls and plugging up my ears. This time even Talia jumped, and I barely managed to suppress a terrified yelp.

"Is it *supposed* to be like this?" I muttered to her under my breath as the Dread Lady continued to shriek. "Because, not for nothing, I am extremely close to pissing myself. And I don't want to fuck up your pretty rug."

"Pottery Barn, thanks. And yeah, she's a little . . . extra spicy tonight," Talia conceded, gritting her teeth against the onslaught— though I could see from the twitching of her lips that she was, shockingly, also struggling not to laugh. "But she's never exactly a crowd pleaser. Part and parcel of being dead and bitchy for centuries, I'd guess."

When the scream finally abated, what felt like hours later, the Dread Lady subsided into a sullen silence, her fearsome gaze shifting between us. I could actually *feel* it when she looked at me, an oppressive menace that loomed over me like an anvil suspended on a very thin string above my head. Not for the first time, I thanked my lucky stars I hadn't been born a main line Avramov. Even for someone who'd seen the kind of shit I dealt with on the daily, this was beyond the pale.

"Spit it out then, you beastly child," the spirit hissed, her features tightening with impatience. "What is it that you want of me *yet again* that is worth interfering with my already tempestuous rest? It had best be a matter of life and extremely grisly death, or there will be consequences for your presumption this time, my kin or no."

"It does concern potentially grisly death, yes," Talia said, still in that composed tone, as if she were perfectly comfortable with managing an unhinged spirit of tremendous power. Maybe she was; it was entirely possible she'd had years of practice. "I would never have dared trouble you otherwise. Something has trespassed on our town—and worse, disrupted the Cavalcade. Something unexpected and malign, that one of our blood has knowledge of. We think it may be one of the dark gods, but we require your sage counsel to discern which one."

The spirit settled down a little, mollified by the flattery, even as her lush black eyebrows drew together in a fierce scowl. "One of the dark gods, on our doorstep," she muttered to herself, tapping a talon-like black nail to her square chin. "Disturbing the sanctity of the Cavalcade. That cannot be allowed to stand."

"No, it cannot," Talia agreed, and for an instant she sounded so much like her great-grandmother many times removed that I quaked at that echoed similarity. "Will you deign to assist us in our time of strife?"

"I will, given the exigent circumstances," the Dread Lady said, those mercurial eyes flicking back to me. "You. Daria. You have seen this interloper? Communed with it?"

"Yes," I replied, as stoically as I could, trying to contain the tremble in my tone. How the fuck did she even know my name? "I'm a devil eater, and the banishing spell we used against him flung me over to the other side of the veil. We . . . interacted."

"Oh, a devil eater!" she exclaimed, a startlingly delighted smile breaking over her face, as if she hadn't been raging at us only moments before. She pressed against her side of the mirror to peer more closely at me, as if it were a window. "What an intriguing notion. The last eater of our line preceded me by centuries—I had not thought to ever meet one. An unexpected pleasure. Tell me, do you find the taste to your liking? I have always wondered what such a power might be like. A talent so literally visceral."

"I don't like the taste all that much," I admitted, holding her eyes with tremendous effort even as my skin crawled at her scrutiny. "Although it feels like something inside me does. And of course, I do it anyway. Whenever it must be done."

"As is your duty," she said approvingly, with a satisfied little nod. "Very well, then. Let us have a gander inside your mind. If you agree, of course. Even I may not read you without consent."

"I'm sorry, what?" I said, squirming with panic. "You want to look inside—inside my *mind*?"

"It's alright," Talia assured me, squeezing my thigh. "It'll only take a second. She's a psychic scryer, and an even stronger one in spirit form than she was alive. It'll be faster and much more accurate than you telling her what you saw."

I chewed on my lip, debating whether it was too late to decide that my desire to keep my mind to myself outweighed my responsibilities to town and family. But like I'd told Ivy, I was done being selfish. If helping meant allowing this horrifying apparition to rifle through my brain, then so be it.

"I consent," I said, trying to dredge up a morsel of conviction. "Go ahead. Please."

Margarita spread her long-fingered, talon-tipped hands, closing her eyes. I did the same, just in case the reflexive connection might help.

Then a thousand ice picks jammed themselves into my brain.

My entire body went rigid, the darkness behind my eyelids turning scarlet with pain. It felt like being raked with frozen claws; long needles speared through my temples, as if my brain had been skewered inside my skull, splayed open like a dissected frog. I could *feel* Margarita's psychic presence inside me, her detached regard like something sharp and alien implanted in my head. I wanted to scream, to thrash, to sever the conduit between us, but I couldn't so much as twitch a finger, every muscle locked in place. She'd immobilized me like a patient under anesthesia, the kind that did nothing to alleviate pain.

Just as I thought I might black out from the intrusive agony of it, the invasion abruptly withdrew. Vanishing as if it had never been, leaving not even a residual headache behind.

"What the fuck?" I demanded through clenched teeth, still bent over double, lifting my head just enough to glare at Talia. "Why didn't you *fucking warn me* it was going to hurt like that?"

"And freak you out preemptively?" Talia retorted, sublimely unbothered, giving me a perfunctory pat on the back. "Would've still felt like corpse fingernails digging in your brain. There's no prepping for that experience. At least this way, you went in relaxed."

"Oh, thanks so very much," I retorted, massaging my temples. "Super thoughtful of you. Highly nurturing."

"They do say I'm a natural caretaker." She bumped my shoulder with hers, tipping her chin toward the mirror. "Look, she's thinking. Maybe she has something for us."

I glanced back up at the mirror, where Margarita did seem to be lost in thought, crystallized into a pensive pose. Only her hair still moved, swirling around her head like an inky cloud. Then her image abruptly thawed back into motion, and she focused on us again.

"I'm afraid you were correct, Natalia," she said grimly, her face darkening like thunderheads. "You are indeed dealing with a penumbral god—one of the masters of chaos and the void. Though which it might be is difficult to say. Many of the penumbral take on a similar aspect to what Daria beheld when they're communing with a mortal they find pleasing in some way."

Nausea rolled through me, mortification at the idea that Margarita had seen us entwined around each other, maybe even felt the way I'd wanted him.

"Thank you, Dread Lady," Talia said, bowing her head. "Is there anything more you might tell us? Names, possibilities. Whatever would help us protect Thistle Grove, should he trespass against us again."

Margarita tipped her head to the side. "As I said, I cannot be certain. But I would imagine that Erebos, Angra Mainyu, and Chernobog might all be contenders. In a sense, they are all one and the same; but in another, they are entirely separate from each other. I'm afraid the sorting out will fall to you."

For a moment, she seemed to lose sight of us completely, her focus turning inward. "We did know it was a risk," she muttered to herself, clicking those talons against the glass. "Elias, especially. Perhaps even an inevitability. Though how could we have been sure, or known when?"

Talia and I exchanged perplexed looks. "Is there anything else we should know?" Talia asked warily. "Something that might help us muster our defenses?"

The apparition's eyes slid back to us, and she gave a weary shake of her head.

"Nothing that I am permitted to disclose," she said, with a touch of something like genuine remorse. "This problem is for you to solve—all you living children of Thistle Grove. But I will say this. When the time comes and the master of chaos and void returns, gather yourselves around this one. Your devil eater. You will need to stand united . . . and you will need her strength."

16

Just Like Rainbow Ruby

BEFORE I LEFT The Bitters, still off-kilter from the harrow-ing encounter with the Dread Lady, Elena had forbidden me from doing any investigating on my own. Moving forward, she'd said, this was a matter for the quorum to pursue. I was also strictly prohibited from traversing the veil until we got to the bottom of the trespass, in case the dark god was still lurking on the other side. Should they need me, I'd be notified, but I wasn't—in Elena's words—to take it upon myself to add "Daria Avramov, Devil-Eating Detective" to my résumé.

In the meantime, my houseguest was still spending most of her time napping, waking only to eat ravenously and sit out on the porch with me for some fresh air before the drowsiness overcame her again. I'd have worried more about the excessive sleep and hunger, but she seemed perfectly lucid and healthy while awake—consistent with Ivy's theory that the spell itself was sapping her of strength, using her own energy to maintain itself. Whenever I left the cottage for work at the Emporium, I reminded her how crucial it was to never leave without me, emphasizing the dangers of venturing into the Witch Woods alone (though I gave it more of a "sinister prowlers and teenage daredevils" slant). She remained adamant that she didn't want to be taken to a hospital or police station under any circumstances, and though I checked the Thistle Grove PD website and searched NamUS.gov each day in case a missing person report popped up, there was never anything new, no one matching her description.

Eventually, I'd have to press the issue. But the truth was, I liked having her there. Even when she was sleeping, it was if I could feel her, her mere presence in the cottage like the serenity hovering in the eye of the storm. As far as I was concerned, she could stay as long as she wanted, or at least until we got to the bottom of whatever was afflicting her.

After work that Wednesday, Ivy had come over for drinks and a tête-à-tête about how to best handle things with her. We'd agreed that it was both unfair and unkind to keep the existence of magic from our stranger; she had a right to know what might have stolen her memory, Ivy argued. Once it returned, we'd always be able to glamour her into forgetting what we'd told her, though the idea already sat poorly with both of us.

When Ivy grew a tiny primrose for her between cupped hands, and I conjured a billow of ectoplasm that swirled like an icy charcoal mist around the three of us, she hadn't balked even for a moment.

"Magic," she'd breathed instead. She gazed down at her own small beringed hands, flipping them over to examine both palms and backs, as if she might discern some proof of the paranormal shimmering under her own skin. "How completely fucking wonderful. I guess I . . . back when I was me, maybe I always figured it *had* to be real, somewhere out there? Because, I don't know. It just doesn't feel like that much of a surprise."

We had also decided that she needed a provisional name, something she felt comfortable using until we rediscovered her real one. So Ivy and I tossed out options, one after another, until we narrowed it down to three contenders: Elise (me), Amanda (Ivy), and Maya (Ivy).

"Maya," she'd decided, with a slow, satisfied nod. "That's the one. I mean, it's not *the* one. But it's close, somehow. Feels good to me."

"So THIS IS Dash's new friend!" Amrita announced as she ushered us in to Saanvi's foyer, where the commingled aromas of Indian and Mexican were already simmering in the air. Since we weren't likely to find any answers to Maya's amnesia in books, I'd decided to pull a few more accomplices into the circle of trust. Once I'd filled my sister in on how I found Maya and what had happened since, she'd immediately offered her expertise in oblivion glamours, along with the obligatory dinner invite. "Maya, right?"

"For now," Maya agreed. "Subject to change. Damn, it smells amazing in here. Thank you for having me. And I have no guest gift for you, I'm sorry. I should have thought to bring something. That Dasha would've had to spring for, ha. *Slightly* defeating the purpose."

"Oh, that's alright. Believe me, we have too much of absolutely everything already."

We shucked our shoes, lining them up under the coatrack before hooking our coats. Something about the way Maya had phrased that last bit niggled at me, but I couldn't pinpoint what it was.

"I have to say, from what Dash has told me, you seem to be taking all this remarkably in stride," my sister remarked. "I'd have expected several more shades of shock and trauma."

"They're probably in there, somewhere," Maya said, straightening up. She was in more of my borrowed clothes, a black V-neck she'd knotted into a crop top so she wasn't swimming in it, over a pair of leggings that were hilariously high-waisted on her. "But I've been too busy either eating or sleeping to really delve into it, you know? Maybe I'll cry some later."

"Fair enough," my sister said equably. "We have a nice weeping couch for that. Mid-century modern, very absorbent upholstery. In the meantime, quick tour before dinner?"

I trailed after them as she led a wonder-struck Maya around a house that, unassuming as it was from the outside, felt like a carnival of antique treasures tucked in every corner. I'd gotten used to it over the years, but Maya's sheer delight at the massive Hermle grandfather clock looming in one corner, with its intricately carved and polished veneer, was contagious. She ran her hands over everything with a child's unabashed enthusiasm, marveling over the clean lines of the walnut Shaker dining table, the carvings of the three storybook bears on the rocking chair in the living room. At some point, Kira slipped loose of Saanvi, who was still in the kitchen, and slunk around our feet like a kitten, pointing out her favorites to a rapt Maya—the cabinet of Lalique crystal figurines and blown-glass flowers, an authentic Ming dynasty vase that I still had no idea how my father had procured. A mirror

of unknown provenance with a frame of lily pads and lotuses surrounding green-tinted glass that made it look like a pond set into
the wall.

"This is incredible," Maya kept saying, smiling so wide her
little face could barely contain it. "Like a wonderland of precious
things. How did your parents afford all this?"

"My mother is a ruthless negotiator," Amrita informed her.
"And it was my parents' favorite thing to do together, for years."

As they moved ahead of us, toward the dining room, Kira
tugged hard on my hand. I dropped into a squat in front of her,
tucking a gossamer strand of hair behind her ear as she gazed at
me with her mother's dark eyes, heavily lashed pools of black in
her sweet face.

"Auntie, your friend," she whispered, biting her lip. "She's really shiny."

"What do you mean, lovey?" I asked, glancing up at Maya's
retreating back, the milk glass pendants in the hallway bringing
out the cinnamon and gold in her curls. "Do you mean all her
rings and earrings? She does have a lot of pretty ones. And really
bright hair."

Kira shook her head, making a frustrated little moue. "No,
it's . . ." She fluttered her hands in a broad, enthusiastic circle. "It's
just all over. Like a unicorn, or Rainbow Ruby? Or Butterbean's
Café? Do you know, Auntie Dash? Do you remember the sparkles?"

"Sure I do, cookie," I said hastily, not wanting to get her
worked up right before dinner. Kira wasn't prone to tantrums, but
when one did arrive, it usually hit somewhere on whatever scale
they used to measure monsoons. "Sure! Sparkly just like Rainbow
Ruby, I'll tell her you said that. She'll love it."

Kira relaxed into a pearly milk-toothed smile. "Yeah, she will.

She's *really* nice, Auntie Dash. I want her to read to me after dinner. Not you, okay?"

I studied her for another moment, puzzled and just the tiniest bit miffed. As boundlessly affectionate as she was with her little family, Kira had a decent stranger-danger radar and was standoffish with new people. Becoming enamored with a guest wasn't like her. But Maya did have a quality of grace to her, a lightness of being at striking odds with her circumstances. How did that play into things, I wondered?

By the time we convened in the dining room, Saanvi had finished ferrying out the night's offerings—dal makhani, butter chicken, garlic naan, guacamole, and pico de gallo. At some point, my dad and Saanvi had started these fusion dinners as a gag, but like many of their longer-running jokes, Mexi-Punjabi Thursdays had become a tradition, even funnier for the fact that neither logic nor alliteration was involved. (I'd invited Ivy to come, given how much she'd once loved them, but she'd declined. Whatever was happening between us, she wasn't ready yet to extend it to spending time with my family.)

"Dasha love," Saanvi said, sweeping over to envelop me in a tight hug. She was still in her meticulous workday makeup, but had changed out of her suit into sweatpants and house slippers, the way she always did as soon as she got home. On her, even velour managed to look regal. She smelled like an entire bouquet of cooking spices, along with the light plumeria perfume that always clung to her long hair. "How are you doing, my girl? Amrita filled me in on all of it, but I wanted to hear it from you."

"I'm okay," I assured her, giving her a squeeze. "Really. It was a little touch and go Friday night. But I got through it, with Ivy's help. I can tell you a little more about it over dinner, if you want."

Saanvi pulled back, her liquid gaze shifting between my eyes, appraising. "No," she decided. "Let's all relax instead. The lost girl . . . poor thing, she must be so overwhelmed. Maybe a little bit of normal—or what passes for it with us—would be good for her. As well as you."

"Yeah. I think so, too."

She cupped my face between her hands, brushing the pads of her thumbs over my cheekbones. "And you're sure you won't come back and stay with us a few nights? We have room for her, too, of course. I wouldn't want either of you to be alone."

I nuzzled my cheek into her palm, thinking of all the nights she'd found me on the weeping couch instead of asleep, then taken my head onto her nightgowned lap and stroked my hair while I sobbed myself raw, yearning for the other side, my mother, my father. The terrible abundance of everything I'd lost.

"I'm fine," I murmured. "I promise. If I wasn't, I wouldn't keep it from you again. Okay?"

She hesitated for a moment longer, then gave a stout little nod. "Okay, my girl. But we're here anytime, whenever you need us. Day or night."

"I know," I whispered back, tears igniting in the back of my eyes. "That's exactly why I'll be okay."

I'D HAD MY reservations about how well we'd be able to skirt sensitive topics, given the maelstrom swirling around us, but we somehow managed it. Saanvi, Amrita, and I took turns giving Maya our complicated origin story—"We're like blended family superheroes!" being Amrita's take—everyone dove back in for seconds, and then we listened to the various dramas that had transpired at Saanvi's office, the Emporium, and Kira's daycare. Next to me, Maya grinned unabashedly through it all, her honey-hazel gaze sliding over all of us with an emotion I couldn't pinpoint, an almost proprietary pride—as if, out of all the families who might have found her, she couldn't imagine a better one than ours.

Watching the joy she took in us gave me a rolling, painful pang, a reminder of everything we were missing. How uproarious these dinners had once been, back when my mother and father were here, too.

"I know, Dash," Amrita said, her voice just a little hoarse as she reached beneath the table to squeeze my hand. "I can feel how much they're not here, too."

At some point, talking about the daycare bully got Kira so riled up that little plumes of ectoplasm emanated from the crown of her head, like some vengeful goddess's crown. Maya watched her in awestruck wonder, her lips parted, rapt. "A baby witch!" she whispered to me, laughter in her voice. "Does that ever happen in her *daycare*?"

I chuckled, shrugging. "Happens to all of us when we're little. Mini manifestations. And she goes to our witches-only daycare, for obvious reasons."

A back rub from her mother quickly soothed Kira; it usually only took physical contact with an adult witch to wind down the kind of minor, emotionally driven spells children manifested by accident. After an ice-cream dessert, the three of us cleared the table, companionably rinsing the dishes and stacking them in the dishwasher while Saanvi whisked a very reluctant Kira off for a bath.

"So, would you mind me taking a look?" Amrita asked Maya, once we'd settled in the living room with wine. "I know Ivy already examined you. But as Dasha probably told you, we—the Thistle Grove witch families—have different talents. Oblivion glamours, the kind of spell that might have messed with your mind, are one of ours. And I happen to be quite proficient at them."

"*Show-off,*" I sneezed into my elbow.

"What? It's just true."

"I don't mind at all," Maya offered. And she did look comfortable, sitting cross-legged on one side of the weeping couch, which clearly wasn't going to get put to its intended use tonight. "What do you want me to do?"

"You're good where you are. I'll just need your hands."

Amrita scooted forward a little closer, wrapping Maya's proffered hands in hers. Curled up in my armchair, I waited with bated breath as my sister closed her eyes, took the long, centering breaths we all used to ground ourselves before casting. I could see the moment her face stilled with concentration as she began searching Maya for any lingering trace of oblivion. I'd have tried this myself, but I was trash at glamours; something about my own talents countervailed the kind of energy it took to cast or even sense one.

After a moment, Amrita hissed in pain, loud enough to make both me and Maya jump. She yanked herself away and pressed the heels of her hands to her eyes, grinding them hard into her sockets.

"What?" I said, leaping straight up out of my chair. "Amrita, what is it? What did you see?"

My sister lowered her hands and gingerly opened her eyes a tiny slit, giving a few experimental blinks.

"Motherfucking *ow,*" she said, petulantly enough that the frantic knocking of my heart subsided a little. "Yeah, no. Whatever that is, it's not the residue of any kind of glamour. Not one I think we'd ever be able to cast, anyway."

"Why not?" I pressed. "What did it look like?"

"Like light turned solid," she said, only the faint tremble of her lips betraying how shaken she was. "Like staring into the sun. I'm still seeing a superimposed afterimage, as if I'd actually been looking at it with open eyes instead of just sensing for magic."

"What does that mean?" Maya asked shakily, her distraught gaze flitting like a trapped sparrow between the two of us. "There's, what—bricks of *light* in my head?"

"More like a barricade of it," Amrita clarified. "Blinding. No wonder you can't remember who you are. How could you possibly see anything past that?"

"Sparkles," I muttered to myself, just loud enough that both of them turned quizzical looks on me. "Like Rainbow Ruby."

"Pardon?" Amrita said, at almost the same time as Maya said, "I'm sorry, but what the hell?"

"Kira told me she thought Maya was shiny," I replied, brow furrowed, as a cold suspicion began gathering inside me. "Asked me if I could see the sparkles, which obviously I can't. But you've seen them now, sort of. And who do we know who specializes in all things flashy and obnoxious and elemental—whose blood Kira happens to share? Whose bullshit does this seem like to you, Ree?"

"I don't understand," Maya said, fiddling nervously with her rings, her eyes still flickering between us. Through her confusion, Amrita and I met each other's gimlet gazes.

"Blackmoore bullshit," we said in unison, my hands clenching into fists in my lap.

17

The Dark Three

I STAYED UP with Maya until almost midnight after we left Saanvi's. She sat with me on the porch, drinking wine as the chill air curled around us like the forest's ghostly breath, watching the unlikely fireflies that sometimes winked at the very outskirts of the Witch Woods. So out of season I'd often wondered if they were tiny sprites.

"She's so precious," Maya said a little wistfully, swirling the gritty dregs of her wine in the stemless glass. "Your little niece."

"Does she remind you of anyone?" I asked carefully, not wanting to probe too hard. "Someone from home?"

She huffed a rueful laugh, shaking her head. "Nah. Even her being that ridiculously cute didn't jog the memory any. But they're all precious, though . . . even the missing. I can see why you cherish them the way you do."

I jerked my head up at that, trying to pick her tidy features out in the candlelit dark. "The missing? What do you mean? How could you . . . how do you know about them?"

I could just make out the sympathetic curve of her smile, her soft cheek rounding above it. Her ringlets floated as if suspended on the breeze, like glistening tinsel. "I could feel the spaces. The energy around you all, it flows like a current." Her voice sounded vague in a way I hadn't heard before from her; untethered, like poetry. She was shaping the air between her hands in a sinuous gesture, as if she were trying to draw what she'd felt. It made her rings glitter in the dark like tiny stars. "And the way it eddies around some places . . . you can feel the imprint of someone who was once there, someone who mattered very much. Two absent pillars, there yet gone. The water of this world still eddying around them."

"That's my mom and dad you felt," I said unsteadily, swallowing back the hot brine of tears. "And I still don't understand how you could possibly have known about them, when none of us even brought them up."

"I have no idea," she replied after a moment, in her normal voice. "If magic exists, maybe so do other things? Things like that? Maybe I was some kind of psychic before all this. Honestly, Dasha, fuck if I know. It's annoying, though, isn't it? The not knowing anything at all."

"I don't know about annoying," I replied with an unsteady laugh. "I would never call you that, no matter what you do or don't remember. Mystifying, definitely. Very charming, for sure."

"Well, I'll take that all night." A wrinkle of that pert nose, another sweet smile in the dark. "And just know you're not wrong to still miss them as much as you do. If even I can feel them, they must have been so special. Larger than life."

"They were," I agreed quietly, that familiar pressure bearing down on my rib cage. "Both of them. Especially to me."

We both went to bed soon after. It hadn't occurred to me to ask her how she knew I still missed my parents, especially my mother, every day. Maybe she was right; maybe she *had* been a sensitive, some sort of non-witch mortal psychic in her pre-amnesia life. Enough that she could sense the ragged edges of the hole that was still gnawed into my psyche by that double loss, the saw-toothed bite life had taken out of me. It made me desperately curious about who else she might have been before I met her, the family and friends and work she'd left behind.

Why wasn't anyone looking for her? Why couldn't I seem to help her at all?

I was still agonizing over it the following night as I sat with Ivy at Tomes & Omens, in the reading section tucked away at the back of the bookstore. As soon as I'd filled Ivy in on what Amrita had felt inside Maya's mind—the possibility of Blackmoore elemental tampering—we'd decided that we had a lead, but not enough of one to bring an accusation to Elena. (Especially since I hadn't yet seen fit to inform her that Maya even existed.) Because if the Blackmoores *were* involved in whatever had happened to Maya, maybe they'd somehow had a hand in the trespassing god's appearance, too. Given their proximity, it seemed ridiculously unlikely that the two events would be completely unrelated. So if we could just discover what deity we were dealing with, maybe we'd unearth our Blackmoore connection, too.

Besides, as Ivy had pointed out, even if I was technically

forbidden from investigating what was now officially quorum business, I *was* the one the god had linked to—which meant I had a personal stake in this. One that even a house elder didn't have the right to prevent me from pursuing, as an act of my own agency.

"Angra Mainyu, Erebos, and Chernobog," Delilah had muttered to herself after letting us in and flipping the Tomes front door sign to CLOSED. It was late anyway, but on special occasions like the Cavalcade, Tomes often kept unconventional hours like all the other family attractions. "Did the Dread Lady say it definitively? As in, only those three are the ones we ought to be considering? Or more as if she were only providing you with examples of penumbral gods, the general category thereof?"

"I'm not really sure," I admitted, still thrown by the much warmer reception I'd received from Delilah than what I'd expected. Whatever Ivy had told her about us had thawed her considerably; she'd even given me a small smile when letting me in, her raven familiar cawing what sounded like a non-pejorative greeting. "I was busy trying to keep my shit together, to be honest. That is one exceedingly scary bitch, and I say that with the utmost respect. But those were the only three she mentioned by name, yeah."

"The annoying thing is, those three deities are very similar," Delilah muttered, eyes bright with curiosity in the bookstore's gloom. I could hear a chorus of soft rustles around us every now and then, as if the books themselves were roosting against each other like birds tucking their heads beneath their wings for the night. "Deucedly so, as Cat might say. They're chaotic, dark—anthropomorphic manifestations of the void that negates all life and light. What is it about them that you want to know?"

"Anything that might help us identify which we're dealing with," I said. "Specific affinities when it comes to herbs, colors, moon phases. Their energies. For what it's worth this one was, uh. Sexy. So, there's that to consider."

To her credit, she didn't even miss a beat. "They do tend to be like that, weirdly enough. Very unfortunate for whatever mortals fall under their sway. Let me see what I can dig up."

THREE HOURS LATER, Ivy let her head slump onto her crossed arms, releasing a defeated sigh. "I feel like I inhaled three whole dust bunnies," she mumbled into them. "Only to find out Lilah was exactly right."

We'd flipped through enough musty old tomes to leave my eyes feeling gritty, too, yet we'd managed to glean only the sketchiest depictions of each deity, with very little to differentiate between the three. All three were affiliated with black and gray— the traditional night, death, and winter colors. Erebos came from Greco-Roman mythology and was considered a primordial being, one of the first five manifested into existence, and either the off- spring or sibling of Chaos. Dark mists, cold winds, and dead things seemed to be his calling card, whenever he was even em- bodied enough for affinities.

Angra Mainyu was a Zoroastrian concept, and eventually thought to be a sort of king of daevas, or demons, known for bringing winter, sickness, and vice. Remembering that icy thrill of his touch, this resonated with me slightly more. Angra Mainyu's affinities were of questionable scholarly provenance, but it seemed like onyx, condor bones, and mandrake root could be considered for sympathetic magic or summonings—which, as the lore made clear, shouldn't be attempted under *any* circumstances, so probably best to forget you ever read about it.

Chernobog came with the most substantiated mythology, though we might have been in more luck if I'd had access to The Bitters' own library. Of ancient Slavic origin, he was half of a duality—the Black God, the dark flipside to the White God, Belobog—and considered the ruler of night, winter, death, famine, and illness. All the undesirable shit, naturally, exactly like the other two. A few of the woodcuts we found depicted him haloed in darkness and sporting what looked like stylized stag horns, but I didn't spot any clawed and feathered wings. His affinities were even more dire: black blizzard stone, wolf's blood, snakeskin, and wormwood. The cautionary tales here were in a similar vein— more grisly examples of what had befallen overeager supplicants who'd dared disturb Chernobog from his slumber in the void.

As far as I could tell, nearly getting to first base on the other side of the veil wasn't among them.

And that was about as far as we'd gotten.

"I'm sorry," Delilah said dejectedly, as though the lack of useful information was a personal scholarly failure on her part. "There's usually at least *something* more concrete to go on. Back when Nina needed to know about Belisama, we actually had one of her artifacts to offer for examination. But we wouldn't keep anything related to a dark chaos deity if it happened to cross our path. Too dangerous, even for a place as warded as Tomes. It'd be borrowing trouble."

"It's not your fault, Lilah," Ivy said, squeezing Delilah around the waist without lifting her head. "All we asked for was your help in sifting through anything you might have, and hey, we even took notes."

"It isn't like we expected any of this to be definitive," I seconded, though that was a lie—I'd been hoping for exactly that, something easy and clear-cut to bring to Elena like an offering. Something that would let us both defend Thistle Grove and restore Maya's memory in one fell swoop. "Thank you again for letting us use Tomes. Your next herb order from the Emporium's on me."

She waved me away, with another flicker of that almost-sweet smile I'd seen at the door. "No need for that. I know I've been shitty to you because of Ivy, and while I'm not sorry, I know you all are . . ." She flapped a hand, clearly at a loss to articulate the evolving relationship dynamic I was also still failing to understand. "Well, whatever you are. And I do still owe you for what you did for Cat. So, maybe let's call it even and keep it moving?"

I blinked. This did not sound like the vehemently grudge-clinging Delilah Harlow I'd known my entire life. "Uh, sure. Fine by me. We can go with that."

"See you tomorrow for brunch with Cat at Wicked Sweet?" Ivy asked as we stood, helping Delilah gather the books strewn across the lamplit table. "Or are you trying to avoid the tourist rush?"

"No, we'll be there," Delilah assured her, flashing a broad smile at the thought of her partner. "Uncle James will be covering for me here. Gods know I'll need a break by then."

We left her to reshelve and lock up Tomes, heading out onto Yarrow, where too many jostling Cavalcade tourists still milled over the cobblestoned street. But even their overbearing presence couldn't diminish the half-musky, half-decaying smell of autumn magic and incense hovering in the nippy air. The darkness of approaching Samhain curled around the corner like a beckoning finger, wispy clouds strewn across the fat slice of moon like tattered lace.

The closer we got to Samhain, the thinner the veil would

become. Maybe that was why I'd been drawn across the veil with him so quickly in the first place, in the spell's aftermath—because the sheering process had already begun, and would only become more pronounced.

And all those gods . . . they were gods of winter and darkness, the coming closeness to the void. The same elements Samhain itself revolved around.

"I'm sorry," Ivy was saying as she fell into step beside me, oblivious to the sudden whirl of my mind. "I really thought that maybe Delilah could—"

"She did," I interrupted, grabbing her hand, my breath pinching short with excitement. "Ivy, I have an idea. You're going to hate it, but I think I know what to do next."

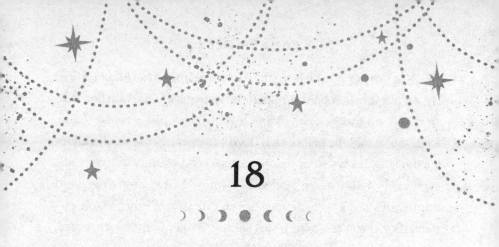

18

Of Blizzards, Blood, and Wormwood

IF YOU THINK there is any world in which I'm letting you do this alone," Ivy said, with that strained equanimity that I knew meant she was exerting herself mightily to keep from raising her voice, "you are out of your entire goddamned mind, Dasha Avramov."

We stood outside my cottage arguing in hushed tones, not wanting to risk the possibility of waking Maya—though she still slept like the living dead, nearly comatose every time her head hit the pillow.

"But, Ivy," I protested, my hands curling into fists by my sides, "I've never even done that before! Does this seem like the best time to try sliding over with someone in tow? When *he* could be there? Besides which, I need you here on this side, to pull me back."

"Not buying it," she retorted, mouth setting in a stubborn line. "If we put a timed binding spell on your garnet and anchor it to an object on this side, it'll yank us both back like a rubber band. And you've told me before that devil eaters can bring others along for the ride. It says so in your super-secret Avramov lore or whatever, even if you haven't tried it. I know I can't stop you—and frankly, it's not a terrible idea, given our lack of other viable options. But if you're going to go sniffing around on the other side, you need backup. *Especially* if he's there."

That was the general plan—now that I knew what the various gods' affinities were, I wanted to do a little sleuthing. I doubted that he'd still be lurking in wait, not when he'd never been there the many times I'd visited over the years. But his presence had to have exerted some effect in a place as otherwise immutable as the other side of the veil. I was willing to bet some godly detritus still lingered like psychic spoor—and if there was a chance it could provide any information about which deity we were dealing with, that meant I *had* to try, Elena's prohibitions be damned.

"But if you get hurt . . ." I trailed off, unable to even finish the thought.

"You won't let that happen," Ivy said stoutly, gathering up my hands between us. But I could feel her autumn-chilled fingers trembling in mine; despite her formidable resolve, Ivy was too smart not to be afraid of what we were going to attempt. "I know you won't. You're the ultimate expert on the other side, Dasha. You'll know if we need to leave immediately—and even if you do get a little carried away, the binding spell will encompass us both, as long as I keep touching you."

I took a long, shuddering breath, then nodded. "Okay," I said slowly, letting it out in a whoosh. "Okay, fine. I'm going to tether my garnet to the porch light." I always kept it on anyway to discourage the shades from hovering too close, but symbolically, it was meant to light your way home. Exactly the energy we needed. "After that, we should be good to go."

"Will I . . . feel anything?" she said, sounding as tense as I felt. "During the transition."

"It's so fast that I barely do, though I can't predict what the other side will feel like for you. Fucking phenomenal, if my experience is enough to judge by. But I can't guarantee anything, because, *like I said*, I haven't exactly had a chance to practice. Not a lot of takers for tours of the other side."

She choked out a brittle little laugh at that. "First time for everything, right? Now cast that bind before I lose my nerve."

I closed my eyes, murmuring the words that would link my garnet to the porch light. I could feel the gem heat at my throat, pulsing like a second heart, and then the shimmering thread, slim but resilient as spider silk, that abruptly sprang up between it and the light. It would allow us the equivalent of ten earthside minutes beyond the veil before it forcibly drew us back. I knew from my experiments that time passed much more slowly there, so we'd have plenty of opportunity to explore, and I could always shift us back earlier if I wanted to. The bind would act more as a fail-safe than anything.

"Alright," I said, squeezing Ivy's hands tight. "Here goes nothing."

The world abruptly wheeled like a top whirling around its axis—and then we landed on the other side with the same dizzying stumble I always experienced, though I made sure not to let go of Ivy's hands. When I opened my eyes, she was already gaping at the blood-rust clouds sprawled against the gray smear of sky, the listless black flowers that surrounded us like a glistening, gothic tableau, the skeletal orchards in the distance heavy with their inedible fruit.

Then her head fell back, mouth dropping open and her neck arching so hard I could see the veins straining beneath her skin.

"Oh my god, Dasha," she breathed, her lips trembling. "It's so wrong here. There's no sound, no air, nothing *at all*. But oh fuck, it also feels *so good*."

"Truer words," I managed wryly, through the blaze of my own euphoria. Because though I was already burning with it myself, I'd known to expect it—and nothing I could have said would have prepared Ivy for its potency. Instead I pulled her close, sliding one arm around her waist, holding her steady like a different kind of anchor as it pounded through her. When she swung her head forward, her eyes were still glazed with pleasure, her chest rising and falling with each rapid breath.

"I want to kiss you," she said, her eyes locked on mine, air rasping through her clenched teeth. "Really, really bad. Is that . . . can we even do that, if our bodies aren't really here?"

"I don't know," I whispered, fighting the tremendous urge to throw caution to the nonexistent wind and do it anyway. "I think we can, but I don't think it's a good idea. Just let it wash over you, breathe through it like you taught me. I know it's intense, but it should recede in a bit. Not all the way, but enough to be manageable."

She nodded frantically, then pitched herself into my arms, winding her own around my neck, as though our bodies truly had been spirited here. I held her close, feeling our hearts beating furiously against each other, her breath warm on my neck. It felt so much like—and yet also nothing like—the last time I'd been here, the almost unbearable ecstasy of arousal coupled with that blazing elation.

But I knew how to weather it now. And I could do it for both of us as she clung to me, her lips hot and plush against my skin, testing me beyond anything I'd experienced before.

"You did it!" she whispered, a tinge of triumph to her tone even through all that languor, squeezing me hard. "You really brought me here with you."

"And you came with me." I squeezed her back, realizing with a shock that I could still smell the familiar creamy sweetness of her scent—as if she were just as real as my own spiritual avatar was on this side. Now the only other living thing here, besides me. "Thank you."

The fact that I could imagine taking us both back, even feeling the way I did with her in my arms, convinced me more than anything else ever had that I'd learned how to exist here in a sustainable way. And the pride that surged through me at that thought only bolstered my conviction.

Finally, *finally*, this world was mine. But I didn't belong to it anymore, except when I chose to.

Eventually, Ivy's death grip on me loosened, and I could hear her slowly wrestle her breathing back under control. Then she took an unsteady step away from me, sliding her hand down my arm until our fingers interlaced so we wouldn't lose contact.

"I think I'm okay now," she said, blinking rapidly. "Very relatively speaking. You?"

"Me, too," I said, leaning forward to nuzzle my nose against hers. "You did fantastic. It took me way longer to get it together in the beginning."

"Well, we do know I'm a champion at . . ." She trailed off as her gaze drifted over my shoulder, eyes widening. "Holy *shit*, Dasha! Is that always there?"

I turned around slowly, careful to keep our hands entwined. And there it was—the castle from the faraway mountain range. Except it was suddenly *here*, right here, looming above us with its glittering black domes and needling spires, towers topped with elaborate finials like spearheads. A sprawling dark palace landed in the field of flowers, not twenty feet away from where we stood.

"No," I said, my insides ringing with shock like a struck bell. "It's never here. I've seen it before, but only in the distance. Out on that mountain range that sits on the horizon. And the mountains are clearly still all the way over there, where they're supposed to be."

"So this *must* be because of him," she said, craning her neck to peer up at its impossibly distant topmost turrets. "Right?"

"Definitely," I agreed, with a sinking heart. "Which means we have to get closer to it."

Hand in hand, we crossed the flower field, our feet making no sound as the petals and leaves caught and brushed at our boots, that oppressively dead silence stoppering my ears. It should've taken longer to reach it than it did, but I knew from my previous adventures that distance here was as unpredictable as time. I'd spent what felt like a day walking to the orchard once; another time, I'd reached it in what felt like two steps, and even passed through it to discover the dead quicksilver river that stagnated beyond.

This time, it was as if we'd thought ourselves directly in front of the castle's shimmering surface. We stood so close I could reach out with my free hand and graze the stone—clenching my teeth against the sub-zero nitrogen cold that emanated from it.

"Well, we have winter vibes for sure," I said to Ivy, my teeth chattering. "Too bad that one's three for three."

"Right, but look closer," she said, peering at the glittering wall. The entire castle seemed to be not laid of stones or bricks but carved like a chess piece, from a single colossal block. There didn't appear to be any visible doors, and the arched windows with their Moorish peaks were set with panes of the same polished stone, revealing nothing within. "Look at that cloudy marbling. Dasha, this is black blizzard stone."

"Chernobog," I breathed, exchanging wide-eyed looks with her as we both remembered what we'd read. "But we have to be sure, don't we? I don't want to go to Elena with just blizzard stone and 'it was super cold.'"

She nodded, fixing her gaze on the glistening surface again. "Then we have to touch it. Touch it properly, feel for the magic. You ready to do that?"

I set my jaw, splaying my free hand. "Yeah. Count of three?"

She nodded brusquely, gritting her own teeth as I counted us down.

As soon as my skin pressed against the stone and I allowed my senses to extend past it, the howl of a winter wind rang in my ears like baying wolves.

I could feel the iron tang of some gamey blood welling in my mouth until it felt like it would choke me, hear the dry rustle of snakeskin as if skeins of it had been wound around my body. My nose filled with the sharp, sagey scent of wormwood, and somewhere in the back of my mind, a pair of tremendous stag horns branched out at the same time as wings unfurled, billowing and flapping, so dark and endless that they blotted out the entire living world. I had the impression of something like the nemeses of stars . . . as if I could *see* black holes, only the entire universe was made of them. Because they'd eaten everything, glutted themselves on light until the very last living speck was dead and gone.

"Child of dark." A silken whisper threaded through my mind, somewhere above and beneath all that overwhelming noise, utterly inhuman and sublimely amused. "With that bright star upon your brow. Is it you, calling for me once more? I would not come for almost anyone, save to tear them asunder and feed their bones to the everlasting void. But *you*. You, child of dark, brimming with the smell of light . . . I *would* come for you."

Gasping, I ripped my hand away from the castle wall, tightening my desperate hold on Ivy. "Did you hear that?" I asked her, panic thrashing in my throat. "Just now? He . . . he's *coming*. He wants to come for me, Ivy!"

"I didn't hear that, but I sure as shit felt *something*," she said, making a face as she scraped her tongue through her teeth. So she'd tasted that rank blood, just like I had—and heard that howling, terrifying cacophony, the echoing din of the void. The roaring silence at the end of the world. The end of *all* worlds. "It's Chernobog, it has to be. So let's get the fuck out of here before he does decide to pull some Hades shit and come snatch you away."

19

Some Private Sun

BACK ON THE other side, we shed our coats and then crawled into my bed together fully clothed, still trembling. That sense of deathly, pervasive winter, the frigid void that lurked at the end of all things, seemed to have crawled into our bones, chilled us beyond what my space heater blowing on full blast could thaw.

"That castle," Ivy whispered to me in the dark, backing up against me until we fit together like nested brackets. I slung an arm over her hips, pulling her closer, inhaling the fragrance of her skin. "You said it's always been there, right? So do you think it's always belonged to him?"

"I have no idea," I admitted, shivering. "I've never understood the other side of the veil; I don't think anyone does. Is that the only world that exists beyond this one? Or is it just where *I* happen to go when I slide over? I don't understand the clouds and those dead orchards and the flowers, either. Or the river that doesn't flow anywhere. Whose is it all? What is it all for?"

"Well," she said grimly, shifting against me with a rustle of my duvet, "I think it's safe to say the palace is Blood, Wormwood, and Winter HQ now, at any rate. The Chernobog Chalet, if you prefer. Chez Chernobog. I could probably keep going."

"Don't forget Snakeskin Central," I said with a little shudder. "Ugh. I'm glad we have something solid to bring Elena, but I could have done without that entire experience. Apparently I'm not *that* into contemplating the terminus of all existence."

"None of us are equipped for facing mortality head-on, right? That's why we're not supposed to be tangling with god shit at all."

We lay together in pooled silence for a moment, thinking. But with the warmth of Ivy's curves nestled so perfectly against me, that icy tingle in my limbs was already transmuting into something else as I thawed, something much hotter and more electric. With the choke hold of winter fading, the bright, sensual blaze of the euphoria we'd both felt came creeping back, the memory of Ivy's glazed eyes and parted lips, the way she'd wanted to kiss me so badly in those first heedless moments.

I could tell she sensed the moment my breathing changed.

"You want me," she said, on her own unsteady exhale. "I can feel it."

"I do," I murmured into the perfumed curve of her neck. "Is that okay?"

"More than okay." She undulated her hips against me, in a slow, inviting motion that made me catch my breath. "I've been wanting you to touch me—really touch me—since we got back."

"I thought you wanted to be talking otherworldly philosophy!"

She chuckled, low. "And now I want to stop. A girl can change her mind."

"A girl certainly can." I pressed a kiss to the nape of her neck, then delicately flicked the tip of my tongue against her earlobe until she shivered. "All I needed to hear."

Slowly, I skimmed my palm over the full curve of her hip and the nip of her waist, then cupped her breast, kneading its heaviness until it overflowed my grip. Spurred on by the way her breathing hitched, I latched onto the nook between her neck and shoulder, sucking and licking at it as I tugged at her hard nipple, until the roll of her hips took on an even more insistent rhythm.

"Turn around," I whispered in her ear. "I want to kiss you."

She rolled over in a single fluid movement, bringing us face-to-face her eyes glittering like gems in the dark. "You're so fucking beautiful," I told her, reaching to cup the back of her head. "There's nothing more beautiful than you."

"Oh, Starshine," she said, with a soft laugh. "That's the thing about you, isn't it? You always make me believe it when you say shit like that, just 'cause you're so goddamn gorgeous yourself."

"You believe me because it's true." I pressed a light kiss to the tip of her nose. "And you know it, too."

In wordless tandem, both of us sat up just enough to drag our shirts over heads and shimmy out of our pants and underwear, until we lay naked and simmering on our sides, hands roaming freely over each other's bodies. I let out a little moan at the velvet of her skin, the way she was always softer than she existed in my sense memory. The atmosphere had shifted between us into something high-pitched and thrumming and insistent, even more urgent than the last time had been.

LANA HARPER

I'd wanted her so many times—I *always* wanted her—but not like this. With this wealth of desperate, ferocious need.

She clearly felt it, too, from the intent way she stared back at me, liquid gaze shifting between my eyes. When she leaned forward to kiss me, it was a full, deep, devouring kiss, open mouths and tongues tangling deeply. I was already so turned on I was practically panting into her mouth, and when I slid a demanding hand between her legs, fingers slipping into the cleft between her folds, I groaned at her slick heat. She went taut as a drawn bow at my touch, then caught my bottom lip between her teeth, biting down hard.

"More," she demanded, in a harsh, unsteady whisper. "I want you inside me."

"You, too," I said, catching her chin with my free hand to keep her mouth open as I slid my tongue against hers. "Please."

I waited, quivering with need, as she stroked her way down between my legs with a feathery brush of fingertips that sent chills spiraling through me. With aching slowness, she slid a finger deep inside me, followed by another, curving them until I let my head fall back. "More. Please, more," I gasped.

She plunged another finger inside me, until I felt like I might die from the sheer pleasure of that fullness, the way she knew exactly how to stroke me from within. When I returned the favor, it was with more care, a slow dip of two fingers, which I knew was usually her max. Ivy hadn't liked nearly any penetration when we first started having sex, and of course I'd never pushed. But something about the way I responded to her inside me had shifted her tolerance, tilted it closer to that ravenous desire I felt for her.

We started moving together in a steady, driving rhythm, never losing the anchoring kiss. With my free hand, I continued playing with her nipples the way I knew she liked, and kept my thumb brushing over her clit in matching circles. The heat that surged through me felt like a stream of melted sugar, so hot and sweet I could barely think, barely breathe, barely remember that I existed separately from her.

We fell into place like celestial bodies orbiting each other, seamless and cosmically ordained, though that was nothing new. Even at our worst, we'd always been fantastic at fucking each other. As if our sex existed in its own sacred enclave, a space not even hurt or anger could touch.

And this wasn't us at our worst, not anymore. The opposite of it.

"Dasha," Ivy breathed into my mouth, breaking the kiss. "Dasha, baby, I love you."

The shock that fractured through me was so intense that I stopped moving for a moment, my limbs going slack. "Really?" I managed, my heart feeling like it was trembling instead of beating. "Still?"

She sighed tremulously, tucking her lips behind her teeth. "Always, I think. Maybe even no matter what."

I bit the inside of my own lip, cheeks quivering and my eyes brimming with tears as I tipped my forehead against hers. "Oh, babe, I love you, too. So much, you have no idea. More than anything."

"Then make me come, love," she commanded, bucking against my hand. "And come for me, too."

We writhed against each other, fingers thrusting in confident tandem, her free hand tangled in my hair and mine curled around her warm nape. Mouths latched on to each other as if we needed that contact to breathe. I could feel myself spiraling inexorably toward my breaking point, the pleasure so intense it made me feel like I was going to come apart, unravel right onto her hand, melt all over her even as she dissolved onto me.

I wasn't usually this loud, but when my orgasm tore through me it felt like a cataclysm, a rippling cascade of clenching muscles and searing ecstasy that coursed all the way down my legs. Seconds later, I felt her own muscles tightening around my fingers, the heat of her bearing down on me in pulsing beats.

"Yes, yes, yes," she kept repeating, dipping down to bite at my neck and shoulders the way she did when she lost all control. I didn't mind—loved it, in fact, hoped my shoulders would be riddled with hickeys and the beautiful imprints of her teeth. The whole world could see how much I fucking loved it when I drove her crazy like this.

Usually, that would have been it—but this time neither of us stopped, couldn't bear to have it be over. My climax segued into another, followed by another, both of us thrusting and stroking with increasingly less precision or control. A beautiful, ragged mess of movement that still somehow managed to feel better than anything else ever had. By then I'd grabbed her ass so hard I was pretty sure I'd leave bruises, dragging her even closer so we pressed against each other everywhere. Chest to chest, the length of our legs tangled up together, bright stars of pleasure exploding behind closed eyes.

So much heat and life glowing between us. Like some private sun we'd conjured with the force of an enduring love that even I, for a miracle, hadn't managed to break apart.

"YOU KNOW, I thought it would make me feel sick. Being on the other side," Ivy murmured hazily to me much later as we lay together, nose to nose. We were both so sweaty we'd opted to lie on top of the sheets, but neither of us had made even a cursory movement toward the shower. "Because isn't death the antithesis of everything we Thorns are? It should have overwhelmed me, sickened me, the way he did that night at the spectacle. But it didn't. It was . . . damn, Dasha, it was something else, being there with you."

"It's because you're you, I think," I mused, tracing the line of her profile. Beads of sweat still shone like dewdrops above the perfect crests of her upper lip. "So alive. So connected to life on this plane. Maybe that makes you burn even brighter over there."

"Well, thank you for taking the risk of bringing me."

I shrugged. "You were clearly right to push me. Thank *you* for coming. And for trusting me to slide you over and back."

"Oh, I knew you could do it, Starshine," she mumbled, already half-asleep. "You can always do anything, once you decide you want to. Part of why I love you."

And she meant it, too, I thought, my heart swelling—that unflagging faith in me. Even after how many times I'd fucked up with her, the callous way I'd treated the precious gift of love she kept offering me, she really did believe I was always worth the gamble of taking that chance.

Thank you, I kept thinking fervently after she fell asleep. A prayer flung into the universe, at the gods, toward anything or anyone who might deign to listen.

Thank you for giving me to her, and her to me.

20

))) ● ((((

You Are Not My Keeper

HE BITTERS, THE Avramov demesne," Maya announced like a court herald, as soon as we walked through the wrought iron gates for the Saturday spectacle. A bright thread of awe glinted in her voice, her avid gaze skimming over the crackling multicolored bonfires, the swirling crowd, the masqueraded Avramov fortune tellers snaking through it.

"Wait, you remember The Bitters?" I asked her, exchanging looks with Ivy. "Have you been here before?"

"I don't know, maybe?" She gave a helpless shrug, screwing up her nose. "I just . . . *know* it. I'm aware that isn't very helpful."

"It's still progress," Ivy said, giving her upper arm a reassuring pat. "And that's why we had you come tonight, right?"

Ivy and I had debated the wisdom of bringing Maya, given the potential dangers. Once I'd gotten in touch with Elena to share what we'd learned on the other side of the veil, the matriarch had been, to put it mildly, displeased with my proactivity. But after she'd dressed me down to her satisfaction—though she couldn't have been *that* surprised, seeing as Avramovs weren't exactly known for falling in line like good peons—she'd come around to the undeniable usefulness of the intel. I'd even sensed some relief there; the Cavalcade hadn't run on magicless spectacles in the entire history of the town, and the elders were clearly growing uneasy with keeping this one mundane. Knowing that it was Chernobog we were dealing with allowed them to plan a strategic defense for the supernatural portion of the spectacle, should he come knocking at our door-veil once again.

"But he's a deity," I'd said, the memory of touching his stronghold still icy fresh, a chill breath of the void drifting over my nape. "Are we even equipped to handle something like that?"

"Together, we most certainly are," Elena had assured me, a silky anticipation to her voice, as if some part of her even relished rising to this unique challenge. "This is what Avramovs were made for, after all. Dallying with darkness when others can't, or dare not try. We'll also have the power of the other three families to support us, should we need it. And we've done it once before, haven't we? Without even knowing what he was."

Even with all the preparation in the world, this could still wind up being as dangerous as the last time he'd manifested. But Ivy and I had felt we owed it to Maya to bring her, especially now that she knew about magic anyway. The odds were excellent that she had been at the spectacle the first time around, given the mask I'd found around her wrist. And if Chernobog made another appearance, that in itself might shake something loose for her.

Not to mention, she'd been adamant in wanting to come.

"No fucking way am I sitting this out." Her eyes had flashed mutinously between the two of us like a rebellious teen, as if daring either to contradict her. "It's just like you said. Maybe I *was* there, and maybe something about what happened did this to me in the first place. Seeing it again might be exactly what I need."

Neither of us had been inclined to talk her out of it, though bringing her was a risk on multiple levels—especially since I still hadn't told Elena about her. The elder would have insisted on examining Maya herself, and I continued to balk at the idea of exposing her to someone who might have very different opinions on what was best for her. And I'd wanted Elena focused on the god rather than the possibility of some Blackmoore mischief, since we'd be working in concert with the Blackmoores tonight.

How did pathological liars even live their lives, I wondered guiltily, glancing down at Maya now. I'd bought her some hard cider and a huge slice of Cryptid pizza, and she was happily enjoying both, those honey-hazel eyes wide, taking everything in. I *should* have told Elena about her by now, no matter what justifications I kept dredging up for myself. That insistent sense of protectiveness aside, keeping her a secret was becoming godsdamned exhausting.

"It's about to start," Ivy said, nudging me in the side as a haunting trill of violin music drifted through the evening air. In response, I looped an arm around her waist; she let me pull her close, shooting me a small, private smile. Even here and now, with all the uncertainty hovering over us, I felt an unspeakable wealth of joy that we were together again. That Ivy Thorn, miracle of miracles, loved me enough to tell me so. "Should we get closer to the front?"

I shook my head. "We have a clear enough view from here. And if some shit does go down, I don't want Maya directly in the cross-hairs."

Maya shot me an irritable look, tossing her coppery ringlets. "I'm not a child," she mumbled around a mouthful of pizza. "I don't need to be coddled like a baby. We can get closer, if you all want to."

"I think we're good right where we are," Ivy soothed, backing me up. "No need for us to be too close to the Avramov circle anyway, if they do light some necromantic shit up. I promise, you wouldn't want to be near all that."

I glanced over to the left side of the stage, where a sizeable cluster of my family had already gathered, ready to fall into a circle formation at any moment. Issa and Talia stood near the center, as two of the most powerful witches of our generation. My sister, whose affinity with glamours extended to whatever spellwork one wielded against invading gods, hovered close by.

Elena stood among her flock, her foxy hair whipping in the wind. As if she could feel me looking, she turned just enough for our gazes to lock. Then she inclined her head in an unmistakable gesture of respect, mouthed, "We are ready for whatever comes," and turned back to her circle, her profile die-cut and adamant against the dusk.

The (very Avramov) moral of this story was, sometimes it really did pay to go rogue.

Slowly, enthrallingly, the spectacle unfolded before us just as it had that first time. Morty's aerialist crew tumbling and twining through the silks, Adriana summoning an army of mock ectoplasmic shades against the Blackmoore-conjured curtain of milky fog, the audience shrieking and giggling, beset by a delicious thrill. I could sense Ivy all but holding her breath beside me as we waited to see if he'd descend upon us again, like a moth drawn to the black flame of necromantic magic.

And then the soaring, eerie music came to a close, the shades dissipating into sooty scraps of ectoplasm against that roiling white fog.

"I can't believe that's it," a familiar voice whined behind me, and I half twisted to find Wynter a few rows back, looking crestfallen as she played with the tangle of necklaces tucked into her deep purple bodice.

"Except, that was awesome," the person beside her countered. "What exactly did you want, beyond a fucking fabulous aerial show and the most elite shadow play I've ever seen? I don't even understand how they pulled that off."

"I don't know," Wynter mumbled, dipping her head. "I guess I just . . . hoped there might be more."

Her friend was still shaking their head in exasperation as I turned back to Ivy. "Maybe we finally caught a break," I murmured to her, tucking her close against my side. She leaned over to brush a grazing kiss over my cheek, and light as it was, I could feel it rush all the way down my side and coil right between my legs, a promise of more to come later. "And he's just lost interest in—"

Then a behemoth roar shook the grounds, so loud it rattled the wrought iron fence that encircled The Bitters.

And there he was—a dark, flickering shape appearing behind the clouded white of the fog, slowly gaining mass and density as he spun himself a body. Again in that doomsday titan form, leathery wings unfurling wide around him, their curved claws framing his head like a dread halo. Only now, I could feel him in a way I

RISE AND DIVINE

hadn't before, the emanating sweep of icy death that rippled out from him. Copper filled my mouth as if I'd bitten my tongue, the scent of wormwood stinging sharp in my nose. And this time, his horns were more elaborate, branching outward like antlers.

"What about that?" Wynter's friend hissed from behind us. "Does *that* do it for you? Because if you ask me, it should have come with a fucking content warning. This, I was in no way prepared for."

It was only then that I noticed Maya standing frozen beside me, her eyes locked on Chernobog. What was left of her cider and pizza tumbled to the ground, her small hands clenching into fists so tight her arms trembled.

"*You*," she spat, in a low, belling voice. Soft as it was, it somehow knelled effortlessly above the hubbub of the crowd. "You dare come *here*, to the sacred ground I claim as mine. Again."

Chernobog's gaze snared hers, as if he'd heard her, too. And then, to my utter shock, an expression of sheer, transcendent joy suffused the bold angles of his face.

"Of course I came to you!" he roared, through a brilliant grin that revealed sharp white teeth. He was even more fully manifested than last time, more divine flesh than ectoplasm. "My light, my sister, my eternal beloved. Did you *truly* think you could conceal yourself from me forever, when you are mine and I am yours? There is no sacred ground you claim in this realm in which I do not belong as well."

Maya bared her own teeth and snarled at him.

"Dash, look!" Ivy breathed next to me, clutching my hand. "Maya's glowing. She's . . . fuck, she's *blue*."

She was, in that dazzling shade of sapphire that I knew well, because I'd seen it many times before—anytime Emmy Harlow

235

communed with the town as the Voice of Thistle Grove, summoning up the latent power that coursed like otherworldly electricity through the land beneath us, fed by the reservoir of Lady's Lake.

But Emmy had never been so blinding. So entirely subsumed with light that she looked nearly made of it.

People began backing away from Maya, shielding their eyes, leaving an open circle around her that contained only trampled grass, discarded masks, and me and Ivy, still clinging to her side. Not that it looked like she needed us. She stood her ground as if she owned it, as if it were somehow a throne to straddle. Her feet planted wide, little chin lifted in a regal mien. And there was still that sense of grace that rolled off her, now so overwhelming it felt like a palm pressed insistently to the back of my neck. A nearly irresistible compulsion to drop to my knees.

"Oh, dearest," Chernobog crooned at her, his brow wrinkling at the sight of all that building blue, clucking his tongue in sardonic disappointment. "*Must* you always be so contrary? I know I wronged you last time. So here I am to prostrate myself before you, beg your sweet forgiveness. And it has been so long since we have—"

"*YOU. ARE. NOT. MY. KEEPER!*" Maya shrieked, and this time we all *did* stumble to our knees, clapping our hands over our ears, bowled over by the shattering force of that inhuman voice. I managed a glance over at the defensive circle of Avramovs, and found them on the ground just like the rest of us. Powerless in this face-off, whatever it was. "*AND IF IT IS WHAT I WISH, YOU WILL LEAVE ME BE!*"

That last "BE" elongated into a wordless, crashing roar like massive breakers folding over each other, a summer squall on the high seas, a lashing monsoon.

As it trailed off, she lifted both clenched fists and aimed them at him, a laser-bright sheet of that radiant blue light surging from them, striking him directly in the solar plexus. He buckled with the force of it, even as the blue enveloped him like licking tongues, the brilliant color at the heart of a gas-fueled flame. And yet the way the flames moved was like water, too, fluid and rippling, surging over his torso and eating through his wings like acid. I could see from the strain in his jaw, the way his head fell back to reveal a neck corded with bulging veins, that it invoked in him both agony and a shade of ecstasy. As if this blue light were something at once dangerous and tantalizing, something he craved as much as it was lethal to him.

"Dearest," he managed, though his voice was weakening. "Dearest, do not do this, please . . . What if I cannot find you again . . ."

"*THEN YOU WILL NOT HAVE ME!*" Maya shrieked back, in that enchanting banshee voice, sweet and decimating all at once. "*NOW GO BACK TO WHENCE YOU CAME, YOU ETERNAL PESTILENCE, YOU EATER OF ALL THINGS!*"

As the light intensified, engulfing him completely, his manifested form began to break down, shredding into wreaths of wisping smoke—like it had when we'd cast our banishing spell. Only faster, much more furiously, burning him away until all that remained was his face. Still ablaze with that odd, desperate longing, and the weight of such a crushing grief that for a single moment, I found it in me to pity him from the bottom of my heart.

And then he vanished with a sound like the suck of a massive vacuum seal being broken, making my ears pop painfully.

Beside me, Maya collapsed to her knees on the grass, all the blue abruptly bled from her. She buried her face in her hands, sobbing into them.

LANA HARPER

"I'm sorry," she keened, rocking back and forth. "Oh, I'm sorry, I'm so sorry. But she had to, didn't she? She couldn't let him have his way *again*."

I sank down beside her, Ivy on her other side, both of us wrapping our arms around her slight form. That tremendous, commanding force had clearly left her body, and now she felt only small and warm and slack, her soft hair brushing my cheeks. She smelled like apple cider and my own bergamot shower gel, painfully familiar and vulnerable.

"Who *are* you?" I whispered to Maya, stroking a palm over her curls, trying my best to soothe her even as my heart still clamored against my ribs. "How did you do that? Burn him away?"

"I don't know who I am," she said wretchedly, lifting her head to give me a tearstained look so woebegone my stomach caved in. She sounded like herself again . . . yet there was still the faintest echo of that crystalline power to her, that prismatic radiance. As if something inside her had been unlocked, a door cracked open, even if not all the way. "But I know who *she* is, now. And I know why he's here, too."

21

Like a Genie in a Lamp

Y OUR GODDESS," MAYA said softly, lifting a hand to brush her fingertips over one temple. She sat in an overstuffed burgundy chair so large it should have dwarfed her, but that aura of enormity hadn't left her entirely. Her curls burned with reflected firelight from the blazing hearth behind her, and flickers of blue still sparked in her eyes, piercing the gloom of The Bitters' library. Sprite-sized as she was, she *felt* immense. Like a tangible dip in the fabric of reality, something that exerted its own gravity. "The one you call Belisama. The piece of her that slept in your lake . . . that's inside me now."

The hush that engulfed the library was so thick and complete that I could hear the rushing gallop of my heartbeat in my ears.

After another large-scale glamouring of the normies—at this rate, we'd be lucky if this crop of tourists left Thistle Grove any better off than Maya—the entire quorum had assembled, along with me and Ivy by Emmy's invitation. I'd never shared a room with all of them before, and the air itself seemed to tremble with the gravity of the occasion. Gabrielle and Aspen Thorn sat to one side on a shared love seat, hands clasped, with Rowan in a chair beside them, his forearms slung between his thighs, locs falling over his face. Next to them was the former Harlow elder, James, now the master recordkeeper, with Emmy seated beside him—though as Victor and Voice and current Harlow elder, she outranked her own father on every level. To their left were Elena and Talia. Closing the circle and representing the Blackmoores, Gareth sat with his sister and advisor, Nina.

Finally, Ivy and I were on either side of Maya in our own wingback chairs—protectively bookending her, like we'd done from the beginning.

I'd never felt so out of place in my entire life, even as we all shared in the collective sense of seismic shock. After the glamouring, I'd finally given everyone the rundown of how and where I'd found Maya, trying not to quail as Elena glared flinty daggers at me. No doubt I'd be dealing with those repercussions down the line.

But there wasn't space for any of that now. None of us could have been prepared for this.

"I know," Maya said wryly, a faint smile tracing over her lips. "It's wild to me, too. But it's the truth. I can feel it. She's hovering in the background right now. There's a . . . a boundary of sorts, between us. A wall in my mind that she built for me, so her presence wouldn't overwhelm me. She took the wheel for a minute there, just to banish him, but she doesn't want to . . ." Her brow wrinkled as her gaze drifted up to the ceiling, sifting for the right words. "Disrespect me? Dishonor me? It's bad enough, apparently, that she chose me as a vessel rather than one of you. But she had no choice; she thought it would be one of the families who answered the call. But I was closest, the one who happened to come when she summoned. Even if I don't remember it."

"Does it hurt?" Ivy whispered, her lovely face alight with painful empathy. "Hosting her?"

I'd had the same thought, my stomach twisting at the unfathomable notion of a goddess—or a slice of one, anyway—writhing like a trapped genie inside the lamp of Maya's mind. But Ivy had actually touched that blazing partition, felt the searing strangeness of it. She had a much better sense of what Maya was dealing with than I did.

Gabrielle and Aspen both twitched instinctively toward Ivy, clearly feeling her distress, though they were too far away to touch her, take her hands the way Thorns did so easily with each other. So I did it instead, folding Ivy's hand between both of mine and nestling it in my lap. She shot me a grateful smile, entwining her fingers with mine.

"Oh, no." Maya's smile widened into something broad and fond. "That boundary keeps it from being too much—and it's also why I can't remember who I am. She did that to protect me; there's not enough room in my mind for both of us at the same time. But I know what she knows, and what I do feel of her is . . ." Her face softened, went misty with awe. "*Wonderful*. She feels like so, so many good things. Dawn breaking over water. A bonfire by a lake at dusk, the light all reflected on the surface, leaves rustling in a warm breeze. Smaller things, even, but still so nice. A hot bath with candles lit around it; your toes buried in lakeside silt. Warmth and water. Liquid and light. All the things life needs to happen, and then to abide."

The way she spoke had become fluid itself, I noticed, its meter and rhythm shifting with each sentence, as if she were slipping in and out of poetry without being aware of it. As if the melding between them had become more integrated, that partition eroding a little now that Belisama had risen to the fore once.

"But why?" Emmy broke in. She had an odd expression on her face, something caught between fascination and envy. I could understand it; before this, out of all of us, she'd been the most deeply connected to the town, to the magic of the lake. The closest to being the goddess's chosen, aside from Nina Blackmoore. But not anymore. "Why did she wake now?"

"Most of her actually hasn't," Maya explained, scrunching up her face. "I know that's confusing, I'm sorry. I understand it because she does, but it's hard to put into people words. The best I can do is say that the . . . the bulk of her is still asleep, locked away somewhere far away, down deep in a different lake." From the corner of my eye, I caught Emmy and James exchanging a conspiratorial look—as if they knew something about this already, more than the rest of us. "Healing, from the last time this happened. The last time he found her and won. But it's the part of her that's here—the very essence of her—that he wants. That he needs, if he aims to get her back."

"So what the fuck *does* he want with her?" Gareth asked bluntly, dragging a hand over his stubbled face, the weary hollows under his blue eyes stark in the firelight. The former Blackmoore golden boy—or abominable fuckboy, depending on how you knew him—looked very different these days from the louche scion I remembered from the Gauntlet of the Grove. It had only been a few years, but taking on the mantle of Blackmoore elder had clearly changed him, and for the better. That old arrogance had been tempered, solidified into something much less mercurial and more dependable. "She's been hidden here for centuries. Like Emmy said, why's he barging in now?"

"Because Chernobog needs her," Maya said simply. "He's her other half. They're a twinned set, two parts of a whole. Light and dark, order and chaos, summer and winter. Siblings. Lovers. Everything all at once, from the moment they came aware to-gether."

Ivy made a face at that, and Maya caught it, the corner of her mouth quirking indulgently, like a parent's at their child's ador-able naivete. "It's not like that for them," she said with a little laugh, shaking her head. "It's not wrong. They're *all* siblings, in a way. The gods, I mean. Living clusters of energy, who sometimes incorporate into bodies if they choose."

"But Chernobog already has a specific counterpart," Elena in-terrupted, steepling her hands. "The mythology has him as part of an existing duality with Belobog."

"Belisama *is* Belobog," Maya clarified, tilting her head. "It's just a different name for the same divine entity, manifested female as Belisama. That doesn't mean there *aren't* others, gods and god-desses that personify other, different aspects of water and light. The names do carry a significant distinction, sometimes—but re-member, we're the ones who gave them these names in the first place. Mortal designations aren't what they call themselves. And in this case, she's both. Welsh goddess of lakes and light, ancient Slavic god of life and day. One and the same."

"Man, how I do loathe that trippy cosmic shit," Gareth mut-tered to himself. Next to him, Nina suppressed a smile, tucking a honey-blond lock behind her ear. "Well, it makes sense to me," she offered gingerly, as all the eyes in the room slid to her. "Back when

I had Belisama's favor and her stone, that's what it felt like to me, too. She's . . . multitudes. I could easily see how she could be both, and more."

"And he's equally vast," Maya continued, idly playing with her fingertips in her lap, a gesture so achingly human that it somehow threw the uncanny reality of her predicament into even sharper relief. "But just because they were made to be together, to yearn for each other, doesn't mean they always get along. The opposite, actually. She's light and life; he's the utter absence of both. He craves her in a way that intrinsically consumes what she's meant to be. It's in his destructive nature, part of how he loves her."

A brisk shiver skittered down my spine at the memory of Chernobog's intoxicating seduction, the way I'd actually considered staying on the other side with him, craved the intensity of that all-consuming lust. But why had I reminded him of her so keenly? Why had he wanted me at all, when it was her he was always looking for?

"And when she can't endure it any longer," Maya went on, "she runs from him, takes refuge somewhere in this realm. Claims a place—a lake, a town, a village—as her own, and shelters there. Until she's ready to both be with and stand against him once again."

"Toxic relationships," Emmy quipped, arching an eyebrow. "Even the gods have them."

"And here everyone thought I was the original shithead," Gareth snarked under his breath, shooting a good-natured half smile at her.

"Oh, but you were," Talia assured him coolly. "Just smaller scale. I mean, *much* smaller."

Emmy snorted so hard she half choked, the stern Victor and Voice façade cracking for a moment.

Gareth rolled his eyes. "Okay, *unnecessary*, Tal."

"You started it, Blackmoore."

"And you don't always have to finish it, Talia, have you considered that?"

Talia bared her teeth like a wolf, her ice-gray eyes glinting. "Why would I ever not, when the last word is so reliably delicious?"

"But the thing is—"

"Gareth. *Dude*," Rowan groaned, tossing his head irritably. "Will you just take your L's for once and shut the hell up?"

"You heard the man, Gareth," Talia agreed gleefully, crossing her arms over her chest. "Suck up all those L's and—"

"Tal." Rowan glowered, shooting her an exasperated look. "He's not wrong, either. You *could* cut it out, yourself."

"*Toxic* about sums it up," Maya agreed, with an amused shrug at their sparring. "At an epic level, obviously. Apparently, the last time they clashed . . . it was somewhere in Scotland, I think? A tiny town near Linlithgow, that doesn't exist anymore—because he destroyed it and most of its inhabitants in a rage, scouring it for her. She was pissed, to put it mildly; you don't fuck with a town under divine protection, not even as another god. They clashed, and he hurt her, very badly. But she had more followers back then, an entire cult of worshippers. And she trusted one of them to hide her essence where he wouldn't find her anytime soon. Someplace she'd have a chance to heal."

"Elias Harlow," James Harlow broke in, eyes gleaming beneath bushy dark brows—so he *had* known something about this, and that it had to do with the Harlow founder of Thistle Grove. "The records *were* correct, then. He brought her here across the ocean, chose the lake as a home for her. And turned the town itself into a magical convalescing mechanism—a haven for witches to gather in, so that her divine magic could fuel their spells, and their spells her healing, wherever she lies. Like a positive feedback loop."

"But isn't that why there's a deflection glamour around the town?" Emmy asked him. I glanced at the rest of the quorum; no one seemed at all surprised by this very well-informed line of questioning. Apparently this knowledge had already been dispensed to a select few, I thought sourly, and the rest of us had been deemed unfit to know. "To keep her safe? There's been a Cavalcade every twenty years since the founding. Why would he have only found her now?"

"The Cavalcades are crucial," Maya explained. "They're like, um, using a magnifying lens to focus a ray of sun, if that makes sense. They enhance the low-level effect Thistle Grove consistently exerts on Belisama. The magic and mortal wonder from the re-creations of the founding—they're what funnel the healing to her like a conduit, all the way on the other side of the water. But this time was different. This time, the magic managed to draw him here, even *through* the deflection glamour. Which means someone had to have issued him a direct invitation."

"And who would do something so deranged?" Emmy demanded pointedly, leveling a much less playful glare at Gareth. "Anyone we know?"

"Hey, it wasn't us!" Gareth protested, lifting both hands. "I swear, on my honor. Come on, Emmy, why would we, especially now? I've cleaned house, gotten our shit together—because you granted me the privilege. I'm not forgetting that anytime soon. Plus, this is a necromantic god we're talking about, and we're a bunch of elementalists tossing around magical glitter. None of us would've known how to even begin summoning him."

Emmy kept that saw-toothed glare on him for another moment, then softened. "Fair enough. It *would* be a monumentally stupid thing to pull, even by former Blackmoore standards—and I know you're running a tighter ship these days. So, who else? Nina, any ideas? You were the one who dreamed about Belisama, before she granted you her favor. Have you had any other dreams? Any premonitions about this?"

"Nothing at all," Nina replied with a dejected shake of her head, a flash of hollow pain in her eyes. I didn't know much of what had happened to her then, but whatever she'd lost had clearly cost her.

"I . . ." My voice emerged as a harsh croak. I hadn't been prepared to speak at all, and I certainly hadn't been expecting to become an active participant in the conversation. "I *did* have a dream. Before I found Maya up on the lakeside . . . it's why I went up there at all. I'm not sure if it matters, though. It was more of a jumble of dream and memory. Strange, that's for sure. But it didn't feel like communion to me."

"Describe it, please," Emmy ordered, with such a crisp air of accustomed command that it didn't even occur to me to be indignant over being told what to do. "Anything is relevant right now. Especially something that brought you to Lady's Lake just in time to meet Belisama-as-Maya and become her de facto protector. Because that's what you've been, isn't it? Her knight, of sorts?"

"She has," Maya said softly, smiling at me with that luminous grace. "My shield and solace. It was Belisama, you know, not me. She needed me away from hospitals or the police, anywhere I could be restrained. Because she knew he was here; she'd felt him come battering at the veil. She knew that she'd have to fight him, eventually, but she's stranded in the lake, without corporeal form. That was why she inhabited me in the first place—and why she needed someone to take care of me just like you did, until I was strong enough. Until the moment came."

"But why me?" I asked plaintively, struggling to understand. "I'm not *anyone's* protector. Until recently, I wasn't even very good at taking care of myself, much less someone else."

"She knows every single one of you, and you're the one she wanted for this," Maya said, flicking a placid shoulder. Wholly trusting of the goddess who'd lodged in her mind like a burr, even though she herself hadn't asked for any of this. "There's a plan, I think. She won't let me see it—or maybe I can't, because I'm mortal and it hasn't happened yet. Possibly *she* doesn't even know the details. But she needs you, Dasha, specifically. An Avramov witch with Harlow blood."

"Why would my Harlow blood matter?" I demanded. "My magic manifests as Avramov. That's how we define ourselves."

"Because the Harlows are Belisama's mortal descendants," Maya said gently, almost wincing at the shock that must have blazed like a solar flare across my face. "Part divine. That was why Elias was able to ferry her essence here in the first place."

I gaped at the quorum, stunned. Ivy caught her breath, too, then squeezed my hand hard in response, trying to anchor me as I reeled with the revelation. "And this—this is something we *know*?" I eked out.

"Yes," Emmy said quietly. "Though only recently."

"Well, shit," Ivy groused, aggrieved on my behalf. "Keeping something like a *divine lineage* from other Harlow descendants *surely* seems fair."

"It wasn't something we wanted widely disseminated," Emmy said, with a hint of apology. "Not until we understood the ramifications better, anyway."

I thought of the way my mother had always been by the lake, so serene, so completely at home up on Hallows Hill. A Harlow through and through, in a way I'd never thought applied to me. So maybe that was it, what Chernobog had smelled on me. A trace of Belisama herself, intriguingly mingled with my necromantic legacy.

"And you're a . . . devil eater on top of that," Maya added with a slight frown, as if she knew the term from her divine hitchhiker, but maybe not exactly what it entailed. "I don't know why that matters to her, but it does. So whatever you dreamed, it *is* important. It matters more than you think. Because he'll be back. The banishment she managed hurt him, but she's terribly weak in comparison. Barely a shadow of the primeval fire she once was. She needs me to hold her—and she needs your help."

Haltingly, my insides still clanging with shock, I walked the quorum through what I remembered of the dream that had led me to Maya.

"It started as a memory," I began. "The first farmer's market of the season, the day I met Ivy." I described setting up the stall with Wynter, Ivy's and my flirtation—omitting some of the juicier *Wanton's Guide* details, because honestly, the quorum had no right to those—and then the malevolent moment in which Wynter had transformed into Chernobog. The way Ivy's eyes had turned amber as she tried to maintain her hold on me, to keep me from drifting back to him. Forcing me to choose what I wanted, to stay with her or return with him to the other side of the veil.

"It was as if someone were speaking through her," I said slowly, mind whirling. "She told me . . ."

"What?" Emmy said intently, leaning forward over her thighs. "She told you what, Dasha?"

"That when the time came, I'd know," I said, but abstractedly, because I'd remembered something else. That unnervingly alien look on Wynter's face, the purple obelisk pendant she'd been toying with at the stall, the sinister smile curling her lips. There'd been other people in the dream—browsing shoppers, fellow vendors. Why had my sleeping brain insisted on twisting her, specifically, into Chernobog?

Maybe it had been Belisama brushing against my dreams, nudging me toward something meaningful. Or maybe it had been my own subconscious, piecing together clues that I'd missed in the glare of daylight, glossed over during my waking hours.

When I'd run into Wynter at the first spectacle, she'd smelled of mugwort and something else, something pungent yet familiar. My mind snared on the memory of her stricken face, those strange, misplaced tears. Then tonight, the way she'd seemed so bizarrely thrilled at Chernobog's appearance . . . as if she'd been expecting him, or something like him, all along.

Wormwood, I realized with a hard jolt. She'd smelled of mugwort and wormwood. And then there were the herbs missing from the emporium—specialty herbs she'd have had direct access to.

"I think I know who summoned Chernobog," I said, lifting my chin, anger licking at my insides like a slow-stoked blaze. "And I know where to find her, too."

22

Will You Be My Champion?

"WHAT IS THIS about?" Wynter said, squirming in the seat of inquisition in Elena's Arcane Emporium office, her eyes flicking anxiously between Elena, Talia, and me. For once, she wasn't wearing her customary mask of Glam Witch™ makeup, and she looked much younger and more vulnerable without it. Tired, too, with bruised shadows raw beneath her eyes. Even her hair seemed listless, the bangs flat and stringy.

She wasn't wearing that distinctive obelisk pendant, but now that I knew to look for it, I could see the way her hand kept twitching up toward her chest, as if to check that it was still there.

"Have you been stealing herbs from us?" Elena asked, in a tone so surgically sharp it sounded like it could part your skin with the barest pressure applied. "And have you been using them to summon the ancient entity of darkness and chaos known as Chernobog?"

The commingling of guilt and surprise that swept like a squall over Wynter's face would have been giveaway enough, even if her jaw hadn't dropped open. "I . . . beg pardon?" she said, ridiculously, her voice quavering. "I didn't . . . How would you . . ."

Elena summoned an entire cloak of billowing ectoplasm, a shroud of roiling, inky darkness that whirled around and behind her like some dark sorceress's cape. There was so much of it I could feel its emanating chill even from where I stood, all the way by the door.

"*Nice,*" Talia hissed under her breath.

"What the fuck?!" Wynter squealed, recoiling so hard that the chair's legs scraped across the floor. "What is that? What *are* you?!"

"A true necromantic witch, you idiot child," Elena snapped, the ectoplasm surging around her like a captive black thunderhead. "As you clearly fancy yourself to be. Now speak, and spare us any further nonsense or prevarication. Tell me what you did, or you'll discover exactly how we deal with the meddling of mundanes who infringe on our territory."

Generally, we dealt with them exclusively by erasing their memories of magic. But from the blotchy pallor that had crept into Wynter's cheeks—and Elena's thoroughly impressive intimidation display—I doubted that was where Wynter's mind was straying.

"I . . ." Wynter began, the word emerging in a sandpaper croak. She swallowed hard, licking her lips. "Yes, okay. I've been . . . Maybe I borrowed some herbs, here and there. But it was for the cause. I'm a darkling, one of Chernobog's chosen. I've been dedicated to him for years."

"You're a what?" Elena demanded, contempt dangling like icicles from each word. Next to me, Talia groaned low in her throat, rolling her eyes so hard she actually let her head fall back.

"A darkling," Wynter repeated a little more sheepishly, a flush mottling her wan cheeks. "That's what the community of the dread lord's followers call ourselves."

"Is this the actual stupidest bullshit I've ever heard?" Talia mused, a finger to her chin. "Or is it *worse* than the stupidest? I can't even tell."

"It does seem to call for its own dedicated metric," I agreed.

"And this community of yours," Elena continued, jade eyes narrowed. "What exactly is it that you do for your *dread lord*?"

Wynter winced at the scathing tone, her shoulders hunching a little, but then drew herself up. "We—we give offerings," she said, with a stout little lift to her chin. "And we celebrate him during the changing of the seasons, when the world tilts toward winter and darkness."

"Hold on a minute," Talia interjected. "Is *that* why you're calling yourself Wynter, *y* and all? As some kind of obnoxious homage?"

Wynter shot her an outraged glare. "It's my craft name," she replied loftily. "Which, as a practitioner, I'm allowed to choose for myself. And spell however speaks to me."

"Oh, for fuck's sake," Talia moaned, dragging a hand over her face. "The *y* speaks to her."

"*Definitely* worse than stupid," I agreed. "Hitting somewhere deep on the negative end of the scale."

"But why Chernobog, out of all the gods?" Elena asked, genuinely bewildered. "Do death and eternal chaos *speak to you*, in similar fashion to the deliberately misspelled names of seasons?"

"My great-great-great-grandma was from Belarus," Wynter replied, bristling. "So the Slavic pantheon is, like, my heritage. And he's . . . well, there's something really hot about all that darkness, right? Like kind of a broody element. The way the end of the world is sort of exciting, if you think about it in a certain light."

"So you worship him because he's sexy," Talia concluded flatly. "Phenomenal decision-making, truly, I applaud you. What better reason to pledge fealty to a deathly chthonic god than fuckability?"

"We don't just worship him," Wynter protested, craning her neck to glare at Talia over her shoulder. "On special occasions, we invite him to show himself."

"You summon him," Elena concluded. "And I assume the Cavalcade would count as an appropriate special occasion."

"Oh, yeah, of course!" Wynter exclaimed, nodding vigorously, guilt and trepidation momentarily pushed aside by a wave of excitement. "The historical re-creation of the magical founding of a town by its witch founders? I mean, *for sure*. I'm sorry about the herbs, I really am. It's just, they're like, seriously expensive. And you need a shit ton of them, at least for the invocation I was using."

"And where," Elena growled through her teeth, her jaw dangerously tight, leaning over her desk far enough that Wynter quailed again, "would a deluded naif such as yourself even find an invocation to summon a primeval deity of death and chaos?"

"Um, Reddit?" Wynter chanced with a preemptive grimace, as if she had a sense of the reception this was likely to get.

Talia burst into a bout of full-throated laughter, leaning over to prop herself against her thighs. "No," she managed through helpless chortles. "Please, I can't. She found the invocation on *Reddit*. Make it stop. Or no, you know what, say *more*."

"Well, the spell itself wasn't on Reddit, obviously," Wynter argued, like, *duh*. "That's just where the community threads are hosted, and there was this AMA from one of the really senior darklings, and then that led me to a Tumblr, and then to an Etsy store where I bought the summoning pendant, and—"

"Enough." Elena held up a staying hand, pinching the bridge

of her nose with the other. "I fear the advent of an aneurysm if you continue speaking."

Absurd as it sounded, it was theoretically possible that someone dedicated enough—as Wynter clearly was, for all her cringeworthy fumbling at witchcraft—could have stumbled across a legitimate spell somewhere in the infinite morass of the internet. The Thistle Grove Grimoire and the other spellbooks kept at Tomes & Omens certainly weren't the only repositories of magical workings in the world, and we weren't the only real witches roaming it, either. Unlikely as it seemed, Wynter had evidently glommed on to something with actual power.

"And how long have you been summoning your dread lord?" Elena drawled with that venomous sarcasm, cupping her chin in her hand. The cloak of ectoplasm still billowed threateningly around her, but it had settled a little, as if even she wasn't completely immune to the comedic undertone of the entire situation.

"Since Litha," Wynter replied. "You know, summer yielding to the colder parts of the year, the balance tipping. It seemed like the right time, so a bunch of us on the group chat were casting it in tandem."

"The storms above the lake," I realized, catching Elena's eye. "Litha is about when they started. Maybe Belisama could feel the casting, knew he might be coming for her, and that was what had her so riled up."

"Shit," Talia muttered. "That makes sense."

"And I wanted to be well practiced for the Cavalcade," Wynter continued, clearly baffled by our asides—so she had no idea her dread lord's counterpart was even in Lady's Lake. So much for the darkling information network. "He hadn't shown himself to me yet, but I thought for sure it would happen then."

Her face fell, lips quivering. "But it's not like it worked. He didn't appear at any of the spectacles, and I figured if he ever would, it'd be at The Bitters. I mean, you Avramovs are supposed to be necromantic witches, right? Like, I didn't know you could actually do . . . *that*"—with a little shudder, she flapped a horrified hand at Elena's ectoplasmic cape—"but I know all about your history. You came from Russia; you're speakers to the dead. Even if you're not full-fledged darklings, I thought probably you worshipped him, too. That's why I wanted to work here in the first place. To see if I could learn anything from you."

"Some of us know better than to court dangerous things we don't understand," Elena retorted caustically—though in fairness, that was a shamelessly far cry from the truth when it came to many of the more daredevilish members of our family. We were just much better equipped to engage in the flagrant disregard of common sense. "And alas, it did work, you foolish child. You just don't remember it."

Of course, I realized. Wynter wouldn't have retained any memory of either of Chernobog's manifestations at the spectacles, because she'd been glamoured to forget them along with the rest of the normies. So she'd simply kept casting and casting—like dropping a pin for him at every spectacle, amplified by the swirling immensity of the Cavalcade's magic such that the spell actually worked for her, unlike all the times she'd futilely tried it before.

"You mean he *manifested*?" Wynter breathed, face suffused with helpless wonder. "The invocation worked? How could I have ever forgotten something like that? It . . . he must have been glorious."

"He was," Talia interjected gleefully, all too delighted to rub salt in the wound. "Super fucking sexy, and did I mention naked?

Babe, I'm talking full-frontal, and packing serious heat. You missed out."

"You forgot because it wasn't a sight meant for the eyes of a malicious little thief like you," Elena responded, as Wynter's face crumpled with abject disappointment. "Now, on to business. First of all, you're fired. That should go without saying, but for you, I prefer to clarify beyond a reasonable doubt. And given the extent of this debacle, I'd suggest you consider leaving town altogether, as the rest of the family won't be any better pleased with you than I am, and will likely show considerably less restraint."

"But Thistle Grove is my home!" Wynter wailed, gaze flitting pathetically between the three of us. "Where am I supposed to go? I built my entire following around living here! And working at the Emporium!"

"Better start looking for a different angle to influence, sweetness," Talia suggested in acid tones.

"And before you leave," Elena continued. "We'll be needing the invocation from you."

Wynter swallowed hard, then set her jaw. "It's *my* spell," she countered stubbornly, her arms tightening over her chest. "I found it. And I don't have to give it to you."

"Ballsy," Talia murmured almost appreciatively, tilting her head from side to side. "Especially coming from someone lucky not to be on the receiving end of at least seven separate hexes. Not to mention the fact that a summoning spell like that draws on *you* as the power source—do you happen to have given that nasty little detail any thought? Cast it enough times, and there wouldn't be much left of you anymore to call it yours."

Wynter paled even further, and Elena grinned like a cat that had sighted a bird within swiping distance.

"And might I remind you that this is *my* motherfucking house, dear," she hissed through that sharp-toothed, crimson-lipped smile, whorls of ectoplasm churning around her, lifting up like a storm brewing behind her back. Inky tendrils of it began to creep over her desk like ghostly, sentient filaments, slithering toward Wynter until she whimpered and strained away from them. "Not to mention my town. And let us not forget that you dared to steal from the Emporium and then lie about it, which amounts to deceiving the entire Avramov family. So you will hand that invocation over as if it were a heartfelt offering to me, in earnest pursuit of my forgiveness. And then you'll never set foot across our threshold again . . . if you're *at least* bright enough to know what's good for you. That much, we will allow you to remember."

THAT NIGHT, WE stood among the surging crowd of normies in the Castle Camelot courtyard—for once absent of its usual jousting knights and beer-toting wenches, the faux castle's crenellated ramparts and turrets soaring above us, the Blackmoore onyx-and-gold pennants snapping in the chill wind. Kitschy as it was during the day, at night the floodlights at the base of the walls, angled up to illuminate the rough-hewn blocks of stone, lent the Blackmoore's mega-sized play castle surprising realism.

It felt a little like having been transported a thousand years back, to when Morgan le Fay, the Blackmoores' alleged ancestress, might truly have been parting the mists in search of Avalon.

Ivy and I stood on either side of Maya with the rest of the quorum gathered near, and Elena's core group of defensive necromancers clustered at the ready close by. The Blackmoore spectacle was already underway—conjured lightning in silver and gold flashed above us in fanciful patterns, splitting the sky into segments like a mosaic of black glass. With each strike, the normies gasped, an oblivious chorus of oohs and aahs that grated on my nerves.

Maya had chosen the Blackmoore spectacle to invoke Chernobog partly because of location; the moat around the castle echoed the lake, Belisama's natural element. Blackmoore magic itself was also elemental and light based, closer in alignment to her aspects than his. "She wants to try reasoning with him one more time, to see if he'll just let her be," Maya had conveyed to us, plainly as skeptical as we were of the goddess's chances of success. "And if he's on the back foot, she thinks she might have a better shot."

We were using the same invocation spell Wynter had cast, for consistency's sake. After all, it had worked twice before, and for a mundane, at that. Talia and Issa had read it over with wrinkled noses—casting something of neither Grimoire nor Avramov origin didn't sit well with them—but agreed to cast it together. Unlike Wynter, they likely wouldn't even need the amplifier of the Cavalcade spectacle to summon Chernobog, but the boost wouldn't hurt, especially if it also put Maya-as-Belisama in a position of relative power.

"You ready?" I murmured to her. "They're about to start."

Maya nodded, nibbling on the inside of her lip, her eyes grave as they met mine. "She's afraid," she said shakily. "She's trying to hide it from me, but I can feel it. She's scared of what might happen if he won't listen to her. But this is the only way. Now that he knows where she is, he'll return on his own, eventually; he never stops trying. She thinks it's best to force the issue with even a slight advantage."

"It'll be okay," Ivy reassured her, sounding about as convinced as I felt. "You'll see."

I'd been seized by deep misgiving as soon as we arrived, a writhing in my stomach like a nest of snakes, almost as forceful as a premonition. Something massive was going to transpire tonight; I could sense it, as if the knowledge itself hovered on the other side of the veil, accessible only to me. And whatever would happen, Belisama had chosen me for it, somehow.

Whatever the cataclysmic fallout would be, I wouldn't be able to evade it—just as I finally had Ivy back, and more to lose than I'd ever had before.

As the lightning continued to fork above us in those gorgeous, geometric patterns, I could feel the moment when Talia and Issa began the invocation, the pungent odor of the herbs burning in a censer held between them abruptly dousing the air. A sticky, icy pall settled over us like an ectoplasmic cobweb, along with a breathless sense of anticipation.

And he answered the call almost at once, as though he'd been waiting just beyond the threshold for another invitation.

Set against the illuminated sky, that striking, demonic form was even more jarring as it coalesced—trapped behind the lightning strikes like prison bars, that web of light acting as the proxy for the veil like the conjured fog had at The Bitters. Whatever damage Belisama had managed to inflict the day before had clearly already been shed; he manifested more quickly than either of the previous times, with a solidity and heft that stole my breath. He looked even stronger this time, more fully realized. And I knew from Maya that Belisama was still terribly weakened from the exertion of the banishment.

"Dearest," he boomed, a terrible smile splitting his face. "You call for me, as I knew you would!"

Beside me, Maya began to glow blue again, though much paler

this time, more diffuse. "I do," she responded, in that belling, other-worldly voice, and I could see from the sapphire and amber sparking in her eyes that the goddess had emerged again. "My brother, my lover, my erstwhile companion. I call for you to ask you to stay your hand, and then hie away. Because we are done, my darling, you and I. I will not have you again, when the price of your love is dearer every time."

Chernobog paused, the smile dropping away like a husk, an awful darkness falling like a curtain across his face.

"You do not mean it," he grated through clenched teeth. "You cannot mean it. We are *one*, my love, as we have always been. As we were made to be. How could you ask me to exist alone in all my darkness, when you have ever been the torch that lights my way?"

"You say you love me, yet you would snuff me out, along with everything precious I have come to treasure here," she called out, and now tears were streaming down her face, eyes bleak with hopelessness. "You would raze everyone in your path, just to seize hold of me once again. I cannot have it. I cannot have *you*. If you do love me, then hear me now—and begone, for the last time. Give me my peace, and find some different light to crave."

"I WILL NOT!" he roared, lifting both clawed hands to batter against the shining grid of conjured lightning that barred his way. I'd been so caught up in their exchange that I'd barely registered the terror of the crowd, but now the muffled screams penetrated my consciousness, the fearful turmoil that surrounded us as the normies woke to the realization that this wasn't part of any planned performance. "I WILL COME FOR YOU, AS I HAVE ALWAYS COME. AND YOU WILL LEAVE BEHIND THIS MEASLY, MEANINGLESS SCRAP OF EARTH THAT YOU

HAVE CLAIMED FOR YOURSELF, AND TAKE UP YOUR
RIGHTFUL PLACE BY MY SIDE ONCE AGAIN!"

"He's not going to stop. Not ever," she whispered beside me,
and this time I couldn't tell which of them was speaking, Maya or
Belisama or maybe both as one. She lifted both hands, gulping
back tears. "Not unless he's destroyed. I will never know peace
while he continues to exist, in this or any other realm. And neither
will this town, not now that he is aware that I am here, that he
might find others of my blood here, too."

Blue light streamed out from her splayed and outstretched
hands, a savage devastation scrawled across her face—because, I
abruptly understood, she *did* care. This was still her lover, her
other half, that she was consigning to destruction, because she had
no choice. She couldn't have peace and freedom and the gorgeous
enchantment she'd made of Thistle Grove, and keep him as well.

This was the end of the line for them.

But nothing happened this time when the blue light met his
embodied frame. The sapphire flames huffed out as soon as they
touched him, lapping against him for only an instant before melting away. The alignments didn't matter, clearly, not in the face of
the colossal imbalance of powers—he a god nearly in his full-
blown and original form, Belisama only a bright seed of herself,
housed in the body of a mortal girl.

"I cannot do it," Belisama whispered, wide-eyed and desolate,
through Maya's trembling lips—and my heart broke at the sight
of that helplessness, goddess or no. "I am too weak to stand
against him, especially in this fragile form. If I burn any fiercer, I
will extinguish all of her, and that . . . I will not do that. Not even
to set myself free of him."

She turned to me, tears still gleaming like pearls in her eyes.

And as soon as I met her gaze, I *knew*, understood at once what she needed from me.

Why I'd been the one chosen to guard Maya in the first place, to stand beside her when this precise moment came to pass.

"Daria Avramov," she said, knelling yet soft, reaching out to thread her fingers through mine. I could feel the privacy glamour that sprang up to encompass the three of us, her and me and Ivy, shielding us from Chernobog entirely. Her eyes glowed both amber and blue like Lady's Lake on a high summer day, rippling with sunlight reflecting off the water's faceted surface. The heat that pulsed from her palms to mine felt like touching the sun itself, and yet the searing warmth of it was welcome, beautiful, beneficent, sinking past my skin like a stream of courage poured directly into my veins. The urge to kneel pressed at the base of my skull once again, but this time it felt like a request, not a command. "You understand, do you not, that my love of loves is merely a devil overgrown? And in so knowing, will you be my champion? Will you allow me to beseech you for your help?"

Abruptly that sleeping hunger stirred inside me, its jaw unhinging, surging up toward my throat. Yes, some gods *were* simply devils, overgrown. Whatever it was that had always lived inside me, ravenous and curled in wait, this was something that it very much understood.

"I will, my lady," I said, dropping to my knees and meeting her gaze with a fierce one of my own, as that sense of destiny fell heavily over my shoulders like a chain mail stole. "Of course I'll help."

"Dasha?" came Ivy's panicked voice from behind Belisama, as she shouldered past to stand next to her, beautiful, furious eyes fastened on my face. "Dasha, what does that mean? Dash, for fuck's sake, *what are you doing right now?*"

"I love you, baby," I said to her, meeting her terrified gaze with as much reassurance as I could muster, though my heart was heaving against my sternum, pounding in my ears until it nearly drowned out everything else. "And I'll come back to you, I *swear*. But I have to do this for her first—you know I do. See you soon, okay?"

"Dasha, please, for once, just *don't*—"

With a furious pulse of the garnet at my throat, I slipped over to the other side of the veil.

23

Devils Overgrown, and Ghosts of Family Past

I LANDED DIRECTLY in front of the blizzard-stone palace—only this time, its glittering façade held a tremendous set of double doors. They were flung wide open, as if waiting for me, a maw of impenetrable darkness gaping beyond.

And Chernobog was there, too, standing in front of them. His divine form sized down to match mine like last time, his flawless face as intoxicating and deathly as a draught of some hemlock-touched wine, those green eyes bright like emeralds. A smile curling the corners of his lips, one hand outstretched to me like a cavalier's.

"Welcome, child of dark, with a star upon your brow," he crooned, tilting his head. His glossy black curls stirred as if in a breeze, though the air here was dead as ever. That consuming rage had fallen away from him like a discarded cloak, as if it had never been; now he was performing entirely for me. "She would not come, my faithless lover. But *you* did—and I am glad for your bright company. Will you walk with me? Will you let me show you what delights may yet be found by my cold hearth?"

Through the immediate, blazing onset of euphoria pounding through my veins, I struggled to think clearly. I'd need time to acclimate before I could even begin to try to best him. And what better way to get his guard down than to let him think I was here out of curiosity or attraction? After all, he hadn't heard any of what had passed between me and Belisama, including my pledge to her. If I had to begin this with a performance of my own, then I could do that for the Lady.

"Show me," I said, lifting my chin like a queen and setting my hand in his.

The touch of his palm against mine felt like mainlining the other side straight to the chambers of my heart.

Icy fire bloomed inside me, vast, frost-furred petals unfurling in my lungs. I stumbled, nearly moaned aloud, before gathering myself enough to fall into step with him as he turned toward the castle doors. I should have been afraid—maybe somewhere down deep, I was, beneath the vast roar of that enchanting inferno—but it didn't feel like I had any room left for fear. Not while I was touching him.

As soon as we stepped across the threshold, the dim space beyond the doors resolved into a dark, shimmering mirage made real. Everything that met the eye was crafted from blizzard stone and smoked crystal flowing seamlessly into each other, from the tiled floor in a whirlpool pattern that evoked maelstroms and black holes to the double staircase that swept away and then met itself on the far-flung second floor. Enormous chandeliers hung high above us, some dripping intricate waterfalls of smoky quartz teardrops, obelisks, and arrowheads, others like massive orreries, with crystal spheres arranged in orders I'd never seen before, as if they spoke of foreign solar systems.

It was breathtaking, the strangest and most beautiful place I'd ever seen, and I'd grown up in Thistle Grove.

"You like it," he noted, lips quirking with delight, in that voice like wildflower honey dripped over coals. "I thought you would. Let me show you more."

Together, we drifted up the staircase, each step and inhale bringing with it a fresh bout of ecstasy. I followed him into a banquet hall furnished only with a table so long it seemed to stretch out into an endless distance, laden with crystal platters of that strange orchard fruit, cleaved in half. Their insides were a winking mess of jagged edges, edible geodes studded with seeds like black pearls. It didn't look like something any human could eat—nor had it ever occurred to me that I even could eat on this side—but somehow I knew that in his presence, it would taste divine. Resurrect every memory I'd ever had of anything heartrendingly beautiful.

"Will you take some?" He motioned to it, one thick eyebrow cocking. "There can be wine as well, if you like."

I shook my head. If nothing else, I knew better than to pick the most obvious Persephone path here. "I'm not hungry. But thank you anyway."

His brow furrowed, but he didn't push. "Perhaps later, then. Come see what else I have for you."

Somehow, only three more steps brought us past that infinite banquet table, and into a chamber like a crystal's heart—its walls rising around us in carved quartz facets, entwined swirls of black and green trapped within. In the middle was a well carved from jet, the water inside it gleaming like black satin.

And it *sang*, a haunting melody like a sylph's song that stole into my ears and nestled into the whorls of my brain as if it were alive.

"Sit with me on the edge," he ordered, and when I hesitated, "and do not fret, it's perfectly safe. The well of worlds would not allow you in, not without me as your escort."

"The well of worlds," I repeated, incredulous, perching gingerly on its freezing edge. "Why do you call it that?"

With a whisper of a smile, he trailed a fingertip over the water, drawing a spiral like a nautilus shell into its surface until it began to ripple. At his touch, colors began blooming far beneath, and I braced myself on one hand to peer inside. There were *stars* in there—and not only stars, but entire milky galaxies, complete with streaking comets and spirals of nebulae. An infinity of tiny, multicolored planets suspended in their gravity wells like marbles.

"More worlds than you can imagine," he said, smiling at my breathless awe. "Worlds upon worlds upon worlds, on every plane and every realm in this mille-feuille universe. You can visit them all, on my arm. We would certainly not be satisfied with this one alone."

"But why does it sing like that?" I whispered, captivated by the jewel-box glow of the water, curiosity blazing inside me like a pyre.

"Have you not heard about the music of the spheres?" he asked, reaching out to tuck a lock of hair behind my ear. I felt even that light touch echo through me like a tremor, had to bite the inside of my lip hard to keep from leaning into it. "It is no metaphor, but simple truth. Life sings, child of dark. It sings *incessantly*, clamoring of itself, until only I can silence it."

"Why would you ever want to silence it? It's so beautiful."

He shrugged a powerful shoulder, folded wings twitching behind him, something like sadness grazing over his face. "Because it is what I am, the purpose woven into me. I am a darkness made to cover light. A silence that snuffs out lifesong and echoes in the void."

"And that's all you do?" I asked softly, meeting his eyes. "Destroy?"

"No," he replied, his eyes dragging over my features with such avid intensity I could feel heat surge into my cheeks, especially when his gaze landed on my mouth. "Not only that. There are many other things I crave. *She* knows. That is why she still yearns for and dreams of me, even as she chooses to flee the love we were born to share."

He rose in a fluid motion, wings rippling behind him, offering me his hand again. "There is something else I would show you," he said. "A final gift. My last offering."

He led me through winding hallway after hallway, ceilings soaring so high above us they nearly disappeared into darkness, the sconces set into the crystal walls flickering with green fire. On either side, rune-embellished doorways opened into decadent bedrooms, with massive canopied beds carved of blizzard stone and crystal, draped with sheets that looked more like swirling mist than anything material.

I could feel his eyes stray to me each time I glimpsed into one, knew exactly what occupied his mind. He'd fuck me in all these beds if I stayed with him. And for as long as I survived being here, it would be a pleasure unlike anything I'd know in mortal life.

"You could find happiness here with me, you know. Be my dread queen, and never leave my side. Perhaps you would be even better than her," he mused, as we walked the long corridors. "Her light has fed your bloodline for these centuries, and yet you are also like me—darkness driving through the branching forest of your veins. You know death. You know the night, as she never did. You would grow to understand me."

And that was the worst of it—maybe I *would*. I could imagine all of it, like a diorama of temptation erecting itself in my mind, what it would be to give in to the indulgence of staying here, with him. Never having to fight the craving for the other side again, but living in it, swimming in it, fucking him in it. Every sensation amplified to excruciating keenness, as I lost myself forever in that churning sea of euphoria.

But beneath that temptation, love for Ivy beat reassuringly inside me like a second heart, human and warm. My grounding anchor, an infallible truth. My reminder of the promise I'd made to her that I'd be back, even as I pledged my help to Belisama.

"Perhaps I would" was all I said, and it seemed to appease him. He smiled and squeezed my hand, drawing me to a stop in front of the chamber at the end of the hall.

"Go on," he urged, gesturing me inside. "I will follow after."

I stepped in, expecting more uncanny wonders. Captive stars, more impossible foods, maybe even clichéd fairy-tale offerings like dresses sewn from the fabric of some overly specific time of day. Instead, I froze as if I'd crashed headlong into a wall—because my parents stood in front of me.

Not flesh and blood, but some swirled-quartz replicas, so uncannily lifelike that I could barely bring myself to suck in another breath. My mother's hair unraveled from a messy braid as it so

often had in life, the expression on her face the one of joyfully animated curiosity I'd seen a thousand times. The way she lived in
my mind whenever I remembered her. And my father with his
crooked grin, his hair curling so familiarly over his brow, arms
spread as if inviting me in for one of his crushing hugs.

Grief and fury pounded through me, merciless and intractable,
cutting through even the liquid heaven in my veins.

"What is this?" I whispered, tears trembling in my voice as I
wheeled around to face him, infuriated by the expectant delight in
his face—as if he'd thought I'd *like* this travesty. "Why would you
show me this? My parents are dead, you must know that. So why
would you taunt me with their likenesses?"

"Because you could have them back," he said, gaze heavy and
magnetic on mine, too cumbersome to let me look away. "If you
chose to stay with me. I could summon their departed spirits with
a single word. I could call their true names and enliven them for
you. And then they could stay here, too, with us. With you."

The sheer gut punch of want took me by complete surprise. I'd
been grieving them for years; I thought I'd finally let them go. But
clearly I hadn't, not all the way, if the idea of having them back in
whatever form was offered could feel like such a powerful entice-
ment. Just the notion of refusing made me want to fall to my
knees, like losing them all over again.

I turned to Chernobog, tears streaming down my face. "You
could really do it?" I demanded, stepping so close to him we were
nearly nose to nose. "Bring them back?"

"I am lord of darkness and chaos, and the master of the void,"
he replied, still in that silky voice but with an edge beneath it, a
blade concealed within a satin sheath. "Of course I could do that,
and more."

I set a trembling hand against his chest, my heart thrumming from the enormity of the choice I was about to make, how desperately torn I was between extremes—life here with him and the parents I thought I'd lost. Life on my side of the veil with the love I'd only just gotten back. Could I go through with this, after everything? Was I strong enough to choose the right thing for myself?

Then the certainty slammed into place, tumblers falling as if a key had turned in a lock. I knew exactly what I wanted. The only door that I could bear to open.

"Then, yes," I said, low and hoarse, looking up at him through my eyelashes. "Yes, I'll stay."

The joy that suffused his beautiful face was immense enough that guilt stirred inside me for the first time. For all his sins against her, I couldn't imagine the loneliness of being denied Belisama's light, of being innately incapable of loving her in a way that she'd accept.

"Truly?" he exhaled, his eyes flitting ardently between mine, his palm sliding to cover my hand on his chest. "You will take her place?"

"I will." I tipped my face up to his, cupped his cheek with my free hand. "And let us seal my promise with a kiss."

My lips parted as he covered them with his own, his mouth lush and cold and deliciously sweet beyond anything I'd ever imagined.

For a moment, I was utterly lost in it, the flood of desire and elation like a wave closing over my head, sealing me under, threatening to wash away all reason. But that hunger inside me still knew what it was for, remembered what it was here to do even if I forgot. It surged inside me at the press of his lips, the sweep of his tongue against mine, hissing, *"Take him for usssss,"* in my ears.

And then my onslaught began.

"Oh, what are you doing?" he managed against my mouth, agony like a thorny wreath wound around his voice. "You treacherous child, what are you *doing* to me?"

"I'm sorry," I whispered back, not letting my will flag even for a moment. "I know it's not entirely your fault, but there's no other way. You wouldn't let her go . . . and she deserves to be free of you."

He resisted me, hard. I could feel him fighting, bucking and yanking against me with his own colossal will, sprawling and barely conceivable, scales of magnitude larger than my own. It felt like wrestling with a black hole incarnate, trying to shred the fabric of night itself, dissolve an entire elemental force that dwarfed me on every level. But though he was a god, Belisama had been right; he was made of the same stuff as all the devils I had eaten. A devil overgrown. And whatever eldritch talent coursed through me—because I wasn't naive enough to think that what I did was wholly, or even partly, good—it had clearly been intended for this, too.

I could feel his shocked gasp against my mouth, his entire body stiffening as he tried to wrench away from me. But the hunger infused me with strength enough to hold on, and I wrapped a hand around his nape, latching him to me.

And bit by bit by bit, I dissolved a god.

He came apart with such an agonizing slowness, like deconstructing an entire universe into a sea of component molecules. Though he shrieked muffled invective into my mouth, begged me to stop, threatened me with everything he could devise, I was far past the point of being swayed even by the deathbed curses of a god. Instead I pulled and pulled and pulled, with the energy flaring like a starburst from the very bottom of my will, unraveling and undoing him—until there wasn't enough cohesion left in him to allow for incarnate form.

When the deed was done, I fell to my knees and tipped my head back for that final drink.

Foolishly, part of me had been convinced that all my experience had prepared me for this, that I was strong enough to swallow the universe that I had melted down—because what was a god if not a collection of forces, a universe in miniature? But Chernobog's essence had flooded the entire palace from keystone to roof, a vast and roiling sea of darkness with me at its epicenter. I drank and drank—and Mother and Crone, it was so terribly cold. Wormwood stinging in my nose and copper twanging in my mouth, the sound of shedding snake husks rustling in my ears, until I felt sure that this ordeal would never end.

That I'd be here not just until my death but the death of all days, the end of ends. The other side of eternity.

I hadn't even realized that the castle itself was dissolving around me, as though it had been an extension of him—chipping away in broken pixels like puzzle pieces that crumbled into ash. But by the time I'd swallowed the last drop, I was on my knees amid the flowers with the charcoal sky above me, those red clouds scudding in their fitful fast-forward—the only witnesses to my collapse.

I fell forward and rolled feebly to my side, knees curled up to my chest.

That hunger inside me not just quiet and sated, but completely quenched, finally overwhelmed by the consumption of a god.

24

Cosmic Jokes (And Gifts)

I COULDN'T MOVE.

The weight inside me felt leaden, impossible to shift. I felt like I'd been pinned down like a moth by a mountain, or possibly a fallen planet, something that had plummeted from the firmament to land directly on my chest. My throat ached as though it had been scrubbed with steel wool, and my insides sloshed from side to side even though I couldn't lift so much as a finger.

Thirst boiled inside my throat, rivaled only by panic. Because no matter how hard I tried, my garnet pulsing against my throat, I couldn't budge myself so much as an inch back toward the other side of the veil.

Normally, the avatar of me that existed on this side—the physical form that my spirit and awareness took—felt exactly like my human body. But I was so spent, so terribly overfull, that the idea of flinging my metaphysical self back across the veil felt worse than impossible.

Like something I'd once dreamed I could do, the way children dreamed of flight.

Tears began pooling in my eyes, spilling hot down my chilled cheeks. Ivy would think I'd broken my promise to her, I thought, anguish splaying itself inside me like a starfish wrapping spiny limbs around my ribs. That I'd chosen to stay, been too weak to do what I'd sworn I'd do. And Amrita and Kira and Saanvi—they'd all think I'd abandoned them, too.

Because if Elena was able to rescue me this time, reel me back in the way she'd done twice before, she'd have already done it.

Maybe not even she could budge me, swollen as I was with godsludge. Or maybe they'd all decided they didn't even want me anymore, after what I'd done. Killing a god was no small thing, even if it had been at a goddess's behest. Who knew how Belisama felt now, if she'd changed her mind after Chernobog's demise. If she hated me for having gone through with what she'd asked me to do in the first place.

So this was it, then, I thought, both grief-stricken and numb, my eyes unfocused on the crimson streaks of the clouds crawling across the sky. This was how it all ended for me. What a pinnacle of irony, I considered, with a faint, rasping chuckle. An involuntarily permanent residence on the other side, now that I didn't want it anymore.

How very fucking appropriate. Trust the universe to get the last laugh, and stick me with one final cosmic joke.

And how long would I even endure like this? What would happen to my physical body, untethered to my essence for too long?

My vision felt like it was compromised already, warbling and fading, splintering the cloud cover above me.

But no; there really *was* something up there, piercing through those scabbed-over clouds. I squinted, trying to make it out. I'd never once seen anything up in this dead sky, no birds or stars, not so much as a floating seedpod. But this . . . this was something brown and green, branching toward me like a growing fractal, arrowing in my direction with tremendous speed.

"What the fuck?" I managed to mumble, straining to lift my head the tiniest bit. "A *tree*?"

It was a tree. Or rather, the enormous crown of one, growing toward me upside down—as though its trunk and roots extended somewhere even higher above, driving *through* the pewter sky and into some other reality. And as it neared, rustling and swaying, boughs reaching toward me, I realized I even *recognized* it. It was a hawthorn, festooned not only with green-and-golden leaves and scarlet berries, but also with the creamy white flowers I'd seen on its branches the first time Ivy had introduced me to it.

This was the heart tree of the Thorn orchards, the one that had been planted by their founder, Alastair Thorn. The one by which he'd chosen to be buried after his death, rather than being interred in the Thistle Grove cemetery along with the other three.

But I didn't remember its flowers shedding a sapphire-blue glow, or the sparks of gold and silver that now crackled along its boughs. There were even misty ferns of ectoplasm curling between the forks of the thinnest branches, filaments of darkness threading up and down the bark.

"Daughter of the void," it greeted me in its creaking, hissing voice, like the shift of boughs caught in a high wind. Its branches drooped toward me, leaves brushing tenderly over my face. "I am sent by the many who owe an eternal debt to you. Will you allow me to do what you cannot? To wrap myself around you and bring you back where you belong?"

"You're here . . . to rescue me?" I croaked, incredulous. "You—did you come through the *veil*?"

"Yes. But it is not in me to linger here." Its boughs shuddered a little, enough to convey distaste. "The air here reeks of death, and the ground could not sustain me, even if it does pretend to breed those false flowers. But it is your choice, daughter of the void. Will you stay, or have me fetch you home?"

I wasn't going to be trapped here, I thought, my heart stuttering through an exhausted attempt at a joyful leap. I was going *home*, back to Thistle Grove, to the world of flesh and blood and moon and sun. I was going home to Ivy Thorn, my best and truest love.

"Take me. Please." I tried to lift my hands toward the boughs to grasp on to them, barely managing to lift them an inch off the ground before they thudded back down.

"Do not exert yourself needlessly, daughter of the void. Nothing more is required of you; I have you now." The heart tree snaked its branches gently under my torso, wrapping them behind my shoulders and knees, lifting me with ease as it curled me against its slim trunk. I closed my eyes, overcome with vertigo at being flipped upside down, because the tree *was* growing inverted, exactly like I'd thought—as though the veil was actually in the sky, the other side hovering somewhere above us. "Rest, if you can. The descent will be slower than what you are accustomed to, when you make the leap yourself. And you have already been through so much."

I didn't need any instruction. As soon as I felt the four familiar, braided magics twining through the hawthorn's trunk, I could feel sleep tugging at me, consciousness dispersing.

I might not have been back in Thistle Grove yet, but in the heart tree's embrace, I was already as good as home.

I CAME TO back in my body, with my head cradled in Ivy's lap, both her hands cupped around my cheeks—so much Thorn magic coursing through me I felt like I might not perish imminently, after all. The heart tree swayed above us, silvery-blue dawn light dappling through its leaves. The brisk air smelled smokily of fall; ripe apples and cider and crisping leaves and the sharp tang of the grass that grew over the root ball of the tree. My deprived senses were so keen I could even smell the dusty earth of the trunk itself, which had held such a sturdy grasp on me.

"*There* you are, Starshine," Ivy whispered as my eyes fluttered, seeking hers. "Finally back among the living. Our conquering heroine."

I attempted a smile, found my lips so dry they immediately cracked. "Told you I'd be back. But . . . *so* thirsty . . ."

Someone else came to their knees next to me, holding a straw to my mouth.

"You're going to want to guzzle, but drink slow," Genevieve Harlow instructed, deftly maneuvering the straw between my lips when I failed to properly lift my head. "Your sister told me what you normally drink after a banishment, but this is a much stronger combination of electrolytes."

"Why . . . *she* here?" I asked Ivy, once I'd chugged down four noncompliantly huge gulps. Genevieve was right; they hurt plenty going down, straining my raw gullet. But they also felt like absolute bliss, sweet and salty and life-sustaining, an IV bag pouring down my throat.

Genevieve's lips pursed, but she couldn't quite maintain the semblance of indignation. "Because the rescue tree was my idea," she said, with preening satisfaction. "So I wanted to be here when you finally came to. Everyone else has been at Honeycake Cottage for hours; you took absolutely forever to wake up."

"Sorry to have kept you waiting," I grumbled. "I was just almost dying for a while. Inconvenient, I know."

"Well, I suppose it was Delilah's idea, too," Genevieve went on, neatly ignoring me. "Credit where credit's due. But I was the one who envisioned the heart tree as the extraction mechanism. Then Lilah nailed down the particulars."

"It's true," Ivy said, stroking hair away from my temples, beaming down at me so brightly I felt like I was staring into a sunrise. "Gawain was involved, too, in the grand casting. We had a whole Cavalcade planning committee redux going on, along with some extra help from Cat."

"Tell me everything," I demanded after more gulps, discovering that between the liquid and the steady flow of Ivy's healing magic being pumped into my system, I was sturdy enough to prop myself up into a half-sitting position, leaning back into Ivy's embrace. She planted a ferocious kiss on top of my head, clasping me tight against her.

"Thought I'd lost you," she said, and I felt the hitch of her chest against my back. "Kindly do not pull any such shit again, no matter what kind of VIP asks you for a favor."

"Believe me, I have no desire to do anything like that *ever again*," I assured her fervently, with a shudder of my own. "But how did you all pull it off? I could feel *everyone's* magic in the hawthorn when it took hold of me. All four families, commingled. How was that possible?"

"Elena was scrying while you were on the other side," Ivy explained, adjusting me against her so the back of my head rested in the curve of her neck and shoulder. "She saw . . . she saw what you did. To Chernobog."

"It sounded foul," Genevieve added, screwing up her pert nose. "I mean, *ick*."

"Maybe we limit any further helpful contributions," Ivy shot back. "Considering Dasha just killed a whole god for Belisama, and for all of us."

"Yeah, dissolving and eating a god, many helpings of *ick*. Also, you're welcome," I added sourly. "So, I figured Elena probably knew what was going down. But she couldn't help."

"No, she said you were too . . . *dense* for even her to move. Issa and Talia tried to help her, but no dice. No one could budge you."

"And that was when I thought, we needed something bigger. A magical ladder, something able to span realms," Genevieve clarified. "And besides the lake and the soil itself, that tree is the oldest living thing in Thistle Grove. We brought you here and asked it for help, explained what we needed—and it agreed."

"But it took all of us," Ivy went on. "The Thorns to actually, physically grow it that enormous size. I took point on that, but we all did it together. A massive empathic link to help us cast something that large, which Cat then magnified, spreading it to encompass the other families."

That would've been the half fae neatly extricating herself out of my debt by assisting in my rescue. We were definitely square now, by anyone's reckoning.

"Then we needed the Blackmoores to turn it into an elemental bridge to extend through the veil, something that would actually function as a portal between two adjoining realms. Gawain—shockingly—was the one who sorted that out, but he and Gareth and Nina cast it together."

"So why the ectoplasm?" I asked, remembering the fronds of sooty black curling around the branches. "And the blue glow, was that Belisama?"

"The ectoplasm was so that the other side wouldn't reject the intrusion of something so large and so alive," Ivy replied. "Like masking its scent. And the blue was actually Emmy—she connected to the root system as the Voice of Thistle Grove, anchored it to the magic of the lake and the town itself. So that once it had you in its grasp, it knew which direction it needed to follow to return home."

"What about Maya-as-Belisama?" I asked, frowning. "She didn't help with all this?"

"She very much wanted to," Ivy said quietly. "But she . . . it hit her very hard, when you destroyed him. For all that she'd wanted it, asked you to champion her. Her grief is . . . Most of the Thorns can't even stand to be around her. So she's hunkering down with James, Cecily, and Emmy at Harlow House. With her closest blood relatives, technically."

"But it was what she *wanted*," I whispered, my stomach lurching with the idea of having caused her pain, done something terribly wrong. "She asked me to do it!"

"Of course it was, love," Ivy reassured me. "And what a sacrifice you made for her. But the right thing sometimes still feels impossible to bear. You'd know about that, wouldn't you?"

I slumped against her, reeling with emotion, and the complexity that it had taken to execute this multidimensional rescue operation. "And *you* came up with all this?" I asked Genevieve, unable to hide the skepticism in my voice.

"Like I said, Delilah helped. But no need to sound like that. Planning is what I do, you know." Genevieve smiled at me, small but unmistakably sincere. "And after everything you did—all that *ick*—we were all pretty invested in bringing you back home."

Was this why, I wondered, the three other families had been drawn to Thistle Grove in the first place, once Elias had planted Belisama's essence here? So that I could be born centuries down the line, the anomaly capable of bringing down Belisama's lover and nemesis—and so that the families themselves could form the precise constellation of magic required to reel me back in once I'd done my part? Were deities really that prophetic and omniscient?

Or was all this simple serendipity, the beautiful, unpredictable dovetailing of fortunate events? A cosmic gift rather than a joke?

Chances were very good, I decided, that we'd never know. Whichever it was, the cards had fallen in the most auspicious way. And I wasn't going to be the one to question the inscrutable divine motives that had slotted them into the kind of arrangement that meant I got to see Ivy's beloved face again.

Against a dawning Thistle Grove sky, under the tree that had managed to tow me home.

⟩ ⟩ ⟩ 283 ⟨ ⟨ ⟨

25

A Song Louder Than Any Other Song

TWO WEEKS LATER, the Cavalcade's closing Sabbat found us all gathered around Lady's Lake at midnight, the moon peering down on us through the pines like Nyx's silver eye.

The families crowded the banks, the watchful evergreens at our backs, all of us careful not to trample the purple sprigs of spiky thistle that ringed the water. Despite the emerald aurora that writhed above as if caught in a celestial wind, like a veil fluttering over the cut-glass stars, all eyes were on the four elders who stood on the conjured island of ice that floated in the middle of the lake.

Of course, the water was perfectly clear and calm. After all that worrying about managing the weather, we needn't have fretted about storms. There hadn't been a single one since I'd destroyed Chernobog.

I was grateful for the reprieve that fortnight had given me; without it, I wouldn't have mustered the strength to be here. Ivy had spent all her spare time holed up with me in the cottage, feeding me, infusing me with more healing magic, cuddling and making love once I was recovered enough for more high-impact activities. I suffered recurring nightmares, too. Horrible dreams in which I didn't manage to defeat the god, or in which I did but remained helplessly trapped on the other side, always out of reach of the heart tree's boughs—or the most awful, the ones in which I chose to stay with him and my resurrected parents in that frigid castle. I'd wake from them sobbing in heartbreak, and Ivy would hold me against her and sing to me for as long as it took me to calm. To remember what had happened, that I'd chosen well.

We couldn't get enough of each other, not after the close call we'd had. I hadn't apologized for my decision, either, even though I knew part of her still resented the fact that I'd done the Lady's bidding at my own risk—and at the risk of never coming back to her. Not even my beloved was so completely selfless, as much as she intellectually understood why it had been necessary.

Besides, she knew better than anyone what it had cost me.

Because I couldn't cross the veil anymore. I'd tried for the first time a few days ago, just to test myself—and even though I'd been almost sure I wouldn't be able to, the knowing hadn't prepared me for the way the boundary felt like running into a stone wall rather than the diaphanous partition I'd been accustomed to my entire life. And when I reached inside myself, I could find no trace of that deep hunger stirring in response.

As far as I could tell, I wasn't a devil eater anymore, either.

Both Ivy and I had been taken aback by the depth of my grief at the loss. On some level, it should have been a relief, this abrupt excision of temptation and responsibility, the need for restraint and self-control taken out of my hands. It wasn't as though I'd lost my ability to practice necromantic magic; I was still perfectly capable of casting other spells, exactly as powerful as I'd been before. But still, I felt like I'd been stripped of some crucial part of me, an integral component of my identity. Ivy had held me through that, too, as I cried for what seemed like hours.

And tonight, even if I still hadn't come to terms with what the rest of my life would look like, at least I knew I'd have Ivy's hand to hold, our love to bolster me through it. She'd even chosen to stand with me rather than with the Thorns, as if our allegiance to each other transcended family.

"We are ready to begin, Lady," Emmy called out from the ice island Gareth had conjured for them. It reminded me of the glacier bridges he'd used in the first challenge of the Gauntlet of the Grove, what felt like a decade ago but had only been a handful of years. "With your permission?"

"Not quite yet, please," Belisama-as-Maya's voice came belling from somewhere in the crowd. A moment later, the witches around Ivy and me parted to let her through, and she and I came face-to-face again for the first time since she'd sent me to destroy Chernobog for her.

She wore a draped golden dress instead of my borrowed clothing, and a gold circlet set with amber and tourmaline sat low on her brow, her eyes beneath it glowing a matching amber and blue. Her smile at me was tentative, both proud and rueful; so she knew I'd been angry with her during my recovery. She hadn't come to

))) 286 (((

visit her alleged champion once, keeping to Harlow House for the duration of my convalescence.

I'd been hurt and resentful, and worse than that, I'd *missed* her. How could she stay away when I was the one who needed her?

"I know," she said, in that impossible, ethereal voice, her lovely eyes pooling with regret—so it was Belisama tonight, Maya in the background. "Forgive me for not coming to you sooner. I did not wish for you to witness my grief for his loss, not after the enormity of your sacrifice. It would have been the utmost disrespect to inflict the sight of it on you. But know that I am grateful beyond words for the gifts of peace and freedom that you have given me, no matter what it may have cost me to accept them. And that I will never forget what you did at my behest."

She offered me her hands, and I hesitated even through the compulsion to sink to my knees and pay obeisance to her, gritting my teeth.

"Did you know?" I asked her, low, refusing to drop my gaze. "That destroying him would mean I wouldn't be a devil eater anymore?"

"Not for absolutely certain," she replied, pressing her lips together, eyes shimmering. "But I knew there would be a strong chance. What was in you was powerful, but he . . . he was a god. That it might strip you of that power was something I considered very possible. Was I wrong in thinking that, if so, it would be worth it anyway?"

I considered it. The trade of the dark gift that had been a gorgeous torment, for the safety of my town and the freedom of my goddess. It *was* worth it, I decided—but still, she should have asked.

"I know I forced your hand by not telling you what you might lose by being so brave," she said, as if she'd anticipated this response, too—the way she might have anticipated all of this, from the moment Elias Harlow lowered her from his cupped hands into this very lake. "But that willingness, that devotion, the fire of that protective spirit—that was what it would have taken, to defeat the chaos and void of him. And now I ask you, Dasha Avramov, do you truly want it back? Would you have me remake you in your own former image, exactly as you were? If you do, it can be done. As *my* gift to you."

I could feel Ivy's hand tighten on mine, the sharp intake of her breath as she considered the implications.

Did I want to be who I was? I wondered. Or did I want this second chance, the opportunity to build myself anew? To see who I could become, without that gift and burden always shaping my path?

Maybe *that* was the truer gift—a new way to exist, a new life to discover. Perhaps less tantalizing and adventurous than the one I'd had before, but calmer, deeper, more reflective. Allowing me to sink into quieter, more meaningful joys.

"No," I said finally, with a firm shake of the head, allowing myself to take one of Belisama's hands without letting go of Ivy's. "I'll stay the way I am and see what I can make of it."

A slow smile curved her lips at that, as warm and inviting as a Samhain bonfire, nearly as dazzling as one of Ivy's smiles. "I am pleased to hear it. That is what makes you human, you know. The power to choose, to reinvent yourself. To break free of cycles and chains that cause you harm, rather than stay unchanging as we divine. Locked into our aspects while everything else in the universe wheels freely around us."

"But you did it, too," I whispered, squeezing her hand. "When you decided to become yourself without him, and asked me to help you. I know it hurt like it might tear you apart. And I—I can't blame you for grieving. How could you not? You lost a piece of yourself, too, just like I did."

Those tears finally spilled over, gleaming an inhuman gold on Maya's cheeks. "Thank you for understanding, my daughter of light and dark. I trusted that you would, in time."

She leaned forward and brushed her lips over mine, the lightest graze. I could taste some of those goddess tears on her, like effervescent honey, light made liquid. Exactly what she was, in essence.

Without releasing my hand, she turned back toward the lake, calling out: "My kin, my blood, my supplicants . . . you may begin the final worship!"

As soon as she spoke the last word, all four elders cast into the sky—a final and true re-creation of the founding, meant for the witch families' eyes alone.

As Margarita Avramov once had, Elena called on the shades that haunted the Witch Woods, bringing them drifting, gray and tattered, in a spinning circle high above them. At the same time, Aspen Thorn emulated Alastair Thorn's avian summoning, and all at once the whole sky seemed to fill with the birds that roosted in every dale and glen of Thistle Grove, the sound of their cries and flapping wings somehow as joyful as it was dissonant. Finally, Gareth lifted an outstretched hand and drew down a skyful of silent lightning, its forking bolts perfectly synchronized as they harmlessly struck the circle of pines around the lake in a blinding display. Just as Caelia Blackmoore's lightning once had, four centuries ago.

And though the Grimoire didn't specify this part, consigning

Elias Harlow's role to that of a modest scribe, it was Emmy who cried out: "Up on this hallowed hill, four families as one . . . we consecrate this lake in the Lady's sacred name!"

That sapphire-blue light poured from her in waves, sliding into the water, illuminating all of the lake as if thousands of massive floodlights had been switched on all at once.

"Oh." Belisama exhaled beside me, her fingers slipping loose from mine. "Thank you. Thank you, my kin and children, for everything you've done, for how you have restored my strength. And now I bid you all farewell—though my stone will always stay with you, lodged in the silt where none may disturb it. This lake will hold my blessing and your magic for all the years yet to come."

Even though the words were spoken in a whisper so poignant I could have sworn all of us teared up, we heard her parting words so clearly they may as well have been a thundering shout. Next to me, Maya flared in a blinding flash of sapphire—and then all that light spiraled out of her, surging up into the sky like a beacon. Pulsing like a tremendous heart, once, twice, three times, before vanishing, melting away into the dark.

For a moment, stunned silence settled over the lake, hushed and bereft. None of us completely able to believe that Belisama, our Lady of the Lake for all the time our town had stood, was well and truly gone.

Next to me, Maya staggered, clutching a hand to her chest. "Ugh," she groaned, gripping on to me as I caught her. "Not that I mind so much, considering everything. But that last part fucking *hurt.*"

Ivy rushed over to her other side, helping me boost her up. "Do you . . . Are you okay?" she asked, peering into Maya's face. "Maya, do you remember who you are?"

"Oh, yeah. My divine roomie cleared all the way out." She tapped her temple with a rueful little wince, her eyes back to that clear, pale honey-hazel. "I'll miss her—how often do you get to host a goddess?—but damn, it's nice to be just me again. And it's Teyana. Maya was just the closest I could come to remembering. Part of her name, mixed with part of mine."

BelisaMA, TeYAna, I realized, just as I caught the flash of matching comprehension on Ivy's face. *MAYA*.

"And you really feel completely fine?" I asked, unable to believe it, after everything she'd been through.

"Better than fine, now that the sting of that abrupt peace-out's wearing off," she replied, moving away from us to lift her arms up and stretch, clearly no longer needing our support. "Could've given me a heads-up that that was going to happen, rude. But she did get rid of all my aches and pains before she left. Shit, I'm probably not even lactose intolerant anymore!"

"You remember your dietary restrictions, that's a start," Ivy commented wryly, and all three of us laughed, puncturing the tension. "And everything else? How you got to Hallows Hill? Why you were here at all?"

"I'm a traveling nurse," Maya—*Teyana*, I reminded myself, *that would take some getting used to*—replied, reaching up to lift the circlet off her curls, as if wearing it was no longer appropriate. "I was here on a job that I timed so I could see the Cavalcade once I was off. I love witchy shit, always have. And I'm from Carbondale, so I've been here a bunch of times before for festivals."

"So close," Ivy marveled. "How was no one looking for you?"

"I used to be a foster kid, so not much in the way of permanent family. I do have a bunch of great friends, but they're used to me kind of dropping off the grid when I'm busy with work. And I'm fairly notorious for forgetting to charge my phone, wherever it even ended up."

"All around convenient," I said.

"For sure. I don't know if she really meant to pick me, though. I was at the Avramov spectacle, right before—and then everything was hazy after. I could only remember snippets of the performance. I'd been drinking, so the glamour hit me even harder, I guess. I wandered around town, looking for somewhere I felt comfortable, and I've always liked being out in the open. So I went to sit at those picnic benches in that little park at the base of Hallows Hill." She wrinkled her nose in bewilderment. "I know it sounds nuts, but it just *made sense* at the time to make the hike up to the summit. Even though it was dark, and obviously I shouldn't have been trying to climb alone. That must've been my divine roomie, calling me."

I thought of Teyana's sweetness and humor, her unbelievable grace and resilience even in a terrifying situation, the fact that she worked with people in a way that required compassion.

"I think she knew what she was doing in ways that we're never going to fully understand," I offered. The crowd around us had begun to disperse, clusters of family members drifting off toward home to process what had happened tonight. We'd lost the goddess we'd only recently even learned we had; we'd survived the onslaught of a god. What happened next, I doubted even the Grimoire could prescribe for us. "And you? What do you want to do now?"

"Tomorrow, I'm going to need to buy myself a new phone and make a whole bunch of calls to get my life together," she said, scrunching up her face at all the logistical annoyances that lay

))) 292 (((

ahead. I felt her on that one. When it came to unpleasantness, bureaucratic paperwork gave even chthonic gods a run for their money. "And then I think I need a little break from this place, to catch up with friends and make sure they know I haven't actually dropped off the face of the earth. But I think I'll be back soon. This town . . . it feels a little like home now, too."

She smiled up at me and Ivy, tipping her head. "And the two of you are feeling a lot like family, I have to admit. So if you wouldn't mind yet another night of me crashing with one of you . . ."

"Yes, definitely, absolutely," I said all in a rush, eager to keep her with us as long as I could. "Want a ride home with us?"

She pursed her lips thoughtfully, then shook her head. "No, I think I'll take the walk down. Kind of retrace the steps that got me here, you know? Clear my head. I'll catch a rideshare at the bottom or see if one of the Harlows will take me. Meet you at your place."

"Okay," I said, knowing it'd be safe for her; plenty of the families would have chosen to walk down tonight, too. Unlike the original ascent, she wouldn't be making this descent alone. "Ivy and I might stay up here for another little while. Just to decompress."

She huffed out a laugh. "Trust me, I get it. I'll see you both soon. And I mean, if you want to pick up some late-night burgers . . . I wouldn't exactly *mind*."

"We'll feed you," Ivy assured her, chuckling. "Don't you worry. We know the drill."

With a wink over her shoulder—did I imagine it, or was there the faintest glimmer of gold in the human hazel?—Teyana turned and disappeared into the receding crowd.

Ivy and I faced the darkened lake, arms around each other's

waists. I felt so strange, both entirely off-kilter and completely content, as if I were exactly where I was meant to be. Even if Belisama was no longer here, would never be again.

"I'm still coming to see you be Glinda, you know," Ivy murmured to me, kissing my ear. "Don't think I've forgotten that beautiful travesty, not even after everything that happened tonight."

"I hope you do," I told her, turning to nuzzle against her cheek. "I hope we both get to see every beautiful travesty that happens to either of us. And I hope we get to see it exactly like this, side by side."

"You're gonna be singing a different tune after I start chanting 'GO, STARSHINE!' every time you set foot on that stage."

"I'm going to keep saying it no matter what," I told her. "Forever."

She held my gaze, her beautiful eyes reflecting the faceted glimmer of the water, a warm half smile curling her lips. "I do really fucking love you, Dasha Avramov."

"And I love you, Ivy Thorn of the Thistle Grove Thorns, blessed by the powers of root and earth, of light and green and—"

"And if you don't cut that cheesy shit out, I'm going to kiss it right off your corny mouth," Ivy warned, struggling not to smile wider.

"What a brazen, wanton threat! I can't *imagine* a worse fate than—"

She cut me off as promised, a hand wrapped around my nape to draw me to her and plush lips pressed soft against mine, sparkling happiness shimmering throughout my veins. And it was perfect timing on her part, because I wasn't about to say it aloud, not yet . . . but maybe one day not so long from now, we'd get married right here, with the music of the spheres from that well of worlds still ringing in my ears. Because a life lived next to Ivy would always sing louder than any other song.

Especially in this fairy tale of a town that had once held a sleeping goddess in its lake and rivers of magic in its blood.

Acknowledgments

))) ● (((

I can't believe we're finally here! Writing the last words in the last book of a series is the most ineffable feeling—bittersweet, triumphant, relieved, a little devastated. (Especially considering the heavier subject matter Dasha had to grapple with; all of it was very close to my heart, and thank you for seeing such a grueling journey through with both me and our dysfunctional devil eater.) Most of all, I feel tremendously lucky to have been granted the privilege of living in my favorite fictional town for five whole books. I've loved every moment spent with the four families, the Lady in the Lake, and Thistle Grove's other denizens, and I'll never forget the way these stories changed everything from my own emotional landscape to the way I approach writing as a craft.

Thank you to Berkley for this unique, life-changing opportunity. My immense gratitude goes to Cindy, Angela, Stephanie, Elisha, Kate, Elizabeth, and the rest of the amazing team who have made these books so special to me. Viki Lester's cover designs have thrilled me for years; no one else could have brought such a distinctive aesthetic to these books. A similarly vibey thank-you to artist @Blacklillybee on Instagram, whose coffin dollhouses inspired the ones featured in the story.

Of course, none of this world would have existed without Taylor Haggerty's loving and expert guidance—thank you for your friendship, wisdom, and patience, Tay, and thanks to everyone at Root Literary who helps me keep writing even through the bumpiest parts of the journey.

As always, huge thanks to my critique group ladies, who were certainly not expecting to critique a book about the consumption of liquified demons but rolled with it admirably. And thank you to the best friends who show up for me every single day. Few things are as precious as friends who feel like home.

To my family—you know I could never have done any of this without you. My Leo, I can't quite wrap my mind around the idea of you being old enough to read this book (presumably with a good bit of cringing) or the rest of the series, but seeing as we're up to five books a night for our bedtime ritual, I know the day is coming at us fast.

Gabe, thank you for all the late-night and cocktail-hour support while I wrapped up what felt like the hardest of the Thistle Grove books. Here's to more Parmesan pigs in blankets and ill-advised wrestling lessons—I love you, babe.

As ever, the deepest of thanks to booksellers, librarians, and my wonderful readers. Thank you for the messages, the reviews, and the beautiful Instagram photos you've shared with me; it's my privilege to know that Thistle Grove seems to have become such a magical beacon of comfort and coziness for so many. Your time and attention have been so precious to me, and I hope whatever comes next speaks to you, too.

And a final thank-you to Thistle Grove, which feels real enough to exist outside of me. I'm so grateful you chose me to be your Elias Harlow.

Rise and Divine

LANA HARPER

READERS GUIDE

Questions for Discussion

))) ● (((

1. We meet Daria "Dasha" Avramov under some unusual circumstances. What were your first impressions of her? Of her relationship with her half sister, Amrita?

2. As a devil eater, Dasha's magical affinity is rare and uncanny even by Avramov family standards. What did you think of her forays beyond the veil? Does the other side sound like a place you'd want to visit?

3. The loss of both parents shaped Dasha into someone very different from the person she once was. Can you identify with the toll grief takes, and does it affect your perception of the mistakes Dasha has made?

4. Do you think Ivy was right to give Dasha another chance? What is your favorite aspect of their relationship?

5. Ultimately, Dasha's fascination with the other side of the veil became an obsession that grew into the equivalent of a real-world addiction. What did you think of this progression? Did this portrayal of addiction or dependence resonate with you in any way?

6. Dasha and Amrita's blended family is both unconventional and increasingly common. What did you think of their close-knit bond and the way they helped Dasha recover from her addiction to the other side?

7. Chernobog is a terrifying chaos god—but also something of a tragic figure when it comes to his inherently unsustainable love of Belisama. What did you think about their turbulent relationship, and the way it echoes toxic human relationships?

8. Maya/Teyana has a special role to play in the events that unfold in this story. What did you think of the way she handled her predicament—is her experience something you'd have been curious to live through yourself?

9. Which of the Cavalcade spectacles would you have enjoyed the most?

See where the Witches of Thistle Grove series began.
Keep reading for an excerpt from

Payback's a Witch

by *New York Times* bestselling author Lana Harper.
Available now from Berkley Romance.

The Prodigal Witch

AS SOON AS I crossed the town line, I could feel Thistle Grove on my skin.

That I was in my shitty beater Toyota made no difference; maybe the town could sense one of its daughters coming home, even after almost five years away. A swell of raw magic coursed into the car, until the air around me nearly shimmered with potential, bright and buzzy and headier than a champagne cocktail. As if Thistle Grove's own magical heart was pulsing eagerly toward me, welcoming me back. No hard feelings about my long absence, apparently.

Made one of us, I guess.

The onslaught of magic after my dry spell was so intoxicating that I hunched over the steering wheel, taking shallow breaths and wondering a little wildly whether you could overdose on magic after having gone cold turkey for so long. From the passenger seat,

Jasper cast me a glinting, concerned glance from beneath his silvery fringe and shoved a clumsy paw onto my thigh.

"I'm okay, bud," I murmured to him through a thick throat, reaching over to stroke his warm neck. "It's just . . . a whole lot, you know?"

That was the thing about growing up with magic. Until you left it behind for good, you had no idea how incredible it felt just to be around it.

And it wasn't only the air that seemed different. Through my spattered windshield, the night sky had changed, snapping into über-focus like a calibrated telescope. Above Hallows Hill, the unlikely little mountain the town huddled up against, a crescent moon hung like a freshly whetted sickle. *Waning crescent*, my witch brain whispered, already churning up the spells best cast in this phase. Its silhouette looked like it could carve glass, impossibly perfect and precise, the kind of moon you'd see in a dream. The constellations that surrounded it like a milky spill of jewels were arranged the same as on the other side of the town line but better somehow, more intentional, clear-cut and brilliant as a mosaic set with precious gems. So enticing, they made me want to pull the car over and tumble out, head hinged back and jaw agape, just to watch them glitter.

This fucking town. Always so damn extra.

With an effort, I resisted the temptation. But when the orchards that belonged to the Thorns appeared on my left, I gave in just enough to roll down my window.

The night air gusted against my face, smelling like the absolute of fall; woodsmoke and dying leaves and the faintest bracing hint of future snow. And right below that was the scent of Thistle Grove magic, which I've never come across anywhere else. Spicy and earthy, as if the lingering ghost of all the incense burned by three hundred years of witches had never quite blown away. A perpetual Halloween smell, the kind that gave you the good-creepy sort of tingles.

And fallen apples, of course. The Thorns' rows and rows of Galas, Honeycrisps, and Pink Ladies, sweet and cidery and indescribably like home.

It all made the part of me that used to adore this place—*oh, cut the shit, Emmy, the part of you that* still *does, the part that will never, ever stop*—throb like first-love heartache. My eyes welled hot with sudden tears, and I knuckled them clear more violently than necessary, angry with myself for sinking into nostalgia so readily.

Sensing my mood plummeting, Jasper gave an aggrieved snort, tossing his regally mustachioed snout at me.

"I know, I know," I groaned, dragging a hand over my face. "I promised not to get too in my feelings. I'm just tired, bud. From now on, it'll be all business till we can get out of here."

He huffed again, as if he knew me much too well to buy into my stoic crap. I might be back here only because Tradition Demands the Presence of the Harlow Scion, but nothing in Thistle Grove was ever that simple. Especially when it came to the heir of one of the founding families.

Ten minutes later, I pulled into my parents' oak-lined residential neighborhood, rattling onto their cobbled driveway. My chest clenched at the sight of my childhood home, fisting tight around my heart. It was a perfectly nice house, though not all that impressive as founding family demesnes go. The Blackmoores had their palatial Tintagel estate, the Thorns had Honeycake Orchards, and the Avramovs the rambling Victorian warren of a mansion they insisted on calling The Bitters, because they thrived on such old-world melodrama.

And we, the Harlows, had . . . lo, a house.

A stately three-story colonial almost as old as the town itself—though you wouldn't know it, to look at its magically weatherproofed exterior—Harlow House has never had a fancy name, thereby upholding the timeless Harlow legacy of being both the least pretentious and least relevant of the founding families. As always, a candle burned in every window; thirteen flames, for prosperity and protection. The flying owl weather vane spun idly in the night breeze, and the dreamcatcher windchimes hung by the front door clinked delicately against one another. A plume of smoke coiled from the brick chimney in a curlicued wisp before vanishing into the velvety dark above.

It looked like a storybook house belonging to your favorite no-nonsense witch—which, come to think of it, sounded like both my parents.

And it was all like I remembered, except that the thought of going inside made me feel painfully stripped of breath. There was an invisible moat of hurt surrounding my former home, years of unanswered questions. Restless water, teeming with the emotional equivalents of piranha and stinging jellyfish.

I couldn't do much about the hurt, and "because Gareth Blackmoore ruined this town for me" still seemed like a shitty answer to the question all the others boiled down to, which was: *Emmy, why haven't you come home all this time?*

So I turned the car off and just sat with my head bowed, listening to the ticks of the engine settling and Jasper's low-grade whine, focusing on my breath. When I'd collected myself about as much as I was going to, I lurched out of the car on travel-stiff legs and let Jas out to baptize the quiet street, then hauled my battle-scarred suitcase and gigantic duffel bag out of the trunk. By the time he came loping back, I'd managed to wrestle everything up onto the columned porch with an admirable minimum of cursing.

I still had my key, but it seemed horribly rude and presumptuous to use it after a five-year absence, so I knocked instead. When the door swung open, I managed to flinch only a little, blinking at the warm light spilling from within.

"My darling," my mother said simply, stepping out to greet me. Her voice was characteristically composed, all British stiff upper lip, but her green eyes—my eyes—were suspiciously shiny. Glossed with the same stifled emotion that burst at my own seams.

"Mom," I half whispered, a lump rising in my throat.

It wasn't like we hadn't laid eyes on each other in five years, because this *was* the twenty-first century. Even a magical haven like Thistle Grove got decent reception and Wi-Fi most of the time, barring the odd magical tantrum disrupting coverage. But seeing her face on a screen wasn't the same, not even close. When I leaned forward to wrap her in a hug, it took all I had not to whimper at her familiar smell, lemon and wildflowers. Though we were nearly the same height, the years between twenty-six and six abruptly melted away. For just a moment, I was small again, and she was the mummy I used to call for in the night after a bad dream, who soothed me with her gentle hands and infinite catalog of lovely British-inflected lullabies.

Then the awkwardness seeped back in between us, like an icy trickle of rain sluicing past your collar. When I pulled away from her, clearing my throat, she bent to offer Jasper the back of her hand.

"A familiar, really?" she said, smiling up at me as he gave her a subdued sniff. "I confess, I'm a bit surprised."

"Ah, no, actually. Jas is just . . . your average cute pup," I said brightly, quelling a spurt of irritation that I somehow hadn't seen this coming. Only in Thistle Grove would your mother assume that your well-trained standard schnauzer must *obviously* be a familiar. "He usually has more pep to him, too, but he's a little wiped out. Actually, we both are, do you think we could . . . ?"

"Right, of course," she said hurriedly, reaching over to wrench my back-breaking duffel across the threshold before I could stop her. "You've both had a terribly long drive, haven't you? Let's get you settled."

Inside, the smell of home hit me like a sucker punch: lemongrass floor polish, tea leaves, the melting sweetness of beeswax candles. I abandoned my monster suitcase in the foyer, shedding my denim jacket and hooking it on the coat tree before trailing my mother to the darkened kitchen. Instead of switching on the overhead light, she flicked her hand at the clusters of pillar candles set on the table and granite countertop. Their flames sprang obediently to life, illuminating the cozy breakfast nook with its vase of peachy tulips, yellow curtains, and my old cat-shaped clock on the wall with its swinging pendulum tail. Lighting candles was a small, homey sort of magic, the kind even Harlows could easily do.

The kind I used to be able to do almost without thinking before I left.

But I hadn't been able to coax so much as a flicker from a candle for almost four years now, and the ease with which my mother did it sent a well-worn ache of loss rolling through my belly. That was why members of the founding families rarely ventured far from Thistle Grove; any amount of distance attenuated our magic. The longer you stayed away, the fewer spells you were able to manage, until your abilities eventually huffed out altogether the way mine have.

I still felt the pain of their absence like a phantom limb, a hollow throb of yearning that never really faded. Seeing even this tiny spurt of magic happen in front of me only reignited the craving.

But, I reminded myself firmly, this was part of the price I'd agreed to pay for my new life. My *real* life, with my real job, real college degree, and unfortunately extremely real assload of student debt. This was the trade-off that I chose—the loss of magic, in return for a life that I could mold into a shape that actually fit.

"You've missed dinner, I'm afraid," my mother said, leaning back against the counter and crossing her arms over her slim middle. I sank down into one of the wooden chairs by the breakfast table, Jasper sprawling out next to me on the travertine tiles, and made an apologetic face in response, as if I hadn't timed my arrival precisely to avoid an hour of mandatory social entrapment with my parents before I had a chance to decompress.

"And your dad's gone back to the shop for a few hours to get the ledgers in order," she added. "The Samhain bedlam seems to set in earlier each bloody year. We're swimming in tourists already, and you know what that does to your poor father's peace of mind."

"I can imagine," I said, wincing in sympathy. "Think of all the *strangers* he has to talk to, the utter horror of it all."

Thistle Grove kicked into high gear every spooky season, starting the beginning of October and sometimes lasting well into mid-November. It was a Halloween destination the rest of the year as well—though of course the tourists had no idea just how deep, and very real, the town's "mythical" magic ran—but quiet enough to be less of a nightmare for my introverted father.

"But if you're hungry, I could make you a sandwich?" my

mother offered, wilting a little when I shook my head. "A bit of tea, then? I could use a cup myself."

I'd been driving for hours, and would much rather take a steaming shower and dive directly into bed before facing any further scenes from the prodigal-daughter-returneth playbook. But she looked so hopeful at the prospect of sharing a cup of tea with me that I couldn't bring myself to say no.

"Tea would be wonderful, thanks," I relented. "And could I have some water for Jasper?"

"Of course. What a terribly polite fellow he's been, too." She squinted at him thoughtfully, cocking her head to the side. "Are you *quite* sure he isn't a familiar?"

"Stone-cold certain, Mom."

I watched as she moved purposefully around the kitchen, all deft hands and competence, her periwinkle cardigan swirling around her, glossy dark braid swishing over her shoulder. When she set my favorite old mug, oversized and painted with a gold foil dragonfly, in front of me, she tapped the side lightly with an index finger to cool it to the perfect temperature. It was a little Harlow party trick, a pretty lackluster one as affinities went. My mother, Cecily Fletcher Harlow, hadn't been born a Harlow, of course; but marrying into a founding family was kind of like marrying into royalty. Only instead of a lifetime of fascinators, anemic finger sandwiches, and wearing nude pantyhose in public, you got to become a witch yourself.

"So, darling," she began, wrapping long fingers around her own mug as she sat down across from me. "Tell me how you've been."

"Really good," I replied, relaxing a little as the rooibos steeped into my chest and loosened some of the underlying tightness. I'd forgotten how medicinal my mother's brews could be. "I, um, even got promoted a few weeks ago. I didn't want to mention anything until the ink was dry, but yeah. Officially creative director at Enchantify now."

"My goodness, that's wonderful!" She beamed at me, though I could see the slight tightening at the corners of her eyes as she registered that this was the belated first she'd heard of my good news. "Congratulations, sweet. What a coup for you."

"Great timing, too. Gave me some leverage for requesting such a long sabbatical."

"And such a treat for us, more than one whole month with you! To be frank, I rather doubted you'd be able to come at all."

I chewed on the inside of my cheek, a little taken aback by such uncharacteristic bluntness. We weren't usually like that with each other, the Harlows. Not insular elitists like the Blackmoores, chaotically codependent like the Avramovs, or nearly empathically linked like the Thorns. We preferred to give the difficult stuff a wide berth, leave each other abundant room to breathe.

Maybe too much room, sometimes.

"'And the Harlow scion shall serve as Gauntlet Arbiter,' remember?" I said with forced levity. "Kind of hard to duck a centuries-old magical obligation. Could I *really* have been sure I wouldn't have turned into a hedgehog for flouting ye ways of old?"

She chuckled, taking a sip. "Not-impossible-though-fairly-unlikely hedgehogification aside, the Grimoire doesn't forbid the next-eldest Harlow of the younger generation from taking your place. Delilah could certainly have stepped in for you."

"Oh, I just bet Delilah could have," I muttered under my breath, trying to stifle the reflexive eye roll my cousin's name reliably provoked.

"Don't be mean about your cousin, darling. She's only a bit . . . eager."

This was one of my mother's epic British understatements, as Delilah was both the eagerest of beavers and the ultimate Harlow stan. She was a year older than me, but unfortunately for her, she wasn't the firstborn of the Harlow main line—which automatically disqualified her from serving as Arbiter unless I stepped down.

Delilah's borderline obsession with our family history had always struck me as kind of hilarious, given the role the Harlows actually played in the founding of the town. Legend had it that a little over three hundred years ago, four witches were drawn to Hallows Hill, lured by the siren song of magical power that emanated from this place. To consecrate the founding of the town below, Caelia Blackmoore conjured a spectacular lightning storm, Margarita Avramov summoned spirits from beyond the veil to serve as witnesses, Alastair Thorn called down the birds from the sky as his congregation, and Elias Harlow drew forth his mighty quill and . . .

Took a bunch of notes.

Seriously, that was it. My esteemed ancestor participated in this magical event of unprecedented majesty and drama by writing it all down in the driest possible manner, diligently avoiding wit or flair lest a historical account actually *entertain* future readers, perish the thought. Making him more or less the equivalent of the accidentally purple-haired lady named Irma who jots down the talking points of every town council meeting ever.

To be fair, Elias was also responsible for the Grimoire, the spellbook that contained the four families' collected spells and the rules for the Gauntlet of the Grove, the tournament held every fifty years to determine which founding family got to preside over all things magical in Thistle Grove. According to the rules, the competition was intended for the rising generation, so that each new Victor started their reign in the prime of their life—which meant that the firstborn scions of each line, the heirs apparent, went up against one another, as long as they were older than eighteen.

The Harlows didn't even *compete*, being so magically stunted that we've historically overseen the proceedings instead. And as the Harlow heir and the other scions' peer, the Grimoire also demanded that I be the Arbiter, rather than my father.

Woot for tradition.

"Well, bully to Delilah," I replied a little sourly. "But, huzzah, here I am! So she still doesn't get to steal my thunder as Emmeline, scion to House Harlow, the magical admins of Thistle Grove."

My mother frowned at me over the rim of her mug. "If you're going to be so glib about it, darling, perhaps you really *should* have let her step in for you. You know respecting the spirit of the thing is terribly important to your father."

I leaned back into my chair, my insides churning. I *did* know that, thanks to the tragically heartfelt and impressively guilt-trip-ridden letter my father had sent me a few months ago. Even thinking about his swooping script across the grainy Tomes & Omens stationery made my stomach twist, with the particular flavor of angst reserved for disappointing daughters.

> *Dearest Scoot, I know you've chosen to make your life a different one—a separate one from us. But, please, consider coming back to the covenstead just this once, for tradition's sake. Consider discharging this final obligation to your history and kin, to your*

*mother and myself, and I promise this is the last we'll ever speak
of duty.*

How could I have said no after that—especially to parents who
had always been so supportive of my choices, and my magicless life
in Chicago? A life they'd never understood, and one that so pointedly made no room for them?

"I know that," I said, not mentioning the letter, because there
was no way my mother would have let him send something so emotionally manipulative had she known about it. My parents were
basically the living embodiment of #relationshipgoals, and I had
no desire to stir the pot between them. "And the *spirit of the thing*
demands that it be me. And since the Blackmoores have won since
pretty much time's inception, it's not like I'll have all that much
arbitration to even do."

This was technically incorrect. The Thorns won once, back in
1921—but only because Evrain Blackmoore was such a roaring
drunk he lit both himself and the Avramov combatant on fire
while transforming a fishpond into a fountain of flaming
spiced rum.

See? Suck it, Delilah, I *did* know my Thistle Grove history.

My mother sighed softly and capitulated, rubbing her temples.
"I suppose that's true. And you'll have a few days to rest up before
the tournament opening on Wednesday. Acclimate a bit to being
back."

At the mention of rest, I tried to stifle a yawn and failed miser-
ably, my jaw nearly unhinging from the force. "Sorry," I barely
managed through it. "I'm just beat."

My mother pushed back from the table and swiftly gathered
up our empty mugs, then set them in the sink. "No worries, sweet.

I have the carriage house all ready for you," she told me over her shoulder as she rinsed them. "I thought, for a whole month, it would be nice for you to have your own space rather than a guest room in the house proper."

"That would be great," I said, my heart lifting at the prospect with genuine pleasure. I'd loved the carriage house as a kid, and spent most of my sleepovers with Linden Thorn sequestered out there, apart from my parents but never too far away for help if any was needed. The kind of distance they'd probably envisioned would carry over into my adulthood, instead of the two hundred miles of Illinois flatlands that now yawned between us, vast and intractable.

Together, we lugged my things out the back door and down the paved path that led through my mother's flower garden. The night bloomers stirred in their beds, swaying toward one another and tittering in high-pitched tones like gossiping fairies. Jasper trotted over to sniff a particularly lively evening primrose, leaping like a rabbit when it leaned over with a tinkling giggle to bop him on the nose.

It was a simple animating spell, though nothing like what a Thorn could have done with one. Flowers in a Thorn-animated garden might have distinct names and personalities and the power of speech, all the trappings of sentience. I knew because Linden Thorn, my best friend of over twenty years, once animated a cherry tree in the Honeycake Orchards for me as a birthday present. Cherry—so styled by yours truly, the world's most literal eight-year-old—whooped my ass at chess a solid four games out of five, and enjoyed regaling me with its gorgeous, uncanny dreams.

Sometimes I still really missed that tree.

We both dropped my luggage at the threshold with a pair of

matching, extremely unladylike grunts, grinning at each other as she handed me a key.

"Your dad may very well sleep at the shop if the night gets away from him," she said, rolling her eyes fondly. "As they so often do. So don't rush to breakfast tomorrow on his account."

"I have brunch plans with Linden anyway." I'd messaged Lin a few weeks ago to let her know I'd be in town for the Gauntlet, and to see if she wanted to get together as soon as I was back. We were still close, mostly thanks to Lin's staunch commitment to keeping us abreast of each other's lives even from a distance, so I figured it was on me to swing our first real-life reunion in years. "But I'll stop by Tomes and Omens right after, if that works?"

"Of course it does," my mother said, leaning over to brush a kiss over my forehead. "Good night, my darling, and give me a shout if you need anything at all. It really is so *very* lovely to have you back."

Photo by Gary Alpert, Deafboyphotography

Lana Harper is the *New York Times* bestselling author of *Payback's a Witch* and four other books in the Witches of Thistle Grove series. Writing as Lana Popović, she has also written *Wicked Like a Wildfire, Fierce Like a Firestorm, Blood Countess,* and *Poison Priestess.* Born in Serbia, she grew up in Hungary, Romania, and Bulgaria before moving to the US, where she studied psychology and literature at Yale University, law at Boston University, and publishing at Emerson College. She lives in Chicago with her family.

VISIT LANA HARPER ONLINE

LanaPopovicBooks.com

🐦 LanaPopovicLit

📷 Lanalyte

Ready to find
your next great read?

Let us help.

Visit prh.com/nextread

Penguin
Random
House